MW01243436

CLOAKS

F. A. FISHER

CLOAKS

EQP BOOKS

CLOAKS

An EQP Book / 2016

UUID: 985FD2E9-9927-42AC-9479-E774FBA276B3

ISBN: 1532948506

ISBN-13: 978-1532948503

ALL RIGHTS RESERVED

Copyright © 2016 by F. A. Fisher

Book cover designed by Deranged Doctor Design

No part of this book may be reproduced or transmitted in any form or by any means, electronic or mechanical, including photocopying, recording, or by any information storage and retrieval system, without permission in writing from the publisher.

http://EQPBooks.com

Editing and interior design by:

E-QUALITY PRESS

The name E-QUALITY PRESS and the logo consisting of the letters "EQP" over an open book with power cord are registered trademarks of E-QUALITY PRESS.

PRODUCED IN THE UNITED STATES OF AMERICA

To
Eleanor Cameron and Evelyn Sibley Lampman
for the spark

and to
Beverly A. Campbell
for the tinder

ACKNOWLEDGMENTS

Hᴀᴠᴇ ʏᴏᴜ ᴇᴠᴇʀ noticed how often authors include a statement at the end of their acknowledgments that goes something like: "There have been so many people who've helped me that I'm sure I've forgotten a few names. If yours is among them, please forgive me"? Authors put that in to avoid receiving poison-pen letters from people they really don't feel like mentioning.

Well . . . maybe *sometimes.*

But it also happens—always—to express a simple fact. No one can write a book in isolation, because no one can grow up in isolation. So many things have gone into shaping a person, which in turn shapes their book, that it's impossible to credit them all. "Don't forget that book you read in fourth grade—and your high school English teacher—and . . ." The list goes on forever.

So, being now in the process of writing my fourth paragraph without having explicitly acknowledged anyone at all, I'll use the rest of this to thank some of the people who've had substantial—and direct—impact on the final version of this book. (And hope that I manage to remember at least those with the *most* substantial and direct impact.)

For the wonderful cover, I have to thank everyone at Deviant Doctor Design, who not only did everything I asked but did it in a most agreeable manner.

Many members of the Writer's Group of the Triad, in Greensboro NC, critiqued versions of this novel, but the standout was James Maxey, who I think read three versions and told me, after the first, that I'd written "a very long book." Well, it's much shorter now, James; thanks! Others in the group with a significant impact were Elizabeth Lustig, Larry Hill, Ryan Anderson, and Karen McCullough.

The Hatrack River online Writers Workshop forum also provided a number of critiques, the most valuable insights coming from Richard Chiu, Mary Robinette Kowal, Danielle Friedman, Susan Buce, and Suzanne Vincent.

I also want to thank my wife, Roberta Horne, who was both my first and my last reader; and my daughter Sarah, who often read over my shoulder as I typed, making spot-on comments and invaluable suggestions. And for simple support, I thank my son Allan, who wouldn't let me stop reading the book to him—or more precisely: as a precocious fourth-grader, but one who hadn't yet learned to enjoy reading to himself— especially a book of this size—he took the manuscript and continued reading on his own from where I'd left off reading aloud. He was just finishing the book when I got up the next morning.

I'll tell you one more thing: although I'm more than happy to acknowledge all these people, I hated *writing* this acknowledgment.

Next time, maybe I won't let anyone read the book at all, and save myself the trouble.

Contents

Area near Kallikot Citadel

outcropping

Post house

Arrick's

Nedick's lake

The Citadel

1 mile

CLOAKS

You can't go home again.

—Thomas Wolfe

You can *go home again, the General Temporal Theory asserts, so long as you understand that home is a place where you have never been.*

—Ursula K. LeGuin

CHAPTER 1

FRIDAY

Heldrick sharpened his knife with slow, deliberate strokes, and wondered if he would find use for it again.

He glanced out the window. From the darkened cupola atop his old house Heldrick could observe the entire neighborhood, unseen. Clouds still darkened the sky, though the last drops of rain had fallen in the early morning. A group of youngsters played ball in the vacant lot across the street. The new boy and a few of the others wore jackets, for the air had an October chill, though August still clung to the calendar.

He expected no danger from the locals; he simply felt more comfortable keeping tabs on his surroundings, so he already knew where the new boy lived. The moving van had unloaded this morning, on the far side of the block across the street. And, later, he'd watched as the other boys pointed out Heldrick's house and filled the youngster with their juvenile tales of terror. Heldrick knew the stories: *Old Mr. Heldrick'll slice you up and put you in his soup. He'll hang you by your ears and torture you in his basement. If you step in his yard he'll come to your house at night and chop off your feet.*

The children's parents, he had little doubt, believed quite the opposite: that, in fact, he rarely ventured past the door of his house. He'd taken steps to ensure that belief. He even had his groceries delivered. And yet—there were doors, and there were doors. He often left the house. The stories told by the children, though foolish, struck closer to the mark. At least they portrayed him as dangerous. He'd lost count of the men he had killed in his time.

Heldrick set the knife aside and picked up the shotgun, checking it over. He didn't expect to need it; he kept it for emergencies only.

Satisfied, he laid the gun down and reached once more for the knife. The clock on the wall ticked away the minutes.

One more trip, he decided.

Soon.

CHAPTER 2

Bᴇss Nʏʟᴀɴᴅ ᴄʀᴀᴡʟᴇᴅ further behind the overgrown shrubbery, cursing her little brother's new friends for believing their own bogeyman stories. They had Jeff believing them, too, and Jeff was smart—almost as smart as she'd been at his age. What made him fall for that crap? Any of them could have crawled back here and fetched the baseball. But no, not with Mr. Heldrick around, waiting to chop off their feet.

Rubbish. Mr. Heldrick wouldn't chase her with a machete. He'd yell at her, that was all—and only if he caught her. Now, where was that ball?

Still on hands and knees, she looked around. She'd seen Jeff wallop the ball over everyone's heads, just as she was arriving to call him home so he could unpack his own junk. The ball had bounced across the street and rolled into the bushes, right here. The mud-encrusted basement window even had a clear spot that might have been made by a ball bumping it. But she didn't see the ball.

It couldn't just disappear.

She tapped a finger, lightly, on the window. It swung open, then closed again. She pushed it wide and stuck her head in.

Sure enough, she could see the ball, dimly, in the middle of the basement floor. Below the window, an empty wooden crate stood on end. Less than four feet separated the top of the crate from the bottom of the window. Talk about invitations.

Before she knew she'd made up her mind, Bess slithered backward through the window. Her toes reached the crate. She pulled her head in through the window and eased the window shut.

The slats under her left foot creaked and gave way. The crate tilted; she tried to hop off but landed wrong. A white-hot needle stabbed through her left ankle and she collapsed, falling on the crate, which splintered with a stale crunch.

She lay amid the wreckage and gingerly wiggled her foot. Twisted, she decided, but maybe not too badly. She'd done that before—it hurt like crazy but didn't last long. With luck it should be okay in a minute, and in two it probably wouldn't even slow her down—if she had two minutes. And she might. The crate hadn't made nearly the clatter she would have expected. Maybe Mr. Heldrick hadn't heard it.

But maybe he had.

She sat up, picked up a slat of the crate and snapped it as easily, and with as little sound, as snapping a soda cracker. "Solid rotten," her brother would say.

When Mr. Heldrick caught her here, in his basement, he'd do more than yell at her. He might even call the cops.

Her lunch clumped in her stomach at the thought. Benton College hadn't been willing to let her live in the dorms until her sixteenth birthday, almost a year from now. It had taken the smoothest talking her parents were capable of to get her in even as a commuting student, despite her glowing recommendations and impeccable SAT scores. The fact that she looked only twelve probably hadn't helped. But her parents had given up their jobs, which they'd loved, to move here so that she could start in the fall. Yeah, they'd found other jobs, but they'd made big sacrifices on her behalf. The possibility of getting arrested, of giving the college an excuse to change its mind, frightened her more than anything. She couldn't let Mr. Heldrick find her.

Carefully, she rose to her feet and limped a few steps. Using the ankle was the quickest way to make it feel better.

A glance around the basement showed her nothing else to climb on, no way to reach the window. She grabbed the window ledge and pulled herself up; but she couldn't open the window unless she let go with one hand, and if she did that she couldn't hold herself up any more. So she dropped back to the floor, making sure to land on her good foot. Going up the stairs, into the house, was not an ideal choice, but leaving by the window was out unless she found something else to stand on. And she *couldn't* take the stairs yet—stumping up with a lame foot would make enough noise to attract the old man's attention.

She hated it when she did something stupid on impulse. It always screwed something up. How many of her recommenders would say "mature beyond her years" if they saw her now? She'd thought her brother might obtain instant status if she fetched the ball from the bogeyman's bushes. And, face it, she wanted to show how brave *she* was, too. But who cared what Jeff's friends thought? Kids didn't matter. Garnering the respect of ten-year-olds wouldn't impress adults.

It certainly wouldn't impress Mr. Heldrick.

Her only choice was to ease up the stairs and then race for the front. With luck Mr. Heldrick would be in a different part of the house. She'd be out before he knew what was happening.

Her ankle barely twinging, she walked to the baseball and stopped, half bent over to pick it up. A deeper shadow hid in the shadows behind the steps. A door? A closet? Maybe she wouldn't have to take the stairs after all. Could be a box or stepping stool in there.

She grabbed the ball and moved closer. Definitely a door, though it looked like a decoration—not in the wall, but against it, as if nothing were behind it but the wall itself. On the other hand, the door seemed thick and was held shut by two massive bolts. So maybe something big and dangerous waited on the other side.

Either possibility seemed ridiculous. She pulled back the bolts and opened the door.

The basement wall did indeed encroach past the doorframe, giving it the look of an oval matte in a rectangular picture frame; but the tall, smooth-edged hole led to a natural cave, with an uneven stone floor and craggy roof. Most of the faint illumination came, not from the small basement window behind her, but from the far side of the cave. The faint outline of another door, cut to fit an irregular opening, leaked daylight. Her heart gave a bound. Another way out was even better than a stepping stool.

She clambered through the hole and walked to the other door, taking care not to twist her ankle again on the lumpy cave floor. Two more bolts fastened this door. Mr. Heldrick really wanted to make sure no one came this way into his house. She pulled back the bolts, wondering whether he secured his front door the same way, and turned the knob. The door swung toward her heavily. Its backside was covered with concrete, shaped and painted to look like the natural rocks of the narrow passage beyond. But she barely noticed the door or the passage; the view at the end held her attention.

Instead of a set of steps leading to the surface, the passage had a down-sloping floor—yet it still exited into the open, not someplace further underground. The fresh scent of damp earth drove the musty odor of Mr. Heldrick's basement from her nostrils. She walked to the end of the passage and a dozen steps past it. A breeze blew by, ruffling her hair. She looked about in a daze.

Downhill and to her left lay a farmhouse. To the right, woodland. Grassy hills and farm acreage filled the area between. The main crop looked like wheat, except for the tiny blue flowers it sprouted. Fog nestled in the hollows, not yet burned off by the morning sun.

But the sun hadn't shone all day. Benton had no hills. She ought to be underground—and in another few hours night should fall.

Bess turned. Instead of Mr. Heldrick's house, an outcropping of rock jutted from the hillside, split by the crevice. Her skin tingled and she felt weightless, cut loose from reality. This was not the way home. She couldn't even tell whether she was on Earth anymore.

No wonder Mr. Heldrick was such a recluse. How far would he go to keep this secret? Might he shoot her as a trespasser? That seemed extreme, but with the stories the kids told . . .

The stairs still seemed to be her only option. And the longer she waited, the higher the odds that Mr. Heldrick would catch her. Gripping the baseball, she took a deep breath and walked into the crevice and past the camouflaged door. A few steps into the dim cave, she stopped, her heart a cold stone in her chest.

Across the cave, beyond the door to the basement, someone approached, silhouetted by the basement's dim light, a rock in one hand.

The person stopped when she did. Bess realized that the figure stood, not in Mr. Heldrick's basement after all, but within what looked like another cave. Some kind of mirror? She lifted her baseball. The other figure imitated her.

But the mirror hadn't been there before. Maybe the old man blocked the entrance to his basement? Bess walked forward again, and the reflection kept pace, step by step, until she could see her own face. She reached out and touched the mirror, her finger sliding as if the mirror were greased, though without leaving a streak. The baseball also glided smoothly and frictionlessly across the surface. She pushed, and the surface gave, like a slippery bag of molasses; her reflection distorted, making devil images at her. Weird. Still holding the ball, she pushed on the mirror with both hands, pushed into it, until with a *pop!* she broke through, stumbling.

She caught herself. Behind her, the mirror had vanished. The hole in the wall, the cave, and the world at the other end of the passage still showed. Strange; very, very strange—but taking the time to figure it out wasn't an option. She had to get out of this house.

Bess circled to the base of the stairs and started up. When she reached the fifth step the door flew open and the old man appeared on the top landing: hunched over, with a thatch of gray hair, a sharp nose, and eyes black like a crow's. The twin barrels of a shotgun in his hands rose toward her faster than she could think.

Bess instinctively flung the baseball at the old man, leaped off the side of the stairway, and dashed toward the cave doorway. Footsteps pounding down the stairs encouraged her to ignore the shout of "Stop!" She grabbed the door on her way through and slammed it behind her as she heard the blast of Mr. Heldrick's shotgun.

Then she was running, running, out of the crevice and down the hillside, as fast as she could go.

CHAPTER 3

DAY ONE

Bess ran zigzagging to the woods' edge, a hundred yards off. Panting within the shadows of the trees, she looked toward the outcropping and saw no sign of Mr. Heldrick.

All right. All right. Good. She could watch from here without being seen. Eventually her brother would tell her parents, and her father would come looking for her. All she had to do was wait. If Mr. Heldrick came out, she would duck behind a tree. Anyone else and she'd run out yelling, "Here I am!"

Bit by bit, her heart rate slowed and she recovered her breath. She leaned against a thick-boled tree and peered around it. It might be hours before her father came through, but she didn't dare stop watching the cleft for a moment.

On a chance, she pulled her smartphone from her pocket and looked at it. No signal—just what she'd expected. She shoved it back.

And waited.

Half an hour passed before a movement caught the

corner of her eye, and she turned her head. Two mounted figures approached from downhill. They were dressed all in black, with long cloaks, and hoods that shadowed their faces. Their horses, unlike those Bess knew, stepped in a curiously mincing fashion that was almost silent. The men rode along the edge of the woods, peering into it. Looking for something.

Of course. How could she have thought for a moment that Mr. Heldrick controlled a portal to this place all by himself? No doubt he'd contacted help as soon as she escaped him. She edged backwards.

At her motion, the heads of both black-cloaked riders swiveled in her direction. One rider tapped the other and pointed straight at her. She stumbled away from the tree and ran, her legs wobbling like a newborn foal's. The horses crashed into the woods behind her. She could hear them now, sure enough, overtaking her from both sides.

She tried to spin and reverse direction, but the blackcloak on her left grabbed her by one arm and lifted her into the air. He pulled his horse to a halt.

"Let me go!" She struck at him with her free arm, but he gave her a shake and held her at arm's length as effortlessly as he might hold a rat by the tail. He looked at her for a moment, his features sharp and unfriendly, before turning to the other and speaking in a harsh, unfamiliar language.

For a minute the two conversed. The arm she dangled by ached. At last the blackcloak who held her shrugged and looked back at her. An unpleasant smile played about his lips. He opened his mouth and spoke a few incomprehensible syllables.

She heard *fffft!* and her captor jerked as the tip of

an arrow appeared, poking at an angle out of his throat. He leaned forward and fell off his horse. Bess landed on her back, the blackcloak face down across her legs. A feathered shaft protruded from his neck. She stared, unable to believe that she lay beneath a dead man. Then she thought, Run! Run!

She pulled her legs from beneath the body and tried to stand, but the dead blackcloak still gripped her wrist. She jerked her arm, but he didn't let go.

The other blackcloak had wheeled his horse. Bess saw a man between two trees with a drawn bow. She scrabbled at the dead man's fingers with her other hand.

Fffft!

With unbelievable speed the second blackcloak lifted an arm, catching the arrow through his forearm rather than in his chest. With his other hand at his lips, he whistled once, piercingly. Then he reached into his cloak and pulled out a long, wide knife.

Another arrow flew and the blackcloak twisted, but the arrow penetrated his stomach. Still, he threw the knife with such force that it flew as fast as any of the arrows and found its mark in the archer's throat.

Bess finally freed her arm from the death-grip of the first blackcloak and staggered to her feet. She turned and fled downhill, deeper into the woods, expecting at any moment to feel a knife thrown by the second blackcloak plunge into her back.

By the time Kierkaven and Cranst responded to the whistle, another vasik and a novice had already arrived. The vasik, twenty paces off, dismounted. Kierkaven watched him bend and pull a knife from the throat of a dead man, a cadril, who still gripped a bow. Two more men, pierced by arrows, lay on the ground beside their horses. By their cloaks, both were vasiks as well. The novice knelt, his ear close to the mouth of one.

"Is he alive?" Cranst asked.

The novice shook his head and stood. "He was when we arrived, though."

"Did he say anything?"

"Tried, but no."

Kierkaven gestured at the dead archer and called to the vasik. "Who's the cadril?"

The vasik looked up, half-amused. "How should I know?"

"Find out. Get some farmer to identify him, and collect the fellow's entire family for the Citadel."

The vasik's expression changed from amusement to displeasure. "Who're you to give orders? You've a vasik's cloak, same as me."

"What's your line of command?"

"I report to Rhun. What's that to do with it?"

"One of Lonnkärin's men?"

"Yes."

"Well, I report to Pandir. Directly."

The other man opened his mouth, closed it. Kierkaven dismounted and walked to the body of the man who'd taken an arrow in the neck. He bent to examine the arrow and then stopped, his attention caught by signs of something dragged from under the man's body.

"Cranst. Someone else was here."

Cranst rode closer. "Are you sure?"

"Of course. You see?" Kierkaven gestured at the trail leading down the hill. "You and these other two take our dead to the post house for identification. I'll follow this trail. Make sure to stay well clear of it."

Bess ran from the woods into a peach orchard. Gasping, with a cramp in her side, she stumbled to a stop. No one followed her yet that she could tell, but when they did they'd outrace her easily. Running was pointless; she needed to think. She needed to *hide*. But where?

She didn't remember passing anything but trees. If she climbed a tree and they discovered her, she couldn't start running again. But she could choose from thousands of trees. They wouldn't know where to look.

She started back to the forest, well away from the place she had entered the orchard—no point in heading right back toward them. Then she paused, aware that she was ignoring acres of free food. She still wasn't thinking. And she couldn't afford that, no matter how good her excuse. Sure, eating was the farthest thing from her mind right now, with fear squeezing her stomach into a tight ball; but her legs trembled from exhaustion and fear. She would need the energy. She plucked two of the peaches, put one in each of her jacket pockets, and went back to the forest.

The trees spread their limbs wide, almost like oaks, yet they grew taller and closer together. Their narrow leaves, barely wider than they were thick, resembled broad pine needles. Dead ones carpeted the forest floor.

She could only reach the branches on the smaller trees, but many large trees had low, broken stubs. Bess chose the first big climbable tree and worked her way up to the branches. Then she heard a distant rustle that grew quickly in volume. She lay flat along a limb of the tree, the bark rough against her cheek, the odor of sap flooding her nostrils, and didn't move.

Five horses rode into view, passing no more than a dozen yards from her position. Three of the horses were ridden by blackcloaks. Well, so were the other two, in a sense—they carried, like baggage, the two who had accosted her. She could see the arrow still in the neck of one. The horsemen rode by without slowing, on to the edge of the woods, into the orchard, and out of sight.

A minute after the sounds faded to silence, Bess dared move. Had the second blackcloak managed to tell the others about her before he died? If so, they would be searching for her. Would they use dogs? Dogs could track her to this tree as easily as sneezing, or to any other tree she climbed.

She noted again how far-reaching the tree limbs were. Without wasting more time she climbed higher in the tree and out along one of its fattest, longest branches. When it started sagging, she switched position and continued hand over hand. The branch drooped lower and her feet brushed branches of an adjacent tree. She edged out further.

The branch bobbed into the other tree and out. Bess waited until it held steady. A stout branch of the other tree was almost within reach. She kicked her legs hard and her branch dipped toward it. She reached out with one hand, caught it.

She let go of the first branch and it snapped up. Her new branch lurched sickeningly, almost throwing her off before she got both hands securely on it. When it steadied, she worked her way closer to the center of the tree. She rested for a minute, then repeated the procedure to the next tree.

Arms trembling, she found a perch where she could rest without falling. No dog could track her now unless it could fly. At least, she hoped so. Just how far could dogs smell, anyway? That was one of the subjects she didn't know a thing about.

She was afraid she might encounter a lot of those, here.

Five minutes later she saw another blackcloak at some distance, on foot, leading a horse and staring at the ground. She watched as he followed her trail to the orchard.

He paused and looked around.

Right. It was probably easy to follow her trail through those needle-leaves, especially running like she was. Now, though . . .

To her surprise, he continued into the orchard, looking at the grass. When he reached the point at which she'd stopped, he angled around, following the path she'd taken out of the orchard. She held perfectly still.

Kierkaven followed the trail to the base of a tree, where it ended. He had the boy trapped now—for surely he tracked a boy. A man would have taken longer strides and at least tried to hide the trail. This cadril, kicking up piles of patula needles with each step—it must be a child. Only the detour through the orchard spoke of any intelligence at all. A few of Kierkaven's stupider compatriots might have lost the trail there.

He raised his eyes. Yes, the boy had used these broken branches to climb the tree. The bark was scuffed here, and here. Yet—

He looked higher, and higher still. The tree appeared empty.

He walked around it slowly, looking up, then again farther from the trunk. Without doubt the boy had departed.

He must have dropped from a limb. Kierkaven walked around the tree again, searching the ground this time, but found no trace.

So the marks on the tree were pretense. The boy never actually went up the tree. Not only that, he must have backtracked in his own footsteps, and done it so carefully that Kierkaven never realized it, never noticed the point at which he left the trail.

Not a boy, then, but a man after all. The short strides were deliberate, to make the backtracking easier. Kierkaven could find the place where the cadril left the trail, now that he knew what to look for, and begin tracking again.

But this cadril appeared far cleverer than Kierkaven cared for. He might lie in wait somewhere, perhaps with more arrows. And Kierkaven was alone.

With a shrug Kierkaven turned away. He'd broken protocol to come this far by himself, and by the time he fetched the others, the cadril would be long gone.

But he'd report this, and the Citadel would double patrols in the area. At least, he told himself, if the cadril had served as accomplice to the archer, he would act again. They always did. And next time, he would not escape.

Bess didn't move, barely breathed, until the blackcloak remounted his horse and rode off. She'd never dreamed they could track her so well even without dogs.

What was going on? Did the blackcloaks really work for Mr. Heldrick? Why did the archer kill them? Whom could she trust?

What little she could see of the sky seemed to be getting darker, and she glanced at her watch. More than an hour had passed since she ran from Mr. Heldrick. Her brother would have returned home by now and told her father that she never came out of Mr. Heldrick's bushes. But how long until they realized she actually went inside the house? How much longer, while Mr. Heldrick stalled her father at the door? Could her father force entrance without a court order? Would he call the police?

Bess hoped so. She didn't want him coming into this place alone.

Wait. Darker? It wouldn't even be getting dark at home, yet—and here . . . When she came through the portal the first time, she'd thought it was morning. She looked at the orchard, where the forest wouldn't block the sky. No direct sunshine anywhere.

Maybe a cloud had gone in front of the sun? But looking straight up the trunk of her tree, she couldn't make out any clouds. Instead, she saw the tip of her tree lit with a reddish glow. Clearly, the sun was setting. In about an hour it would be dark.

Being trapped in the woods at night would not be good. She'd wait five minutes to see if any other blackcloaks came tracking her; if not, she'd head back uphill, toward the portal. In the meantime . . .

She pulled a peach from her jacket pocket. Though she still wasn't hungry, she needed the sugar. She trembled all over.

The fruit was fuzzier than the peaches she was used to, almost furry. She pinched at the skin and half of it tore right off. She set the skin on the branch and sniffed the fruit. It smelled like a peach and, when she bit into it, tasted like one, except for a bitter undertaste. Not quite ripe, perhaps.

With the first bite, she realized that she was hungry after all. Ravenous, in fact. She gulped several bites before noticing the bitterness again, noticeably stronger now. She stopped eating and licked her lips. They burned. Maybe eating this wasn't such a good idea after all. She brought the fruit to her nose and sniffed again. Something odd . . . The remains of her hunger collapsed to a burning, oily queasiness.

Maybe it was just a stress reaction, but she couldn't count on it. And it wouldn't do to toss the fruit somewhere it could be found by her trackers. She reached out to spear it on a small, broken twig, but the distance seemed to grow as she reached. She almost lost her balance. The fruit dropped twenty feet to the ground.

What had she eaten?

Her tongue and lips were swelling now, sudden strangers to each other. Her fingertips tingled and her limbs grew weaker than ever. A spasm of nausea hit her, and she bent over her tree limb; then it passed, leaving her dizzy and adrift. The whole world rolled around, while she floated, unbearably light, in the center; and she didn't realize she'd fallen until she struck the ground.

CHAPTER 4

Bess landed flat on her back and bounced once on the needle-leaves that cushioned the forest floor. She lay in a daze, conscious only of her thickened tongue, a throbbing headache, and a shoulder that felt dislocated.

A bout of shivering brought her to fuller awareness. Though her shoulder hurt, she could move her arm. But the foliage showed stark black against the twilight sky, and all about lay shadow. She'd soon be in utter darkness.

Struggling, she rose to her feet. The ground tipped beneath her; she stumbled to a tree and held the trunk until the ground steadied. Which way to go?

Uphill. The portal lay uphill.

But she could hardly see the ground, let alone which way it tilted. She took a deep breath and let her feet lead her in the direction they thought was correct.

The shivering stopped soon after she started moving. She held out her hands as she walked, to avoid bumping into tree trunks, and counted the trees that she touched to distract herself from the ache in her shoulder and the sting in her mouth.

But darkness swirled at the edge of her mind, and she kept losing count. Her aches grew more insistent with every step. The pain in her mouth spread, and her throat burned every time she swallowed.

What if her throat swelled like her tongue? She could suffocate in this strange place and her father would never find her. The people who did find her wouldn't know where she'd come from. A mystery on both sides . . .

She walked in an open grassy area lit by a full moon. Had the moon been full at home, she wondered? Then she stopped, confused. Where had the trees gone? She couldn't remember leaving the forest, couldn't think—

She was hot, but when she wiped the back of her arm across her brow, her nylon jacket and the dry skin of her forehead rasped together like two dead leaves. Her tongue scraped against her lips when she tried to lick them, and she felt desperately thirsty. Water would be in low areas, so she turned downhill, pulling off her jacket as she went. She tied the sleeves around her waist.

The stinging sharpness of her mouth faded to a dull throb. Her tongue was so numb it might not have been there. She poked a finger into her mouth to check on it and found the inside of her cheeks covered with blisters.

DAY TWO

The next thing she knew she was struggling up a steep hill, gasping for breath.

Down! I'm supposed to go down!

Though she had a reason to go uphill, too; but she couldn't quite remember the reasons for either choice. Sweat from her brow ran stinging into her eyes. She untied the jacket from her waist and mopped at her forehead with the felt lining. Too tired to retie the jacket, she held one cuff in her fist and let the rest drag along the ground.

She lay face down in a meadow, shivering. Her back and shoulder ached, and only her bulging tongue kept her teeth from chattering. One hand still clenched her jacket. She pushed herself to her feet and started to pull the jacket on, then stopped. It was heavy and cold. Wet. Her shoes, too, and the cuffs of her jeans. Somewhere she must have walked through a stream. That seemed a shame, though she couldn't think why. She concentrated on placing one foot before the other. . . .

In the distance, she saw a barn. The moon, large and ruddy, had dropped near the horizon, while the sky opposite glowed with the coming dawn. The barn was a gray shape in the predawn light. A farmhouse lay a short distance beyond. Maybe the people there could help her. She no longer cared whether they would be in league with Mr. Heldrick, or the blackcloaks, or the archer. If she didn't get help, she'd die.

She struggled forward, trying to hold the intent firm in her mind. The farmhouse slid away, keeping its distance as she staggered toward it; and the next thing she knew, the house and barn had disappeared. She stared at empty fields.

But—

She'd cycled out again. She turned until she saw the farmhouse, much closer now. She stared at it, unmoving.

Walk!

Yes, walk. Toward the house, toward help.

Her feet began to move, and move, her heels kicking the dirt, kicking the dirt. She stopped kicking. Why was she lying on her back?

She couldn't remember. She tried to sit up, managed to roll to her side, and saw the barn not twenty yards distant. Tears sprang to her eyes.

She didn't want to die here. She had to reach the barn. That would be good enough. Dying in the barn wouldn't be so bad.

She struggled to her feet and staggered toward the barn. The world spun, and the barn moved from side to side. But she followed it, step after step, until she squeezed through the gap between the barn doors, pulling her jacket after her.

Then the floor swung up and smacked her in the side of the head.

CHAPTER 5

KALE HATED MILKING Maisie but complaining didn't help. "Be glad we've a cow to milk," his mother would say. "Lot of folk round here got none a'tall, have to buy their butter and cream from the dairy."

Kale pushed the large sliding door of the barn aside, letting as much of the dawn light into the barn as possible. Course he didn't mind the cow, and his mother knew it. 'Twas rising with the sun what put the burrs in his shorts. The one time he complained about that, though, Pa had heard, and out came the switch. Kale hadn't groused about milking since, but that didn't mean he'd changed his mind.

In the barn, he set the bucket down, opened his jacket, and stuck his hands under his arms. Maisie wouldn't stand for cold fingers on her udder.

From right at Kale's feet came a low moan. Kale jumped back, then bent forward and took stock. It looked, in the gloom, like a girl on the floor, half covered with loose straw. He leaned closer.

It *was* a girl. Something funny about her lips, though, like a cat that'd found the cream. Flecks of spit, maybe.

Struck by panic, he straightened and stood paralyzed for two long seconds. Then he turned and ran out of the barn. "Ma! Pa!" he shouted at the top of his lungs. "Wellen!"

Wellen appeared first at the farmhouse door. "Cork it, Kale."

Kale tried to hold back his tears. "There's a dead girl in the barn. She's caught plague, I think."

Wellen straightened. "Dead?"

"Well, she will be if she ain't already. And I was standing right next to her!"

"What kind of plague?"

"I— Just plague. How many kinds are there?"

Wellen made a face. "Moonbrain. You don't know what you're spouting about." Wellen started running toward the barn.

"But Wellen, you'll catch it too!" Wellen ignored him, so Kale went on into the house. "Ma! Pa!"

Wellen stepped into the barn and saw the girl right away. He knelt at her side. About twelve years old, he thought. He could see her breathing. With her pale skin she looked like an ice sculpture. He touched her hand and it was cold as ice, too.

Her clothes were . . . odd. Wellen placed his hand against her forehead. To his surprise she jerked away from him and her eyes snapped open. But they unfocused again and her lids drooped. She moaned.

Wellen noticed the small blisters on the girl's lips and the protruding tip of her tongue. He pulled down her jaw without encountering resistance and peered into her mouth. Her dark, parched tongue filled her mouth, and more blisters covered the inside of her cheeks.

Wellen scooped the girl into his arms and stood. She fought a moment, then stared at him and made some meaningless sounds. She began to shiver.

He carried the girl back to the house, into the sitting room. The girl curled against his chest for warmth.

"Put her here." Ma spread blankets on the floor before the fireplace. "Poor thing, must be half froze."

Pa had started some tinder burning and now added wood to the fireplace. "I wonder where she's from."

Wellen set the girl down. She clung to his jacket, but when he covered her with a blanket she clung to that instead. "She's got funny clothes," he said.

"Do you reckon—maybe. . . ." Ma looked back and forth from Wellen to Pa and blurted, "Could she have escaped?"

Pa came and took her hands.

"Needa, there ain't none that escape."

Ma looked down and heaved a deep sigh. "Yeah. Yeah, I know. Anyhow, she don't look old enough."

Pa frowned at the girl. "We help the girl till she's well. But then we find out where she's from and why she's here."

"I think she needs water, Ma."

"Kale," Ma shouted. "Bring some water."

"I ain't coming in there," Kale called from the other room. "I don't want to catch plague."

"Kale!" Pa's nostrils flared. "The girl's sick, needs our help. You bring water or you'll catch a lot worse than plague."

Kale brought water.

CHAPTER 6

DAY THREE

-
-
-
-
-
-
-
-
-
-

CHAPTER 7

.
.
.
.
.
.
..
....

Shadows.
A flickering candle.
A woman sat knitting. Who?
Her name popped into Bess's head
and out again. Other bits of memory surfaced
and vanished, like vegetables in a boiling stew. A few
had staying power: falling from a tree; a man with an
arrow through his neck; reaching the barn; an arm
supporting her in front of a crackling fire while someone
tipped sips of water into her mouth.

But this was no barn, and no one held her now
except heavy blankets and a soft bed.

Yawning gaps splintered her memory, large enough to swallow whole months, strewn with hazy and indistinct scenes from a dream that never ended: strangers appeared and disappeared, saying words she did not understand. Sometimes she thought she talked back, though with no idea what she might have said.

She wore a nightshirt instead of her clothes. Another memory surfaced—gentle hands sponging her clean. Or was that happening now? No, the woman still sat knitting. But memories kept fusing with the present, making it difficult to work out what had happened, when.

She couldn't manage it now. Her eyes closed and she went back to sleep, to strange dreams, to nothingness.

When she next woke, a young man sat in the room, reading by yellow candlelight. How long had she been sick? Weeks must have passed since . . . since—

She ran her tongue around the inside of her mouth. The blisters were gone.

But where was she? She pulled the covers close under her chin, and the young man looked up. He set his book down and spoke softly: *"Dom po evert. Enawbiddy noss urar."*

"I . . . don't understand."

His eyebrows rose. He stood, went to the door, and called, "Ma!"

That word, Bess had heard, was common to nearly all languages.

Within moments a thin woman in a heavy dressing gown entered the room. Sleep filled her eyes and dull brown hair fell in front of her face. She looked at Bess and started to speak, but her son interrupted her. The woman frowned and replied. The two talked back and forth, while Bess listened. The language intrigued her with its familiarity. She must have heard it before, but it couldn't be the language the blackcloaks had used. That had been harsh and guttural.

The woman turned to Bess and asked a question. Bess turned her palms up and shrugged. The woman made eating motions, and at the thought of food a voracious hunger descended on Bess. She nodded.

The woman left and the young man returned to his chair. He thumped himself on the chest and said, "Wellen." Bess repeated it and said her own name.

Wellen nodded and began talking. His tone soothed Bess. Surely these people meant her no harm.

The woman returned with a bowl of thin broth containing a few bits of beef and vegetables. Bess hid her disappointment. She had hoped for a more substantial meal. Wellen jumped up and performed introductions: "Needa, Bess. Bess, Needa." Bess forced a smile and said, "Thank you, Needa."

Needa stroked Bess's hair once with a sad sort of smile, and left. Bess began to eat. To her great surprise, a few mouthfuls filled her. Her stomach must have shrunk to the size of a walnut. She couldn't finish.

Wellen took the bowl away. Bess fell asleep before he returned.

Still dark. Bess raised her head. Wellen was slouched in his chair, asleep. The candle burned low.

She had to go to the bathroom and vaguely recalled Needa leading her there before. She eased out from under the covers, set her feet on the icy floor, and stood up, too quickly. A wave of dizziness hit her and she staggered, bumping Wellen's chair, waking him.

He stood and grabbed her shoulders, steadying her, concern written on his face.

"I have to go to the bathroom," Bess said; but Wellen jabbered and pushed her gently onto the bed. He thinks I'm delirious again, she realized. "Please," she said, and struggled to rise, but he refused to allow it.

Bess bit her lip. This incident could become mortifying. She tried to make Wellen understand, but he wouldn't budge.

So she took a deep breath:

"Needa!"

Wellen's eyes widened and he said "Shh!" followed by more of his irritatingly familiar language. Couldn't he see that she'd regained her senses?

Needa appeared and spoke sharply to Wellen. He took his hands off Bess's shoulders. Needa looked in Bess's eyes, then at the way she sat with her thighs pressed together. She spoke again to Wellen.

He turned red as a brick. Needa shooed him out of the bedroom and led Bess downstairs to the bathroom. The toilet held no water; instead, a board slanted down into a dark hole. No odor rose from it, though; instead, a draft of air flowed constantly down it.

After they returned, Needa brought Bess another bowl of the soup, which Bess managed to finish. Needa took the bowl, snuffed the candle, and left Bess in the room alone.

The small breakfast that Needa brought in the morning filled Bess's stomach but left her soul empty. She wanted to believe that everything was a dream, that she *still* dreamed. But the touch of the sheets and the odors of bacon and wood smoke pinned her to reality like a butterfly to a display.

Wellen's book still rested by the candle on the side table. Maybe she could identify the language if she saw it in print. That might give her a clue to her whereabouts. She tossed back the covers and sat up. This time she waited several seconds, then eased to her feet. The floor hadn't warmed up one bit. She stepped to the table, grabbed the book, and hopped back into bed.

When she looked at the book, her jaw dropped. The cover bore the inscription, *"Travels in Kendali-Land,* by K. V. Emberston."

English?

She opened the book with care and turned the brittle, age-browned pages. It was all English. But they hadn't been *speaking* English.

Had they?

Thoughtfully, she closed the book and considered. Whatever the language was, it had the same sorts of sounds as English: no rolled r's, no gutturals, no oriental singsong. That, she realized now, was why it had sounded familiar. And the flow, the rhythm, was English-like as well. If she'd heard it spoken at a distance, too far to make out the words, she probably would have thought it was English right away.

Which didn't mean it *was.* But with the book being in English—

Still, she couldn't just assume it. It would mean that transpositions had occurred, that the mapping of letters to sounds differed from one world to the other.

If—and it was a big *if*—it actually turned out to be English, then it was English with a difference. *Otherworld* English. She had wondered if the portal might—possibly—have transported her somewhere on Earth, since the old familiar moon had lighted her wanderings through the countryside. But she didn't believe that anyone on her Earth spoke English like this.

Wellen knocked on the doorframe and, ducking his head, spoke words she couldn't understand, still embarrassed from the night before. He stepped to the side table and stared at it.

"Wellen." Bess held up the book.

He looked, started to speak, and stopped. Bess set the book in her lap and made writing motions on the palm of one hand, but he frowned, puzzled; so she gestured that he should bring the chair over to the bed. He'd catch on soon enough.

Wellen brought the chair. Bess handed him the book, opened to the first page, and moved her finger along the first few lines to suggest that he should read. Wellen, puzzled, began reading silently.

"Aloud, you fool!" Bess snatched the book and started reading it herself. She moved her finger under the words as she read:

"One of the most fascinating aspects of travel in Kendali-Land is travel *to* Kendali-Land." She handed the book back.

Confusion clouded Wellen's eyes, but he took her meaning, and read:

"Oan if thaw mast vosnaytink uzbex if driffel on Gentoli-Lint uz driffel *dow* Gentoli-Lint."

Otherworld English it was. Bess took the book again and tried to reread the sentence in Otherworld, as Wellen had. Wellen blinked and corrected her pronunciation of "aspects." He read another sentence, and Bess repeated it.

Then his eyes lit up, and *he* made writing motions.

"Yes!" Bess almost forgot to accompany the word with a nod.

Wellen set the book down and left the room. In a minute he returned with slate and a lump of chalk. Bess grabbed them from his hands, scrawled "Where am I?" and returned the slate to Wellen. He looked at it, glanced at Bess and back at the slate. He shrugged and shook his head.

Maybe in her excitement she'd scribbled her handwriting. She retrieved the slate: only a bit messier than usual. But Wellen might not know cursive.

She erased the slate and printed the same question, carefully and neatly. Heavens, this would make for slow communication.

Wellen nodded this time and, for Bess's benefit, said the words in Otherworld before erasing them. Bess repeated them.

Wellen took the chalk and printed his answer laboriously, with his tongue in the corner of his mouth. Bess realized that the effort went less into writing the words than drawing the letters. He knew how to do it, but the knowledge was a rarely practiced skill: in his head, not his hand.

He held up the board and said the words in Otherworld, and Bess read, "Kallikot district." She said it aloud in Wellen's pronunciation, hiding her disappointment.

What had she expected? She and she alone knew where she was: through the portal. She had asked a foolish question.

She took the slate. "How long have I been sick?"

He answered: "We found you at dawn, two days past."

Only two days! That meant she'd passed through the portal less than three days ago. Her father wouldn't have given up the search for her already—unless the blackcloaks had captured him.

Why, he might have come here.

She wrote, "Has anyone come asking for me?"

Her anxiety must have shown, for Wellen shook his head in answer before writing his reply:

"You're safe here."

Safe? From the blackcloaks? Or from a danger she didn't know about yet? She wanted to ask, but telling Wellen about her father came first.

"My father will search for me."

"Describe him."

She filled the slate describing her father in as much detail as she could. Before she finished, her hand began to tremble. Wellen must have sensed her exhaustion, for after reading the slate, he stood and took it and the chalk away. Bess slumped back on her pillow and fell asleep in moments.

When she woke, the afternoon sun shone through her window. Needa looked in a few minutes later, then left and returned with lunch. After Bess ate, she and Needa read back and forth from Wellen's book. Bess could sense Needa's own uncertainty of how to pronounce some of the words, but that didn't matter. The way she sounded out the words gave Bess as much information about Otherworld English as anything did.

Within an hour, Bess had gathered a general sense of the transformations and could understand some of what Needa read before seeing the sentences. Understanding someone else speak Otherworld came more easily than speaking it herself. They began reading entire paragraphs at a time, but shortly after that Needa left to prepare supper.

Bess wondered where Wellen had gone. She wished he'd return so she could keep practicing the language. She tried to think in Otherworld, but unless she said the thoughts out loud, unless she used her tongue and lips to hold the sounds down, they kept slithering back into their accustomed pronunciation.

Eventually she heard the outside door open and recognized Wellen's voice, and his father's. Soon afterward Needa brought Bess supper on a tray. Bess ate quickly, hoping to practice speaking more after eating, but by the time she finished supper she was drowsing off. She decided that perhaps she hadn't entirely recovered, and that was her last conscious thought of the day.

A glint of light from the ground ahead flashed and vanished as Grayvle rode out of the stream. He pulled his horse to a stop.

Corck turned. "What's the problem?"

"Saw something shiny."

"So what? Probably some rock."

"No." Grayvle began to back the horse up, hoping the glint would reappear.

It did. He rode forward again, keeping his eye on the spot. It looked like a piece of metal. An artifact, tilted toward the sun by a rock beneath it, perhaps.

"What the hell are you prancing around for?"

Corck sounded annoyed, but Grayvle looked up and saw him smiling. Good. Grayvle was pleased to have been paired with Corck for these training patrols. Some of the other vasiks were so hidebound, he might easily have done something they considered poor judgment, and they'd have written him up, ruining his near-perfect youngling record. Corck was flexible enough that he could extend some flexibility to Grayvle, as well.

Of course, if Grayvle did something really wrong, he knew Corck would be merciless.

He dismounted and bent over. Definitely an artifact. It resembled a key, though he'd never seen another like it. He plucked it from the mud.

Instead of a rock, another artifact lay beneath the key, stuck halfway into the mud and connected to the key by a very small chain. He stepped back to the stream and rinsed the things off.

The chain, like the key, was metal, but the second item was not. Nor was it wood, nor glass.

Grayvle had no clue what it was, and that disturbed him.

"Where do you think this came from?" He tossed it to Corck, who looked at it carefully, his face now utterly serious.

"I don't know," Corck said at last. "What do you think we should do about it?" He glanced at the tracks in the mud.

Grayvle hesitated, also looking at the tracks, but after a moment he dragged his eyes away. "Make sure the

Citadel knows. That's the first step. They can decide whether to send someone back here to follow the trail."

Corck smiled again. "Absolutely correct." He pocketed the item. "Let's go. At least it's an excuse to return from patrol duty early."

CHAPTER 8

Arrick and Wellen were gone again, but Needa read with Bess practically all day. Bess progressed so quickly with her reading that, by the time Needa left to fix supper, Bess could outpace the older woman. She continued to read aloud, to herself, until Needa arrived with her food.

"Sorry it's so late," Needa apologized. "Arrick and Wellen was late getting back."

"Where have they been?"

Needa hesitated. "You can ask them yourself after you eat. I think you're ready to get up." She set out a fresh set of clothes. "These are warmer than what you come in," she said. "When you're dressed, come downstairs."

Bess ate and then pulled on the clothes—leggings, a long skirt, a blouse, and a sweater. Her own clothes were there, too, along with the meager contents of her pockets: a couple of dimes and her smart phone. She wondered what Needa had made of that. When dressed, she went downstairs to join the family sitting around the fireplace.

Most of her interactions so far had been with Needa and Wellen. She'd seen Kale several times, peeking into her room, before Wellen caught him. Arrick she'd seen just once, when he had introduced himself then left without another word. But now he spoke first.

"What town d'you hail from?"

"Uh . . ." Somehow she hadn't expected that to be the first question. "It's called Benton, but that won't mean much to you. How did you know I was from any town? I didn't even know you had towns here."

"Course," Needa answered. "Nearest is fifteen miles. Nigh-on five hundred folk. Where do you think we find glass for our windows, oil for our lamps? Don't they sell things like that in your town?" She looked almost accusatory.

"I . . . suppose they do. We just moved there."

"From another town?" asked Arrick.

Bess nodded. "Almost everyone lives in town where I'm from. Is that a problem? You don't seem too happy about it."

Arrick frowned in doubt, and Wellen said, "Maybe you better tell us how you came so far from home."

"Well, it's hard to believe—"

"Just tell."

She started her story with the baseball her brother hit, thinking a familiar beginning would make the rest more acceptable. But she knew she hadn't managed when Kale asked first thing, "What kind of a ball's that?"

Arrick shushed him, and from then on they listened without interrupting, until Bess told of opening the door in Mr. Heldrick's basement and seeing another world through it.

"Ah," Arrick said. "A mousehole."

"Pardon me?"

"Old man had a mousehole in his basement. Smart of him to cover it. Never can tell what might come through one of those, though a door's a bit of overkill. Go on: What happened next?"

Bess stumbled mentally, as if she'd stepped on the top step that wasn't there. "I didn't know what to call it. I'd never seen one—"

"Go on with you," Needa said. "Did you grow up in a closet then?"

"No. Don't you understand? I grew up on the other side."

"Of what?"

"Of the—the mousehole! What are we talking about?"

And now the disbelief she'd expected earlier hit.

"Oh, no, Bess," Needa said, as if to a small child. "You can't go through a mousehole. They're too small. That's why they call them mouseholes."

"This wasn't small, and you're the ones who called it a mousehole. I call it the portal. The point is, Mr. Heldrick caught me. He tried to shoot me, and I didn't know what to do but run through to this side. Now I don't know whether he's sent out other people to search for me, or where my father is, or how to find my way home, or, or . . ." She stopped and bit her lip.

Arrick stroked his chin. "Grandpa said he once saw a mousehole big enough to toss a fox through."

"Aye, and you never believed him, neither," Needa said.

"Still, a mousehole that size'd be almost big enough for this girl to squeeze through."

"But I didn't squeeze through," Bess said. "I ran through. Any of you could go through standing up. How can you believe in it so easily and still quibble about its size?"

Arrick and Needa's faces continued to express doubt.

Wellen asked, "Can you find the mousehole again? If you're able, we could see for ourselves."

"I think I could, if you could take me partway. There's an orchard nearby. When I ran from Mr. Heldrick I turned toward the woods. . . ."

She stopped. Everyone else had turned their heads away from her, their attention captured.

Bess listened but heard nothing special.

Needa stood. "Quick. We must hide her."

"Every trace," added Arrick. He turned to Kale and Wellen. "Clean her room. Change the linens, make the bed—"

"What's going on?" Bess asked.

"No time for linens!" Needa said. "But straighten the bed."

She pulled Bess from her chair saying, "Up, girl." She took the chair and set it in an inconspicuous corner of the room.

Bess identified the pounding hooves of a galloping horse, distant but approaching.

"Where can we put her?" Needa asked Arrick.

"I'm thinking!"

"How about the bed drawer?" Needa adjusted the other chairs around the fireplace to suggest that four had sat there all along.

Arrick nodded. "Come."

He ran up the stairs and down the hall to his and Needa's bedroom. Bess stayed close behind. Arrick flipped up the edge of the coverlet, revealing a solid bedstead without legs or under space. He hooked his hands into two inconspicuous nooks at the bottom, pulled, and out came a huge drawer.

He pulled enough clothes and linens out to make room for Bess. "In."

While Bess climbed in, Needa brought the boys into the room and told them to put with the laundry everything Arrick had pulled out.

Bess sat up suddenly. "The clothes I came in— they're in my room."

"I've taken your things out," Needa said. "Now lie down."

The hoofbeats sounded very loud as Arrick pushed Bess into darkness.

Arrick's heart pounded as he stepped outside to greet the rider. Tall, gaunt, and hooded, the rider dismounted and held out the reins of his horse. Arrick took them and flipped them around the rarely used hitching post. The rider started toward the house without waiting. Arrick hurried past him and opened the door.

The rider entered the house without breaking stride.

Wellen waited inside with Needa behind him, her arm around Kale's shoulders.

Arrick closed the door. "What do you want from us?"

The rider pushed his hood back. He looked to be in his mid thirties, with a sharp nose and dark eyes. "You have a fire. The night is cold."

Arrick motioned to the fireplace.

The rider stretched his hands toward the fire. His shirt and pants, like his cloak, were black. For a moment he warmed himself, then he turned and faced the family. His eyes moved around the room, taking in every detail.

No one asked him to sit.

He said, "I search for a girl."

Needa tightened her lips and the old anger rose in Arrick's chest. He quelled the anger, crushed it like a beetle; but he worried about his son. Wellen knew to hide the anger, right enough; but not how to kill it, nor how to dig out the dangerous thoughts that burrowed into the heart with it. "We ain't got no daughters."

"No. I seek a particular girl. She stands this tall—" The rider held his hand palm down. "—with brown hair, brown eyes, and a somewhat large nose. She would be too young for work in the Citadel, and a stranger to these parts. She might speak another language, or perhaps like a town girl. Have any of you seen such a person? Despite her youth she is a dangerous criminal and must be apprehended."

"Ain't seen any strangers, except yourself."

"You speak for your family?"

Arrick shrugged. "Anyone else seen any strangers?"

Everyone shook their heads.

The rider considered. "I will inspect your house."

He began to move from room to room, picking up and examining occasional knick-knacks. Everyone followed him. When he went upstairs, he stopped first at Kale's room.

"Who uses this room?"

"The boy."

The rider nodded, moved to Bess's room.

"And this?"

Arrick struggled to harden his face into a wooden mask, to show no more emotion than a fish. "Vacant, now."

Arrick saw tears run down both of Needa's cheeks, but the rider didn't notice. He made a circuit of the room, opened a drawer, glanced under the bed.

"Vacant, you say?"

"Aye."

The rider allowed himself a faint smile and moved on.

In Arrick and Needa's bedroom he walked around the bed to the far side of the room before flipping up the bed covers. Seeing the solid underframe, he frowned. He took a step back and examined it from end to end, then kicked it once. Slowly, he walked to the foot of the bed. Again, he ran his eyes over the wood.

He stepped to the near side, lifted the covers, glanced at the solid construction beneath, and dropped them. Then he paused, lifted them again, and flipped them onto the bed. He bent and traced the almost invisible line of the drawer with his finger.

"Very clever."

He took a step back, dropped to his knees, and pulled the drawer open.

Bess wasn't there.

Needa's hand rose to her mouth. Arrick elbowed her and she lowered it.

The rider's nostrils flared and his lips turned white, and he stared for several seconds into the empty hollow where Bess had lain. Then he shut the drawer and stood.

"I will return in several days. If you see or hear of the girl before I come back, do not bother to report her. Give me the information when I return. Is that clear?"

Everyone nodded.

Without another word the rider strode from the room, down the stairs to the sitting room, and on to the door.

He raised his hood as he went, and paused at the door until Arrick opened it for him. Then he went out, remounted his steed, and cantered off into the darkness.

The moment Arrick closed the door, Needa said, "Where—" but Arrick clapped a hand over her mouth. He couldn't figure it. Why'd the rider left so easy?

He opened the window and listened until distance muted the thudding of hoofbeats to silence. At last he closed the window and nodded to Needa.

"Where'd she go?" Needa asked.

"Don't know." Arrick led the way upstairs to the bedroom. He opened the bed drawer again and frowned at the empty space.

"We'd best find her," Needa said.

"Aye. Easy to say. But she could be anywhere."

Wellen said, "Not anywhere. She must be in the house."

"Rubbish. He'd a knowed it."

"He'd a knowed it if she left. There ain't no way she could slip outside tonight without letting in a gust of cold air. We'd all know it."

"Nor no way she could slip out of the bed drawer neither, a girl like that. But she did, didn't she?" Arrick stared at the empty space in the drawer. "And a good thing too, or it'd be all our necks."

A muffled thumping followed, and the open drawer jiggled and moved out another half inch.

Arrick gaped for a second, then motioned to Wellen. They grabbed opposite sides of the drawer and yanked it out. A moment later Bess poked her head out of the cavity.

Wellen said, "You can come out now."

"I should hope so." The girl rolled onto her back, grabbed the edge of the bed, and pulled herself from underneath, collecting balls of dust on the way. "Do you think I'd make a racket like that otherwise?"

"But how'd you know he left?" Arrick asked.

"I could hear you talking." She knocked the bigger clumps of dust off her shoulders and out of her hair, and sneezed. "Who was he?"

"A rider. As you must've guessed."

Bess frowned. "Well, yeah, I heard the horse, I knew he was riding. But—wait, he wasn't wearing a black cloak, was he?"

"He was a rider, Bess," Wellen repeated. "What else would he wear?"

Bess stared at him blankly.

Arrick, puzzled, said, "If you didn't know who it was, why'd you hide?" Maybe this girl really had popped through a mousehole. What place on earth didn't know of the riders?

"You're the ones who hid me. I figured you must have had a reason, so when I heard footsteps by the bed I grabbed the slats under the mattress with my fingers and toes, lifted myself up, and let the drawer slide out without me. Did I do the wrong thing?"

"Gracious no, child!" Needa said. "You couldn't have done righter."

"But," Bess asked, "why did you hide me? Even before you knew who it was?"

"Strangers ain't allowed here, Bess," Arrick said.

"Pardon?"

"On account of it being a crime to leave one's home province." Arrick felt awkward declaring what any fool should know. "Also to travel after dark, which I reckon you must've done to wind up in the barn at dawn."

"Um, yes. I did. All night long, in fact."

"You're lucky not to've got spotted by a patrol. But this one here tonight—he wasn't just making trouble. He was looking for you particularly."

The girl's eyes widened. "What makes you say that?"

"He described you exactly."

"Oh." Bess closed her eyes for a long moment. When she opened them again she said, "I guess I'd better tell you the rest of the story. Maybe then you can figure it out."

CHAPTER 9

"... AND THEN I ran," Bess said, "before any more riders came."

"The archer might've been Pry," Wellen interrupted. "Did you see an orchard nearby?"

"Yes!" If they knew where the orchard was, they could show her how to get home.

"That's who, then," Wellen said.

"Damn fool," Arrick said.

"But Pa, he took two down with him!"

"And what of it? He's dead! You think that's a good trade, two of them for one of us?"

The two locked stares until Needa said, "Don't forget about Bess. He got her loose, too."

Both Arrick and Wellen jerked their eyes toward Needa, then looked at Bess. "Well, yeah," Arrick admitted. "That's worth something."

Needa snorted. She asked Bess, "What happened next?"

Bess explained about the fruit and falling from the tree. "Why did—Pry?—grow those awful things?"

"For the pits. Here." Needa lifted the lid off a candy dish. It held nuts resembling small almonds. "Try one."

Bess shrank back.

"They're good, Bess." Wellen popped one into his mouth.

"I'd rather not."

Wellen shrugged and took another. Needa quickly recapped the dish.

In the corner, the clock softly chimed eleven. Bess realized she had been hearing the chimes all evening without paying attention. "Is that clock right?" she asked.

"Aye. Pretty near," said Arrick.

She looked at her watch. It read eight fifty-seven. Fat lot of good that did her. She reset it to eleven o'clock.

Needa observed her as she pushed the buttons. "I ought to've looked closer at that. Thought it seemed an odd bracelet."

But Arrick said, "What happened next?"

Bess shrugged. "I wandered until I reached the barn. You know the rest better than I do."

"Aye," Arrick said, but continued to frown.

"What is it?"

"We heard no news of your pa," Wellen said. "That's where we been the past two days, talking to neighbors. Nobody's heard tell of anyone to fit the description you gave. Seems they should've, if he's out hunting for you."

"But that's not possible! It's been—" She quickly counted the days, hoping she'd understood how long she was asleep. "—four days since—"

"Now, now," Needa said. "Sit back down. That don't mean nothing. They couldn't out and ask, you know, without raising questions. They told folk nearby they'd heard tell of someone like your pa wandering near Pry's place, and no one picked up on it."

Bess didn't remember standing. She sat, but on the edge of her seat. "Do you think the riders might have caught him?"

Arrick shrugged. "If they did, that'd explain why this one came here tonight."

"My father would never tell them about me!"

Arrick shrugged, reluctantly. "Your pa's human, Bess. The riders ain't."

"What do you mean? Of course they're human."

But Arrick shook his head. "They're riders. Don't count on your pa to've kept no secrets from them, if they chose to ask."

The words chilled her, but she shook her head. "My father's a smart man. He wouldn't set off into a strange world alone. He'd go back and call the police. And if anyone had captured him, then my mother would have called the police. Either way, there ought to be a crowd of people searching for me."

"But there ain't." Arrick spread his hands. "Your pa must never of made it through. I think you guessed right—Mr. Heldrick works with the riders. Some would've helped him hide the mousehole so's your pa couldn't find it, and others would've gone hunting you, like that one here tonight."

"But those two that Pry killed—why didn't they drag me to the portal when they first caught me?"

"Expect they weren't really looking for you. On patrol, more'n likely, and chased you cause you ran. The old man wouldn't've had time yet to contact the riders."

In other words, if her father weren't here already, she couldn't count on his arrival any time soon. "If you took me to Pry's orchard, I think I could find my own way back to the portal."

Arrick shook his head. "Can't take you to the orchard now."

"Why?"

"Too many riders about. They took his orchard for themselves when they killed him. They'll take this year's crop, then let it go. It's too much trouble for the Citadel to keep up permanently, even with town help."

"What's the Citadel?"

"Their base. Where they live when they ain't out hounding folk."

"And the town people help them?"

"Sometimes. Town folk are merchants and craftsmen, and riders are their best customers. So they shine up to the riders and imitate their highfalutin way of talking—"

Arrick stopped and rubbed his shin where Needa had kicked it.

"Ah," said Bess. "So that's why you thought I was from town? From the way I talk?"

Arrick nodded.

"What about the riders?" Bess asked. "Where did they come from?"

Arrick pulled at an ear. "You really don't know?"

"How could I know? We don't have such things on my side of the mousehole."

". . . Right. Well, I reckon we don't know where they came from neither, not really. Stories say—and mind, they're old stories, hundreds of years old—that the riders came through a mousehole, like you did. I always figured that idea was crazy. Actually, the stories say a different folk, called the Settlers, came through and built the riders after they got here. But that don't make no sense either. The riders ain't machines. Anyway, they just left."

"Who left? The Settlers?"

"Yep."

"Why? It doesn't make sense that they'd have 'built' the riders and then gone off."

He shrugged. "Didn't like it here, maybe; nobody knows."

"Tell her about the Renegade, Pa!" Kale said.

Arrick grimaced. "She didn't ask that."

Well. *That* piqued her curiosity. "Ask what? Who's the Renegade?"

"A rider who fought for common folk," Wellen answered. "But no real rider would ever do that. Anyway those stories are old, too."

"They say he still comes back," insisted Kale.

"Oh, for—!" Arrick looked annoyed. "It's just the stories that come back. It can't never of happened. And it's way past your bedtime."

"Aw, Pa!"

"I'll take him," said Needa. "Come along, then."

Kale reluctantly followed Needa up the stairs.

Bess wasn't ready to drop the topic, though. "Why do you say there never could have been a renegade?"

Arrick rolled his eyes. "Past your bedtime, too."

Bess didn't move, and after a moment Arrick sighed. "Because no rider would do that, ever."

"That's easy to say. But people aren't all the same—"

"Riders ain't 'people.'"

"All right, then, horses aren't all the same. Dogs aren't all the same. I don't see why it should be so impossible that at some time, some rider didn't like what his people were doing and decided to fight against them."

"But Bess," Wellen asked, "what difference can it make? Pa's grandpa heard those stories when he was a boy, and they were old then. It ain't like the Renegade could still be around to help us."

"No, of course not. You're missing the point. You're so set on thinking the riders are all bad that you wouldn't recognize a good one if he saved your life."

"That'd be the day!" said Needa, coming back down the stairs. Her voice had never held anything but kindness, but now she spoke with such bitterness that Bess was taken aback. She must be missing something.

Well, okay, she was missing lots of things. Renegades, Settlers, riders who were built not born . . . it all ran together in her mind. "Why do you say they're not human?" she asked. "They looked human enough to me."

Arrick said, "Aside from the stories? They're too strong to be human, too fast. It's said they can hear what you say in your house from a distance of a mile."

"It's said! Who says? That's got to be an exaggeration."

Arrick shrugged a bit sheepishly. "Well, yeah. Maybe so. But we can't beat them, and that ain't no exaggeration. There ain't no point resisting."

"But all of you resisted, tonight. You hid me."

Arrick frowned. "Didn't think straight."

"Why, Arrick Verdanit!" Needa said. "You never thought straighter in your life, you rattleheaded lout."

A grin split Arrick's dour face, and Needa turned to Bess. "We couldn't let him take you off, that's all."

"But you resisted and got away with it."

"Ah, and you should've seen his face when he opened that drawer and you wasn't there."

"*His* face?" Arrick said to Needa. "What about your own, then?"

"I may've been a mite surprised, I admit. But no more than you yourself."

"Well, mayhap I was. A bit."

Arrick smiled and Needa laughed, and Wellen said, "You took us all aback, and if the rider'd thought to look at our faces we'd a given the whole thing away, as well as if you never disappeared in the first place."

"What would have happened then?"

Wellen shrugged. "He'd a started tearing the place apart. And when he found you—well, that depends on the mood of the rider. He might've done nothing except haul you off, since he'd found what he wanted. Or he might've killed us all on the spot. Most likely he'd a sent us to the Citadel for a term. They're not always vicious, though you never know."

"But why couldn't you all have jumped on him at once, or hit him over the head with a kettle, or something?"

Arrick muttered, "Girl don't understand a thing."

"Bess." Wellen gave a little shake. "The riders have weapons. We don't. Besides, that one here tonight could've torn this house down, except maybe the fireplace and the foundation. It might've took him a few hours—maybe a day—but he could've done it, and without help, and left not a wall standing. If we attacked him . . . well, he'd a killed us sure. That'd be suicide, not resistance."

"Then why do some people decide to fight back? Why did Pry?"

For a moment no one spoke. Needa clenched her fists and stared at her feet. At last, Arrick said, "Pry's wife died a year or so ago. They only had the one child, a girl, a few years older than you. About two months back the riders took her."

Bess grew warm outside and cold inside. *The riders took her.* A dozen things clicked together in her mind, and she knew that Pry's daughter wasn't the only girl the riders had "taken." She ran her hands over the clothes Needa had given her.

Girl's clothes.

She had never thought to wonder why Needa kept such clothes in the house when no girl lived there to wear them.

"Oh, Needa, Arrick . . . I'm so sorry."

Needa leaned forward and rested a hand on Bess's shoulder. "In a few weeks they'll decide you lost yourself in the woods for good, or drowned in Nedick's lake, and they'll stop hunting you. When that happens, we can try to help you back to your mousehole. Meanwhile it'll be nice to have a girl in the house again."

"But I can't stay a few weeks, Needa. You've been good to me, wonderful really, but my parents must be frantic."

"And the rider'll come back in a few days," Wellen said. "If we can't return Bess to her mousehole we'll have to find some other place to hide her. That rider won't fall for the same trick twice. Fact is, we'd be safer taking her back to the mousehole and going through with her."

Needa's face hardened. "We can't leave Corlene."

"Oh, Ma, Corlene's gone. But if the riders think we know about the mousehole, they might send us all to the Citadel to make sure none of us try to use it. So we got to use it, whether we want to or no."

"Why would they care if you used it?" Bess asked. "It can't hurt them."

"It can," Wellen said. "Course, the riders don't want no one here sneaking off; but even more, they fear the mischief folk they don't control could do them."

Of course. The riders must dread having the mousehole discovered by Bess's world, given the difference in technology. No wonder they wanted to find her! They would never consent to her return. Not on her life.

At that moment a cold draft blew through the sitting room and the fire guttered in the fireplace, then sprang up more brightly than before. There followed the sound of the back door to the house being shut and latched.

CHAPTER 10

Everyone jumped up. Bess couldn't think where to run, so she stood frozen. Needa stepped to her side.

The sound of footsteps crossed the kitchen, and a tall rider, hooded and cloaked, appeared in the doorway.

"No one outside to greet me this time?"

"Didn't hear you coming," Arrick said, his face a blank mask but his voice thick with fear, or anger.

"Indeed. I see you've already found the one I search for. Commendable of you."

"No!" said Needa; then more quietly: "No, this is our niece. She's spending the evening. She didn't show up till after you left, see, and—"

"Out after curfew, then? A serious offense, that." The rider waved his hand. "—No matter. I'll not punish her for it. But she must come with me."

"But she ain't the stranger you asked for! She's our niece—"

"Yes, yes. Your niece or not, she is the one I seek."

He pushed back his hood and said to Bess, "You remember me perhaps?"

And all at once she did; for although he looked thirty-five, with dark brown hair, and stood tall and straight, she couldn't mistake his gaunt face, black eyes, and sharp nose.

"Mr. Heldrick. . . ."

"In this world, my friend, the word 'Mr.' possesses no meaning. These people would no doubt think it part of my name. Call me Heldrick."

My friend. Bess was too angry to speak until she noticed everyone gaping at Heldrick and herself and realized that Heldrick had spoken to her in regular—Homeworld—English.

She relayed the conversation in Otherworld.

Arrick frowned, and murmured to Bess, "Thought you said he was an old man."

Heldrick looked at Arrick a moment before speaking. "I found the disguise of an elderly recluse useful in that world." His Otherworld English flowed as smoothly as his Homeworld. "In this world, such a disguise would serve no purpose."

"So instead you disguise yourself as a rider?" Bess said, still angry. "What's the point of that, to frighten—"

Heldrick turned as Needa clapped a hand over Bess's mouth.

"In this world," he said, "I wear no disguises."

Bess swallowed.

"Please sir," Needa whispered, "forgive the child. She ain't familiar with things here."

Heldrick stretched out his hand.

"The time is short. The girl must come with me now."

But Needa cried out, "No!" Then, more quietly, when Heldrick's eyes narrowed, "No, she's my niece, she's not who you think. It would be a mistake—"

"Stop. Tell me your name, woman."

The hand that Needa held against Bess's mouth trembled. "Needa, sir."

"Needa." His black eyes turned to Bess. "And yours, girl? —Needa, you must remove your hand from her mouth before she can answer."

Needa did so, but Bess remained mute.

"Come girl. Don't vex me."

Bess swallowed again. "Bess, sir." She tried to sound as frightened of riders as Needa's real niece would—an easy task, for her anger had shriveled, exposing the fear at its root.

"Now, Needa, I know that Bess is not your niece. I watched her as she entered this world, and so I *know*. You hold no claim upon her." Again he stretched out his hand. "Hand her to me and no harm shall come to any of you."

But Needa hugged Bess closer and began to cry. "Not again," she said as she wept. "Please, not again."

Heldrick frowned. He stepped back with a thoughtful expression and looked around the room. His eyes came to rest on a thin plaque of wood with finely inscribed symbols, sitting on the mantel.

"They took your daughter," he said.

Arrick was breathing hard. "Three years ago."

"You had no other?"

"Not alive. One reached five years, before the red pox took her."

"How old was the one they took to the Citadel?"

"Fourteen."

Heldrick rubbed a thumb and finger together. "A bit young, perhaps." His eyes flicked at Wellen. "The two must have been close in age."

"Aye. Twins."

"Sir," Needa asked, her voice strained. "Sir, her name is Corlene. Do you know anything of her? I think about her most every day, and if I knew—" She broke off under Heldrick's cold stare.

He said, "I can tell you nothing."

No one else spoke.

"You understand that the incident with your daughter gives no protection here. This girl does not belong to your family. She is as much a stranger to you as I."

"Never," Needa whispered.

"Come, come. Don't miss my point. She is not a relative, or even a girl whom you've known for years. You can't have that strong of an attachment to her. Give her to me; I shan't hurt her."

Bess might have laughed aloud at that, under other circumstances. But why did Heldrick argue? Why didn't he simply take her? She took a deep breath. "You tried to shoot me."

"I did no such thing. I fired the gun to scare you into stopping—not the most effective tactic, perhaps, but my call to you had already gone unheeded."

"You tried to shoot me on the stairs, before you said a word."

"I lifted the gun, yes. I expected you to be someone dangerous. But note that I didn't pull the trigger at that point. If I had, you would be dead. Surely you can see that."

Bess frowned. "I do see that." But she didn't see what Heldrick was up to. "You really are a rider, then?"

"The only requirement for that is a horse."

"Yes, but—"

"We call ourselves quistrils."

"Whatever. You really are one?"

"Yes. Born and bred, like my brother, and our father before us."

"Born? Not built?"

He looked puzzled. "Do you think I'm some kind of robot?"

Bess said, "No . . . I just—I heard stories about the Settlers, and—" She didn't know what Heldrick would find offensive. Had she already gotten Arrick's family in trouble?

"Ah, of course. They wouldn't understand." Heldrick didn't seem angry. He glanced at the rest, then back at Bess. "We're quite human, as human as you cadrils. The Settlers were extremely skilled in genetic manipulation, that's all. They modified us slightly for their own purposes, made us stronger, faster. Nastier."

"But why do that and then leave? If that's what happened."

"The details don't matter. It's enough that they left." He spoke to the others. "I presume Bess told you that I live in her environ, across the world margin."

"World margin?" asked Bess.

"He means through the mousehole, I think," said Wellen. "She told us, yes. But we thought you were an old man, a gatekeeper working for the—the quistrils, not one of them yourself."

Heldrick looked mildly annoyed at the last part of Wellen's statement. " 'Of them,' yes; 'with them,' no. I hide in Bess's world from the quistrils of this world. They would kill me if they could find me, and Bess has made that finding much more likely. The sooner I return her, the easier I shall breathe. Do you understand?"

Bess looked at Arrick, then back at Heldrick.

"You mean the other quistrils don't know about the mousehole? No one's guarding it? I can go back?"

"That is why I'm here."

Bess stepped forward, but Arrick's large hand landed on her shoulder, stopping her.

"What's wrong?" she asked him.

Arrick didn't speak, but the doubt and mistrust on his face answered for him.

"You think he's setting some sort of trap?" she asked. "But he doesn't have to. He can take me by force if he wants. You've all told me so. Why doesn't he, unless he's telling the truth? Don't you see? He's a renegade, just like in the stories."

"Well," Heldrick said. "Not 'just like.'"

"You mean," Wellen said doubtfully, "you're *the* Renegade?"

"He can't mean that, you blockhead," Arrick said. "He ain't old enough. He means he's different from the Renegade."

"But he's still a renegade," Bess insisted. "It's the only thing that makes sense."

"What don't make sense," Arrick said slowly, "is why he was acting like a normal rider earlier, and now he acts like a renegade. Or why he says he's got to hurry and get Bess back to the mousehole before the other riders find her, when it took him four days to show up, four days where no other rider bothered us one bit. Or—"

"Enough!" Heldrick pinched the bridge of his nose. "I've never heard such an argumentative bunch." He ran a hand over his face. "I acted like a regular quistril because I thought frightening you would be the quickest way to secure Bess, without all this pointless argument.

It didn't work. But you're right, under normal circumstances I should have gotten here much earlier. Listen carefully; I don't want to have to repeat this:

"A margin conjunction cannot open between two universes, unless they are in close temporal alignment—" He broke off, presumably seeing the same incomprehension Bess saw on the others' faces. "Ah . . . think of two boats floating on the same stream, barely moving relative to one another. A loose plank dropped from one to the other can serve as a passage."

"And a margin conjunction is like the plank?" Bess asked.

"Exactly. But the situation is unstable. If a current catches one of the boats, that boat moves faster than the other, and the plank begins to slip. My metaphor is stretched, but the effect is real—the temporal motion of Bess's universe tugs at this end of the conjunction, sliding it into the future. It's moving now at such a rate that if I went to Bess's world for six hours of sleep, I would return here close to a year hence."

"You're saying that's what took you so long to show up?" Needa asked.

Heldrick nodded. "Had I crossed the margin one second after Bess, the time differential would have allowed her nearly half an hour to hide. I couldn't avoid tracking her, but to do so without the quistrils disturbing me required fetching proper dress. So I ran upstairs, grabbed my garb, and ran back down. By that time, if I interpreted her trail properly, Bess had already eaten the maracot, made her way to this house, and I would guess lain in bed for a day. And as the trail was already getting old by then, it took me even longer to track her all the way here."

"But Bess said she came through the mousehole twice," Arrick said. "How come she didn't notice no time change between?"

Bess caught her breath. "You're right, Arrick. It was morning the first time and afternoon the second. I did notice, but thought I'd made a mistake." This certainly made sense out of why Heldrick hadn't immediately followed her out of the conjunction. But the other implications staggered her. "You are the Renegade—the original—aren't you? Kale was right."

"That's crazy," Arrick said. "Look at him, so young."

Heldrick's eyes flicked toward Arrick, but he said nothing.

"It's the time difference, Arrick. All he has to do is go to my world for a day, and when he comes back here four years will have passed. A month there, and, um, over a hundred years go by here. It's why he can keep coming back. Am I right, Heldrick?"

Heldrick nodded slowly, his eyes on Bess.

Arrick muttered, "I don't believe it."

Heldrick shrugged abruptly. "That's your affair. However, the quistrils of the Citadel would find your doubt perplexing. *They* know when I've been here."

Needa said. "But why do you do it? What made you a renegade? That's what I want to know."

Heldrick paused a moment, and the utter flatness of his voice, the supreme lack of emotion in what he said next, astonished Bess as much as anything.

"I hate them." Heldrick's features held no expression. "I hate them all."

He shrugged again. "What's more important right now is the state of the conjunction. It didn't always have such a large time differential. Eleven years ago, in Bess's world—and about a hundred fifty years ago, here—the time differential was hardly noticeable. But it's been growing ever since. That's a sign of decay. Any conjunction with a time differential as large as this cannot last much longer, just like the plank between the boats cannot avoid falling into the water. That's why I'm in a rush to get Bess back. I trust, now, that none of you still intends to block her from going home?"

Arrick and Needa glanced at each other, then back at Heldrick. Arrick said, "Go ahead and take her, if she wants to go."

But Bess drew a deep breath. "I don't believe I do."

Heldrick scowled. "What is it now?"

"If what you say is true, then nobody's guarding the conjunction after all, and my father must be here now, looking for me. I can't go back and leave him trapped on this side, even if the conjunction might fail. *Especially* if it might fail."

Heldrick's eyes bored into her. "Haven't you been listening to a word I said? Your father is not here! Five minutes haven't gone by, over there, since you left. Months will pass, on this side, before you're late for dinner."

Bess bit her lip. She should have thought of that. "That's *if* you're telling the truth. I still don't trust you."

He smiled grimly.

That annoyed her. She hadn't said anything funny. "I don't like your smile, either."

"No? Is this better?" He flashed a full smile at her, revealing a set of disquietingly sharp teeth.

The better to eat you with. . . .

No, not that sharp. Not wolf's teeth, nor vampire's teeth, yet enough sharper than normal human teeth to give her a grave sense of unease.

"No. I don't like that better." Fortunately, Heldrick's expression reverted to its usual grimness. Bess had to ask: "So, what did the Settlers design those teeth for?"

"To frighten. What did you think, that we eat little girls?"

Needa gasped. Her hand flew to her mouth. She turned, ran up the stairs to her bedroom, and slammed the door.

Heldrick watched her without expression, then turned to Arrick. "The girl and I should leave as soon as possible."

Arrick glared. Heldrick turned to Bess and raised an eyebrow.

"I'll go with you," she said. "But don't expect me to like it."

"There's no need to like it, as long as you do it. Collect your things, all of them. You mustn't leave anything behind. Change out of those clothes you're wearing into the ones you came in, to avoid carrying a bundle. And hurry."

Bess nodded, returned to her room. Needa had already replaced her belongings, and Bess changed quickly. She scooped up her dimes and shoved the smart phone back in her pocket, but hesitated before going back down. She would miss this family, though she'd known them such a short while. And once she returned to her own world, time would sweep her up in its headlong rush. She could never come back and visit. Goodbye was forever.

A soft knock at the door startled her. "Come in."

Needa entered. Bess ran and gave her a hug, which Needa returned.

Then Needa held her at arms length. "You sure you're making the right choice?"

Bess wasn't sure at all, but why saddle Needa with her doubts? She nodded.

"You'd best go, then. But not in that thin jacket. You'll freeze! Here." Needa rummaged through a chest and pulled out a heavier coat. "Take this. It belonged to Corlene, and even if she comes back it won't fit her no more."

Heldrick stood gazing into the fire, hands folded behind his back. He appeared utterly calm, but Bess sensed tension within him, as in a whip held poised: dangling, but ready to be cracked without warning.

He lifted his head, frowned.

"You did not come with that coat."

"I gave it to her," Needa said, almost defiantly.

Heldrick shrugged. "Do you have everything you did bring?"

"I didn't bring anything. Except my clothes."

"No loose change? Hairpins? The quistrils would accept no excuses for finding such otherworldly things possessed by this family."

The thought chilled Bess, and she began searching her pockets. But she'd already gotten her dimes and smart phone.

Wait. Her jacket. She pulled aside the heavier coat and stabbed her hands into the jacket pockets. Nothing.

She turned to Needa. "Did you find anything in my jacket pockets when you cleaned my clothes?"

Needa shook her head. "Naught but mud."

"Mud?" Dear God, what had she done?

"You must've dragged it on the ground in your fever."

Heldrick stepped away from the fire, his eyes narrowed. "What is it?"

"I brought a key, my house key—"

"Any words on it? 'Made in U.S.A.'? Anything at all?"

"I'm not sure about the key. But it was on a key chain, a blue plastic Liberty Bell. They sold them at my old school, and—"

"Describe it!"

"Well . . . about this big, with white lettering on the back. You can see through it."

"I followed her trail to the barn," Heldrick said to the others. "Perhaps one of you saw the thing there? It would be softer than metal but harder than wood. You could not mistake it for a thing made in this world."

No one spoke.

"Who found Bess?"

Arrick said, "Kale."

"Fetch him," Heldrick said. "Quickly, or I shall fetch him myself."

Arrick's fists clenched, but he walked up the stairs to Kale's room and returned a moment later with the sleepy boy in his arms. Heldrick put his face near the boy's. Kale's eyes widened as sleep left them.

"Listen to me, boy. The day you found Bess in the barn—did you also see a small key attached to a blue bell-shaped object lying near her? Or anytime later, did you see such a thing?"

"I never. What'd it look like?"

Heldrick repeated Bess's description.

Kale shook his head. "I never seen it."

"But," said Bess, now that she'd had time to think, "the key probably fell out of my pocket in the woods. They can't blame anyone here for a key chain they might find in the forest."

"A key chain they did find. Had it been where you dropped it, I would have found it while tracking you."

Heldrick grasped Bess by the hand and started across the room as the clock began to chime midnight.

"Since they found the key before I tracked Bess to that spot, and since they have not already come here, the finder must have taken it to the Citadel to obtain orders rather than tracking Bess himself. That could take a day or two, but who knows when they found it? And the orders will call for a search. They won't necessarily wait for daylight to show them trails to follow; they'll go house to house. More than anything else, they fear the possibility of a new group of Settlers."

He pulled Bess toward the door with relentless determination. She tried to say her farewells.

"Needa, Wellen . . . oh, goodbye. I'll miss you all."

Heldrick let her go for a moment to raise his hood.

"Tell them, when they come, that the girl was here . . . knocked at your door . . . but you didn't let her in because it was past curfew, and then a quistril came and took her away. Her trail will make liars of you if you try to claim that you never saw her."

He opened the door and pushed Bess through ahead of him; then, without warning, the pressure at her back eased. Heldrick might have disappeared. Bess stopped, confused, until she saw two horses at the hitching post. A tall, dark figure, looking much like Heldrick himself, stood examining one of the horses. As she watched, he turned lazily toward her and smiled, his sharp teeth glinting in the moonlight.

She scrabbled blindly behind her for the knob, stepped back, and slammed the door.

CHAPTER 11

DAY SIX

"There's another quistril out there," Bess said. She didn't see Heldrick anywhere.

"It's as he said, then," whispered Needa.

"He could've planned it," Arrick said, "making all that talk to give this other time to get here."

"Oh, Pa, for what reason?"

"But where *is* Heldrick?" Bess whispered like the rest.

No one answered.

Bess heard the cold crunch of boots on grit and moved away from the door, closer to the others. Wellen pushed her behind him, so that he and Arrick stood in front. Needa took Bess's hand, and Kale's.

The door opened, letting the cold air swirl in. This quistril had the features and brash bearing of a man younger than Heldrick, twenty-one or twenty-two years old.

"I am accustomed," he said, "to having the door opened for me, not slammed in my face." He paused a moment, while his eyes rested on Bess. "You offer no explanation?"

Arrick took half a step forward. "I'm sorry, sir. My daughter's affrighted. My other daughter was already took by—"

"You have a plaque?"

"Yes, sir, in the—"

"Then she had nothing to fear, did she?"

"No, sir, I'll see that she's punished."

The quistril glared. "I'll see to it myself."

"Yes, sir." Arrick swallowed. "Please, come in sir."

"But Pa!"

Arrick turned toward Wellen with a violent, "Hush!"

The quistril stopped with one foot across the threshold. "My, my. I've not seen this much impudence in a long while. Apparently I'll be punishing two of you tonight. At least."

He grinned again, and the chills ran like spiders up and down Bess's spine. Heldrick hadn't conveyed such a sense of menace even when he tried. This man would burn other people's good intentions, incinerate them in his soul and radiate evil as waste.

The quistril stepped into the room, no longer grinning.

"You have a stolen horse outside. How did you come by it?"

Bess glanced behind her. Where had Heldrick gone? Why?

Arrick shifted his feet. "We ain't got any horse at all, less someone left it there."

"No? And where did this girl plan to go on a cold night, eh? For a walk, perhaps . . . or a ride? One can break curfew so much more effectively on horseback— which, of course, is why ownership of horses is disallowed."

Bess felt skewered by the quistril's gaze. "I, um, heard a noise. Sir. I was curious—"

"You heard no noise. I didn't make any. And besides—" His long arm snaked between Arrick and Wellen to grasp Bess's coat. "You wouldn't have worn this merely to peek out the door. . . ." His voice faded and he let go of Bess's coat, but he reached further and fingered the now exposed nylon windbreaker underneath.

"What is this? What's the material?"

"It's . . . I don't know, sir."

"Where did you obtain it?"

Bess had no answer.

He tightened his grip on the jacket. "Where are you from?"

She had no answer to that, either. But the quistril didn't wait for one. He lifted his head.

"What made that noise? Who else is in the house?" He pushed his way past everyone to the foot of the stairs.

Needa pulled Bess close and whispered into her ear. "Now—run and hide."

The quistril stopped halfway up the steps, turned, and looked at Needa. "You will pay for that advice, woman. All of you, come with me."

Bess heard a short scraping sound, and the quistril turned away and raced up the stairs. Almost against their will, everyone followed the quistril to Arrick and Needa's bedroom. He yanked open the door and strode in.

"You! Stop!"

Heldrick stood frozen, his arms stretched out an open window, something dark in his hands. He had traded his black quistril garb for some of Arrick's clothes. Other clothes lay scattered around the opened bed drawer. Naked terror filled Heldrick's expression.

"I'm sorry, sir," he said, trembling, "I didn't know you was in the house."

Bess's stomach turned. Heldrick lacked the courage to stand up to a real quistril.

"Let me see what's in your hands," the quistril said. "Quickly!"

Heldrick brought his hands, full of his own garb, back through the window. The quistril glanced at the bed drawer and the scattered clothes.

"You should have left them in the drawer, you know. I'd never have thought to check there."

He looked at each person in turn. "A stolen horse outside and stolen vestments inside. Obviously you've colluded in murdering one of us. I'd like to know how you frail beings managed it, but there is a penalty, to be applied without delay. I'm afraid I must administer it."

His gaze returned to Heldrick. "Since you have the clothes, I'll assume that you acted as ringleader. Therefore, you'll go first."

A long, wide knife appeared in his hand. Heldrick saw it and quaked, but he took a step forward. "No, sir, it wasn't me that did it. 'Twas the girl. She's, like, not human, sir." Heldrick's long finger pointed toward Bess.

The quistril's eyes flicked at her. "I suspected as much. Unfortunately, she's the one of you who mustn't die. I'll have to take her with me for questioning. But the rest of your lives are forfeit."

He stepped toward Heldrick, and Heldrick's outstretched arm—the one pointing at Bess—moved like lightning to grasp the wrist of the quistril's knife hand. The clothes dropped from Heldrick's other hand to reveal his own knife, which he thrust toward the quistril's ribs.

For a moment the quistril's face showed utter astonishment. But he grasped Heldrick's knife hand before the blade had entered half its length. With a yank on Heldrick's wrist the quistril pulled the knife out. The wound bled and bubbled, but the quistril kept Heldrick's knife at arm's length while he backed Heldrick against the foot of the bed and inched his own blade closer to Heldrick's throat.

Sweat broke out on Heldrick's brow.

The quistril kept advancing his knife, overcoming Heldrick's resistance. Yet he seemed perplexed that Heldrick had the might to resist him at all. When his knife came within two inches of Heldrick's jugular, he opened his mouth as if to speak but coughed instead, spraying blood over Heldrick and the bed behind him. He drew breath wetly, while the wound in his side sucked air, and he coughed again. The knife stopped moving.

The tableau held, as the quistril's breath rattled in his throat and blood dribbled out of his mouth. Finally his eyes glazed. Heldrick pushed the quistril's knife further away. The quistril's knees buckled. Heldrick pressed him to the floor and thrust his own knife between the quistril's ribs, to the hilt.

Bess felt numb. She had never seen so much blood in her life—and it was her fault. If she had never come here—if she had never gone into Heldrick's basement—

Heldrick removed the knife from the quistril's dead fingers, and took the leg sheath as well. He said to Arrick, "I would leave his knife for you, but it would mean your death if discovered."

Arrick looked up from the dead quistril, awe on his face. "I understand."

"In my day they always traveled in pairs." Heldrick poked the body with his toe. "This was careless. I can take the body away, but Bess and I shouldn't stay here any longer. I must impose upon you to clean up the mess."

Arrick nodded.

"Please." Heldrick's voice had an earnestness that Bess hadn't heard before. "Don't wash the sheets; don't bury them in your vegetable patch. Burn them, along with these clothes of yours I'm wearing. And scrub the floor well. When it's clean, dry it with rags, and burn the rags. Do you understand?"

Arrick nodded again, his mouth still slightly agape.

"All right, then. If you'll permit me, I'll put my own clothes back on."

When Heldrick emerged from the bedroom, he looked again as a quistril ought. He had rolled up the quistril's body in a sheet off the bed and carried it over his shoulder.

"If we reach the conjunction they'll never find this body," he said. "And if we're caught with it, they'll blame me, not the rest of you."

"That's not what *he* said," Needa said, nodding at the sheeted body.

"He assumed I was a cadril, like the rest of you, and that it must have taken all of us together to murder a quistril. They won't assume any such thing if they catch me in my garb. But do your best to remove all traces that this quistril or myself entered the house tonight. Don't touch the hoofprints, or footprints, or anything else outside. Just tell them that two quistrils, not one, took Bess away."

Then Heldrick surprised everyone. He said: "Good luck."

Heldrick asked Bess, "Do you know how to ride?" Before she had a chance to answer he went on: "No, never mind." He lopped the sheeted figure over the back of one horse. "You can ride with me."

"I've taken lessons for years. I've even competed. I can ride fine."

"No. This will be better. It may be that a patrol will not question my being without a partner, since *he*" —Heldrick nodded at the dead quistril— "came alone. But they would certainly look askance at my letting you ride your own horse, with your hands free, without a companion to guard your other side."

Bess clenched her fists in frustration. She couldn't argue with Heldrick's reasons, but she suspected that if she knew more about this world, she'd be able to identify them as hogwash. Would she never meet someone who could see past appearances and treat her as an adult?

Heldrick studied her a moment. He reached into his cloak and fetched the extra knife and leg sheath.

"Wear this," he said, to her surprise. "I'm not much better with two knives than with one."

She wanted to strap it on casually, as if she'd worn such things thousands of times before, but idle gestures would get them nowhere. "I'm no good with even one. You keep them both."

"They won't expect you to have one. It might help us if you take it."

"There's no point." She could never bring herself to stab someone deliberately. It was bad enough that she bore the responsibility for one death tonight, already. "I won't use it. I don't want to kill anybody."

"Oh, you needn't worry about that. Any quistril could disarm you easily. But it might serve as a momentary distraction, enough for me to intervene. Now, let's waste no more time." Heldrick adjusted the belt around her leg.

Then he mounted his horse and pulled Bess up behind him.

"Hold tight," he said.

She expected to take off at a gallop, but Heldrick kept the two horses to a walk. The near silence of the horses unnerved her. She wondered whether the quistrils trained their horses to be so quiet, or whether they'd been bred for it.

The methodical rhythm of the horse beneath Bess almost hypnotized her. That, the moonlight, and the hour could have put her to sleep under kinder circumstances. Her tensions began to ease, and she relaxed her grip on Heldrick's waist.

Heldrick slowed the horses, stopped them. Bess's vigilance returned. Her eyes tried to pierce the darkness, her ears to filter out the ordinary night sounds. What had Heldrick heard? What had he seen?

He twisted and put his lips near her ear. In a whisper quieter than the forest sounds, he asked, "What did I tell you to do?"

Bess couldn't think. She opened her mouth but no sounds came out.

"I told you to *hold tight.* You never know when we may have to make a run for it."

Heldrick straightened, and the horses began to move.

After that, Bess maintained her grip. Her senses tried to outperform one another, reporting rumors as well as facts. A dozen times she saw to one side a dark figure astride a horse, which vanished when she turned to look at it, or heard a gentle *clop-clop-clop-clop* that resolved, after a few seconds, into the sounds of the night. Heldrick sat straight and unconcerned, and they continued riding at a constant, maddeningly slow walk.

Heldrick kept their path close to the trees. He took long detours to stay close to the woods rather than cutting straight across a glade. Bess knew it decreased their visibility. But who, or what, might hide behind a tree, waiting to ambush them? She peered into the woods, searching for anything, any shape, that might resolve itself into an enemy.

Heldrick plodded along.

They entered the forest proper. Bess's heart gave a bound in spite of the increased darkness. Perhaps these were the woods near the portal.

A minute later, through her grip on his waist, she felt Heldrick tense, though he kept the horses moving at the same steady pace. She heard nothing but the gentle hooting of an owl, and then of another, farther away, as if in answer.

Her heart grew cold.

Heldrick drew the other horse forward and gave it a sharp slap on the flank. It bolted, carrying its burden into the darkness, making a racket painful to Bess's ears.

Bess heard two other horses in pursuit of the one Heldrick had sent off. Heldrick himself merely turned right and continued at the same, slow, silent pace. Moonlit ground showed ahead. Heldrick picked up the pace, and they broke out of the woods.

Bess looked for the outcropping that hid the portal, or the farmhouse near it, but saw instead a black silhouette that grew, accompanied by the sudden thunder of hoofbeats. . . . She sucked in her breath. The quistril was almost close enough for her to touch.

He tried to pull ahead and cut them off.

Heldrick reached out, seemingly without effort; the quistril dropped the reins and fell backwards off the horse.

The horse continued at their side a moment before veering off. Bess saw the knife in Heldrick's hand. She shivered.

And gripped Heldrick even tighter; for he made good his warning, and they charged off at full gallop. Over his shoulder he said, "This is not a chance patrol." To the right she saw two more of the black silhouettes and heard their thundering horses. They forced Heldrick to veer left, back toward the woods, from which another quistril emerged. Heldrick's horse reared, and Bess held on in terror.

But not tightly enough. A strong arm encircled her waist and pulled, squeezing the breath from her. She found herself moving away from Heldrick. In panic she reached for the leg sheath, drew the knife, and slashed; but the quistril caught her wrist and squeezed until the knife dropped to the ground.

He brought his horse to a stop and dismounted, never releasing Bess. Then he pushed her face-first onto the ground and held her, with a knee pressed into her back.

CHAPTER 12

A FEW MINUTES LATER, the quistril turned her onto her back. A second quistril now stood watching, arms folded. Bess didn't move while the first tied her hands in front of her. Then he dragged her onto a blanket, lifted her hands over her head, and rolled her up in it. He threw her, like a sack of potatoes, over what she realized was the back of an unsaddled horse, and lashed her hands and feet together with a strap passed under the horse.

The horse began to move, faster than she'd expected. The jolting shook her entire body. The drumming of hooves sounded dangerously near her ears. She began slipping, sliding further with every round of hoofbeats, and her arms and legs squeezed the horse in a desperate attempt to keep her position.

By the time the horse stopped, she'd realized that the slipping was an illusion; but her arms and legs could not be convinced. She ached all over from straining to maintain her position, and the constant pounding at her stomach had nauseated her.

A pair of hands untied her, lifted her off the horse, and hefted her over something. Not until that "something" started to walk did she realize a quistril carried her on his shoulder. He went up two steps. A few paces farther, he set her down and unrolled her by yanking hard on the blanket. She spun up against a wall.

Behind her she heard the quistril walk off. Other quistrils moved about and talked in their own language. What chance of escaping did she have when she couldn't even understand what they said? Tears welled in her eyes.

But she blinked them back. She needed all her faculties intact. She rolled away from the wall and struggled to a sitting position. The large room contained a central fireplace and more quistrils than the sound of conversation had led her to expect, but none showed any interest in her.

A shuffling to her left caught her ear; she turned. Heldrick shifted toward her.

The ache in her throat eased. She thought he'd escaped, and she held no illusions that he'd risk capture, himself, to rescue her. But now . . . Heldrick must have been in this situation a dozen times. He'd know how to get out, and he might as well take her with him.

"No point sitting up," he said when he got close. "You should sleep."

"Why?"

"It would be the smart thing to do. Though I suppose that may put it beyond your abilities."

Bess pressed her lips together. She expected people to underestimate her age, but no one had criticized her intelligence for a long time.

Heldrick gave her an appraising glance. "Well, perhaps I'm wrong. I'm merely going by my observations: You break into an old man's house in the middle of the afternoon and smash the furniture in his basement, practically begging to be caught. When that event occurs, you run to someplace far removed from your own neighborhood, of which you have no knowledge, yet you depend on people back home to rescue you. You eat poisonous fruit. You leave a trail any moron could follow, including dropping an item which screams of foreign manufacture. Did I miss anything?"

Bess couldn't believe what she was hearing. "Yes, you did. Who could have prevented this whole thing by putting a lock on the basement window? Who wasted hours in hopes of frightening everyone instead of explaining things . . . and then wound up explaining anyway? And what genius explained all the unimportant things before letting me know how important it was that I might have dropped something?"

"Softer," Heldrick said, though to what purpose she couldn't imagine. The quistrils could hear them anyway, if they bothered to listen.

He sat for a moment, eyes straight ahead. Bess hadn't anticipated that; she'd thought he'd retort.

"I still recommend rest," he said at last. "In the morning they'll move us again. You'll get no sleep then."

"And you will? Hadn't you better get your sleep too?"

"I need very little. It's a quistrilian thing."

"Oh." She sat for a moment. "I'm not tired right now. I feel like I've been sleeping since I ate that darned peach. I wish we were alone."

"Why? So we could discuss escape plans?"

Bess blinked in shock.

Heldrick looked around the room at the other quistrils, then lowered his voice a bit more.

"You think they're listening? Maybe some are. Maybe not. But they don't care. It doesn't matter. There's nothing

we can do. You think we need simply apply our brains
and our wills to the problem? You're wrong. Bad things
do happen, you know, and quistrils are masters at
making them happen. That's why I've always taken such
care never to get into this situation before."

Bess's last reservoir of hope drained away. Heldrick
had no more escape experience than she. But in place of
the hope grew anger: it sounded like he didn't even want
to try.

He continued, his voice growing ever softer. "Barring
some unforeseen miracle, they'll take us to the Citadel
before noon; and once we're there, escape is out of the
question. They'll kill me within a day—if I'm lucky—and
you'll be a prisoner for life. Those are the facts. Ignoring
them won't help. But if you do have any ideas, tell them
to me this way."

And she realized that Heldrick hadn't entirely given
up, after all. He'd made his little speech an uninteresting
murmur to the quistrils so they wouldn't notice the last
bit of murmur, which he spoke in Homeworld.

For a while, Bess said nothing. She had no ideas for
getting out of this mess. But maybe Heldrick could
elaborate on his previous, rushed explanations. He might
say something that would give her an idea.

"Heldrick?" She spoke softly, in Otherworld,
reserving Homeworld for secrets.

"What?"

"Tell me about the Settlers. Why did they make the
quistrils? Why did they leave?"

He shrugged oddly with one shoulder; she decided
he'd meant to rub his chin, or tug at his ear, but unlike

her own bound hands, his were tied behind him. His legs were also tied. Obviously he was considered more dangerous than she.

"What I know comes from old stories—"

"That's what Arrick said!"

"My stories are undoubtedly more reliable. They come from records in the Citadel's archives. But they weren't written until many years after the events, so they may not be completely accurate. What exactly did Arrick say?"

She told him.

"Basically correct, as far as it goes. The Settlers came from a universe with far more conjunctions than this one, and—"

"Conjunctions are more likely in some universes—?" She stopped and thought of mouseholes: common here but unknown at home. "Of course. Go on."

"—and they used them to offload surplus population. Whenever a big one opened they sent a group through to genetically engineer a portion of the local population into an army, which they used to subdue the rest—a multi-generational project. But here, the conjunction became unstable when the quistrils had subdued only a small portion of the planet. Knowing it would collapse before this world was ready, the Settlers abandoned it. They knew another conjunction would open soon enough."

"But why leave the quistrils behind? They could have used them at the next place. Or did they expect another mousehole to connect back here?"

"A second conjunction never occurs between the same two universes. No, they simply didn't want quistrils on their home world. Here, quistrils functioned as a useful tool; there, they would pose a hazard."

"I would think they posed a hazard here, too."

"Yes, but not to the Settlers—"

"No, to girls!" The anger that she'd felt since learning about Pry's daughter, and Corlene, boiled over. "Why can't they stick with their own wives? Why—?"

"Stop." Heldrick's voice held such intensity that it cut her off cold, though he hadn't spoken loudly. "Look around. What do you see?"

She gave the room a quick glance. Nothing seemed changed, except . . . the sound of conversation had grown a bit softer, and one or two of the quistrils had turned their heads her way. She'd attracted notice.

Okay. She understood his point. But she couldn't say so without revealing that they didn't want attention. The best way to lose the quistrils' interest would be to answer Heldrick's question literally. In a soft voice.

"I see quistrils."

He nodded once, accepting the answer. "Do you see any females?"

"Well. . . ." She looked again. "I can't be sure, with that garb, but it doesn't look like—"

"There are none. Quistrilian women don't exist. The Settlers designed our immune systems to destroy gametes that either lack the quistrilian genes or contain an X-chromosome, thus keeping the gene pool undiluted and preventing the conception of females."

Then he frowned at her. "Did any of that mean anything to you?"

She rolled her eyes. "Yes, yes. Go on."

He gazed at her thoughtfully a moment. "All right. The result is that quistrils cannot sire girls. Well, I shouldn't say 'cannot'; genetic accidents happen occasionally, but the rare female baby is destroyed. If she weren't, she'd still be sterile, her ovaries attacked by her own immune system."

"But why did the Settlers do that? To make the quistrils more hated?" Like they wouldn't have been hated enough, anyway.

"Not at all. They wanted an easy way to eliminate the quistrils after they'd served their purpose."

Bess frowned. "It wouldn't be that easy. I mean, it's been hundreds of years and the quistrils are still here."

Heldrick nodded. "No one can be certain, of course, but the conclusion the quistrils came to, after the Settlers left, was that the Settlers planned to eliminate humans from this planet altogether. That's the task they designed the quistrils to perform, but once the job was done, the all-male quistrils would have died out. If that's correct, this world is lucky that quistrils are the worst it's had to endure."

Wipe out all humanity? The concept was unthinkable. Had the Settlers really done it, numerous times, in other universes? Bess could think of nothing to say.

Heldrick went on. "The result of all this is that cadrilian females command a high value. The quistrils will keep you safe, after questioning you to find out where you came from, until you grow old enough to bear children."

"You mean I'll be part of a harem."

"Essentially, yes; except that the harem is communal, rather than belonging to a single individual."

"That helps a lot." She took a breath and said in Homeworld, "I'm already a year older than Corlene was."

"You're kidding." Heldrick stared at her. "Well, don't tell anyone. Your appearance will buy you a bit of time."

"If I'd planned on telling anyone, I wouldn't be speaking Homeworld, would I?"

Heldrick shrugged, then smiled slightly. "'Home-world'? And 'Otherworld,' perhaps?"

Bess nodded.

"Those are the same names I use," he said. "Though in my case, the meanings are reversed."

"What do you call your own language?"

"Vardic. We learned it from the Settlers."

"Do all the quistrils speak both Vardic and English?"

"In this part of the world. Elsewhere they speak Vardic and French, or Vardic and Japanese, or whatever second language is appropriate."

"So you could speak to any quistril in the world?"

"If I had the opportunity. It is unlikely to arise."

"What do you think they'll do with you, then?"

"Oh, they'll execute me, and soon. Not that it'll earn them anything, or cost me much. Quistrils don't live more than thirty-five years, anyway."

"Oh. . . . —How old are you?"

"It's hard to be certain, with the time differential confusing the issue, but I think I'm about thirty-one. My reflexes have already begun to slow. It would go downhill quickly from here."

"But that's awful!"

"You needn't fret over it," Heldrick said. "Execution's tomorrow."

She did sleep then, for a time. When she woke she looked at Heldrick. He sat against the wall with his eyes shut, but at her first movement he opened them and looked at her.

"Ah, there you are. They'll be taking us in soon."

"Already?"

He nodded and switched briefly to Homeworld. "So if you've come up with any ideas, we'll want to implement them quickly. Once at the Citadel, we're doomed."

"Why so much more hopeless then, than now?"

He leaned forward and wiggled the fingers of his bound hands. "This is makeshift. Escaping from rope bindings is child's play compared to getting out of the dungeon. And it's unlikely that any of these—" His eyes indicated the quistrils around them. "—are particularly intelligent. Most aren't."

"Really? That's not the impression I got."

"You're thinking of the one I killed? They often adopt a supercilious air, especially when dealing with cadrils; but, believe me, the Settlers' intent was to create soldiers, not generals. They're incredibly good at what they do, but they don't do everything."

"Actually, I was thinking of you."

"Me?" His head turned sharply toward her, and Bess was pleased to see that he could be startled. Then he frowned. "You called me a genius earlier, but the tone was clearly sarcastic."

"Oh, that." She shrugged. "I was angry. I can't really tell how smart you are, but you're not below average, that's for sure."

He leaned back against the wall. "I was angry when I spoke, as well, but with myself. Everything you said was correct, and I already knew it."

An apology? She hadn't expected *that.*

"The point is," he continued, "that those of greatest intelligence rise to leadership positions, so there's a higher density of them at the Citadel. If you plan to outthink anyone, now's the best opportunity."

But only a few minutes later, two quistrils took Bess and Heldrick from the post house, as Heldrick called it— one of many, where quistrils could procure some food or a change of mount. The quistrils untied Heldrick's legs, re-bound Bess's hands at her back, and set the two of them on horses. The reins hung free, but the well-trained horses followed the lead quistril, while the second quistril kept watch from behind. Even if Bess managed to free her hands and grab the reins, an attempt to dash into the forest would earn her a knife in the back. She began to understand what Heldrick had been saying: You didn't always need to be smart to be very, very good at your job.

Yet they had to escape before reaching the Citadel. There must be a way, but try as she might, Bess couldn't think of one.

Then, as they passed a lane that led from the road to a farmhouse, she stiffened in her saddle. The farmhouse looked familiar, and behind it, high on a hill, she saw a rocky outcropping.

The portal.

She turned her eyes away, relaxed her shoulders, and began to pay attention to the route. She could find her way back here, if she could get free before they reached the Citadel. But how? How? She didn't know when they would reach the Citadel, but she did know that time was running out.

She was still racking her brains an hour later, when they rounded a hill and saw the Citadel spread out before them. Squat, square, and ugly, it stood three stories tall and covered so much ground that it made her think more of a city than a building. A high stone wall enclosed the immense compound that contained the Citadel and several smaller buildings.

Once they entered the compound, they were met by other quistrils who took Heldrick in one direction and Bess in another.

CHAPTER 13

THE DUNGEON CONSISTED of a spiral staircase leading down to a long, dim corridor lined with cells on each side; maybe a hundred altogether. The quistrils placed Bess in the fourth cell on the left and marched off without a word. As they left the dungeon, the dim light at the top of the stairs went out.

Bess, her arms around her knees, sat on the pile of straw without touching the cold wall behind her and breathed the scents of mold and rotting wood. Now and then she heard the scratching and scrabbling of small rodents. But no eyes glowed at her from the dark; that required at least a tiny bit of ambient light.

Heldrick had warned Bess that the quistrils kept the dungeon unilluminated, but she'd imagined it no darker than a moonless night. This utter blackness was unnerving. She sat for a long time, hoping that her eyes would adjust, but they never did.

After a while she closed her eyes, because the effort of trying to see gave her a headache. Then, afraid that she would miss any bit of light that did creep in, she opened them again.

Nothing.

The quistrils had taken her nylon jacket, but they'd let her keep the coat. She was glad to have it, in this chill place. But she really wished they'd left her with her smart phone, or at least her watch; in this darkness, either would have served as a flashlight.

She stood and felt behind her for the damp wall, then walked straight across the cell, her arms outstretched, searching for the door. Her hands touched rough stone. She took a step to the left, and her shoulder bumped a wall. Other way, then.

Two steps and the toe of her right shoe bent down, unsupported. She crouched and searched with her fingers.

A hole! She traced the hole's circumference, and her excitement faded. The hole spanned six inches. She reached into it the length of her arm. The hole maintained its diameter. She couldn't reach the bottom; it could have been three feet deep, or three hundred. No matter. Neither she nor anyone else could escape through such a tiny opening.

Except the rats. She snatched her arm back.

Straightening, she took another small step to the right. And another. Her right hand found the low, ironbound, wooden door—she'd bumped her head on the lintel coming in. The iron had rusted but remained solid, and the wood was thick. Brute strength would not break this door down.

Again, no matter. She had no brute strength to apply.

Bess moved to the center of the door, felt around at the height of her shoulders, and found the grating. She curled her fingers around the bars, crouched, and pressed her face to them. She put one arm through the grating and tried to see her hand.

No light whatsoever. She pulled her arm back.

She called Heldrick's name, then shouted it, hoping that the quistrils had put him in a different cell before they brought her here, but got no response. They'd probably taken him right out and killed him, as he'd warned her. She had to face it.

In fact, it sounded as if she was the only inmate of the dungeon. She called out again—to anyone, this time—and heard only echoes.

She returned to sit in the pile of straw, her hands in her lap. After a drowsy interval she thought she could see her hands faintly and knew she was dreaming. But then she heard the door to the dungeon open and lifted her head. The grating in her cell door showed as a crosshatched square, black against the faint, yellow light of the dungeon corridor. She listened. Footsteps descended the spiral staircase.

She bit her lip. Somewhere, in a secret compartment of her heart, she had still hoped that she could escape before they came for her. But maybe Heldrick was right; maybe his hopeless attitude wasn't resignation but a simple acknowledgment of the truth. They could never escape from the Citadel.

Cloaks flashed by her grating. The footsteps passed her cell and continued. She heard another sound, a scuffing, as if they dragged a heavy object behind them down the corridor. Another prisoner? Heldrick? Her heart leaped.

But why couldn't he walk for himself?

Someone must have stopped outside her cell door after all, for she heard something slide underneath it. A voice said, "Food."

The other sounds came to a halt. Someone fumbled with keys. A cell door creaked open, she heard a thud, and the cell door banged shut. The footsteps headed back.

Again they passed her cell, and Bess watched the grate on her door until the light winked out, a second after the dungeon door closed.

She crossed to the cell door again. "Heldrick?" she shouted.

No response.

She reached down to the floor and found a wide, flat brick of some dry, crumbly substance, about the size and shape of a news magazine. She broke off a piece and nibbled it; it tasted like a bread crust so dry and old that all flavor had departed. Still, it made her realize how hungry she'd grown. In a minute she ate the entire thing and washed it down with a ladle filled from the water bucket.

She called Heldrick's name again. Still no response.

If she could only see! She returned to the straw pile and sat, despondent. She held her knees, put her head on her arms, and tried not to weep.

And so she didn't notice the light once again shining through her grating, until the sound of footsteps alerted her. She looked up only a few seconds before the footsteps reached her door. A key grated in the lock, and the door opened.

Two quistrils stood in the dungeon corridor. One bent down and said, "You will come with us."

She rose and stepped out of her cell. One quistril waved for her to proceed. As she walked, they fell into step beside her. They left her cell door open, which she took as a sign that at least they meant to bring her back.

They took her up stairs and through long, tunnel-like corridors constructed of dark wood. Intersections occurred at surprising angles, and the corridors occasionally swerved oddly, though she once saw a corridor that must have stretched straight for a hundred yards.

The corridor walls curved together overhead to form a rounded, Romanesque arch, intensifying the tunnel impression. Bess imagined that she walked through the burrows of an underground maze: a rat's warren, mysteriously enlarged. But the corridor's floors were polished flat hardwood, and the lighting was electrical—though scarcely brighter than the oil lamps at Arrick's house.

The quistrils ushered her into an office and closed the door behind her, leaving her alone with a single occupant clad in a tan cloak, who sat writing at his desk. He wore glasses; had thinning hair, gray at the temples; and unless the seat of his chair was unusually low, he was either the shortest quistril she had yet seen, besides being the first with less than perfect vision—or he was a cadril.

A collaborator.

Grayvle hated contests where they had to injure each other. Why couldn't they save that for rebellious cadrils? Maybe because so few cadrils rebelled, anymore. Only the cowards remained.

He dodged Thuvwald's vicious but clumsy swipe and, disregarding all three fatal strokes that Thuvwald had opened himself up for, touched the point of his knife to

Thuvwald's earlobe. A single drop of blood swelled. Grayvle stepped back and bowed, sheathing his knife.

A sudden murmur from the spectators made him look up. Thuvwald had turned on him with his knife raised. The fool didn't realize he'd lost!

Grayvle blocked Thuvwald's descending stroke with his forearm and kicked Thuvwald's legs out from under him. "Your ear, Thuvwald!"

Thuvwald touched his ear and stared at the red on his fingertips, looking puzzled and somewhat foolish. Of course, that was his regular expression. Grayvle extended his hand and pulled Thuvwald to his feet.

Thuvwald belatedly returned the bow, and Grayvle glanced at the judges. A figure wearing the charcoal-gray cloak of a mastron was just leaving the court. No question, then; he was a candidate for promotion directly from youngling to vasik, bypassing novice—a singular honor given to at most one youngling from each graduating form.

At least, *one* of them was such a candidate. But he couldn't believe that the mastron had come here to watch Thuvwald.

Corck pushed past the other spectators. Grayvle's form-mate, Enfarad, followed him. "Excellent fight Grayvle, Thuvwald," Corck said.

"Me?" Thuvwald asked. "I never came near him."

Corck shrugged in a manner that somehow expressed disagreement without being dishonest. "Grayvle, may we speak with you?" He cocked his head. "This way."

Grayvle followed Corck and Enfarad to an unoccupied classroom.

Corck shut the door. "Some news on that item you found a couple of days ago. They're pretty sure they found the person who dropped it: a girl, tenth form from the look of her, or whatever corresponds to that among the cadrils. She's in the dungeon now."

"The dungeon!" Were they afraid of a child?

"Well, she's too young for the Nest."

"But . . . why keep her at all?"

"Sit down, both of you." Corck found a seat for himself. "I shouldn't be telling this to either of you, so don't let it go any further."

Grayvle and Enfarad glanced at each other. Grayvle wondered what other privileged information Corck might have shared with Enfarad. During his senior three years as a youngling, Corck had been Enfarad's mentor. Now, three years later still, they'd maintained that bond. Grayvle's own mentor had gotten himself killed a year after graduation.

"How closely," Corck asked him, "did you look at the artifact attached to that key?"

"Only enough to know that I didn't recognize the material. You never gave it back to me. Is it valuable? I suppose the girl is a thief. Or a runaway from another district, perhaps." Except that he saw no reason for other districts to have materials that Kallikot didn't. So what source could the girl have found from which to steal it?

"A thief?" Corck shrugged. "It's possible, but we've no reason to think so. From outside the district? Well . . . I think that's a bit of an understatement. They're pretty sure she's a marginal."

"You mean there's an active margin conjunction open?" Enfarad asked, leaning forward. "One large enough for people?"

Corck nodded. "Not only that, but she had a companion. . . ." He paused, for no reason that Grayvle could detect other than dramatic effect. "A quistril. Think about what that might mean."

Slowly, Enfarad sat down. Grayvle kept his face expressionless. Oh, he knew what Corck was getting at: quistrils on both sides of a conjunction. Yes, an interesting problem.

But it didn't interest *him*. Not at the moment. What concerned him more was that some poor girl had done nothing at all, except perhaps stumble through the conjunction. And for that misfortune, she was now spending time in the dungeon.

Well, she was only a cadril. Probably a sneak and a coward. Probably an honorless worm. Probably deserved everything she got.

Probably.

But *I'm* the one who put her there. I'm the one who found that key.

Somehow that thought made him uncomfortable.

CHAPTER 14

Bᴇss sᴛʀᴜɢɢʟᴇᴅ ᴛᴏ ᴋᴇᴇᴘ disgust from showing on her face. It probably wouldn't have mattered; the collaborator barely glanced up as the door closed behind her. He spoke while he wrote.

"I'm Casternack. Please take off your clothes."

"I will not!"

Casternack looked up at that, giving her a close appraisal. "Are you wearing underclothes?"

"What business is that of yours?"

Casternack sighed. "If you have underclothes, you may keep them on. The rest has to go." He made a few more marks on his papers. Bess didn't move. Casternack's diction was noticeably different from the members of Arrick's family, and she thought: Of course. He's a town man.

He looked up again. "Well? Are you going to take them off or not?"

"Why should I?"

"So I can examine you, for God's sake! Surely you don't expect me to conduct an examination through all those layers of clothing." The man frowned at her. "Didn't they tell you I was a doctor?"

"They didn't tell me anything."

"Well. All right then, I'm a doctor."

"You're not *my* doctor."

"I am now, and from now on, unless and until they replace me. Now, off with the clothes. Or I'll call your guards to do the job for you."

With reluctance, Bess complied, stripping down to underpants and camisole. When she finished, the doctor told her to sit on a high stool and listened to her heart and breathing. He stood back and frowned at her flat chest.

"Had your first bleeding yet?"

Bess flushed. "No, I . . . no," she lied.

"How old are you, anyway?"

She could tell her answer had irritated him. "Um. Twelve."

"That's ridiculous. They should never have brought you here at this age." And then his face cleared. "No. I forgot: you're the prisoner, aren't you?"

"Isn't everybody, here?"

"I mean they're keeping you in the dungeon. Not the usual case. What's it like there?"

"Dark."

He looked into her eyes and ears and mouth. Then he examined her palms and the soles of her feet and tested her reflexes.

At length he stood back, motioned for Bess to dress, and went back to his desk. He resumed writing.

While she dressed, she asked, "Is there some place around here I can go to the bathroom?"

"Can't you wait until you get back?"

"There's no place in my cell."

"No? I understood that each cell had a hole in the floor."

"Oh! Yes, I guess . . ." She should have figured *that* out. It hadn't smelled; that was her only excuse, and it wasn't good enough. Embarrassment turned her contempt for the doctor into anger. "I hope they pay you a lot for this kind of work!"

Casternack didn't move. After a moment, without lifting his eyes, he said, "Yes, they do. My own daughter is here. This is the only way I can keep an eye on her."

Bess bit her lip.

A few seconds later, he looked at her again and asked in a friendly voice, "Where're you from?"

She froze. She didn't know a place name on this world. But perhaps Casternack didn't want a place name.

She said, "Out in the country. A farm nearby."

Casternack nodded. "You don't sound much like a farm girl. You have an unusual accent."

Bess decided to speak as little as possible. She shrugged, and after a few seconds the doctor went back to his writing.

Soon the two quistrils entered the office without knocking and took Bess back to her cell.

In the darkness, Bess slid her hands over the rocks of her cell wall, at first feeling only their sameness. Then, as her fingers became sensitized, they began to dwell on each tiny bump and crevice. Here a tiny crack ran through the middle of a stone; there some mortar had broken out; here a stone shifted when pressed—but no more than a millimeter.

For hours she persisted, pausing only to eat the midday food wafer. Though she grew more attuned to the patterns in the rock, nothing suggested itself as a means of escape. At length, a growing tiredness in her fingers breached her concentration and convinced her to sit back on her heels for a rest.

She tried to think. It didn't do any good.

She felt her way to the cell door and called Heldrick's name again. A rustling preceded the word, "Yes?"

Her heart leaped. "You're still alive?"

"Yes, Bess." He sounded tired.

"What are they doing to you?"

"Asking me the questions I expected they'd ask you."

"I heard them drag you to your cell this morning."

"Yes. The experience left me a bit weak. No permanent damage. You might find this amusing: they don't realize I'm the Renegade. They think a new margin conjunction's opened, to a world so similar it has quistrils, and that I'm the advance guard for an invasion. They're unpleasant about the way they interrogate me, but I'm thankful for their mistake. It's keeping me alive, after all."

"Uh . . . is it safe to talk about all that?"

Heldrick took a moment responding. "I should have thought of that. If I hadn't gone through an interrogation recently, I would have. It probably *is* safe; quistrils aren't much for subterfuge. But if someone is hiding in another cell, I'm afraid my secret is out."

"Maybe we should talk in Homeworld from now on," she said, doing so.

"Good idea."

Bess changed the subject. "How did you find the conjunction in the first place?"

"Pure luck. I'd have passed right by it the day it opened if Mildred Cavendish, the old woman who used to own my house, hadn't been standing outside the crevice, staring around her with as much wonder as if she were seeing the world for the first time. Of course, as far as this world went, she was."

"Someone else used to own your house?"

"Of course. Did you think I had it built around the conjunction myself, with no money and no job?"

Bess had never thought about it. "What did she do, just give the house to you?"

"In her will, yes. Along with her money. She had no living relatives, and by then we'd set up the pretense that I was her crotchety, reclusive brother. I powdered my hair when in the house and wore extra makeup if I expected to meet anyone."

"But why did she do that for you?"

"She approved of the work I did."

"You mean your Renegade raids?"

"Yes. Although she somehow got the impression that I fought for freedom, that I had a goal other than mayhem. She didn't understand the situation here. She thought I had left the Citadel to escape oppression, though that didn't make much sense, as I would have been one of the oppressors."

He sounded finished, and yet he hadn't told Bess why he, a quistril, hated all the other quistrils so much; why he hadn't just picked up the old woman and brought her back here.

"Heldrick . . ."

"Shh!"

Bess held still. The light went on, almost at the same moment that the dungeon door opened. A number of footsteps descended the stairway.

This time they took Heldrick. A long time passed before they brought him back, and when they did he didn't answer her. A quistril brought her another food wafer, which she devoured. Sometime later she fell asleep and slept for a long time.

DAY SEVEN

When she awoke, it was still dark.

Bess stood, stretched, drank some water, and used the hole in the floor for its intended purpose.

Should she try to go back to sleep? For all she knew the sun had risen hours ago, although the morning food wafer hadn't come—assuming that the wafers came three times a day.

Anyway, she was awake. And Heldrick had said he didn't sleep much. She went to the grate and, softly, so as not to disturb him if he slept, said:

"Heldrick?"

Ten seconds passed, fifteen. No answer. She turned away.

But then, "What do you want?"

She swiveled back to the grate. "Did I wake you?"

"I don't know."

"Uh—pardon?"

"I was drifting. A residual effect from my questioning sessions, I suspect. Not a thing I would normally do."

"Are the sessions bad?"

"Could be worse. They haven't questioned you yet?"

"No. Do they—I mean—"

"You'd like to know what to expect? They'll ask questions and inflict pain when you give no answer, or an unsatisfactory one."

She swallowed. "Torture, then." She'd known that would lie at the end of the road. She suspected she'd be no good at resisting.

"In our case, yes. They use a machine called a 'stressor.' It functions as a training tool—"

"Training?"

"Perhaps I should say 'character building.'"

"They use torture to build character?"

"I said that in our case—yours and mine—it was torture. In the case of the young quistrils, it is milder. Psychologically, quistrils possess certain predispositions, genetically encoded, that stressing helps to bring out. Quistrils must follow orders, lack innovation, act ruthlessly, and be loyal to the Citadel. The Citadel instills the ruthlessness and loyalty by treating the young quistrils ruthlessly but impartially in the stressor."

Bess's stomach churned. "You're talking about children, Heldrick."

"Yes. But the children build up a resistance, and the stressors cause pain but no disfigurement. It's endurable."

"Endurable? I understand how torturing children could make them ruthless when they grow up, but not how it can engender loyalty!"

"I said they were *not* tortured—"

"It hurts, doesn't it?"

"Yes. Resemblances exist, I admit, but it's a different thing." Heldrick sighed. "The boys all go through it together, you know. Eventually they realize that the older quistrils went through it too, in their day. It's a bond, like the survivors of an army unit from your last war might share."

"It's not like that at all. It's sick."

"Without doubt. As I say, the quistrils have an innate tendency to interpret these events in the proper way, and therein, no doubt, lies a built-in sickness of the quistril mind. But remember that many of your college fraternities and sororities conduct hazing rites which amount to a milder version of the same thing and are every bit as self-perpetuating. Sickness is not an exclusive property of quistrils."

Bess had heard about some of those hazing rites and could hardly disagree. But it annoyed her that Heldrick saw any resemblances between her own world and this.

"Anyway," Heldrick went on, "they ask me any number of questions, but mostly they want to know the location of the conjunction. When I don't answer, they crank up the stressor."

Bess had trouble imagining herself withholding that information. "What does it matter if they know where it is? It's so close to collapsing, they can't use it. They won't have time to hurt anyone."

"Think about yourself for a change. If they find the conjunction, they'll guard it. We won't have a chance in the world of going back."

"Oh. —I thought you said we didn't have any chance, anyway?"

"We have no reasonable chance, but you can never be sure a meteorite won't smash into the Citadel, killing most of the quistrils but leaving us alive and somehow blasting open our dungeon doors. It's not something to count on, you'll admit, but why should we do anything that would make such a freak opportunity useless to us?"

"Well—I see what you're saying, but if that happened I doubt that continuing to guard the conjunction would be a high priority for the remaining quistrils."

"Actually, they wouldn't guard it for very long, anyway. They'd close it. Hurling a few tons of rock through would do the trick, in its present state."

"Really? You mean that would accelerate the time differential?"

"Well . . . it would, but that's not what I meant. The conjunction is twisted and strained by the relative motions of the two universes. Anything passing through also strains it, and sufficient strain can snap it. The weaker it gets, the less mass is required. Once the quistrils find the conjunction, they won't stop short of closing it. Anyway, once they know where it is I, personally, will become useless to them, so if I tell them, I'm dead. I'll accept a few hours of pain each day for the privilege of keeping my head on my shoulders. Especially since they're using the stressor to inflict the pain."

"How does that help? Because you were trained? It doesn't hurt you that much?"

"Gods, no! At the power setting they're using, it hurts more than I would have believed. Next time it'll hurt more, and sometime, if I live that long, it'll hurt enough that I'll tell them what they want to know. But all the time they're doing it, I know that when they let me go the pain will stop. They're not putting out my eyes or cutting off my fingers. Keep that in mind when your turn comes."

Bess swallowed. "I'll try."

"Try hard. Did you want anything in particular?"

"No. But I wish I knew the time."

"About 3:20 a.m."

"How—? Do you have a watch? They took mine away."

"No. Built in time-sense. Very useful at night and in dungeons."

"Oh. I guess I should try to go back to sleep then."

"If you wish. You've already slept a long time. I don't think it matters much."

"You really believe there's no hope for us, don't you?"

"That's right. I know the quistrils too well. They don't make mistakes."

"No? What happened with you, then? I'd say their loyalty training didn't work so hot."

A minute passed.

"Yes," Heldrick murmured at last. Bess had to strain to hear him. "I guess you could call that a mistake." And then louder, his voice tense with buried anger: "They killed my brother."

CHAPTER 15

Bᴇss ᴄᴏᴜʟᴅɴ'ᴛ ᴛʜɪɴᴋ what to say. She had never known Heldrick's brother, she barely knew Heldrick, and it had happened so long ago. Frankly, what surprised her more than Heldrick's revelation was that it seemed to bother him. She found it difficult to imagine that quistrils could feel intimacy with anyone, even a relative, even in childhood. In fact, she could hardly picture them *having* a childhood. But they did, of course. Quistrils were people too, though nobody wanted to admit the fact.

"His name was Ankvar," Heldrick said. "We were closer than most quistril children, though we didn't know, for years, that we were true brothers. Small children are raised in the crèche, where all wear the title 'brother' equally. Besides, the mothers themselves rarely know which quistril sired which child, so the crèche can track no relationship closer than half-brother. But Ankvar and I were twins, so the crèche staff knew, all right. They didn't tell us, but they passed the information along to our preceptors when we left."

"And your preceptors told you?"

-119-

"Yes, eventually. When we turned seven. But only because—well, you should know that quistrils discourage strong friendships between children, as that tends to weaken loyalty to the group."

"Then . . . why—?"

"They thought our kin relationship indecently intimate. They expected us to feel the same, and informed us in an attempt to shock us into withdrawing from one another. Foolish of them. What do children care for decency? Still, Ankvar and I could see their intent, and knew they would take a different tack if this one failed. We did as they expected, in public. But the need to restrict our friendship to private meetings made us resent the Citadel bureaucracy, so that we grew closer to one another, instead—the exact opposite of what our elders had intended."

"And they found out?"

"Not about that. But Ankvar had a sense of humor, if you can imagine that virtue in a quistril. He played practical jokes. When we were twelve, little more than a year from finishing with the stressors and becoming full-fledged adult quistrils—"

"Whoa! You said 'twelve'?"

"Not so young as you think. Quistrils reach full maturity early. Younglings graduate to the novice rank before turning fourteen. That quistril who accosted us at Arrick's house was probably fifteen."

"My age!"

"Not in any reasonable sense. A one-year-old dog is not a puppy, and a fifteen-year-old quistril is not a boy. Think of Ankvar and me as having been Wellen's age, if it helps. Anyway, Ankvar recalibrated the dials on some of the stressors. The next day many boys were supplied with more of a jolt than they expected, while others received close to nothing. A day and a half passed before the stress proctors realized that immature stress reactions—cries of pain and whatnot—kept coming from the same stressors. The boys themselves had recognized it earlier, but they knew that the adults would have regarded any complaints as sniveling.

"As a result, for a while at least, the children saw the adults as capricious and uncaring, and the ordeal of stressing divided rather than united the Citadel. My brother thought it hilarious. For that day and a half, no one but I knew what he had done. I didn't share his amusement, but I did do my best to take one of the friendlier stressors when my turn came.

"Then the proctors corrected the problem, and for the next several days I didn't happen to see my brother. When I learned that no one else had either, I began to worry. They must have known that no one but Ankvar would play such a trick. Had he pushed the graycloaks too far?"

"Graycloaks?"

"The highest ranking members of the Citadel. If they had merely sequestered him in a room with guards, everyone would have known about it. I could think of only one way for the graycloaks to isolate him secretly: incarceration in the dungeon.

"I came here in the middle of the night, after the corridors had emptied. I didn't dare risk turning on the dungeon light, so I walked in silent darkness, with nothing but the faint rustling of my cloak to remind me that I was alive and awake."

"Did you find him?"

"Yes. The graycloaks had tortured him with the stressor."

"Like they're doing to you now?"

"That's right. Nothing in my life had ever shocked me so much."

"Really? I thought you grew up with the thing."

"Understand, Bess. The explicit purposes of the stressor are to build strength of spirit and resistance to pain, and to engender loyalty. I could imagine applying it to a cadril to break his spirit, but to use it that way on one of our own seemed a kind of blasphemy, a far worse crime than Ankvar himself had committed. No wonder they'd kept their actions secret! This was worse than executing him."

Bess had trouble seeing it that way, but had to grant that Heldrick did. "So . . . why did they do it, then?"

"Partly, I suppose, they viewed what Ankvar had done with much the same horror that I experienced on learning of what they had done to Ankvar. To them, Ankvar's joke was a more serious offense than he or I had thought; it was a subversion of a crucial tool in maintaining the Citadel for future generations. They probably wanted to know who'd assisted him in his prank. No one had, of course, and Ankvar would have said so. But I knew about it; I could have reported it. The Ascendant of the day possessed an uncanny ability to detect falsehoods. He would have known that Ankvar held something back. Ankvar should have told them—my punishment would have been light. But I suppose his reticence convinced them that he protected an accomplice. They meant to torture him until he revealed the person, then kill Ankvar."

Bess felt ill. "I can't believe that torture was insufficient punishment for them."

"Punishment was no longer the issue. The graycloaks would want no one to learn of the perverted way they had used the stressor. It had to remain confidential."

"But you—"

"Exactly. I had become an unexpected party to their confidence. My failure to denounce Ankvar for his foolish joke seemed suddenly a mere peccadillo. The moment I realized that, the dungeon light went on.

"I should have known. Had they taken Ankvar to the stressors anytime other than the middle of the night, someone would have observed them. Everyone would have known about it.

"I flew toward the far end of the dungeon corridor and hid under my cloak. In the deep shadows, they didn't notice me. I waited five minutes after they took Ankvar from his cell, and then left the dungeon. I never returned to my bed. When Ankvar broke now, he would tell them more than they'd expected.

"As a youngling, I had no permission to leave the Citadel in the middle of the night. I headed toward the kitchen instead, trying my best to appear on legitimate business. I have no idea if I succeeded: I didn't meet anyone, and was not put to the test.

"I packed some food to last me a few days, then found an empty pantry and slept the sleep of a condemned man. In the morning, I slipped out of the kitchen and went to the stables, where I took a horse and rode out of the Citadel uncontested. Late that day, shortly before dusk, I found the conjunction. You know the rest."

"But Heldrick, they're torturing you now in the daytime. Don't they care anymore if it's secret?"

"They think I'm an outsider, a foreigner. Nobody cares how I'm treated. Of course, I'm not an outsider at all. It's almost funny," he said. "Here I am at last, in the same situation my brother was in generations ago. They finally caught me, but they don't know who they've caught. They don't even ask me my name."

Heldrick said no more that night. Eventually Bess went back to sleep, and in the morning—or at least, not long after the next time she woke up—four quistrils took Heldrick away for about an hour.

A vasik—Grayvle recognized Kierkaven, Pandir's chief henchman—pushed his head into the duty room while remnants of the previous shift were still exiting. "I need three of you to come with me to the dungeon."

Just what Grayvle wanted. He jumped to his feet, but Kierkaven pointed at the ones crowding to get out the door: "You, you, and you. Come with me."

Of all the luck! Any other time, the doorway area would have been clear, and—

Bad luck for the three going off duty as well, he realized, as they glanced at one another in dismay. Grayvle stepped to the door and caught the last one before he went through. "You're off duty," he whispered. "I'll go." He pushed through before the other had a chance to refuse.

If Kierkaven knew that youngling and noticed the exchange, Grayvle and the other fellow could be hauled up for insubordination. But since the other hadn't come chasing after him, that was unlikely. Grayvle would accept the risk. He just wanted to see the girl. He wanted to see that she was a typical cadril: stolid, gritless, and treacherous. Then he could relax.

And he'd managed it! Swapping his own gate assignment for Fendrig's on-call duty had been a long shot, on the off chance something like this would happen; he couldn't believe it had paid off so quickly.

At the dungeon door, Kierkaven paused. "We'll be taking the prisoner to the crypt's adjunct, for interrogation. He's extremely dangerous. You must each keep a hand on your knife at all times."

He? Grayvle's heart sank. Of course the near-quistril would be the one of concern to anyone but himself. By attaching himself to this first group, he'd effectively exiled himself from the duty room for a while. He might miss his only opportunity to see the girl.

"Any questions?" Kierkaven looked at each youngling . . . then his eyes returned to Grayvle's face. He frowned. "What's your name?"

Grayvle tried to keep his face expressionless. "Grayvle, sir."

After a moment, Kierkaven turned away, flicked on the switch, and opened the dungeon door. Grayvle swallowed. Kierkaven couldn't have known the youngling whose place Grayvle had taken, or he would surely have said something more. And since he'd barely glanced at the three when he chose them, Grayvle hadn't expected him to have the least idea of their appearance. Yet, at some level, he'd noticed something amiss with Grayvle, even if he didn't quite know what.

The man was sharp.

Waiting in the hall for the interrogation to end, Grayvle decided, could be no less agony than what the prisoner endured in the stressor. But at last Pandir opened the door and said to Kierkaven, "Return him to his cell. We'll try again later." Then he stalked out, his cloak flapping against Grayvle as he went. Grayvle had never been quite so near a mastron before; this was the first time he had seen Pandir closely enough to clearly make out his features.

Kierkaven led the way into the crypt adjunct and walked to the stressor. Pandir hadn't even bothered to turn it off. Grayvle could scarcely credit how high the setting was. He had experienced that level once, for a moment, on a dare. The near-quistril had endured it for nearly an hour. He abruptly changed his mind about the agony of waiting.

Kierkaven slowly turned the dial, and Grayvle heard the prisoner's extended sigh as the pain gradually faded. Kierkaven pulled off the mesh. "Get him dressed and back to his cell. He'll have to be carried or dragged."

It took five minutes to dress the near-quistril, and ten more to get him back to the dungeon. As they dragged him from the bottom of the stairs to his open cell door, Grayvle saw the girl peer out from her grating. Still here, at least. Maybe he could yet be assigned as her escort—if she needed one today.

The girl paid no attention to him or any of the rest of them. Her eyes were fixed on the near-quistril, so Grayvle could study her a moment without her noticing. She didn't look frightened. She didn't look stupid.

Damn.

They threw the near-quistril into his cell, and Kierkaven closed the door. When Grayvle glanced back at the girl's cell, she had left the grating.

At least he'd managed to see her once. He hadn't seen what he wanted, though. Let that be a lesson to him. Don't pick up strange items out of curiosity. Either that or learn to live a with guilty conscience.

Kierkaven sent the three of them back to the duty room, and headed off in a different direction. Grayvle hurried well ahead of the others—just in case—

Turning the last corner, he almost collided with two younglings coming the opposite way.

"Hey!" one said.

Both were in the nineteenth form—one behind Grayvle's. Grayvle didn't know their names, but he recognized the one who spoke as having been in the duty room earlier. "Sorry. Where are you going?"

"The dungeon. We're to take the marginal to meet the Ascendant."

What? The Ascendant wouldn't bother with the girl, would he? But the near-quistril couldn't even walk yet. "Which marginal?"

"You don't think they'd only send two of us to get the near-quistril, do you?"

Grayvle shook his head. "I had to make sure." He glanced behind him; his companions were still distant. "I was told to intercept you and substitute for one of you. Which one is up to you."

The two looked at one another.

"Come on, you don't want to keep the Ascendant waiting! Who has the keys?"

The one who had spoken raised them in his hand.

"Fine. You come along." To the other: "And you can return to the duty room." He turned and began walking. In a moment the one with the keys had caught up to him.

"Where, exactly," Grayvle asked, "are we taking her?"

"To the empty sub-proctor's office. Weren't you told?"

"No time." Grayvle shrugged. "He just said to make sure I caught you; you'd know the details."

"Who said?"

"Kierkaven. Works for Pandir."

"Ah . . ." The other youngling stopped asking questions.

CHAPTER 16

No more than five minutes after the quistrils brought Heldrick back, two more fetched Bess from her cell. This is it, she thought. It's my turn now.

Her escorts looked college-age. That meant that, in fact, they were probably younger than she was. They took her through corridors different from those leading to the doctor's office, although soon the twists and turns so confused her that it might simply have been a different route.

At last they stopped. One of the escorts knocked at a door. When no one answered, he opened the door and motioned her into a room containing nothing but a single wooden chair.

"Don't sit in the chair," he said. "The Ascendant will arrive shortly." He closed the door behind her.

The room was dimmer than the corridor. The single light over the door reached to the corners solely because the room was so small. Perhaps quistrils, with their better eyes, found the gloom no impediment. Or perhaps they intended the dimness to irritate her. If so, they'd missed their mark. She found it a relief. Her eyes had ached all through the corridors after a day in the dungeon.

The door opened and the Ascendant entered. He was dressed like the other quistrils she'd seen, in black—except for his cloak and hood, which were light gray.

His hood shadowed his face. He moved slowly for a quistril—like a monk, with his head bent forward as if in contemplation. He sat on the chair before raising his head. But when he did, neither the dim light nor the hood could hide his wrinkles. She hadn't seen any old quistrils before. Of course, old quistrils didn't live long, did they?

The Ascendant pushed his hood back, revealing a cruel but meditative face, with none of the impetuosity exhibited by the quistril Heldrick had slain. His gaze drilled right through her. She felt transfixed, like a doe in the headlights. He continued to stare, and her throat went dry.

At last he asked, "Where are you from?"

Bess swallowed, tried the answer she had given to the doctor. "A farm nearby."

"Yes, yes. But before that. I want the location of your margin conjunction."

Bess swayed. If she told them now, she could save herself from torture. Wouldn't she tell them anyway, in the end?

"Perhaps the term is unfamiliar to you," the Ascendant continued. "I wish to know the location of your mousehole."

"I . . . don't understand," she managed, but with little hope that he believed her.

He reached into his robe and withdrew a small object. "Ever see this before?" He held it high.

Her key chain. Bess's hand rose halfway to her mouth before she stopped it.

"I see that you have. No one on this world made it—'Value Liberty,' it says. Clearly it came by way of a mousehole. Careless of you to have dropped it. We'd never have come looking for you else."

"But—"

"And brought a quistril with you. The two worlds must resemble each other closely indeed, despite this curious sentiment," and he waved the key chain, "to have both produced quistrils."

"But I didn't—"

"There's no use denying that you came with the quistril. He's not one of ours, any more than this material—" He tapped his fingernail on the plastic Liberty Bell. "—is of our manufacture. I'm afraid that only a mousehole can explain either; and for two mouseholes to crop up at the same time, each big enough to allow a human to pass through, is too much to swallow. So you must have come with the quistril. I ask only the one question: Where *is* your mousehole?"

"I don't—I didn't mean to come through at all, and then I got lost—"

"Lost! I could believe that of you, perhaps, but not of your quistril friend."

"I never saw him before I came here. He didn't come with me; he followed me to take me back. He must know where the mousehole is, but I . . ." She remembered that she'd seen the conjunction on the way here. She did know where it was.

The Ascendant narrowed his eyes. But instead of telling her to finish her sentence, he asked, "He came here only to find you?"

She swallowed, nodded. How could she keep him from asking about the conjunction's location again? If she lied outright, he'd know. She felt sure of it.

The Ascendant thought a moment. "So they're not scouting yet. They aren't ready to invade. This is good news. But we still need the mousehole's location. If you know it, I suggest you tell me now. Understand that if we choose to question you more forcefully—well, you have no training on our equipment. If we must use it, it could damage you beyond repair on the first session, or even kill you. Well?"

Anything to keep from answering directly. "I can't answer your questions if I'm dead."

He frowned, and squinted at her. "You see to the heart of things. Surely you cannot be the innocent that you claim."

She didn't want him thinking that, either. Better to arouse anger than suspicion. "You think I'm guilty because I'm intelligent? What sort of foolishness is that?"

The quistril's expression changed again, became unreadable, like a snake's. "Calling me foolish is itself foolishness." He paused. "You have spoken correctly on the first count, however. We do not want you dead. And so we interrogate your companion first. He has no doubt received training on similar equipment in your own world. He has already shown us that he will resist, which means that he may expect many painful sessions before his obstinacy breaks. By telling us what you know, you could save him from this. And of course if we fail to get the information from him, we will interrogate you without hesitation."

Bess closed her eyes. She didn't need to save Heldrick from the stressor. He could do that anytime by talking. So what could she say now, without giving anything away? Could she avoid telling the central lie?

Maybe. "I went through the mousehole by accident, and then I got lost, like I said. That's why that quistril you found me with came through, to find me and take me back. I just want to go home."

"You insist that you don't know the mousehole's location?"

"I tell you I got lost. But I—I think I would recognize the place if I saw it again."

The Ascendant looked at her for a long minute. She kept her mind on the true things she had said, rather than the false impression she hoped she'd given.

Finally he stood and said, "Come with me; there's something you should see."

Grayvle's companion said, "Have you ever seen the Ascendant before?"

Grayvle shook his head. "Except at graduations and things. Never close up, like this."

"What is he, thirty-four? He doesn't look too healthy, does he?"

Grayvle turned to meet the other's eyes. "I can't believe you just said that."

His companion shrugged.

The door opened. The Ascendant came out and beckoned to the girl. "Follow me."

She did. Grayvle kept pace on her left, his companion on her right.

With a start, he realized where they were headed. The crypt annex, again. Of course, he'd expected it eventually, but with the meeting in that empty office he'd assumed that questioning was not, yet, in the works.

Something grabbed his stomach and twisted. The near-quistril was one thing, but the girl—she had no training. It could kill her.

He never should have arranged to escort her. It was just making him feel worse.

But the Ascendant bypassed the annex and continued on instead to the crypt itself. Surely he wouldn't interrogate her here, with all the younglings? Yet he stopped before the double doors. Grayvle stepped forward and opened one. The Ascendant motioned for the girl to precede him.

Bess suspected the old quistril was taking her to the stressing room. She had already built a mental image of it: rows of tables with open, rounded lids full of spikes, like iron maidens. Well, she could stand seeing that, as long as he only wanted to show her.

But when she stepped into the huge room she stumbled to a stop, for though the stressors looked much like she'd expected—except that simple mesh coverings replaced the heavy spiked lids—she hadn't expected to find them occupied.

The old quistril stepped past her and to her right. She looked beyond him at all the stressors, with the reflective mesh shaped by the forms of their occupants. In the closest stressors she could see through the mesh to the young men beneath, apparently fourteen or fifteen years of age but, taking into account what Heldrick had said, probably about ten. Though their bodies under the mesh shone with perspiration, none struggled, none cried out, and perhaps, as Heldrick had said, when used for training it was "not that bad." But it made her ill.

No. It made her *angry.*

"The younglings, I fear," said the quistril, "refer to this room as the crypt and to these stressors as caskets. The mesh above and the table below conduct impulses which stimulate the pain nerves. This dial controls the intensity—" He stepped to the nearest stressor and twisted the dial one way, then back. The young quistril's jaw and fists clenched in response and he emitted a soft grunt. "—as you see." Bess noticed that the old quistril hadn't returned the dial quite to its starting position; the poor youngster continued to receive an unaccustomed dose. He made no more complaint, but it made Bess angrier than ever.

"The training starts quite young." The quistril walked across the center aisle to Bess's left, where small children, looking no more than three years old, occupied the stressors. Bess raised one hand to her mouth, and she backed away from the sight, until she bumped into the stressor of the youngling who had served as the old quistril's exhibit. A pins-and-needles sensation tickled her back. She jerked away.

How could children that young have any understanding of the reasons for this "training"? They couldn't! But she could just imagine Heldrick telling her that understanding the reason was not necessary for the training to be effective

"Of course we keep the small ones at an extremely low dosage. The object here is not punishment. However, as I'm sure your near-quistril friend could tell you, the stressor serves excellently for that purpose, also."

Bess stared back at the quistril, hating him, and realized that she had the power to undo one small evil he'd committed. Without thinking further, she shifted her weight, moving her body a couple of inches, and felt behind her, keeping her fingers below the level of the mesh. Her fingertips brushed the control dial.

The quistril stared at her as he had earlier. But he watched her eyes, and her hands were behind her. She gripped the dial, turned it—just a short way, enough to put it past where it had started but no further than might be attributed to the old quistril's carelessness—and let go.

CHAPTER 17

GRAYVLE HAD NOTICED the Ascendant's carelessness in returning the dial to its proper place and wasn't surprised that the girl noticed it, too.

What did surprise him, what shook him to his very core, was the way she went on to correct the problem, at no possible benefit to herself, under the gaze of the most powerful quistril of the district, while surrounded by devices that could induce pain of the highest order. Why, that went beyond brave, to foolhardy; beyond honorable, to suicidal; beyond confident, to insane.

But, by the gods, it proved she was no coward.

She had kept her eyes locked on the Ascendant from the moment she reached for the dial until she released it. Now she looked for a second at Grayvle and his companion. Grayvle had no time to feign disinterest before she turned her eyes back to the Ascendant. But, though she must have recognized the possibility that he'd seen her turn the dial, she kept her expression neutral. Grayvle glanced at his companion, who stood gazing blankly at the far wall. At least no one had seen her but himself.

But that meant that, unless he reported her, she'd gotten away with it. No matter how foolhardy, suicidal, and insane her action had been, it had worked. He found himself standing straighter, and his chest expanded, filled with a strange emotion . . . no, not strange. He'd encountered it often enough, but never like this, never in this context. He was . . .

He was proud. Not of himself, of the girl. The cadril. Incredible. Who would believe it? He could hardly believe it himself.

"I believe you," the Ascendant said. Grayvle jumped and turned his head. But the Ascendant was still looking at the girl. "You came through the conjunction accidentally and got lost, so you don't know the way to your conjunction. Yes, it fits. But you may actually know more than you think. Understand that if your near-quistril friend proves intractable, we will bring you here to make certain. Come this way." He walked between two rows of the stressors. The girl followed, Grayvle and his companion accompanying. What did the man plan to show the girl now?

He stopped near the end of the line at an empty stressor and flipped back the mesh. "This will be more effective if you remove your clothing first."

The girl paled. "I—"

"Do it now, or these younglings shall remove it for you."

She glanced to either side, her expression unreadable, and began undressing.

What was the Ascendant up to? Hadn't he just said that he wouldn't interrogate her unless the near-quistril gave them no information? Grayvle's stomach began to twist again.

The girl stopped undressing when she was clad in nothing but skimpy underpants and a sleeveless shirtlike garment that didn't quite reach the top of her briefs.

The Ascendant frowned, then shrugged. "Good enough. Lie down here."

She did so and sank a bit into the table as it molded itself to her form. "Please, I—"

"Just a taste. So that you know what's ahead." The old quistril laid the mesh over top of her.

The mesh was easier to see out of than into. Bess watched the old quistril plug several attached jacks into the table below. "I believe three seconds should suffice," he said.

He reached for the dial. She closed her eyes, clenched her fists, and had taken one deep breath when the world exploded, forcing all the air back out of her lungs. Needles jabbed her from every direction, to the bone and beyond, then twisted and jiggled. Pressure built up in her eyes until they verged on bursting. All her fingernails and toenails were bent backward, and someone knocked her teeth out with a hammer. A rod covered with bits of broken glass was shoved down her throat and pulled back and forth.

She couldn't scream because there was no air.

Couldn't breathe . . .

It went on well past the allotted three seconds, and she realized what had happened. That youngling must have seen her and told the Ascendant, once the power was on; and so the Ascendant had decided to leave the machine on until she was dead. She found herself grateful for that, knowing it would end soon.

But it didn't end soon enough. Another minute passed, and she couldn't think of anything at all, except the agony. The rod in her throat turned to a snake that devoured her from within. All thought receded, fell away from the agony into a black pit with no bottom, but awareness remained. Time went on. . . .

And on—

"Three," the quistril said.

Bess didn't recognize him. She didn't know what he meant.

She watched as he unplugged the jacks and rolled back the mesh, but she didn't understand what he was doing.

She saw his face change, heard his words:

"She's not breathing."

A youngling appeared beside the old quistril. "She's conscious." The words almost made sense to her.

The youngling's hand swung back and forth in front of her face. Her head moved of its own volition to follow it. She heard two smacks. She felt nothing.

The youngling's hand moved again. Smack! Smack! This time her cheeks tingled.

"Breathe!"

She knew that word, but there was no air. To prove it she expanded and contracted her rib cage. Everything moved fine, but—

No air.

Black spots formed before her eyes.

"That's better," the old quistril said. Bess wondered how he talked without any air. "She must be more sensitive than I'd realized."

The spots grew together until all was black except for a space in the middle, filled by the Ascendant's face.

He watched her from the bottom of a deep well that grew deeper as she watched . . . his face fell away from her, shrinking with the distance as the black closed all around it, until it disappeared.

The Ascendant was a fool!

It was a terrible thought, but Grayvle couldn't help thinking it. Anyone should have known the setting on the stressor was too high, even for three seconds, for someone with no training. He could only hope the girl would suffer no permanent damage.

At least she was breathing again. The Ascendant nodded after a moment and said, "Very good. I doubt she'll forget that." He sounded pleased.

It made Grayvle ill. Couldn't the Ascendant see that this cadril was not like all the others?

"Get her dressed and drag her back to the dungeon. I'll leave you to it." The Ascendant turned and shuffled off.

Grayvle stared at the Ascendant's retreating back and wondered for the first time whether *any* cadrils were like what he had been taught. Was his entire education a bundle of lies?

The moment the door had closed behind the Ascendant, Grayvle's companion looked at the scantily dressed cadril with a speculative look in his eye. What he was clearly considering was forbidden. At least he had the sense not to say anything. But he glanced up at Grayvle with a questioning expression.

Grayvle stared back as coldly as he knew how. "You are not going to touch her."

His companion jerked back, but without suspicion. After all, Grayvle was the one following strict protocol.

Grayvle carefully pulled the girl's clothes back on. Then he lifted her in his arms. "Let's go."

"You're going to carry her all the way?"

"It's not far. She's light. And you can open all the doors."

As they passed through the huge room filled with occupied caskets, he couldn't help but wonder: had all those years of pain the Citadel put him through really been worth it? The adults claimed that stress training was required to strengthen courage and will, but if the girl's action didn't demonstrate willfulness and courage he'd eat his cloak.

A voice in the darkness. Had it awakened her? Had she been asleep? Bess sat up, trembling all over, and concentrated on breathing, savoring each fetid, stale, wonderful inhalation.

"Bess?"

Her name. Someone had called her name.

"Yes?"

"Ah, that's a relief. You were so quiet I feared they'd taken you away."

She began to cry.

"Bess! What's wrong? Did they interrogate you?"

"No . . . Heldrick? Is that you?"

"Of course. Who else?"

"I don't know. I can't think."

"What happened?"

"There wasn't any air." She couldn't stop crying. Her brain was turning to water and leaking out her tear ducts, running down her face, gone forever. She tilted her head backward to help keep it in.

"What did they do?"

"They put me in a casket."

"A stressor?"

"Yes. For three hours."

"Bess," Heldrick said quietly, "that's not possible."

Bess thought. She remembered the face in the bottom of the well saying "three."

"Three something," she said. "He counted."

"Three seconds?"

"That . . . may be." Her tears slowed, and her brain remained in her skull. She felt greatly relieved.

"What setting did he use?"

"I don't know. He didn't say."

"He could have killed you." Heldrick paused. "I didn't expect them to start with you until they'd finished with me. They'll never believe that you don't know your way to the margin conjunction."

"But . . ." *But I do.* The knowledge startled her, as did the suspicion that she would be safer, somehow, to conceal it. "But they do believe it."

"Pardon? What do you mean? Why did they put you through the stressor, then?"

She wiped her eyes, beginning to remember. It seemed that all her thoughts had been absorbed by rolls and rolls of cotton batting. She was having the devil of a time squeezing them back out. "For a taste."

"A taste! Great gods!"

"They came by this morning, right after they brought you back."

"Ah. No wonder I didn't hear them. Bess, listen. Will you do me a favor? Go back to sleep."

Fear clenched her by the throat. "I might dream—"

"No. That's one thing you won't do. Believe me. Your brain requires rest. Try it."

"Well." She moved back to the straw and lay down. "But I don't feel . . . very . . ."

Bess's eyes snapped open. Heldrick had been right: she hadn't dreamed. And her mind felt clear. But what had wakened her?

She heard footsteps on the stairs and noticed the dim light at her grating. Who did they want this time? A single set of footsteps, and they sounded hurried.

The footsteps slowed as they approached. A hooded shape appeared at her grating, black against the dim light of the corridor. A hand pushed something through the grate, which fell with a heavy clink to the cell floor. The footsteps retreated down the long dungeon corridor, faster than they had arrived.

Bess didn't wait for the quistril to leave. She bounded across the cell to the door. Despite the corridor light, the shadows at the base of the door were too deep for her to see what the quistril had dropped. She swept her hands from side to side on the cell floor, and her left hand struck something which skittered away.

She lunged and hit the floor so hard it expelled her breath in a rush. Carefully she moved her hands around the floor and found the hole under her face.

If it had gone down there . . .

She raised up, slid her hands around the hole, and found the thing right away: two things, to be precise, held together by a small ring. One of them lay at the edge of the hole; the other dangled into it.

She gripped them and rolled away from the hole, then raised the objects to the grating before the light went out, to let her eyes confirm what her fingers had already told her.

Keys, large and old-fashioned. One for her cell and one for the dungeon door? What else could they be?

Who had brought them? She could only think of one possibility: the youngling whose casket she'd turned down in the crypt. But how could he have known which cell to bring a key for? Maybe . . . maybe he'd brought a pass-key, one that would work on any cell.

The dungeon door closed and the corridor light blinked out. Heldrick immediately said, "Bess? What was that?"

"Someone brought me keys."

"Ah, Bess, Bess."

She reached through the grate with an empty hand to locate the keyhole. Then, poking one finger through the key ring to keep from accidentally dropping it, she took the keys in her hand and reached again through the grate. She inserted one key into the lock, turned it, and with a satisfying *snick!* her cell door opened.

"Bess! What was that?"

"What did I tell you? I've opened my cell door."

"Great gods! You have keys?"

"I said I did. I wouldn't joke about something like that. Keep talking so I can find your cell."

"I thought the stressor had damaged your mind. —Here, I can do better than talk."

Two seconds passed, then light burst from the grating of a cell a short way down the corridor. Bess gasped. But her eyes adjusted, and she saw that Heldrick shone only a keychain flashlight.

She hurried to his cell. "Where did you find that?"

"I always carry one with me when I come to this world. I keep it in a special pocket in the neck of my cloak. The gathers hide it well. Now, who brought you the keys?"

"A youngling. I turned down his casket earlier." She pushed the key into the lock of Heldrick's cell.

"His casket—? Bess, what are you doing?"

The key seemed tight, but she pushed and jiggled it until it went all the way in.

"Bess?"

It would not, however, turn more than a hair.

"Bess!"

"What, already?"

"Your key won't work on my cell."

"But it must. The youngling can't have known which cell I was in. I figure he brought a pass-key."

"He wouldn't have needed to know: all of those cells are keyed alike. So I guess you might as well call it a pass-key."

Bess stopped jiggling the key in astonishment. "How could they be so foolish?"

"If they make a pass-key anyway, what's the difference? The prisoners don't—usually—have access to any keys."

"All right, all right. But if all the cells open to the same key, why can't I open yours? I can't even pull the key back out." She tugged. "I'm sure it's the right one."

"I said all of *those* cells. This and the next two, as well as the three across the corridor, are different. Here, take my light." He passed it to her through the grate. "How many keys have you got, then?"

"Two." Heldrick's cell door displayed a rectangular metal plate, with an inscription in unfamiliar characters.

The two doors farther along the corridor bore a similar decoration. "What does the sign say?" she asked.

"That other key should fit the door at the top of the stairs. The sign translates as . . . well, it doesn't really translate well. Just say these six cells are extra-secure. They're keyed individually. A steel plate is sandwiched inside the door of each and a steel box encases the entire cell behind the stonework."

"You're kidding. I thought my cell was strong enough." Bess shone the light at her key in the lock, aligned the key's handle with the keyhole, and then gave another yank. It came out.

"I thought so, too," Heldrick answered, while Bess tried the second key.

She couldn't even fit it into the keyhole.

"But you're out now, aren't you? In any case, these extra-secure cells result from quistrilian paranoia and are used when the individual imprisoned represents any special risk."

"So how do we get you out?"

"We don't, as I've said all along."

"You said I wouldn't escape either."

"Nor have you, yet. But at least a chance exists. Don't waste it. Go back to your cell and put that flashlight out."

"But, I—"

"Before somebody comes."

"Well . . . okay."

She returned to her cell and pulled the cell door shut. The bolt that locked the door shot automatically. She flicked off the light and darkness sprang at her from the corners of her cell, swallowing her in an instant.

CHAPTER 18

"I'LL WAKE YOU at midnight," Heldrick said as soon as the light went off. "At that time, you leave your cell, steal a horse from the stables, and ride as fast as you can to the margin conjunction. I'll instruct you on how to reach it. And I think we can push my cloak through the grate; it's too big for you, but it may allow you to ride out the gate unchallenged. Ride to the top of the rock outcropping, then abandon the horse and send it on its way. Climb down to the crevice without stepping on anything but bare rock, if possible, so as to leave no footprints. Can you remember all that?"

"Yes, but—"

"I'm not finished. Once you're through the conjunction, go immediately up the stairs and out of the house. I can keep from talking for another couple of days, perhaps, but in your world that will translate to a mere couple of minutes. They'll pursue you through the conjunction, but they won't go outside the house. Not for you. They'll settle for closing the conjunction. If they find you waiting in the basement, though, they'll bring you back. Clear enough?"

"Yes."

"Good. Now, to reach the stables—"

"You don't have to tell me all this," she said. "You're coming with me."

Heldrick sighed once. "That's a pleasant thought but not a kind joke."

"I'm not joking. I won't go without you. I swear."

"Don't be foolish."

Bess scowled. "I'm not foolish!"

"Well . . . no, not usually. How will you manage my escape, then?"

"I don't know yet. If I did, I wouldn't tell you. You might spill it under . . ."

"Stress. Yes. Well, humor me and listen to my instructions anyway. It can't hurt."

"Okay. Give me a minute." She still held the keys, the cell key in her palm; now she removed the second key from the ring so she would be able to tell, later, which was which, and placed the flashlight and the keys in a back corner of her cell. Then she covered them with straw and returned to the grating.

"I'm ready for directions to the stables. But don't tell me how to find the conjunction until I'm ready to leave." If Heldrick found out that she knew how to find the portal, he might reveal it in the stressor. Of course, he could also tell them that she had keys, but they'd be unlikely to ask about that.

"Fair enough." He told her how to reach the stables and added, "If you lose your way, pick a bearing and do your best to stick with it. This place isn't designed as a labyrinth, though it gives that impression. With any sense of direction at all, you'll find your way outside; from there, you can find the stables on your own. But try to stick to the path I've described. It will keep you in the least populated corridors and bring you out of the Citadel at the point nearest the stables."

He made her repeat the instructions and, after correcting her errors, repeat them again, until she said them right.

"I guess that's all for now," she said.

"Not quite. I'd like to know how you managed to turn a youngling's stressor down, if I heard you correctly."

She told Heldrick everything that had happened that morning. He didn't interrupt once, and when she finished he still said nothing for so many seconds that she began to wonder if she'd put him to sleep.

At last he said, "And you said you weren't foolish. I can't complain, considering the outcome, but if the Ascendant had caught you, it might have convinced him that you'd come here to interfere with quistrilian activities. Try to remember that the quistrils, including the young ones, are your enemies. If you persist in this sort of behavior, you'll never get back home."

"If it hadn't been for 'this sort of behavior,' I wouldn't have the keys now."

"I understand that. You were incredibly fortunate. Don't do it again."

Bess returned to her straw pile and thought. She thought hard, and for a long time, but could imagine nothing that would allow her to release Heldrick from his cell. She kept thinking of the same impossible things over and over again, kept bumping up against the hard fact that she could do nothing to open Heldrick's cell door. At last, exhausted, she lay back on her straw and tried to clear her mind.

She had to open up. She had to ask a different question, think of the problem in a different, maybe a crazy way. Like, accept that she couldn't release Heldrick from his cell: could there be any other way to rescue him?

She thought again and the answer came to her at once.

Pandir paced in annoyance. Ascendant Arvinblöd wanted him to push harder for the location of the conjunction, although the near-quistril revealed more sensitivity to the stressor than he ought. Perhaps stress training was less rigorous across the conjunction?

He shrugged, perturbed more by the Ascendant's behavior than by that of the near-quistril. Did the Ascendant want him to fail? That made no sense. No, he decided, the Ascendant wants to distance himself from me, should I fail, and to minimize the accomplishment should I succeed.

Irksome.

All right. He recognized that he lacked the vaunted mentality of the Ascendant and of the Ascendant's favorite, that prig Lonnkärin. So what? He had other strengths: a good sense of practical realism and the ability to watch out for himself. He'd never have become a mastron otherwise.

He had to guard his own back. How could he ensure that he succeeded with the near-quistril? Or at least improve the odds? Perhaps he could add a second approach to the problem.

After a moment's thought, he sent for Kierkaven. He really ought to promote the fellow sometime; perhaps he would if this enterprise succeeded.

"I've a bit of tracking for you," he said when Kierkaven arrived. "I'd like you to follow the trail of the marginals backward to its source."

Kierkaven frowned. "How old is the trail?"

Pandir shrugged. "Some days. It might be hopeless, but running the near-quistril through the stressor until he's pliable may take even longer. With enough men, tracking can be done faster, if it can be done at all."

"How long do I have, then? With all the backtrack-ing—"

"Report back by sundown. You've no hope of following a trail that old in the dark anyway. Take an additional fifteen men, however. That way you can split up and do your tracking and backtracking at the same time. You choose the men. Give me a list of their names before you go so I can grant them dispensation from their regular duties."

"At least it hasn't rained in the past few days." Kierkaven hesitated. "I should think it a shame to abandon a promising trail on account of darkness."

Pandir waved a hand. "Then send a message. Or come back and start again in the morning. I don't care. But make sure no one goes anywhere without a partner."

Kierkaven bowed in assent.

"You know where to pick up the trail?"

Kierkaven hesitated. "That farmstead we visited this morning?"

"Right. That's all."

"I'm hungry," Bess said.

"Yes. Lunch is overdue. Don't expect too much concern for our creature comforts, Bess. Try to make do with water."

A few minutes later the grate brightened again. Several pairs of footsteps this time. Two quistrils always came for Bess and four fetched Heldrick, but maybe one of these was bringing food.

The tramping feet went by her cell to Heldrick's. Still no lunch, then. She listened: keys clinked, a lock turned, a door opened. Then came a word in Vardic and, after a moment, footsteps leaving. She stood by the grate and watched them pass. They walked in a box formation, with Heldrick alone in the center.

There. Heldrick was out of his cell, and the quistrils themselves had done the job for her. Now came the trick: to keep them from putting him back.

She retrieved the key to her cell, and the flashlight, and waited until the dungeon door banged shut and the light went out. She had maybe an hour, by previous estimates, until Heldrick was returned; but who knew if her estimates were correct? And they might come to get her at any time. She would simply have to work as quickly as she could.

She turned on the flashlight, let herself out, and closed the cell door behind her. The bolt shot back, automatically locking the door. The quistrils had left Heldrick's cell door open, as they did with hers when they fetched her. She used her key to open the cell immediately to the right of Heldrick's, shone the light into it, and then into Heldrick's cell, comparing them, looking for any visible differences. In appearance, so far as she could tell, they were identical.

Of course, she needed to move the straw.

She put the key into her pocket and held the light in her mouth. She stepped to the back of Heldrick's cell, bent to grab an armful of straw, and had the sudden, horrible conviction that the cell door was swinging shut behind her. She dropped the straw and spun.

The door hadn't moved. She took two deep breaths, then pulled off her shoes and jammed their toes underneath the door. Reassured, she returned to the straw, gathered an armful and carried it to the new cell.

Heldrick lay in torment. His jaw ached from the clenching and his eyes were screwed shut. But, he thought, it won't last. It will stop. The agony will be but a memory.

The thought formed a shell of sanity that held him together. If he forgot it for an instant he would explode from pain.

The familiar, hated voice of his inquisitor returned to the central question:

"Tell us where the conjunction broke through. Tell us and the pain will stop."

Heldrick said nothing.

He heard a shuffle, a consultation that he couldn't make out over the pounding in his ears. The stressor induced virtual paralysis, but he could open his eyes. He did so on hearing the voice of a new questioner.

"Tell us this: does the girl know the conjunction's location?"

The voice belonged to an old quistril, with a cloak lighter in color than the dark gray of his interrogator's. The Ascendant's cloak. Heldrick struggled to release his clenched jaw but couldn't. Finally he curled back his lips and grunted, as well as he could, "No."

For a long moment the Ascendant kept his eyes upon Heldrick. Then he nodded. "It is as the girl says."

Heldrick's eyes closed again as the Ascendant walked away. He didn't see the mastron interrogator twist the dial off, but the sharp absence of pain was so abrupt that it seemed, everywhere under his skin, like sudden knives of ice. For a moment it hurt worse than the stressor-induced pain, and in that moment Heldrick passed out.

Pandir, furious, watched the younglings dress the near-quistril before dragging his limp form away. The Ascendant had given him, Pandir, the job of interrogation. Everyone knew it. But few comprehended how much the Ascendant disliked Pandir. Pandir himself had taken years to understand it.

The Ascendant's interferences were petty, but they added up. So he'd interrupted the interrogation to ask a question of his own? A minor point. But it was a no-win situation for Pandir. If the near-quistril had admitted that the girl knew vital information, then the Ascendant scored vital points at Pandir's expense. But although the near-quistril had denied the Ascendant's suggestion, the question had misdirected the thrust of the interrogation and Pandir could accomplish no more at this session.

The Ascendant meant to ensure that Pandir did not become the next Ascendant, obviously. He was grooming that invertebrate Lonnkärin for the job. Well, it took more than grooming. But Pandir knew he had to come up with some way to make the Ascendant's interferences backfire, to shed bad light on himself instead of on Pandir.

Some way. If it existed, he would find it.

Bess had moved most of the straw. She examined her work and decided it would do. She took the light from her mouth, shone it around, and saw that she'd left a trail of straw between the two cells. She kicked at it with her feet, but the bits of straw clung to the rough floor. So she dropped to her hands and knees and picked up each little piece, the flash once more in her mouth.

Her mouth was growing quite tired by the time she finished. She took the flashlight into her hand, stepped to the new cell, and threw the last bits of straw to the floor. She checked the corridor floor again.

All clear.

One last task. She picked up the empty bucket in the new cell, took it to Heldrick's cell, and poured half of his water into it. Then she lugged the half-filled bucket back to its position in the new cell. As she set it down, the dungeon light clicked on.

She clicked the flashlight off. If this was Heldrick being returned, he'd have to go through one more session before she could put her plan into effect. But if they were here for her, she was in trouble. She didn't have time to get back to her own cell, and they would find it empty; her only recourse right now was to hide where she was. She began to pull the new cell door closed as the dungeon door opened. But at the last second she stopped in despair. No quistril could miss the crash of the bolt shooting home as the cell door closed. But an open cell door was equally obvious.

No, wait. With the key in her hand she put her arm through the grate, inserted the key into the lock, and turned it. Then, gripping the key firmly, she pulled the door closed. She heard the tiny click of the catch which released the bolt. Nothing louder than she might have made with the ladle in the bucket. Only the pressure of her hand holding the key now kept the spring-loaded bolt back.

Slowly, she let the key in the lock turn back, as the bolt slid into place. Then she pulled the key from the lock and in through the grate.

The footsteps—they sounded like only a single set this time—still spiraled down the stairs at a steady pace. That guaranteed nothing, of course; quistrilian eyes might well have seen her hand sticking through the grate, even in the dim light . . . if the quistril had looked. She hoped that he hadn't.

The quistril took slow, weary, steps. It sounded like the quistril who delivered their meals. An older quistril might not possess such phenomenal eyesight.

The footsteps stopped a short way up the corridor, at her own cell. A short shuffling sound, then, and a single word, as before: "Food." Bess exalted. If he'd noticed her, he would have come straight to this cell.

The footsteps continued on past Bess's current cell, to the next one, Heldrick's.

Not until the footsteps stopped at the extra-secure cell did Bess remember stuffing her shoes under the cell door.

CHAPTER 19

BESS BIT HER LIP. The quistril could not miss seeing the shoes.

He mumbled something in Vardic. But after a moment the mumbling stopped and the slow footsteps plodded back, past her location and along the corridor. She wished she could have understood the mumbling. Could the quistril be simple-minded, or old enough to have lost his faculties? If they had a failing elder they might well use him for menial jobs. Maybe he wouldn't report the shoes. Not likely—but either way, what could she do about it now? She had to follow her plan and hope for the best.

When the dungeon door closed she let herself out of the cell, moved the food wafer to the new cell, and retrieved her shoes. Then she closed the door of Heldrick's original cell and left the door to the new cell open. The biggest danger was the lack of a sign on the new cell door. She would have moved one of the others there, if she'd had the tools. But they couldn't see that side of the door while it was open, and once they closed it, why look? At least, she could imagine herself missing something like that, especially in this light; and if what Heldrick had said about the average quistril's intelligence was true, they might be less likely to notice than she.

She could only hope.

She returned to her own cell. Within a minute, the light blinked back on. Would it be Heldrick, or other quistrils sent to check out the food deliveryman's story?

Many feet started down the staircase. Among the footsteps came the thump, thump, thump of Heldrick's heels on the stairs. The quistrils dragged Heldrick past her own cell, on to the cell she'd prepared, and threw him in. He landed with a thud. The cell door slammed, and the quistrils marched back along the corridor. The dungeon door closed.

Moments later Bess opened the door to Heldrick's cell.

Heldrick lay on his back, unconscious, his upper body on the straw. The flashlight showed circles under his eyes.

Bess had no time for finesse. She filled the ladle with water and threw the water in Heldrick's face.

His eyes snapped open, but he didn't move otherwise. Then he murmured something unintelligible.

"I'm sorry?" Bess said. "I didn't catch. . . ." Heldrick turned his eyes up and sighed. Bess came closer and put her ear near Heldrick's mouth.

Still, she could barely make out the slurred words. ". . . could have just . . . shaken . . . shoulder. Only asleep."

Bess hesitated. *She* hadn't been asleep when they'd brought her back. She'd been out cold.

"Why don't you get up then?"

"Nerves don't work . . . overloaded. Need a few minutes. Anyway, could at least have *tried* shaking shoulder."

"I'm sorry. I was in a hurry. I—"

"Can't hurry," Heldrick muttered. "Must wait." But Bess noticed the words getting clearer.

She turned the light off but couldn't sit still. She kept flicking the light on and off, moving from Heldrick to the grating, listening for sounds, then back to Heldrick. Finally Heldrick said, his enunciation barely impaired:

"All right. I give up. How did you get in here?"

"My key."

"Bah! Don't play games with me. How did you do it?"

Bess explained and told about the old quistril who'd seen her shoes. "He must be a simpleton, or senile—I'm pretty sure he's old, and I heard him mumble—but still. That's why I wanted to hurry. I'm afraid he'll report it to somebody."

Heldrick had already started trying to sit up. "You should have told me that right away. Here, help me."

Bess took the outstretched hand and pulled. With a small grunt, Heldrick managed to sit.

"Does it hurt much?" she asked.

"No. A mild case of pins and needles. Mostly I'm numb, anaesthetized. Let's see if I can stand." He managed it without Bess's help.

"All right, we have to find a way out of the Citadel as quickly as possible. But it's still daytime, late afternoon. In the middle of the night we would have had a good chance of walking through the corridors undetected, but now it's impossible. I might make it; you, never."

He paused in thought.

"Would you trust me with those keys of yours for a bit?"

"Of course, but—"

"I'll need the flashlight too. And you'd better get back in one of these cells. How do you unlock this?"

"Here." Bess took the key. Heldrick's arm was longer than hers, but thicker as well. He probably couldn't have gotten it through the grate far enough to reach the lock. In any case, she didn't want him trying, in his shaky condition, and dropping the key outside the door where they couldn't reach it.

She unlocked the door. They stepped out. Heldrick flashed the light along the cells on the opposite side.

"That one yours?"

"Yes. The other key is still there."

"All right. Get it."

She did, and handed it to him.

He took it. "Come on. We don't want to leave you in that cell." He closed her cell, led her up the corridor to the cell nearest the staircase, and unlocked its door. "Lie down here by the hole. If anyone comes before I return don't move. Open your mouth wide, cup your face, and breathe into the hole; they might not be able to hear you that way."

"They can hear me breathe?"

"It's possible, if they're listening. Especially if you breathe harder when they come in, which is likely."

As Bess stepped into the cell, she said, "But where—"

"No time. Must hurry." Heldrick closed the door and strode off to the steps.

Bess lay down immediately beside the hole, while no one but Heldrick could hear the sounds she made. Now all she had to do was roll onto her stomach with her hands by her face.

Not two minutes passed before the light went on. Heldrick already? He hadn't said where he planned to go, or for how long. She rolled over, hands cupping her nose and mouth, and opened her mouth wide, breathing as regularly as she could. The air, though dank, did not smell foul, and she gave thanks that prisoners rarely occupied the dungeon.

Voices. And several sets of feet descending the stairs. Her lungs abruptly cried for more air.

She didn't try to fight it; she'd wind up gasping. She breathed more deeply but kept it regular, kept her mouth wide, kept her hands cupped.

The footsteps passed by her cell, continued down the corridor, came to a stop. A cell door opened.

Now the voices again, sounding alarmed. Another cell opened.

The footsteps returned at a run, passed her cell, went up the stairs. She heard one voice call. The dungeon door closed; the light went out.

The voice continued calling, and now she heard the shuffling footsteps of the quistril who'd brought them their food.

He moved too slowly. The others hadn't waited for him. But his hearing might equal theirs; Bess couldn't rest now.

She kept her mouth to the hole.

Heldrick heard the banging on the door even before he turned into the corridor that held the dungeon. What in the world did Bess think she was doing? With his bundle under his cloak he hurried to the dungeon door, a rebuke on his lips that he bit off at the last instant.

He'd left Bess locked in a cell, without keys.

He opened the door, uncertain what to expect but completely unprepared for what he saw. A quistril stood before him, tears streaming down his face. Heldrick had never seen such a sight in his life. No wonder the man had been assigned this duty.

"They, they went off without me. I'm not so fast as I once was, but they took my key and left me no light, even!" The quistril sniffed and rubbed at his nose.

Heldrick found his voice. "All right, old man. Wipe your eyes. If you've a complaint to make, go to your supervisor."

The old quistril started off. Heldrick let the door close and waited until he could no longer hear the shuffle of footsteps before he opened it again. Then he slipped in and hurried down the steps.

"Here," he said, opening Bess's cell. "Put these on." He threw his bundle—a complete set of quistril outerwear—to the floor of the cell, handed her the flashlight and stepped several paces down the corridor. "When did they come?" he asked.

"Just a couple of minutes after you left."

"Damn. We've got no time to waste."

"I guess they'll be all over the Citadel looking for us."

Heldrick didn't contradict her. He wanted her to dress, not talk.

After a moment she stepped out wearing the quistril garb. "You have a good eye," she said. "It all fits. Even the boots are okay."

"Good. Put your old clothes down the hole; if they find them they'll know you've changed."

Bess stepped back into the cell.

"Where did you get the clothes?" she asked.

"A stressing session. I took these from the lad that looked closest to you in size. I kept his knife for myself, though the haft would probably fit your hand better."

"Of course." Bess stepped out of the cell again and closed the door. "How come my cloak has these two thin brown stripes along the edge of the hood?"

"Youngling's cloak." Heldrick glanced at her as they walked. "Stand straighter. Tenth form younglings are a pretty proud bunch."

She stood straight and looked ahead.

"Pull the hood forward and push the hair back." She raised her hands, but he could see what needed doing better. He reached over, tucked her hair behind her ears, and pulled the hood as far forward as it would go. "Like that. Let's go."

The moment Bess stepped out of the dungeon she must have lowered her head, because Heldrick reminded her, "Head up!" She really wanted to slink along the wall in hopes that they wouldn't meet anyone.

When they neared a curve in the tunnel-like corridor Heldrick started speaking in a berating tone, though at conversational volume. Bess stared at him in astonishment, for he spoke Vardic. At that moment another quistril came around the bend toward them.

Bess jerked, but thought, *Head up!* and kept walking. Heldrick continued his monologue. The other quistril passed without a glance, but Heldrick kept talking until some time after they had gone around the bend. Then he whispered:

"Good job. You had a properly chastened look."

" 'Terrified' might be more accurate. What were you saying?"

"Just a tongue lashing I once got for letting imperfectly cleaned silverware pass inspection when I served on kitchen duty."

Heldrick repeated the scolding several times before Bess recognized a three-corridor intersection that she'd noticed near the crypt. Yes—the double doors lay ahead.

They were just passing the doors when Heldrick stopped and tilted his head. He looked behind them. Then he grabbed Bess's arm and practically dragged her to the doors. In two seconds he had yanked one of the doors open and shoved Bess through ahead of him. He let go of Bess's arm as he pulled the door noiselessly shut, but then he grabbed her arm again and propelled her along the wall. The younglings they passed all had their eyes tightly shut. Some had clenched their jaws and others showed their teeth in a rictus. The sight repelled her but she couldn't look away. She would bet they didn't even know she and Heldrick were there.

Heldrick stopped at some empty caskets.

"Boots and cloak go under here," he hissed. "Quickly!"

Bess stared at the casket and remembered the needles, the snake.

"I can't—"

Heldrick pulled the cloak from her shoulders and lifted her to the platform, then yanked off her boots and covered her with the mesh. He stowed the clothes beneath. Then he strode off, heading toward the doors.

Don't leave me! She almost screamed it before she realized he was heading to the opposite side of the crypt, where the stressor occupants were more nearly his size.

Still, it took all her will to lie still. Heldrick hadn't merely thrown the mesh over top of her; he'd plugged in the jacks. What if the machinery went on accidentally? Or if a quistril discovered her and turned it on?

She could no longer see Heldrick, and his footsteps had stopped. How long would they have to lie here? What if the stress proctors returned to let the younglings out, and she and Heldrick were still here?

Through the mesh Bess saw the crypt door open, and a quistril entered. Three more followed him. The first walked along the center aisle out of her sight, but she heard him open the opposite doors and call. In a moment he and two other quistrils came back. The six held a brief discussion.

Four of the quistrils then walked slowly along the central aisle, out of her sight. The other two split up, one walking along the wall toward her, the other going in the opposite direction. The one approaching stopped as he passed each row and scrutinized the spaces between the rows. Bess bit her lip and hoped he was only looking around the stressors, not in them. She still wore most of her clothes. The mesh, though hard to see through from a distance, wouldn't hide her state of dress from more than a cursory glance up close. And then it wouldn't require an accident for the stressor to go on.

She didn't dare move her head, so she was only able to watch the quistril until a couple of rows before he reached her. The footsteps stopped, moved on. Stopped. Moved on.

Stopped.

She fought a desperate desire to tear back the mesh and run, and concentrated instead on keeping her breathing slow and even. After a moment the footsteps continued, then stopped again . . . the pattern continued until the quistril reached the back wall. Then he walked slowly back to the center aisle, not stopping along the way this time. At the doors he waited for his companion, then both headed along the central aisle. By the sound of the voices, the six quistrils were holding another impromptu conference. After a minute, the voices ceased, and three of the quistrils came back into her line of sight, heading for the door.

Bess closed her eyes in relief but snapped them open as she heard an exclamation of surprise. The three quistrils had stopped. One of them spoke, and another voice, a bit higher, replied. The other quistrils arrived. More conversation ensued. If only she understood the language! Had they been seen after all?

The quistrils divided again, three hurrying to the double doors and out. The others headed in the opposite direction, and she heard the doors on the that side open and close.

She couldn't stand it any longer. She pushed on the mesh, the jacks popped out, and she sat up and looked around. The quistrils were gone. She didn't see Heldrick. She hopped off the stressor, pulled on her cloak, and grabbed her boots but didn't put them on. She padded toward Heldrick's end.

She anticipated little trouble finding Heldrick, knowing that he'd be near the rear and probably mostly clothed, but the glittering mesh disguised him better than she'd expected. Before she found him, he raised his mesh on his own, sat up, and put his finger to his lips. He looked angry; and she knew why, but too bad. Sure, she should have waited for him to give the all clear, but she'd reached the point where it was either get out or scream.

Heldrick stepped down, picked up his boots and cloak and carried them to the nearer pair of doors. Bess followed. He put his ear to the crack between the doors.

She looked around. The empty stowage area beneath a nearby casket caught her eye. Heldrick must have taken her clothes from this youngling. Would the older quistrils punish him for it? She stepped closer to the stressor. The youngling looked twelve but was probably about eight. Still, five years and he'd be an adult. With a start she realized that, unlike all the others, this one had his eyes open.

He must be the one the adults had talked to. So they'd noticed the missing clothes, too. That's what the fuss had been about.

The youngling made a growling, threatening noise. At the sound several nearby younglings opened their eyes as well. Heldrick looked up and beckoned to her sharply. He began to pull his boots on.

She stepped back to him and did the same.

Heldrick fumed. What was wrong with the girl? Climbing out of the stressor on her own initiative, and disturbing one of the younglings, as if to ensure that he knew of her presence—perhaps her experience in the stressor had softened her mind, after all.

He waited for Bess to get her hood pulled well forward, then led her into the corridor, to a door which accessed a stairwell. He ushered Bess ahead of him.

Once in the stairwell, he whispered, "They're less likely to look for us one floor up, though it'll take us longer to reach the stables."

"How long till all the quistrils in the Citadel know we've escaped the dungeon?"

"It may not happen. Mistakes are poorly tolerated here. Even the graycloaks don't want to lose the confidence of the rank and file by revealing that we've escaped the dungeon while under their supervision. And they must have every expectation of capturing us simply because you're a girl, who ought never to be out of the women's quarters. Anyone seeing you would know to grab you."

He ran a hand over his face. "Except that, now, they know you've got a youngling's outfit. I'm not sure what they'll do."

He paused at the top of the stairs to put a finger to his lips—though any nincompoop ought to know enough to keep quiet—and opened the door.

He chose a roundabout path through the twisty corridors, sacrificing speed and directness to avoid the heavily trafficked corridors. After a bit he led Bess down another flight of steps, and a few more paces brought them to an outside access door. He opened it and waved Bess through. In the huge compound only a few quistrils went about their business.

"They don't look like they're searching for us," Bess whispered.

Heldrick shook his head. "They wouldn't alert anyone at this point, except perhaps the gatekeepers. And the gate is usually manned by elder younglings. I think I can bully our way through."

He led Bess across the expanse of scrub grass to the stables. "Wait here," he said, and pushed his own hood back.

He walked into the stables, picked out two horses, and asked the youngling stable hands to saddle them. When they'd finished, he led the horses out to the courtyard, handed one to Bess and mounted the other.

"Follow me." Heldrick pulled up his hood and headed toward the gate at an easy walk.

As they neared it he called out "Ho!"

A youngling appeared on the platform. Heldrick waved and the youngling saluted, then returned to the gatehouse. The huge gate began to swing outward.

—And stopped.

"Halt!"

Heldrick drew rein and looked up.

A quistril in the charcoal-gray cloak of a mastron stood on the platform. Heldrick cursed himself for a fool. Of course they wouldn't have depended on the younglings to handle this. The younglings probably hadn't even been told about it.

Heldrick saluted as Bess drew up beside him. The gate had only opened far enough for one of them to pass through at a time, and it would take but a moment for the younglings to close it again.

He edged his horse back two steps, leaving Bess in the lead.

"Hoods off," the mastron snapped, with a mastron's characteristic arrogance. Heldrick began raising his hand but then brought it sharply down on the rump of Bess's horse. "Go!"

Bess, unprepared, yanked on the reins. The horse reared.

"Close the gate!" the mastron called into the gatehouse. He turned back with a knife raised in his hand.

But Heldrick's knife was already cocked. He threw it as hard as he could, impaling the mastron's forearm and pinning it to the wood of the doorframe.

The gate began to close; Bess controlled her horse and raced out. Heldrick pulled his legs up and dashed after her. The closing gate scraped his horse's flanks as he went.

Behind him he heard the gatekeepers call the alarm.

CHAPTER 20

BESS GLANCED OVER her shoulder at the reopening gate.

"Two of them!" she shouted.

Heldrick didn't turn. "More will follow."

They rounded the bend and Heldrick directed his horse into the trees. The first place the quistrils will search, Bess thought; but before she could protest Heldrick said:

"Hurry! We've got to get through these woods."

The trees and undergrowth cut down on their speed. Soon Bess could hear their pursuers behind them. But at last they came to a second road. She followed Heldrick as he galloped to the right and then turned into the woods on their left, before their pursuers reached the road. She understood: his tactic forced the quistrils to follow a trail, rather than track them by line of sight.

A third road. After galloping a hundred yards Heldrick wheeled his horse about and headed back. Bess didn't hear or see anyone coming up the road, but she trusted Heldrick's senses. She followed without protest.

After a mile Heldrick eased the pace and turned again into the woods.

"That ought to slow them a bit," he said. "We can ride faster than they can track. And if we're lucky they may continue off in the wrong direction, searching only for the place where we left the road, rather than carefully following our trail on the road itself."

"How can they track us on the road at all?" It was a dirt road; but surely other quistrils rode their horses on the roads all the time, leaving their own tracks.

"Every horseshoe looks slightly different, Bess. And our prints will be the freshest, the clearest. Quistrils can tell, though not easily on a dry, dusty road. They won't track us to this point for at least ten minutes. We can travel with more care, now, and use more subtlety."

"Where are we, anyway? You've turned me all around. I have no idea how to reach the conjunction now."

"So? You never did. I never gave you those instructions."

"I noticed it after we'd been captured, when we passed it on the way to the Citadel."

Heldrick frowned. "You didn't say anything."

"I figured you wouldn't want to know I knew."

"That's . . ." Heldrick turned toward her, his expression wooden. "That's right." He faced ahead once more.

"Hey, what's wrong?"

"Nothing. You surprised me, that's all."

Kierkaven sat on his horse and stared at the patula tree. Cranst dismounted. All the others had gone to follow less promising trails earlier. This late in the day, they probably wouldn't catch up.

"It just ends here," Cranst complained, kneeling at the spot. "Like she fell out of the tree. Except there's no sign she ever climbed into it."

Kierkaven barely listened. He looked right, then left. His eyes fixed on a huge, nearby tree. "I know this place."

He rode to the base of the larger tree. "Yes. She climbed this one. See?"

Cranst walked over, nodded. "What made you think to look here?"

"I already followed this trail from the other direction. I thought it ended here. Let's go: I can save us some time."

Kierkaven rode up the slight rise, disdainful now of any track or trail. Cranst ran back to his horse and hurried to catch up.

Kierkaven stopped near the edge of the wood. "Recognize this spot?"

Cranst turned his horse in a circle. "A week ago. The archer."

"Right." Kierkaven dismounted. He could still see signs of the girl's trail as she left this spot; not how she'd arrived, though. Of course, the patrolling quistrils had come from the wood's edge. He couldn't imagine the girl running in any direction except away from them. Their horses had no doubt obliterated her trail.

He tied his horse and walked forward until he peered out from the last row of trees.

Straight ahead stood a farmhouse, perhaps a quarter mile distant. Downhill and to the right lay the fields. To the left the hill sloped up; near its top jutted a rocky outcropping.

She might have stopped at the farmhouse, but after this long he'd have a hard time proving it, even to his own satisfaction. He stepped from the wood and turned a slow circle, searching for something, anything. . . .

The murdered quistrils had entered the wood at this point, but the girl might not have. He moved along the wood's edge, searching.

Nothing.

He stood again and examined the surroundings. The fields. The farm. The outcropping.

The outcropping. A crevice split the front of it.

"Cranst—"

"I see it."

Kierkaven rubbed his chin.

"I guess we'd better check it out."

"Where are we now?" Bess asked. Heldrick had maintained a slow pace for the last hour to avoid attracting attention, but he'd never stopped obscuring their trail. Now they left the road and trotted across a meadow toward a creek. A ruddy glow filled the western sky. "Will we reach it tonight?"

Heldrick nodded. "Arrick's place is over that rise. Other side of the trees." He led them into the creek and headed upstream.

Bess gazed up the incline. "I wish we could stop and see them—tell them I'm all right."

Heldrick looked alarmed. "Stop! For a visit? You're mad. We can't do that."

"I know. I know. I just wish, that's all."

They abandoned the stream after several minutes for some open fields. About fifteen minutes after that, as they rounded an arm of the forest, the portal came into view. Bess gasped. So close to Arrick's! And she had wandered so long that first night, nearly a week ago.

Heldrick turned his horse sharply, away from the outcropping and toward the nearby farmhouse.

"Follow."

Puzzled, Bess did so, past the farmhouse, out the lane to the road.

Heldrick said, "Did you notice the two quistrils near the outcropping?"

"No!" Bess twisted around, but the farmhouse blocked her view.

"Stop that! Act calm." He frowned. "I fear they traced your trail to its source. But I erased the more obvious tracks; it can't have been easy." He shrugged. "Perhaps they're after something else altogether; at worst they can't be sure they've tracked you correctly. They may assume that the cleft leads nowhere, and—who knows?—the camouflage door may fool them. But we can't go through the conjunction while they're there."

"You only saw two of them?"

"Two is enough."

"There's two of us—"

"If you're thinking of a fight, you can't count yourself. And, if you'll recall, I left my knife back at the gate." He grimaced and shook his head.

"What?" She didn't get the impression that he'd want to fight two quistrils even if he did have his knife.

"Eh? Oh, we're taught not to throw knives except in a life-threatening emergency."

"Well, it seemed pretty life-threatening to me."

"It was, for us. But not for that mastron. If he hadn't been about to throw *his* knife—which he should *not* have done—I'd still have mine. Anyway, we'll check the cleft again in an hour or so. By that time those quistrils will have left, unless they find the conjunction."

"And if they do, won't they leave anyway, to report?"

"Not likely. They'll whistle for help."

Bess swallowed. She wouldn't give up now. She couldn't. Not this close. "Where should we watch from?"

"We shouldn't. They might see us and realize that something worth finding is nearby."

"Well, then, what do we do for the next hour?"

Heldrick considered. "You might as well get your wish. It shouldn't cause any harm."

They returned to Arrick's by way of the stream, so as to leave virtually no trail at all. As they left the stream to climb the rise that hid Arrick's land, Bess caught the scent of wood smoke and remembered the meals Needa had cooked.

But the wind shifted, and the smell was suddenly too strong. Could the barn have burned?

They saw when they emerged from the trees that it had. The house was burned, as well, and razed. Not a timber stood. Even the chimney was demolished. The rubble piles still smoked and smoldered.

The cow and the plow ox lay still, all covered with flies. Bess couldn't speak.

Heldrick said, "The quistrils must have worked in pairs, after all, but split up to check on Arrick's house and their neighbor." Heldrick pointed left, toward another farmhouse half a mile away. "When the one I killed failed to return, his companion came to this house and found the evidence, before Arrick's family could clean up the blood."

"They're all dead then?" Bess felt empty inside, hollowed out like a pumpkin, ready for carving. This would never have happened if she hadn't come here.

"No. A typical quistril would take into account the absence of the quistril and his horse, indicating the action of a party no longer present. He would whistle for a patrol, and . . ." He hesitated. "This explains the band of quistrils hunting for us that night. I'd wondered about that."

"But the one you killed said the death penalty—"

"For murder, yes, and he assumed that all of us together colluded in murdering a quistril. For lesser offenses, as in guilt by association, the quistrils find an advantage in keeping the guilty parties alive."

"You're sure?"

Heldrick waved his arm at the destroyed homestead. "This is a punishment for Arrick and his family, for when they come back. Why punish them if they're not coming?"

It made some sense. She *wanted* to believe it. But the quistrils might have intended the destruction as a warning to the neighbors. How could she know for sure?

All at once Heldrick reached out and slapped the back of her head, pushing her forward on the horse. A small, fast-moving object whistled past her ear.

She heard someone crash through the trees. With her head down she looked around. Heldrick's horse stood calmly beside her own, but Heldrick no longer sat on it. Her eyes searched and found him seconds before he disappeared into the trees, running in silence.

"Lemme go, lemme go!" The cries stopped as suddenly as they had started. Bess lifted her head higher, and Heldrick reappeared, with Kale struggling under one arm.

Bess dismounted and ran to them. Kale relaxed, once Bess pulled back her hood and showed her face. On questioning, he confirmed Heldrick's guesses. The quistrils had taken the rest of his family off to the Citadel. Kale himself had clambered through a window and run off.

"I don't believe they couldn't catch you," Bess said.

"I'm fast. I bet I can run faster'n you."

Heldrick said, "A child so small isn't worth chasing. He'd be useless on the work crews."

"I'm not useless!"

Bess said, "Work crews? You mean slave labor!"

"Don't make so much of it. A two-week field conscription catches every able-bodied man several times during his life. It's nothing new to these people."

"That doesn't make it right! Anyway—" she stopped and looked at Kale. "Kale, I need to talk to Heldrick in private for a minute, all right? Just stay right here."

"Aw—"

"A minute or two, that's all. Heldrick, over here." She stalked off, her insides in turmoil. If they'd reached the conjunction just a little earlier, before those quistrils, she'd be back in her own world by now, happy that everything had worked out so well. Except that it hadn't. She just wouldn't have *known*.

Ignorance was bliss, right? She really understood that expression now for the first time, but that didn't make her like it any better. Bliss like that she could do without.

She stopped and faced Heldrick. "This'll be a lot longer than two weeks. Won't it?"

"A few years, I suppose. Maybe two. Maybe ten."

"Ten years! And I bet they're not treated very well. I bet lots of people that are kept that long die before they get out. Don't they?"

Heldrick sighed. "It happens. We can't do anything about it."

"Of course we can!"

"Well, yes. We can at that. We can take the boy with us. Keep him safe."

"But what about his family? We can't take only Kale. What if the portal closes while he's on the other side?"

"I don't suggest we take him through the conjunction. I meant that we take him with us now and find a place for him; then, if we can, you and I go through the conjunction."

"No!" Bess hissed. Her heart sank, but she couldn't go back home. Not now. "This is my fault, Heldrick."

"Nonsense."

She stared at him, surprised.

"Don't confuse 'fault' with 'cause,' Bess. If you carelessly set a cup on the edge of a counter, and it falls and spills when you let go, is it gravity's fault? Of course not. Did you kill the livestock? Did you burn the house and barn? Did you haul Arrick's family off to the Citadel? No. Did you order or even ask for any of those things to be done? Absolutely not. The quistrils chose to do this, and then they did it. The fault is theirs and theirs alone."

"But if I hadn't come through the conjunction—"

Heldrick rolled his eyes. "If your family hadn't moved to Benton, you wouldn't have come through the conjunction. Are you going to blame your family?"

"No, but they only moved so I could go—"

He cut her off with a wave of his hand. "You're not getting it. If your grandparents hadn't decided to marry and have children, your parents wouldn't exist, nor would you. You never would have come through the conjunction. So it must be your grandparents' fault. Is that what you're saying?"

Oh. "I . . . I see your point."

"Good." He turned to go.

"But, Heldrick—"

He waited, his back toward her.

"That's not all there is."

He turned around slowly. "No? What else, then?"

"After I'd eaten the maracot, these people helped me. They probably saved my life."

He hesitated. "That's possible."

"I owe them. If I can do something now to help them, and I don't do it—then that *is* my fault."

Heldrick looked over his shoulder at Kale for a minute. She wondered what he was thinking. Finally he turned back. *"If.* The point is, you can't. There's nothing to be done."

"No? What about getting them out of the Citadel?"

"Hopeless, Bess. Nobody—"

"Nobody what? Nobody ever escapes from the Citadel?"

Heldrick scowled. "We barely made it, and next time they'll be on guard."

"But we can prepare too. We aren't captured prisoners anymore."

"And what do you plan to do if you free them? As it is they'll be free, anyway, in a few years—"

"If they live that long."

"—but if they escape, they'll be fugitives for life—or, if recaptured, prisoners for life."

"They can go with us through the conjunction."

"You don't even know if the conjunction is still open. Anyway, if they did that they'd be exiles for life. What makes you think that's what they want?"

"It probably wouldn't be for life. I bet if they spent a few hours over there they could come back and the quistrils wouldn't be looking for them anymore."

Heldrick threw his hands in the air, turned, and began walking back toward Kale and the horses.

"It's the best alternative!" She slapped her thigh in anger and started after him. "I can't just leave them there and you can't talk me out of trying to get them free. So don't try to stop me."

Heldrick climbed onto his horse. "I wouldn't dream of it. You're too stubborn for your own good. It's a flaw in your personality you'll have to come to terms with someday. But don't expect any help from me."

"That idea didn't even occur to me, Heldrick." Though of course it had. All at once her anger felt like mere bravado. In the Citadel, alone?

But she could do it. She had an outfit and a horse, and she could obtain more outfits from the crypt, as Heldrick had. The keys to the dungeon still clinked heavily in her pocket, and—most importantly—the quistrils would never in a million years expect her to come back.

She could do it.

Heldrick pulled Kale up to sit behind him. "Let's go," he told Bess. "No rush, now, in returning to the conjunction. We'll find you a place to spend the night. I'll stay with you until morning; we can check out the conjunction before you go on." He started off.

Bess scrambled onto her horse and followed Heldrick down the hill to the stream. They sloshed through the water for a mile and a half before Heldrick said, "Everybody off," and dismounted. The flowing water gurgled around his boots. He plucked Kale off the horse.

"Hey—"

"Quiet." He set the boy atop his shoulders.

Bess hesitated. "What are we doing?"

"Confusing the trail. Don't worry about the water, your boots will keep your feet dry."

"But—surely they couldn't track us even this far."

"Probably not. Remember, though, that horses leave identifiable tracks. With a bit of luck—theirs, not ours—the quistrils could identify the trail at any point and begin tracking again from there."

"So . . . when we went to Arrick's, they might have tracked us? We could have been endangering them?"

"The chances of anyone finding the tracks in that small stretch were trivial. Besides, I had no intention of riding to the house. I'd planned to leave the horses in the woods and walk the last bit. Now, off."

Bess dismounted. What did Heldrick plan to do, scratch new marks on the horseshoes with rocks? She watched. He led the horses to the side of the stream opposite Arrick's property, tied their reins loosely together and sent them off with a slap on their rumps.

"Heldrick!"

"Hush. They'll separate when that knot slips off. By the time either is found, we'll be well away. In any case, the quistrils won't know where we were when we turned them loose, especially if we move on a bit before leaving the stream." He began to walk downstream once again.

"But Heldrick, I need the horse!"

"You can reach the Citadel on foot. You can't do anything if you're captured. You must ensure, first of all, that the quistrils can't track you."

Bess followed, angry. Heldrick's explanation made sense, but she didn't buy it for a moment. "Heldrick," she said when she'd caught up with him. "Don't think you can make me give up by taking my horse."

Heldrick glanced at her. "I can't imagine what would cause me to entertain such a foolish notion."

From Heldrick's shoulders Kale said, "You gotta let me go with you, Bess."

Bess gawked at Kale in surprise and dismay. Having Kale along would be a worse setback—far worse—than not having a horse.

Heldrick shook his head in disbelief. "You two can discuss that in the morning. We'd best keep silent now until we find shelter. Patrols increase after curfew."

CHAPTER 21

KALE HAD ASSURED them that Glasshugh, the nearest neighbor, was a good neighbor and a decent man. "Fat, though," he'd added with a faint scowl, as if it were a moral failing.

Now they stood at his back door. Bess, her hands at her back, held Kale's hands to keep him securely hidden behind her.

Heldrick raised his fist and rapped. "Open at once!"

The sounds of conversation stopped, footsteps clumped across the kitchen floor, and the door cracked open. Heldrick pushed it wide and strode past the heavy man who stood gaping behind it. Bess followed, pulling Kale along, keeping him hidden. Heldrick reached past her and closed the door, which had slipped out of their host's nerveless fingers.

"Please, sirs—" Glasshugh began, glancing with obvious puzzlement at Bess, though her hood hid her features. She supposed that younglings were rarely seen outside the Citadel.

"Close those shutters," Heldrick directed. While the man obeyed, Heldrick closed the shutters on the other side of the kitchen. Bess kept Kale behind her and hoped he would stay quiet. On the short trip from the creek to this house he'd seemed unable to think without speaking, or to speak without shouting.

"Have you any guests?" Heldrick asked.

"No—"

"Good. You have now. Assemble your entire family here."

The fellow's face went ashen. He didn't move or respond.

"Right away," Heldrick prompted.

"Yes. Yes, sir." Their host turned. "Lenkas," he called. "Mariel, Vandelise, Robelle, Sarona. Come."

His wife, whose lankiness made up for her husband's bulk, entered the kitchen, followed by four daughters, from perhaps eight to seventeen years old: all lovely, all frightened. The older two shed silent tears. Bess knew in a moment that this family had never—yet—lost a daughter to the quistrils.

"All of you, sit down," Heldrick said. He reached behind Bess as they did so and drew Kale forth.

The youngest girl cried, "Kale!"

"Sarona! Mind!" Glasshugh said, though in fact everyone had betrayed recognition. Realizing this, Glasshugh said, "Our neighbor's boy, sir. We don't know what they done, nor was any of us involved."

"I'm aware of that. Kale ran from the quistrils, and they didn't find it worth their while to retrieve him. But he'll require a place to stay until his family returns . . . I should think in a couple of years, but perhaps five or even ten. He holds no interest for the other quistrils, and they will not care if you take him in."

Glasshugh glanced at Kale, then back at Heldrick in puzzlement.

Heldrick continued. "My friend and I will need lodging here for the evening." He waved at Bess. "Your hood."

She pushed it back. They all stared for a moment.

"You're no quistril," Glasshugh said, and stood. His face darkened. "I don't like tricks and I won't have no illegal costumes in my house. The boy can stay, but the two of you go."

"But," Heldrick said, "I *am* a quistril."

Glasshugh sat again with a thump.

"It's agreed then?" Heldrick asked.

"Yes, of course, of course. Pardon my presumption."

"Forget it. There is one thing more. Bess and I will leave in the morning. But I would advise you to tell no one of our visit—for your own good."

The words painted a horrible image in Bess's mind of arriving here with Arrick's family and finding this house burned to the ground as well.

"Uh, Heldrick, maybe we should go now."

"Don't be silly." He hesitated, and said to Glasshugh. "I don't believe anyone could track us to this house, but should they ever learn of this visit, it won't help for us to have left. I'm sorry if we've placed you in jeopardy, but if we leave now—quistrils with no horses—the odds of a patrol capturing us and tracing us back here will only increase. In the morning, however, if you'll provide us with clothes, we can leave safely as a farmer and his daughter."

Glasshugh's jowls hung in confusion. "But— who. . . ? I mean, why. . . ?"

"It doesn't matter. Come morning we'll be gone."

"Oh, Heldrick," Bess said. "Of course it matters." And to Glasshugh, "He's the Renegade, that's who he is."

No one believed her, of course; at least, not until Kale backed up Bess's claim and explained why his family had been taken. He talked until Lenkas brought him a plate of food, then fell asleep at the table before finishing it.

Heldrick obtained a backpack from Glasshugh and an old shirt, too tight for Glasshugh to wear now. The sleeves ended two inches short of Heldrick's wrists—but he simply rolled them to the elbows. He kept his own pants and boots, but the shirt and absence of cloak would obscure his quistrilian identity from anyone who didn't scrutinize him.

Bess accepted a shirt from Mariel, who was twelve, and pants from Robelle, the fourteen-year-old. The pants were roomy enough to hide the tops of her quistrilian boots, though nothing could hide their sharp toes. It might be a slight risk wearing them—especially with Heldrick shod similarly—but she would need them later, and they wouldn't fit in the backpack with the other garb.

Heldrick suggested that Bess write a note to her family informing them of her situation. He promised to deliver it after they separated.

"Make sure to explain that the conjunction may close before you return. Your parents are unlikely to believe me on that score if all I can show them is a door in my basement with a wall behind it. Now good night. I need my rest."

"You? I thought quistrils didn't sleep much."

"Under normal circumstances. But I never got my recovery sleep after this afternoon's stressing, and there's a cumulative effect, besides. I'll sleep till morning."

Grayvle lay wide awake in his bed. Giving the girl those keys was treason, and utter foolishness, besides. What if she tried to use them? Once out in the corridors she would be picked up in a minute, and then they'd find the keys and . . .

Well, he didn't know what they'd do. The girl would probably be in a worse situation than ever, and if they managed to figure out where she'd gotten the keys, he was done for. He hoped she'd have the sense not to use the keys during the daytime. Maybe in the middle of the night, in the empty corridors, she could make it outside. But then what? She couldn't get past the gate; escape was still hopeless. Yet giving her the keys had seemed so clearly the right thing to do. He couldn't help smiling when he remembered dropping them through her grate. That action had taken more courage than anything he had done in his life.

Of course, it would also require courage to jump off the roof of the Citadel. It just wouldn't require any brains. Why hadn't he planned better? Perhaps he should sneak to the dungeon now and retrieve the keys, before the girl got them both in trouble.

Perhaps? Of course he should! But he wouldn't; foolish and disloyal though it might be, he was committed. If he had it to do over, he would still choose the same path. But maybe he could take her a cloak. That way she might have a chance. It would be safer for both of them. More certain still, he could escort her out, but that act would also be more traceable back to him.

And it was treason. When they came for him, they would show no mercy.

A door creaked. Light flooded the dormitory room.
"Grayvle!"

Damn! He sat up and saw a figure silhouetted by the dorm room entrance. But only one figure. And the voice was familiar. "Enfarad?"

Enfarad let the door close and walked down the row of bunks to Grayvle's. "Get up. Get dressed."

"Why?"

"I don't know," Enfarad said, and Grayvle's heart chilled. "Corck wants to talk to both of us."

"Corck?" Grayvle breathed again.

"Hey," said a voice, "would you two shut up? I'm trying to sleep!"

Enfarad smiled. "Get dressed and let's go."

A few minutes later they arrived at the Archive. "He said to meet him over here." Enfarad led Grayvle to a study room. But when he opened the door, the room was empty. Grayvle pulled back.

"What's the problem?" Enfarad entered the room, and Grayvle followed. "You're a little jumpy tonight."

"I guess I'm not awake yet."

"Being tired makes you jumpier? I wish I had reactions like that."

The door opened a minute later and Corck slipped in. He put his finger to his lips until he'd closed the door behind him. Certainly he didn't act as though he'd been sent to seize Grayvle for treason.

Enfarad frowned. "Who are you hiding from?"

"Anyone who outranks me. Listen, I have some news you'll be interested in. Before morning, someone will have ordered me not to mention it. So I wanted to tell you tonight." He turned to Grayvle. "Remember how that key you found led to the capture of those marginals? Well, there's been an escape."

Gods! He was too late. The fool girl had left already and been caught. . . . Was Corck warning him, then? Out of friendship, perhaps? Unlikely; and why bring Enfarad into it, in that case? But . . . surely Corck didn't mean a *successful* escape?

"Impossible," he murmured.

"But it happened," Corck said. "The marginals escaped from the dungeon and have not been recaptured."

"They *both* escaped?" Grayvle bit his tongue but too late.

Corck nodded. "That seemed significant to me, also. I wouldn't have expected him to take the girl along."

"But . . ." Grayvle felt turned upside down. "The near-quistril was in one of the high security cells." He hadn't given the girl keys for that.

"Really?" Corck regarded him. "I hadn't heard that part myself, though it makes sense. How did you know?"

"I was on call this morning. I escorted him to an interrogation session. Do you know how they managed it?"

Corck shook his head. "No one knows how they left the dungeon. But they apparently rode out the gate, both in cloaks, not too long before dinnertime. There were a few witnesses to that. The younglings on gate duty have been sequestered, and all the known witnesses have been ordered to silence. But of course the story began to leak before those measures were taken. By the time you get up tomorrow, the rumors will be flying. I wanted you two to know the true story—what there is of it—before then."

"What makes you think," Enfarad asked, "that they'll be looking for you? They can't be going through the

Citadel telling everyone not to tell the story, not without giving away that there's a story to tell."

"Right. I talked to several people who'd talked to the original witnesses. The last one recently told me that, after I'd spoken with him, he was asked who else he'd told. He was also ordered not to tell anyone else, so I probably shouldn't, either. Of course, he couldn't order me not to. But the graycloaks are trying to track things down, and now they've got my name. They're probably already looking for me, to give me that very order. As soon as I realized that, I sent for the two of you, to tell you before they catch up with me. And if you'll each give me your word to tell no one else, I don't see a need to mention you to the graycloaks. I'm sure they're not happy with having to chase down more and more people."

Grayvle managed to say, "Of course," only a moment after Enfarad, but his mind was spinning. How had the near-quistril left his cell? And where did the girl get garb? Had someone else helped them, as well?

Difficult as it was to let go of such questions, Grayvle knew they didn't really matter. Corck had lifted a great weight from his shoulders. The girl was gone! Six hours and more had passed without recapture. They would have gone back through their conjunction by now. For the girl's sake, she would be safe; and for his own, she would no longer be available to point any fingers, willingly, unwillingly, or even unwittingly, at him.

For, whatever else the girl did, she would certainly never come back.

CHAPTER 22

Bess awakened to Heldrick shaking her shoulder. He tipped his head to indicate she should follow him. She grabbed her boots and tiptoed after him. He led her to the bathroom and whispered, "Meet me in the breakfast room after you've finished here."

When she arrived in the breakfast room, she wondered why they were being so quiet. Glasshugh's entire family had obviously been up for some time and were busy with chores.

Then she remembered Kale.

Heldrick pulled on the backpack. He looked odd in Glasshugh's flannel shirt, less forbidding. The blousiness of the shirt made him appear skinny and weak, instead of lean and hard. He opened the door and motioned Bess out of the house.

They'd gone less than fifty paces before a shout came from behind them. "Hey, you two! Wait!"

Bess turned. Kale raced toward them.

"Now what'll I do?" she muttered to Heldrick. "He'll start to shout whenever I have to hide."

Kale reached them, puffing. "I said I wanted to go with you, Bess. It's my family, you know."

Before Bess could protest, Heldrick said, "If you wish to help, you must learn to speak softly. Does anyone know you've gone?"

"Uh . . . well, yeah, Glasshugh saw me as I was leaving, and I said I was going with you. I lit out 'fore he could stop me."

"Good. So long as they know. No more talking."

Heldrick turned and went on. Bess fumed. Heldrick must have decided to use Kale's presence as an unspoken argument against her going to the Citadel—and it was a good one. What could she do? She wouldn't give up. How could she possibly convince Kale to stay behind? Because she sure couldn't allow him to come along.

She worried at the problem, uselessly, until they came out of the woods and saw the outcropping which hid the portal. No guards stood outside the fissure. Heldrick waited at the edge of the woods for several minutes, watching and listening.

"We may be in luck," he said at last. "Wait here."

He headed up the slope. When he reached the outcropping he paused, listened again, and at last peeked into the crevice. He nodded and waved them up.

"Great! Nobody's—" Kale cried before Bess slapped her hand over his mouth.

"Sorry," he said. "Forgot."

At the cleft Heldrick put out a hand. "Your letter."

Bess pulled it from her shirt pocket and handed it to him. "If I'm lucky," she said, "I'll be back here with Kale's family before you know it."

"And me, too!" said Kale.

"Kale," said Heldrick. "I need you for a moment." He turned and stalked into the cleft. "Come on, both of you."

Bess pushed Kale on ahead of her, and they followed Heldrick between the walls of rock, which came to a dead end. She would never have known, in the semidarkness, that nothing more than concrete and wood blocked the end of the passage.

Heldrick stopped and shook his head. Bess feared for a moment that the conjunction had already collapsed, that what they stood before was truly rock, until she remembered that the conjunction existed on the other side of the camouflage door. Its collapse would not affect the door at all.

"What's wrong?" she asked.

"Nothing; but I'm surprised this door fooled the quistrils. Whatever they searched for, a casual glance must have convinced them they wouldn't find it here."

Heldrick's hand slid through a crack and Bess heard the catch release. The door swung open, revealing the small cave, with the strange mirror opposite them. They filed in, Bess warily. Why hadn't Heldrick sent them off and come in alone?

"Kale," Heldrick said, "Bess wants her father to receive this letter. We need only put it in the basement of my house, through the mousehole. You're the smallest of us, and your passing through the conjunction will perturb its integrity the least. You can cross through, drop the letter, and come right back. It'll take you two seconds."

Kale's eyes widened. "Sure!" he blurted.

"Great." Heldrick didn't even remind him to lower his voice. He handed Kale the letter. "Now remember, no exploring or goofing around."

Kale nodded with impatience, barely listening. He touched the glistening interface.

"Push hard," Heldrick said.

Kale leaned forward against the pressure, and the mirror snapped over him, coating his backside liquidly. His left leg, buttocks, and lower back projected, scattering the dim light in all directions.

Heldrick's grim smile held a trace of smugness. "The time flow's got him," he said. "Now—this is the last chance you'll have to give up this mad scheme."

Bess could hardly believe that Heldrick had disposed of Kale so easily. She pulled her gaze from Kale's motionless, quicksilver backside. "No way, Heldrick. If I did I couldn't live with myself. Hand me the backpack."

"I ought to pick you up and carry you through the conjunction myself."

"No!" Bess bit her lip. "I doubt I could stop you, Heldrick. But I'd never forgive you if you do. Never. Not in my lifetime."

"Which is no doubt numbered in days. Besides, why should I care?" He grimaced. "All right. Let's go. By the time Kale drops the letter and turns around, we'll be long gone."

"But—" She raced to follow Heldrick as he strode across the cave.

"I suspect strongly that he will spend a minute or two looking around, which will translate to a day or two our time. If we ever manage to return, it should be before then." He closed the camouflage door. "I hope that if he does come out immediately, he has the sense to go back to Glasshugh's. And to shut this door when he leaves, too, though nobody's apt to happen on this place in a single day." He cocked an eyebrow. "Ready to go?"

Bess nodded. "But Heldrick, I don't understand why you changed your mind. I wasn't trying—"

"Great gods!" Heldrick said in disgust. "Why don't you just shut up?"

To Bess's surprise, Heldrick insisted on keeping to the roads.

"No one will expect us here. They'll search first where we turned the horses loose and then farther afield. The more closely we approach the Citadel the safer we'll be, so long as we don't attract attention by appearing furtive."

"But this is taking hours! We could have been there by now."

"I'll admit this is an indirect route. I'm looking for something."

Throughout the morning quistrils sometimes passed them on horseback. This caused Heldrick no concern, but he ushered Bess into the ditch each time.

"Required deference," he said. "And don't stare at them, even when they're far off."

The quistrils never glanced sideways. Bess thought it pretty foolish of them, but when she said so Heldrick shrugged.

"Most of the quistrils we've encountered wouldn't know of the escape even if the graycloaks publicized it. They haven't any radios, you know."

They walked and walked, Heldrick keeping silent. But at length he asked her, "What do we do when we arrive?"

"Um." Did he seriously want her opinion? "You know the Citadel better than I do. I thought you'd decide."

"You expected to do this by yourself. Surely you have ideas of your own. I'd like to hear them."

"Well, all right. But remember, I didn't originally plan on turning the horses loose. I thought I could put on my quistril clothes, ride in, and steal extra quistril cloaks like you did. I could use the dungeon key to let the others out after midnight. And we'd ride out together, all the way to the portal. It should be easier with you along, but if you can't find us horses before we reach the Citadel . . . would it look too suspicious if we walked through the gate on foot?"

"Yes." Heldrick frowned. "But I told you last night that they'd not be in the dungeon. The quistrils will put Arrick and Wellen to work as slaves, probably in the fields. Remember?"

"But don't they go to the dungeon at night?"

"Oh, no. The quistrils save the dungeon for short-term problems. Besides, it wouldn't hold all the men on crew. They have barracks for that purpose. And of course they'll put Needa in the Nest, with the women."

It took a moment for her to realize what that meant. "But she's too old!"

"Hmm. You think so, do you?"

"I mean, she has children, a family! A husband. How can they—?"

"It's punishment, Bess. And Needa's only in her late thirties. No reason she can't produce more children. While she's with the quistrils they'll use her the one way they know."

Bess walked in silence for a few moments, trying to get her thoughts in order. "If we free Needa first, the quistrils may discover her absence before we can find the men, and vice versa."

"Yes. Besides, you could do little to help me fetch the men from the fields, and I'd be more conspicuous in the Nest than you. So we should split up."

"But—"

"You expected this morning to do the job on your own."

"Yes—"

"And now you need bring out but a single person."

"Yeah, except instead of the dungeon, I've got to search the women's quarters, and how big is that?"

"Sizable."

"That helps a lot. Where is this Nest? Do they post guards? Do the women wear some kind of uniform, or can I keep these clothes?"

Heldrick shrugged. "I've never been inside the Nest, you know. Younglings aren't generally allowed. I suspect the women wear what they arrive in until the clothes fall apart, and then they're given something else. Or perhaps they make clothes themselves. The Nest comprises a good portion of the third floor. They may well have looms and spinning wheels and all whatnot in there. You'll find out."

He thought for a few seconds. "A single door accesses the Nest. As with the dungeon, you'll need a key to open the door from inside. Not the same key, I'm afraid."

"I can jam up the catch before I go in."

"And the next quistril to use the door will notice that it's jammed and fix it. If he can tell that the condition resulted from an intentional act he'll raise a hue and cry that you wouldn't believe."

"All right. I'll find some other way out."

"I admire your confidence."

Bess studied Heldrick's expression. Was he making a joke? She decided to ignore it.

"Once I'm inside, how do I find Needa?"

"I've no knowledge of the inside. But one thing I can tell you: since younglings may not enter the Nest, no one must see you enter; and as soon as you're in, you should divest yourself of the youngling garb. To keep from encountering a quistril inside, you should go in before the dinner hour. The first hour after dinner is the Nest's busiest; I would suggest you try to hide somewhere during that time. You don't want to risk some quistril selecting you."

"Yeah, that's for sure. —And once we're out, what? We steal horses from the stable? How do Needa and I find you and the other two?"

"You can't get horses out except through the gate, and that won't be as easy as last time. Following any breach of security, the graycloaks issue stringent procedures for gate passage. After a month or so everyone grows weary of the annoyance and starts to ignore the protocol. Do you want to wait a month before doing this?"

"No."

"All right, then, we'll put you over the wall. And at midnight I'll throw a rope over the wall at the point where you went in. Tug on it and I'll get you back out. If you're there, anyway."

Bess walked in silence. Her task had grown several magnitudes in difficulty. The Citadel was so huge that even a quarter of the third floor might contain miles of corridors and hundreds of thousands of square feet of room space.

Heldrick must have noted her unease. "Here," he said. "Have a sandwich."

CHAPTER 23

Two quistrils galloped past them, trailing clouds of dust. Bess moved to the side of the road almost as quickly as Heldrick.

The road here curved through the woods, and the quistrils disappeared around the bend, but moments later Bess heard the horses slow down and come to a halt. Heldrick stiffened.

"Not another word," he breathed. Then he started along the roadway with such long strides that Bess trotted to keep up; she nearly bumped into him when he stopped short. A hundred yards off she could now see the two quistrils conversing with a third.

The two made some sort of salute, turned their horses and came charging back. Bess skittered off the road to let them by but Heldrick lingered, almost enough to attract attention from the two.

The third quistril remained on his horse, watching them. Why had Heldrick moved so slowly? She glanced at him and saw in horror that he stared openly at the quistril.

"Eyes down!" she hissed.

Heldrick lowered his gaze. Maybe Heldrick was deliberately baiting the quistril? But why? Even though she could see the quistril approaching from the corner of her eye, she resisted the temptation to look up and kept her eyes on the sharp toes of her quistrilian boots. They seemed particularly obvious right next to Heldrick's.

The quistril stopped his mount a mere fifteen feet off. She risked a quick glance. His cloak was charcoal gray rather than black, and his hooded gaze radiated suspicion, not anger.

Her stomach twisted with sick fear and the certainty that this quistril knew of the escape and was neither careless nor a fool. If Heldrick was baiting the quistril, he'd picked the wrong one.

The quistril opened his mouth to speak, but Heldrick stepped up on the road.

"Please, sir, please." Heldrick drifted, cringing, toward the quistril. "Can you help us? It's about my daughter, sir, my oldest. She was took when I was away from home, and I've come to petition, and perhaps if you'd help us . . ."

The quistril's features relaxed. He allowed Heldrick to come within a yard before he lashed out with his boot and caught Heldrick full in the face. Heldrick's head snapped back; he fell and moaned. Bess gasped and took a step toward him but stopped under the quistril's gaze.

"Petition all you like." The quistril turned his horse and started off.

Before Bess could move, Heldrick rolled onto his feet and took two swift steps toward the horse, his hands rising.

But the quistril wheeled his horse around. Heldrick stumbled to a stop, off-balance, and the quistril's swinging foot connected just below Heldrick's ear. Heldrick went sprawling.

"You thought to fool me with a farmer's accent?" The quistril reared his horse over Heldrick's position.

"Heldrick! Roll right!" Bess shouted, in Homeworld.

Heldrick did, and the hooves crashed into the ground where he had just lain.

The quistril spared Bess a glance, while Heldrick pushed to his hands and knees, shaking his head. The quistril reared his horse again.

"Roll again, Heldrick! And get up!"

Heldrick rolled but not far enough. One hoof caught him in the stomach. He curled.

The quistril looked hard over his shoulder at Bess. "What language was that?"

"Wouldn't you like to know?"

But the quistril was rearing his horse once more. It looked to Bess as if Heldrick wasn't going to move. She ran forward and, at the moment the horse had reached its height, kicked it viciously in the back leg with the hard pointed toe of her boot, then danced out of the way.

The horse screamed and fell over backward, pinning the quistril. It thrashed, snorted and rolled over, then regained its feet and backed away from the scene, limping. Bess ran to the stunned quistril, pulled his knife, and held it to his throat.

"Hurry, Heldrick," she said. If the quistril recovered before Heldrick arrived, he could reach up and take the knife right back. No way she could kill him. She only hoped he wouldn't know that.

After a few seconds that dragged like ages, she heard rough breathing behind her. Heldrick's hand reached over her shoulder and took the knife. "Back off," he rasped.

She did.

He knelt beside the quistril, recovering his wind; then he stood and rolled the still form over with the toe of his boot.

"Broke his neck," he said.

"He's dead?"

"Yes. Lucky. And thank you. That was good work."

She swallowed once. "I didn't mean to kill him, I only—"

Heldrick turned to face her. "You only wanted to give me a chance to regain my feet so that *I* could kill him, eh? Well let me tell you something. You made the decision to go back to the Citadel, and the responsibility for anything that happens as a result falls at your door."

"I didn't ask *you* to come," she said, piqued. But she regretted her words instantly. Maybe she hadn't asked, but Heldrick had come for her sake. And he was right. The freedom of Arrick's family—the possibility of freedom even—meant more to her than the life of this quistril, or of any others who might block her. That wasn't a judgment; it was a fact, a priority. Maybe it exposed a moral flaw in her character; she didn't know. Her conscience could wrestle with that later. For now, the fact stood. She felt worse about injuring the horse than killing the quistril.

She'd changed. She didn't know if she liked the change; but, again, that was something to deal with later. "I'm sorry. You're right. I shouldn't have said that."

Heldrick shrugged. "We mustn't waste more time. Try to pull him out of sight while I check the horse. I'll come help in a minute."

Bess hadn't crippled the horse, but she'd bruised the leg. Heldrick ordered the first quistril who passed by to give them his horse and to take theirs back to the Citadel, or a post house, as he preferred.

The quistril obeyed without argument because Heldrick now wore the charcoal-gray cloak of the dead quistril, a mastron. Bess sat on the new horse behind Heldrick, her arms around his waist, a rope wound around her wrists for appearance's sake lest they meet any other quistrils. The contents of Heldrick's backpack had been moved to the horse's saddlebags.

Bess leaned sideways to better see Heldrick's face. Even though he didn't want to be here—even though he would *not* have been here, would not have been attacked by the mastron, but for her—his thanks for helping him in that attack had been genuine. Not until she'd tried to decline responsibility did he flare up about the circumstances.

"What's the matter?" he asked.

"Nothing." She straightened up. "I'm just trying to figure out when I started to like you."

"Hmmph."

They rode for a minute.

"Heldrick? Why do you use a knife?"

"Pardon?"

"Why didn't you ever bring a machine gun, or something, through the conjunction?"

"Oh, I thought about it once, after Mildred died. But you can't use a weapon like that without revealing your position; they'd have swarmed me. And even if I'd escaped, they'd have known a conjunction had opened, and would have concentrated all their efforts on finding and closing it. They might even have pulled out their own guns."

"The quistrils? I've never seen any guns here."

"Well, they're primitive, unreliable, and inclined to blow up. Since any quistril could take on half a dozen or so unarmed cadrils, they find knives more than sufficient. But they do keep some firearms handy in the event of any serious uprising. Also some explosives, although these days those are pretty much used for mining operations."

They rode for another minute.

"Heldrick?"

"Yes, what now?"

"What made you decide to come with me? I thought at first I'd said or done something when we dropped off Kale, I couldn't imagine what. But you packed food for both of us. You planned to come all the time."

"Ah." He said nothing for a few seconds. "Observant."

"But why?"

Heldrick shifted. "You may be willful and pigheaded, but you're trying to do a good thing—the kind of thing I might have attempted myself, when younger, if I'd known then that quistrils aren't as invincible as everyone thinks, themselves included. But I still don't see any happy ending if you try this all by yourself."

"That's your answer? You're hoping for a happy ending?"

"No, I'm not that optimistic." For a time he remained silent. At last he said:

"All the time in the dungeon, especially after you'd acquired the key and could have left at any time, I believed that you considered escape without me impossible. I knew the Citadel, I was the expert on all things quistrilian, and I alone knew the location of the conjunction. But when you told me you'd known the way to the conjunction all along you exploded that theory. The other factors didn't weigh that heavily. I'd already told you how to reach the stables and that the corridors would be vacant late at night. You could have waited until midnight, taken my cloak and gone."

"Oh, come on. Do you think I'd have felt confident running around the Citadel by myself?"

"Not the point. I don't believe you risked your freedom in order to bolster your confidence. If the quistrils had brought me back much earlier you'd have lost your keys, lost your one chance of ever escaping them, and you knew it."

He hesitated again, and when he continued his voice had grown soft. "You did, for me, what I failed to do for my own brother."

Then, in a more cheerful tone, he said, "Besides, I— well, I guess I like you too. Flaws and all."

From a distance, the Citadel had dwarfed the stockade around it. But now that they were closer, the wall loomed. And it had watchtowers, which Bess found worrisome.

"Surely the watch sees us coming," Bess said.

"What's to see? A quistril bringing in a girl. They won't think twice."

"Until we turn off."

"We won't turn off until we reach the wall, and they don't watch that. They're charged with monitoring the open expanse that takes time to cross."

"But if we're recognized out here . . ."

"Not a chance." Heldrick sighed. "Listen—you're used to a world with television and newspapers, instant access to pictures of celebrities from every corner of the planet.

There's none of that here. They could say, 'Watch for a girl that meets this description,' but any verbal description of you would match thousands of girls."

She supposed that made sense. "What about you, though? Are there enough mastrons that you can blend in anonymously?"

"Well . . . the mastrons' names are far more widely known than their appearance. So if I stay away from other high-ranking quistrils, who might know all the mastrons by sight, I can use the power of this one's name with a fairly small risk."

"You know his name? How?"

Heldrick reached into his cloak and extracted a small wooden implement. "His chop. It's a stamp of his name used in place of a signature. All quistrils carry one."

"And if you escorted me all the way into the Citadel, they'd require that name at the gate?"

"Yes, which they'd record. Then, should other quistrils find the mastron's body before I return, they'd know what we've done. Far better if we leave no record."

"But if they see me going over the wall—"

"Make sure no one's looking. Believe me, no one will be assigned to the task; watching for insane cadrils trying to break *into* the Citadel is not a priority on anyone's list. All right, it's a risk, but less so than sending you through the gate. Now, quiet."

Heldrick returned the chop to his cloak and edged the horse off the hard dirt road into the grass, to muffle the already quiet hoofbeats. Bess understood that Heldrick didn't want the gatekeepers to hear them and uncover the spyhole, or he'd be committed to taking her in after all. They continued straight ahead until the wall rose up before them. Then Heldrick reined left, hugging the wall, and continued on till they'd gone around the corner, to hide them from the road and any gate traffic. It also put them almost directly under a watchtower and therefore effectively out of view of its windows.

It was time. You can do it, Bess told herself again. She pulled her hands from the loose rope and dismounted. Heldrick handed her the youngling outfit from the saddlebag. She pulled it over her other clothes and tucked the pants inside her boots.

Heldrick passed her the dungeon keys and the flashlight. She slipped them into the pockets of her garb. Then he pulled her up, put his hands under her boots, and lifted her high against the sloping stone wall of the stockade. He pushed her higher until her eyes reached the top of the wall. Bess studied the scene between the pointed stones that crowned the wall.

No quistrils stood nearby. She peered over the edge to the ground.

Good God.

She remembered her terror the first time she jumped off the high dive at her pool. This looked about the same distance but without water at the bottom. She glanced over her shoulder. It didn't seem so frightening on this side; the slope of the wall softened the height. On the Citadel side, the wall leaned in, supported only by occasional buttresses.

But she didn't plan to jump off. She'd dangle from her fingertips and drop. That'd put her maybe six feet closer to the ground than jumping. She could do it.

Still no quistrils in view. She signaled Heldrick to raise her higher. He stood in the stirrups. She pulled herself up the rest of the way and clambered over the sharp rocks; then, holding onto the inside ledge by her fingertips, she lowered herself to arms' length. For a second she dangled, then took a deep breath and opened her hands.

Almost instantly she jerked to a halt. Something ripped and she fell again, spinning out of control. The ground rushed up at her.

CHAPTER 24

BY SHEER GOOD FORTUNE, Bess struck the ground feet-first, though she pitched forward and hit as hard with her hands, and with her face, as with her feet. That's what it felt like, anyway. She understood well enough that if she'd landed on her back, or her head, she'd be dead or at least incapacitated. Even a slight change in angle might have meant a broken leg. She'd been lucky.

But, somehow, she didn't feel lucky. She felt sick to her stomach.

She lifted her face from the dirt. No one was running toward her; she hadn't been seen. But that would change soon if she didn't get up. She started to push herself up but stopped as pains pierced her left wrist, and a wave of nausea flowed through her. Using her right hand only, she got to her knees, then stood. She brushed the dust and dirt from her outfit and face as well as she could and then noticed blood on her fingertips. She touched her stinging cheek and her hand came away with more. She'd probably smeared it all over her face.

Also, a strip had torn loose from the hem of her cloak, undoubtedly the cause of her wild fall. She raised her gaze to the top of the wall and saw the piece of black cloth, snagged on one of the sharp crest rocks, waving in the breeze like a flag for all to see.

But no one had noticed. Not yet. She began to walk across the expanse of dirt and scrub grass, aching and wretched. She must look a mess. She didn't dare let anyone see her close up. Getting into the stockade should have been the easiest part of this business, and already she'd blown it. But she couldn't go back and start over.

Heldrick had described a number of buildings located within the stockade: she recognized the smithy, the armory, and the stables. She couldn't identify a dozen smaller buildings, but she used them to give her walk a semblance of purpose, always walking toward one or another of them, never reaching any before changing direction. As she neared the back side of the Citadel the labor force barracks came into view. She turned toward it.

The barracks sat hundreds of yards from the Citadel but gave a clear line of sight to the door she meant to enter. And Heldrick had told her that dinner for the quistrils would begin at six, well before sunset. She couldn't imagine the quistrils bringing their cadril workers back to the barracks while the sun shone.

Maybe she could do this after all. The barracks might have a place where she could wash her face, and if she avoided the Citadel corridors except at dinnertime and late at night, she would encounter few quistrils that might notice her torn cloak.

The barracks door opened and four or five young-lings came out with mops and buckets in their hands. Bess spun on her heel toward the nearest projection of the Citadel. She couldn't let any other quistrils see her close up. She couldn't.

She heard a splash as the younglings emptied their pails, followed by the clanking and knocking of the supplies being put up. She glanced over her shoulder. The younglings now followed in her footsteps. She angled her course to take her farther along the side of the immense building. She could hide around a projection of the Citadel till the younglings went inside, and then return to the barracks.

A door opened on that side of the Citadel and two quistrils came out, deep in discussion. Not younglings, either. They started to walk toward her.

She changed direction again, this time toward the nearest doorway. She had no choice. So long as she didn't encounter another quistril on the other side of the door, she could still pull this off.

In moments, she reached the door and turned the handle. Her heart thumped in her chest like a child falling down an endless flight of steps. She took a breath and pulled the door open; the corridor, at least the few feet of it that she could see before it turned left, was vacant. As she stepped in, she glanced back and saw two of the younglings split from the group and head toward her.

Oops.

Bess closed the door. Bad luck? Or had they seen her torn cloak, noticed her zigzagging path? She started along the corridor, hoping to find an empty room, and soon.

Instead, she found, twenty feet past the turn, another corridor, busier than any she had seen in the Citadel while with Heldrick. For a moment she stood paralyzed. But the younglings coming behind her had most likely noticed *something* odd about her, either her changes in direction or her torn cloak. If she turned and went back, when she passed them again they'd scrutinize her. The quistrils in the hall might not pay her any attention.

She took a breath, tugged her hood around her face, and strode toward the busy corridor. She heard the younglings open the Citadel door behind her as she turned right.

Head up, she remembered; but she didn't dare, not with her filthy face.

A quistril approached from the opposite direction. If she'd understood Heldrick properly, the single brown stripe on the hood of the cloak identified this one as a novice. She touched her right thumb to her left shoulder with the fingers extended, as Heldrick had shown her. The novice didn't bother to return the salute.

A youngling went by next, whom she ignored. Then a menodral, with one gray stripe down the front edges of the cloak and along its base, and a vasik.

Salute. Salute.

No one glanced at her, but she knew that the real danger came from whomever walked behind, staring at her back. How long before they noticed the torn cloak? They might reprimand her, or they might inform her out of courtesy.

It didn't matter. If they tried to talk to her, they'd expect her to answer in Vardic, and she'd never see home again. She had to find a place to turn off.

The corridor forked and she took the emptier branch. The footsteps sounding closest to her continued on the other path. But she glanced back to see the two younglings from the barracks turn into the corridor behind her.

She saluted another vasik, who squinted at her a moment before passing on; then she turned right.

The younglings followed.

She turned again, and they followed still.

She began to sweat. But if they wanted to catch her, wouldn't they shout for her to stop? Wouldn't they run her down?

Another right, into a long empty corridor. The footsteps grew louder behind her and then softened again, as the younglings reached the intersection and passed by.

Her footsteps faltered and she leaned against the side of the corridor. Sweaty, almost feverish, she pushed her hood back and wiped her brow with her arm. She'd really thought, for a moment—

But what now? Her left wrist still ached abominably, and she didn't know how to reach the Nest from here. She did remember the turns that had brought her here. Should she retrace her steps through the busy corridors, or try to find a less traveled way out of the maze-like tunnels of this place?

An almost subliminal tapping sound reached her awareness. She turned. Another quistril had turned into the corridor, far down its length. She pulled her hood forward and started walking again, but certainly he'd seen her lounging and, probably, with his quistril eyes, the blood on her face. And the length of her hair! Why hadn't she just cut it?

He called out behind her.

Perspiration slicked her palms, but she kept walking.

"Wait! You! Stop!"

English. He'd recognized her as a cadril, then. Behind her she heard the quistril's footsteps increase their tempo. She glanced behind and saw that he had already cut a substantial portion off the distance separating them.

She ran. She could run pretty well for a girl; maybe even for a boy. But for a quistril? No way.

She cut left at the first corridor, also empty. If she could reach another corridor while out of her pursuer's sight . . . but before she found one she heard him round the corner after her. She turned again and again, fortunately into empty corridors; but she could hear his footsteps grow closer each second and imagined his hands already raised to grab her by the neck, and shake her. . . . She managed not to scream.

Instead she ran faster.

A modest fence enclosed the field acreage. At the gate station, an aging vasik saluted Heldrick.

"Where's the overseer?" Heldrick asked.

"One moment, Mastron." The vasik disappeared into the station for a few seconds. When he returned he said:

"You can find Senoral Durnstaff at the spring apple orchard. Follow the fence to the corn fields, then turn left and keep going."

Heldrick nodded; the fellow opened the gate for him. Heldrick rode through, disturbed.

Senoral Durnstaff. A single rank below Heldrick's feigned mastron. Heldrick had thought the overseer would be a menodral. Browbeating a senoral could present difficulties. And a senoral was more likely to have known the mastron Bess had killed. Heldrick should withhold the name, if possible.

Only two guards rode around the spring apple orchard to keep the workers from loafing. That meant that these were conscripts, not criminals. Wellen and Arrick would be elsewhere. Heldrick rode up to Durnstaff and returned the offered salute.

"I'll require two of your workers as soon as you can give them to me," he said.

Durnstaff stared. "That would be next week. Why don't you order a quick conscription?"

"I've no time. I didn't mean when you can spare them, I meant the moment you show me an appropriate group to select from."

"What's this for? What do you mean, 'appropriate group'?"

"Can't say." If he admitted that he wanted to select from the criminals, Durnstaff would balk. The Overseer of the Fields regularly contended with the Overseer of the Mines for criminals, as they were used for the nastiest jobs and were often in short supply. Best to get Durnstaff's agreement first.

But Durnstaff continued to stare, and Heldrick shifted uncomfortably in his saddle. This man did not respond well to unexplained orders.

Heldrick remembered another Citadel, which in his time owned a reputation for strange projects, and said, "It's to do with Norvenmot Citadel. Other than that I cannot say."

"Those bastards," Durnstaff muttered. "Always up to something." He chewed on his lip, glanced at the Kallikot emblem on Heldrick's clasp.

"Well, all right. How long will you need them?"

"Perhaps a day or two. Perhaps forever."

"You mean they might die. You want to select from the criminals then."

Heldrick shrugged.

"Damn! Why didn't you say so in the first place?"

Heldrick turned his head and gazed into the distance.

"All right, be that way. But you'll wait until I'm through here."

He's trying to make me angry, Heldrick thought. "How long will you take?"

"An hour and a half."

Absurdly long. "I'll wait."

Durnstaff nodded and rode around the field, checking the work. Within ten minutes he returned.

"Let's go. The criminals are at the slog paddy today."

Heldrick let Durnstaff lead. The man didn't seem in the mood for conversation.

A half dozen alert guards, mounted, surrounded the paddy and the thirty or so workers within. Heldrick couldn't see the faces of the hunched-over workers. Durnstaff said, "Wait here," and rode his horse to one of the guards, to explain what Heldrick wanted. He plans to leave then, Heldrick thought. Ideal.

Heldrick tried to see which of the workers had the leg ulcers that came from working in the alkaline mud of the paddy. Arrick and Wellen wouldn't have had time, yet, to develop them. But even though the men wore only shorts, mud covered everything. The men were anonymous.

Durnstaff returned and gestured toward the criminals.

"Take your pick, but only two; no more. And sign them out with the stationmaster when you go." He turned his horse and rode off.

Heldrick rode into the mire, peering closely at each worker. Covered with muck as they were, he could not make a positive identification any other way. He found Wellen almost at once but completed the circuit without having found Arrick.

He sat on his horse wondering what could have happened. It didn't make sense that one, and not the other, would be here.

The nearest man squinted up at him.

"Back to work, you!" Heldrick turned his horse and headed back in the direction of the guard captain.

CHAPTER 25

BESS NEARLY PASSED the solitary doorway before recognizing it as the dungeon entrance.

She snapped her hand out and grabbed the handle, yanking her to a stop. She barged through and slammed the door behind her, but it never closed, bouncing instead off the hands of her pursuer.

She half ran, half fell down the spiral staircase, holding tight to the handrail with her good hand to keep from going head over heels.

At the bottom she moved away from the stairs and looked up. The light from the hall silhouetted the quistril. The framing doorway gave her a perspective on his size: about as tall as Wellen: somewhat short for a quistril. He was still a youngling, then; no wonder she'd managed to elude him as long as she had. Bess went to a cell door and shook it. Anything to make herself look clueless. She shook another door and glanced again at the open doorway.

The youngling stepped out of the dungeon and pulled the door shut, plunging the dungeon into the deepest black.

Bess kept still until her breathing returned to normal. She'd feared the youngling would have a key or, forgetting that the dungeon door closed and locked itself, would come after her anyway.

She flicked the tiny flashlight on and off to fix her position, then felt her way to the steps and up them. In the dark, and with her quistril boots, silence would have been impossible. But she didn't want to be silent; she wanted him to hear her, if he was there. She halted on the top step, separated from the door by the landing. She dared approach no closer. She scuffed one foot across the landing. Nothing happened so she grabbed the handrail and raised her foot to jiggle the handle once.

Nothing. She had to hope he'd left to fetch help.

She stepped onto the landing, unlocked the door with her key, pulled it open a crack and peered out. No one. But that youngling would return soon. She couldn't hide here. Her best bet was to leave the Citadel and find the outside door by which Heldrick had told her to enter. Then she could follow his instructions to the Nest. That would put her back on track.

Except that, now, they knew she was here. Trying to hide out in the Nest with Needa until midnight seemed foolish—surely that would be one of the first places they would search. And the only earlier time to get Needa out with relatively empty halls would be during dinner. That meant she had maybe two and a half hours to find Needa and get them both out of the Nest, as well as finding another place to hide until midnight.

Two and a half hours. It seemed both too short a time to accomplish her task, and too long a time to hope that the quistrils wouldn't begin the search. In any case, though, the first thing was to find Needa.

She followed Heldrick's earlier instructions for traveling from the dungeon to the Citadel exit nearest the stables. The route took ten minutes but avoided all the busiest corridors. Outside again, she glanced at the stockade. The strip of black cloth looked tiny from this distance, and she might have missed it but for the breeze shifting it back and forth. But the quistrils had better eyes than she.

She spent another ten minutes walking around to the barracks side of the Citadel. This time, she managed to make it inside. It was apparent that the quistrils provided no luxuries for their cadril workers. Row upon row of thin sleeping mats covered the floor. Dozens of exposed latrine seats lined one wall. From the relative lack of odor, she supposed they were constructed like the toilet at Arrick's house.

She took off her cloak and gave it a good shake, and washed her face and hands with water from a wooden barrel. Then, for two minutes, she plunged her swollen left wrist into the water. The water wasn't particularly cold and didn't help much, but her wrist had been feeling slowly better anyway. As long as she didn't try to use it, anyway.

At last she left the barracks and walked to the entrance Heldrick had instructed her to use. She reached it and entered, this time without incident, and followed the empty passage until it joined another passage, equally empty. Heldrick had chosen her path well.

Up a flight of stairs and along another corridor—one quistril, going away from her, no problem—turn right . . . another quistril approaching. Salute! Up another flight of stairs . . . another corridor.

At a place where the passageway turned sharply right, she came to the door Heldrick had described. She turned the handle, pushed and . . .

Of all the strange things Bess had seen since going through the Portal, this was the strangest.

An electric clock hummed on the wall. Bess hadn't seen one of those since she'd left home. Several sofas lined the walls and a couple of tables had games set up on them, though no one sat, no one played. This room was some kind of lounge, for goodness' sake.

But why would the quistrils give the women a lounge? She must have reached the wrong place.

Still, the door's inner handle resembled that in the dungeon: a mere attachment to pull the door open after the key had been turned. Perhaps she'd found the right place after all.

No one approached along either branch of the corridor, so Bess tested her dungeon keys on the inside of the door, but neither fit. No surprise, but it left her with a difficult decision. If this was the Nest, fine, she'd risk being locked in. But she couldn't afford to be locked into the wrong area of the Citadel. Think!

Every second counted. She glanced again at the clock. It read 4:09. Without her watch, a clock would come in handy—

Wait. Quistrils didn't need clocks; they had their time-sense. The clock had to be for cadrils. And the only cadrils she would expect to find inside the Citadel were the women.

She couldn't call it proof, but with this room being at the end of the path Heldrick had given her to reach the Nest, it was enough.

Bess barely considered trying to jimmy the lock. Heldrick had reasoned correctly there. Tampering would attract the very attention that she wanted to avoid. She closed the door until it was nearly flush with the wall, then let go of the handle, hoping that the door might stay in that position. It didn't; it moved the last hair's width and she heard the lock click.

Okay then. First task was to stop being a youngling. She removed her youngling garments, except for the boots—which she mostly hid again by pulling Robelle's pants over their tops—and pushed the clothes behind a sofa before starting down the left-hand passage. The first door she tried opened upon a small room with a bed—a far cry from the Spartan barracks accommodations. But the bed wouldn't be for the convenience of the women, exactly, would it? And the room was equipped with neither closet nor dresser. The quistrils had designed it for breeding, not inhabiting.

She followed the passage to the first intersection, turned right and then right again. She opened several doors along the way, and all the rooms looked the same. Fine, but it didn't help her locate Needa. And she hadn't even considered yet how to escape. Maybe they could tie sheets together and go out a window. Or climb through the ventilation shafts.

Unlikely. All such obvious exits would have been blocked by now, if they'd ever existed. Anyway, thinking of a way out took second priority to finding Needa. The vacancy of the place indicated that the women had other jobs, in a different part of the Nest, during the daytime. That's where she would find Needa. This route had simply brought her back into the lounge by way of the middle passage.

She heard a sound from the entrance door and jumped, crouching, behind a chair. The door opened and footsteps hurried past her. She lifted her head.

Casternack, the doctor, rushed down the middle passage.

He had a key?

Of course. He probably discharged the bulk of his duties in the Nest. He could let her out—

She stopped herself from running after him. He did report to the quistrils, whatever the reason.

Instead, she turned and watched the door as it finished closing. If she'd already found Needa, if they were ready to leave, if she'd been prepared, she could have caught it.

Which meant she'd discovered one way out of the Nest—at least, if she could learn how to initiate an emergency call to the doctor.

For some reason, Heldrick decided, the quistrils must have sent Arrick to the mines. How in blazes could he abduct him from there?

And he'd asked for two prisoners. He couldn't leave with just one.

He pulled his hood far forward and rode to Wellen.

"You! Go over to that guard and wait for me."

Then he returned to the last man, the one he had ordered back to work.

"Come with me," he said, and rode off without seeing if the man followed.

Wellen reached the guard before Heldrick. Heldrick glanced over his shoulder and saw the other man approaching.

"I'll take these two."

The guard nodded. "Durnstaff asks that you sign them out with the station master when you leave."

The same instruction Durnstaff had given to Heldrick earlier. Heldrick smiled to himself. By giving him the same message twice, Durnstaff insulted him. Now, if he were really a mastron, then he might really be insulted.

"I will need two horses also," he said.

The guard's eyes widened.

"I require more speed than these men can provide by walking. I'll return the extra horses to the stationmaster by the end of the day. Two of you can manage to walk from here to there. Tell Durnstaff I appreciate his compliance in the matter."

The guard bit his lip, but Heldrick knew that, without grounds, the guard would not dare defy a mastron. "Yes," he said at last. "Of course."

Heldrick ordered two of the guards off their horses, took the reins in his hand, and told Wellen and the other man to mount.

"Try to flee," he said, "and you are dead men. Understood?" He started back toward the entrance station without waiting for an answer.

What to do with the second man? He could let him go, but the quistrils might catch him before Heldrick and Bess finished their work and interrogate him. He knew nothing, but his story would be strange enough to heighten alertness. Or Heldrick could kill him; Bess would complain about that, no doubt, if she found out.

He could take the man into his confidence and try to use him to help find and rescue Arrick, if Arrick still lived. But could he trust the man? Or he could put him out of action some way . . . knock him out, tie him up.

That course carried the same risks as letting him go, though to a lesser extent.

They reached the station and the stationmaster opened the gate.

"Durnstaff stopped by and said you'd take two of the criminals with you. He'd like you to sign for them."

Heldrick frowned. This senoral began to annoy him. He recognized Durnstaff's insistence as a ploy to obtain his name, without breaking protocol by asking directly.

It couldn't be helped. "I presume you know all the criminals? You write the names of these two. I'll sign." If the stationmaster recognized that Heldrick's face didn't match his assumed name, Heldrick would need to dispose of him. And if Durnstaff did . . . well, that wouldn't happen for hours.

The stationmaster wrote. Heldrick read the paper— Kinsett Wonfall was the other man's name—and stamped his chop. The stationmaster folded the paper without looking at it. Heldrick rode off with the two men in tow.

After a bit he asked them what each had done to incur a stint on the long term labor force.

Kinsett answered first. "Wouldn't get out of the road for the ornery devil."

"Ornery devil? You have a free tongue."

"You asked."

"And that's all? This ornery devil rode by, you failed to hop into the ditch, and so he came back and hauled you in? I expect you received a short sentence, then." He noticed that the man's breath wheezed and his voice rasped and hoped the cause was not contagious.

"Well, I didn't say that was all now, did I? I'm here for life."

"Life! You must have stood in the very middle of the road, then."

"I did. Nor wouldn't move neither. A bit of an argument ensued, you see. Like with tongues and fists both. I think I killed his horse."

"With your bare hands?"

"No. His knife. I snatched it before he knew I meant business, but when I went for him he moved too quick for me. Got his horse instead. Felt bad about that."

A cadril who could disarm a quistril? That might be useful, if true. . . . "I'm surprised he didn't kill you on the spot."

"Aye. He said this'd be worse. But I'm still alive and enjoying a pleasant ride."

"You're an insolent rascal, Kinsett."

"Aye."

"Foolish too, I think."

"The more so when I'm drunk."

"Ah, so that's the way of it." Kinsett's claim of disarming a quistril was hard enough to believe; that he could do so while drunk was preposterous. The man couldn't be trusted. "And why did he put you in the fields rather than the mines?" Or had he? Heldrick suspected, the moment he asked, that Kinsett had in fact spent time in the mines. That would account for his lung congestion.

"The fellow that nabbed me keeps an eye on me, like. He says he don't want me to die right off so he rotates me out of the mines now and again. A right bastard he is, a mastron like yourself."

Heldrick allowed himself to smile. "I won't kill you for provoking me, Kinsett. You'll not escape your sentence so easily."

Kinsett didn't respond.

"And you?" Heldrick asked Wellen. "What did you do?"

"I did nothing."

Heldrick didn't press, since he already knew the truth. Anyway, he found he preferred Wellen's answer to Kinsett's. No boasting.

Still, Kinsett could come in handy. Heldrick abruptly knew how to use him. He could leave Wellen in a safe place and take Kinsett to the mines, and there trade him for Arrick—a common enough procedure with Kinsett, it appeared.

Heldrick left the road and headed toward a stream. When they reached it, he directed the two men to dismount.

"Why we stopping here?" Kinsett asked.

He had thought the reason obvious. "Because the two of you need a bath."

CHAPTER 26

HELDRICK LED THE MEN into the woods. A hill blocked the late afternoon sun and, with the thick foliage, made it seem an early dusk. Heldrick pulled to a halt and listened for patrols. Hearing none he turned to Wellen.

"Do you recognize me?" he asked, his voice soft.

"Not with your hood up, Heldrick. Not in this light."

Heldrick frowned. "Then—"

"Well, I did peg your voice a long ways back."

"You didn't say anything."

"I couldn't know it for a fact."

"You might give your brother some lessons in caution."

"I was exactly like him at his age. You seen him, then?"

"Yes." Not wanting Kinsett to know of the conjunction, he said, "We left him at Glasshugh's."

"What's this?" Kinsett asked Wellen. "You some sort of spy?"

"Later, Kinsett," Heldrick said. "Wellen, do you know why they didn't put Arrick in the fields with you?"

Wellen's shoulders drooped. "He resisted when they came for us."

"Arrick did? You're kidding."

"I wish. And after all them lectures he gave me! But he took a swing at a quistril, who twisted Pa's arm 'hind his back. I thought at first they'd broke it. I guess they figured he'd do no good in the fields, leastways till it healed. At least, I hope?"

"Damnation! He couldn't use his arm?"

"He could move it a bit but couldn't lift it nor carry nothing. Do you think that's bad? They wouldn't up and kill him for it, would they?"

"You're certain the arm didn't break?"

"I'm sure. He declared it felt better already by the time we reached the Citadel, and he could raise it a bit."

Heldrick chewed at his lip. Kinsett would be useless, after all.

"You're right," he said at last. He dismounted and signaled the others to do the same. "For a broken arm they might dispose of a prisoner, but not for an injury that heals in a few days. They'll give him light work to do till he recovers."

But not, he thought, in the mines. No more than in the fields. Not till the arm healed enough to make him usable. They'd use him in the Citadel itself. Worse, far worse than the mines.

"That's what I'd hoped for." Wellen face showed relief, a reverse mirror of Heldrick's own feelings. "Did Bess get—?"

"Not yet," Heldrick interrupted before Wellen could mention the conjunction, and glanced meaningfully at Kinsett. "It's her doing that I'm here now."

"Who's Bess?" Kinsett asked. "Who's Arrick? What're you two up to?"

Heldrick said, "You got a lucky break, Kinsett. I told them I required two men; when I couldn't find Wellen's father I picked someone else. Count your blessings."

"And who are you, then?" Kinsett demanded.

"He's the Renegade," Wellen replied.

Kinsett, to Heldrick's surprise, believed at once.

"Well, Lord love us. I never thought I'd see the day."

Sometime later Heldrick said, "I must leave again, for a few hours at least. During that time a patrol might chance upon you—though I doubt it, if you keep silent. Kinsett—" He felt foolish even asking. "Could you really disarm a quistril?"

"Aye. With help from this young'n I'd expect no trouble."

"How can I help against a quistril?" Wellen asked.

"A little bit of distraction's all I need. I'm mighty fast." And before Heldrick could stir, Kinsett gripped him by the ear. Without waiting for a response, he released the ear and stepped back. "Begging your pardon," he said.

"Quite." Heldrick cleared his throat. He had never seen a cadril move so quickly. Perhaps the man was not an idle boaster after all. "I'll leave your horses about a hundred yards off. In the event that they make noise and attract attention, it shouldn't mean your discovery. I expect to return with Arrick, Needa and Bess by midnight. If dawn arrives before us, take the horses and flee. Go as far as you can, to the jurisdiction of another Citadel if possible. Don't wait past dawn and under no circumstances come in after us. We possess one advantage—secrecy—and if they catch either Bess or myself we'll have lost that. Understood?"

Wellen nodded. "But must Bess go in with you?"

"She's in already."

"By her lone? She's but a girl!"

"Don't underestimate her," Heldrick replied. And then, with a grimace, "Let me do that. —Best you both keep quiet now, until I come back."

"Why must we only keep quiet when you're not with us?" Kinsett asked.

"Quick you may be, my friend, but I'll not believe your hearing matches a quistril's. The patrols will hear you long before you hear them."

Kinsett frowned but nodded.

Bess was almost cheerful. She'd found two stairwells—Heldrick had been mistaken, or out of date, about the Nest being on a single floor. She guessed the stairwells led to the women's work areas. That explained the emptiness everywhere else. Better yet, she'd found the mess hall. She could find Needa there at dinnertime without difficulty.

But in all her exploring, she still hadn't found a good way out of the Nest.

And now she heard a faint, repetitive, whimpering noise. It gave her the chills. She walked along the passage and the sound grew louder. Someone weeping? A door on the left stood barely ajar. Bess tiptoed toward the door and opened it wider. The crying doubled in volume. She peered into a small room with four chairs. A short hallway ran to the right, with three doors along its left side. The crying came from the open first door.

Bess almost turned to go. Here, anything related to a crying woman seemed likely to involve quistrils. And yet—the place seemed so empty, of both quistrils and women, that she suspected this was something less usual.

She slipped in and stepped to the open door. In astonishment Bess recognized the crying woman.

Needa.

And on a bed in the room—

Bess didn't move, didn't speak. Her tongue, her arms, her legs, had all gone wooden, like a tree. She was rooted.

On the bed lay another woman, much younger than Needa. Needa knelt by the bed. Her hands grasped one hand of the woman lying there. A third woman, also young, sat on a wooden chair behind Needa and rested a hand on her back.

The pale face of the woman on the bed shone with sweat, and perspiration plastered her hair. She was entirely naked. Blood covered her groin and thighs. Much more had soaked into the sheets beneath her. Her eyes stared.

Time stumbled, moved forward in fits and starts, left blank areas of nothingness between the moments. A buzzing filled Bess's ears. The other woman saw Bess and spoke, but most of the words fell into the cracks between moments.

A door in the back of the room opened and a man came through. He carried a small bundle. The bundle squirmed.

Bess swallowed, loosened her tongue. "I . . ."

She knew the person with the bundle—Casternack.

He glared at her without recognition. "Bronli, get her out of here."

The woman stood. Bess found her voice.

"Wait! —Needa."

Needa raised her head.

"Bess? Oh, Bess! I thought you'd made it home." Then Needa began to weep anew and turned her face back to the dead woman.

Casternack and Bronli hesitated. Bess managed to take a step, then another, and another, until she reached Needa.

Casternack watched Bess.

"Say," he said, "you're the one . . ."

But Bess crouched down beside Needa and put her arms around her.

"It's Corlene, Bess," Needa whispered. "My girl. It's over for her. She's free. I'm crying for myself."

Three years, thought Bess. For three years she's dreamed of seeing her daughter again, and now . . . This is the girl whose bed I slept in, whose clothes I wore.

The bundle in the doctor's arms began to cry also. Another quistril, Bess thought. A murderer already.

Needa wiped her eyes and asked, "Please, may I see the baby?"

Bess unwrapped her arms from Needa, surprised that Needa would want anything to do with the infant. The doctor handed him to Needa. She took the baby and smiled at him, then put him on her shoulder and patted him. For a moment he grew quiet.

He started to cry again, and Needa said, "I think he's hungry."

Bronli took a bottle from Casternack and handed it to Needa. Bess wondered about the woman. She knew the doctor's reason for working with the quistrils; what was Bronli's excuse? But then she chided herself. Helping the women here took precedence over blocking the quistrils.

Needa took the bottle but frowned and did nothing with it.

"It's milk," Bronli said. "From the new mothers. Most goes to the crèche but we cycle some through here. See?" She took the bottle and coaxed the infant into sucking, then gave the bottle back to Needa. Bess watched the tiny hands wave and the unfocused eyes wander, and her hatred popped like a bubble.

This baby couldn't help what had happened. He wasn't a murderer, not yet. Maybe he never would be.

Needa still wept silently, and Bess found her own cheeks damp.

The doctor pulled the sheet over Corlene's body. "Why don't you go into room two? Bronli, go with them."

Bronli nodded and went to the door.

"Let's go Needa," Bess said.

"I'll keep the baby," the doctor said.

Needa jerked. "No!"

"The baby goes to the crèche. It's rules."

"Oh, hang the rules," Bess said. "Can't you give her a few minutes? What if Corlene had been *your* daughter? Would you hurry the baby off to the crèche then?"

Casternack's expression didn't change. But he lowered his hands.

"A couple of hours, maybe. That's all. You'd better stay here in the infirmary so I know where you'll be. Don't make me come find you."

"I'll name him Lantry," Needa said. "After Arrick's father."

"They'll name him in the crèche," said Casternack.

"Then it'll be a false name!"

"Please, Needa, not now. Let's go to the next room."

Needa looked at the form under the bloody sheet and her eyes filled with tears again.

"Yes . . . let's go." She stood with the baby.

Bronli took her by the arm and led her into the hallway.

Casternack grasped Bess's elbow before she could follow and held it while he shut the door. "Why are you in here?"

The black strip of cloth remained tantalizingly out of Corck's reach. "Here, push me up a bit higher and move a step closer. Not that way!" But a breeze lifted the cloth enough for Corck to snag it— "Stop jiggling, you idiot—"

Too late. He found himself falling.

Oof!

He climbed to his feet, dusted himself off, and glared at his companion. "I said *closer*."

The other, still astride his horse, rubbed a shoulder where Corck's boot had dug in. "I'm not an acrobat, you know. What's wrong with letting the younglings keep the wall clean?"

Corck, examining the cloth, failed to answer. He ran the bit of quistril cloak through his fingers. Youngling, novice, or vasik. Not enough to tell more. An odd thing, certainly; odd enough under any circumstances, but coupled with yesterday's escape . . .

He mounted his own horse. "Find another vasik for patrol duty today."

"You're skipping out? But that's—"

"This takes priority." Corck turned his horse back toward the stables, disturbed.

Strange doings were afoot.

CHAPTER 27

BESS JERKED HER ARM from Casternack's grip and winced as pain shot through her wrist. She grabbed it with her right hand and spoke through gritted teeth.

"They decided they didn't want me in the dungeon." Where did Casternack stand? Whose side would he take, if forced to choose?

But now he took her arm again, more gently.

"What'd you do to your wrist? And your face?"

"Fell."

"Hmm. Hang on." He went out the room's back door and returned in a minute with a roll of gauze and a damp pad. He set the gauze down and cleaned the scrape on her face with the pad. It smelled like medicine and stung like it, too.

Then he picked up the roll of gauze. "This'll give a bit of extra support," he said, wrapping her wrist. "Too tight?"

"No." In fact, it felt much better.

He said, "You're too young for this place."

"I'll grow."

"Why be so anxious, with this ahead of you?" Casternack pointed to Corlene. Then he shook his head. "I don't understand. How could you. . . ? Well, anyway, I won't say anything unless they ask me. You understand? But if they ask me, I'll say what I know."

"What are you talking about?"

"I'm saying something's fishy, and don't tell me what. Keep your nose clean and stay out of my sight. I might forget you that way."

Bess didn't even nod, for fear that Casternack would take it as some sort of admission. "Thank you for the . . . medical attention."

He shrugged. "It's my job."

"I'd better go see Needa, now."

He nodded, and she decided it could have been worse. He wouldn't help them. He would never intentionally use his key to let them out. But he wouldn't turn her in, either; not if he could avoid it.

When Bess opened the door to the middle room, Bronli broke off speaking to Needa. Her eyes roved over Bess, not seeming to like what they saw.

But she only said, "Needa should eat. You, too. I can bring some food back from the mess hall if it's not already too late."

Bess heard Bronli without listening to her. She glanced at the clock, which read ten past six. Only fifty minutes remained for their escape, if they wanted to take advantage of the vacant dinner hour hallways. And she didn't even have a plan, yet.

Then Bronli's words penetrated.

"'Too late'?" For what? "Didn't dinner just start?"

Bronli shook her head. "At five-thirty."

"Since when?"

"Since . . . well, since before they brought me here." She frowned at Bess. "I should be back in fifteen minutes. Sooner if the food's gone. Needa, remember what I said."

Bess's stomach contracted to a heavy lump. Heldrick had been wrong about dinnertime, too. No way she could effect their escape in twenty minutes. Maybe they should wait until midnight after all.

But before midnight Casternack would certainly hear about the youngling who'd chased her to the dungeon. He'd no longer be able to pretend that he thought she'd been transferred to the Nest. And then he'd be bound to report her.

They needed to start now and figure out what to do on the way. She touched Needa on the shoulder the instant Bronli left.

"Come with me. We have to move fast."

"Go with you where?"

Bess bit her tongue and told herself to be patient. The woman had just lost her daughter and had never considered the possibility of escape. She needed time to process.

But they had no time to spare. Bess took a deep breath. "Needa, listen. I intend to leave this place, I intend to take you with me, and I mean right now. Can you just do what I ask? I'll answer questions later."

Needa stood, her face brightening. "Arrick and Wellen?"

"Already out. But the baby—"

"Lantry goes with me, Bess."

Bess sighed. Why had she asked the doctor to leave the baby? Acting on impulse, as usual. And she didn't have time to argue with Needa now. "Fine, then." But what would she do if the baby started crying? "Bring that bottle along."

She yanked the door open and stopped, waving Needa back. The door to the next room stood open. Could Casternack still be here? Of course. Only five minutes had passed. And she'd made no effort to keep quiet when opening the door. She took a step into the hall.

Casternack appeared at the other door and frowned at her. "I thought I said to stay here."

"I . . . wanted to know, do you have a bathroom here?"

After a moment, he grinned. "You ask me that every time we meet. Through here." He took her through the other room's back door, which led into a larger area filled with equipment and supplies. The two doors to her right would be the back entrances to the other treatment rooms. Casternack directed her to another door. When she finished, she thanked him and returned to the middle room directly, then closed both the room's doors.

Five minutes wasted! And Casternack remained. "If he doesn't leave before Bronli returns, we'll never get out," she said.

"Ah, Bronli," Needa said. "She doesn't trust you."

Uh-oh. "She doesn't?"

"At least, she told me that *I* shouldn't trust you. I said nonsense, I knew you better'n she did. But she insisted, said you were too friendly with the doctor."

"Ha. That's a good one. She's the one who works with him." And she remembered the appraising glance Bronli had given her. "Needa, she must know who I am. A youngling saw me earlier, and I bet anything she's heard about it already. You must have noticed from her speech that she's a town woman. She's probably reporting that I'm here right now. And I bet if she returns before we're gone, she'll try to keep us here until her friends arrive. But we can't leave yet." Bess wanted to pound on something.

As if in answer to her thoughts, a couple of thumps sounded at the door. Bess put her finger to her lips; Needa nodded her understanding. Bess opened the door and let Bronli in, carrying several plates and sets of chopsticks on a tray, the top plate heaped with food.

"What I wouldn't give for a knife and fork!" Needa said, as Bronli divided the food. "But the quistrils don't trust us with them."

"Can't blame them," Bronli said. She opened the back door and invited Casternack to eat with them. For the next fifteen minutes, no one said much of anything. Then the doctor rose to leave, saying he had an appointment he was already late for. Bess hoped he would take the baby now.

But he said, "I'll come back at nine to fetch the baby. No later. Stay right here till then."

And Bronli said, "I'll keep them company."

I'll bet you will, thought Bess. But I don't plan to stick around.

She began to pick up the plates the moment Casternack stepped out.

Bronli said, "I can get those."

"Okay." Bess waited until Bronli's hands were full, then stepped behind her. She wrapped an arm around Bronli's neck, pulling her backwards, and swept the chopstick she'd kept in her hand up to Bronli's right eye. Bronli dropped the plates with a crash. Needa gasped.

"Don't move, Bronli. This thing isn't sharp, but your eye is soft."

Bronli didn't move.

"You told your friends about me?"

Bronli hesitated. Then, "Of course. What would you expect?"

"Needa, go into the back area and find something to tie up this . . . this informer."

Needa went out.

Bronli stared after her, looking incredulous. "You convinced *Needa?*" she asked. "What in the world did you tell her?" Bess didn't bother to answer.

Needa came back with a roll of wide tape.

"Wrap it around her ankles first, Needa."

"Needa, surely you don't believe—"

Bess tightened her arm on Bronli's throat. "It's a little late to start denying things now, Bronli. Okay, Needa, now her wrists." Once Needa finished, Bess let go of Bronli's throat and removed the chopstick. What would she have done if Bronli had struggled? She honestly didn't know. "Needa, wrap a few lengths all the way around her. Tape her arms to her body."

Needa finished that in moments. Bess and Needa tilted Bronli backward and lowered her to the floor.

"You're making a mistake, Needa," Bronli said.

"Aye, and I might think so too, despite your own words, if you hadn't tried to turn me against Bess earlier."

Bess ended the discussion by tearing off a strip of tape putting it tight over Bronli's mouth.

"All right, Needa. Let's go."

Grayvle still couldn't believe he'd done it. Only a day had passed since he gave the girl those keys, but it seemed a lifetime; and in a way it was. He was a new person. He kept catching himself smiling. But he had to block that, had to keep everything inside. No one else must know.

He tried not even to think about it. Yet, unknowing, others kept bringing the crucial events to his attention. Thuvwald went on, waving his fork dangerously: "Listen, the younglings who had gate duty say—"

"Did you talk to them?" Grayvle asked. He sliced his meat, stuffed a bite in his mouth.

"No," said Thuvwald, "but—"

"Neither has anybody else, so you don't know what they said. All right, security's augmented and your friends are in isolation, so something unusual happened at the gate, but that's no reason to conclude that prisoners escaped the dungeon."

"Well," persisted Thuvwald, "the dungeon did hold prisoners, you know. —Wipe your chin."

"Yes, I know. Yesterday I escorted the girl to a meeting with the Ascendant and the near-quistril to an interrogation with Pandir."

"Well, then. And now they're gone!" Thuvwald said.

"I knew that, too. It doesn't mean they escaped." He felt himself beginning to smile and turned it into a scornful laugh. "Did you know that the vasik occupied a high-security cell? And do you think no one would have spotted the girl? You've ignored the rational assumption that they were disposed of in the usual fashion. Do you plan on eating that muffin?"

"Here." Thuvwald handed it over. "But don't try to change the subject. I can see your big shot friends have told you to suppress the story."

Grayvle said nothing for a moment. He knew he had come to the notice of several senorals, even a mastron or two. Yet none of those acquaintances—Thuvwald spoke wrongly to call them friends—had mentioned any escape to Grayvle, or told him to suppress it. Only Corck, and Corck could hardly be called a big shot. But if Thuvwald wanted to believe otherwise, so much the better.

"I don't wish to discuss it further," Grayvle said.

Thuvwald smiled knowingly but went on. "I'll bet I've got news that you haven't already heard."

Grayvle sighed. "What?"

"Have you talked to your protégé since midafternoon?"

"Horvöl? No."

"I saw him before dinner. He seemed agitated. I asked him what was up and he said he saw her in the Citadel today."

The urge to smile vanished. Grayvle carefully placed his fork on his plate. "Saw her? Who? What does that mean?"

"The girl from the dungeon. She wore a cloak but he recognized her face."

That wasn't possible. "At what distance?"

"Close enough."

"I . . . presume he seized her, then."

"Well, no. She ran to the dungeon."

He struggled to think of what he would normally say. "Of her own will? How considerate."

"Don't be snide. Horvöl didn't have a key so he didn't follow her in; but he shut the door so she couldn't leave, went to fetch a key, and when he returned she'd disappeared." Thuvwald's eyes held a triumphant gleam. "So you see, it's possible to escape the dungeon after all."

Horvöl had bungled the capture, then. Grayvle began to relax.

"What are you grinning about?"

"I'm laughing at your critical faculties. According to your own story, there's no evidence."

"Well . . . Horvöl's word . . ."

"Horvöl reported this to his duty-master?"

"When he let her escape? Hardly."

"Horvöl's a fool and a liar."

Thuvwald's eyebrows rose. "I thought you liked him."

"Irrelevant." In fact, Grayvle hated Horvöl, but he generally did his best not to show it. "As his mentor I'm duty bound to criticize him where it's due. He's a liar because he never saw the girl in the dungeon. So if she did escape, and he did see her, he still couldn't have recognized her as he claims. And he's a fool for telling anyone stories, true or false, that he's afraid to report to his duty-master. Think about that, if you like him, before you spread the story further."

Thuvwald frowned and sat back, and Grayvle returned to his dinner, his mind spinning. Why would Horvöl claim seeing the girl, if he hadn't done so? How could he have recognized her, if he had? But who else could he have seen? And it made no sense that she was still in the Citadel today. Why would she have stayed? How could she have remained hidden? Perhaps Thuvwald had made up the whole thing.

He would talk to Horvöl after dinner. He wanted to know who was lying. And why.

Pandir ate alone at a table in the graycloaks' mess and fumed. The Ascendant had blamed the marginals' escape on him for not posting a guard outside the dungeon door after the last interrogation. Ridiculous! Nobody posted guards at the dungeon. The Ascendant should have done it himself, if anyone should. And that fool Mastron Ollagh had let them past him at the gate!

By the gods!

But of course the Ascendant didn't accuse Pandir of anything. As always he used innuendo and rumor. And he'd given another mastron charge of tracking the marginals after their escape. Pandir hadn't really wanted that hopeless task, but the Ascendant snubbed him doubly by blaming him for the escape and then withholding responsibility for retrieving the prisoners.

Fortunately, Pandir had already dispatched Kierkaven to track the marginals backward from that farmhouse before the Ascendant gave his orders. An old trail, but perhaps the marginals hadn't hidden the evidence of their passing with such care before anyone searched for them. All the rest of that group had returned by nightfall yesterday except Kierkaven and the man with him, and they hadn't so much as sent word.

Well, maybe bears ate them, or maybe they rode off a cliff in the dark, or maybe they quarreled and murdered each other. On the other hand, maybe they found the conjunction, in which case their failure to report back indicated that an armed group of marginals guarded it.

At his scheduled audience with the Ascendant, Pandir planned to ask for a large force to investigate. The Ascendant would agree, thinking, no doubt, that they'd track Kierkaven and his companion to the bedroom of some farm girl, and Pandir would become a laughingstock. But Pandir knew Kierkaven better than that. And when, in fact, they found a conjunction . . .

Let the Ascendant try to make him look bad after that.

CHAPTER 28

WELLEN THOUGHT HELDRICK astonishingly quiet as he led the horses away. Before Heldrick went twenty feet the sounds blended into the chirping of crickets and the sigh of leaves in the breeze.

Kinsett remained standing nervously, head tilted, listening. Wellen sat down against a tree and closed his eyes. It would probably be a long wait—might as well rest a bit. But after a moment, something poked him in the side of the leg. He opened his eyes.

Kinsett was prodding him with a toe. "A poor way to grow old, following a rider's advice."

Wellen stared and Kinsett went on: "This is our chance lad. The sooner we leave, the likelier we live."

"But—"

"Come on! We'll never find a chance like this again. Outside the stockade, no guards, and horses to boot."

Wellen frowned. "Keep still, man. Hold your tongue. Sit down."

"Aye, keep still. But somewhere else, eh? Not here, where our location's known."

"There're none that know we're here."

"Lad! The rider left but five minutes ago! Do you think he's forgot so quick?"

"But that's Heldrick. He's helping us."

"Oh, for . . . He's a rider, man! Wake up!"

"But he's the Renegade!" Fat lot of good saying that would do now, if Kinsett hadn't swallowed it the first time. He might have known something was up when Kinsett accepted it so easily.

"You believe that lot? Are you simpleminded? There's no Renegade, never was. That's a pack of tales."

Wellen shook his head. "It's the Lord's truth. I saw him kill another rider, with these very eyes, in my own house, but three nights past."

"Huh. And for that he goes free while you pull a stint on the work crew." Kinsett shook his head. "I say he's fooled you. I say he's setting up a training exercise and we're the prize. In ten minutes, this whole wood'll crawl with riders searching for two damn-fool humans, and the one that finds us first earns a commendation while you land five extra years for trying to escape. You can be quiet as a cat in the snow, they'll find you 'fore the night's out."

Wellen shook his head. "It ain't so. I can see there's no convincing you—"

"Damn straight."

"—but I wait for Heldrick. So if you want to go, go. If you stay, hold your tongue. Agreed?" He'd rather Kinsett stayed here quiet, as Heldrick had asked; but if he couldn't keep quiet, best he were gone.

Kinsett snorted. "On your own head, then," he said, and Wellen relaxed against the tree trunk, letting his eyes close.

A viselike hand clamped his arm and another his

neck. The two hands hoisted him to his feet, and the one holding his arm twisted the arm behind him painfully.

Kinsett whispered into his ear, "If you think I'll leave you here to tell them which way I've gone you're highly mistook. I'll break your neck first. Well?" He squeezed Wellen's neck with his large hand. "What'll it be?"

"I . . . guess I'll come . . . along, then."

"Good." Kinsett let him go. "Mind, if you go running I'll catch you in a flash, and I won't give no second chances."

Wellen rubbed his shoulder, then his neck. He nodded.

"Good," Kinsett said. "Let's fetch those horses."

Wellen shook his head. The faster they went, the harder it would be for him to get back here. "The horses are tempting, I'll allow, but we'd go quieter on foot. We might not travel so far so fast, but in the end the riders are less likely to notice us."

"Don't think so. Maybe after a bit, but to start we need distance."

"Besides—" He thought fast. "If it's a trap the horses are part of it. Maybe they dunked their hooves in bear scent, or some such."

He could see the doubt in Kinsett's eyes. "Mayhap," the man muttered. "This way then."

They started out. For a long time Wellen walked next to Kinsett, but finally he drifted a bit to the side.

And a bit more.

Kinsett glanced at him.

"Don't think to run," he whispered. "You know I'll catch you."

"I know." Wellen didn't plan to run, he planned to walk. Just a few paces distance was enough. "Kinsett."

"What now?"

He stopped moving. "I'll scream if you take a step toward me," he said, and drew breath to do so.

Kinsett spun, his hands raised. His eyes gauged the distance to Wellen.

But Wellen knew he had already won. The sole danger was that Kinsett might have lunged without thinking. Wellen breathed out.

"You can catch me right enough but not before I let out one good yell that'll stop your blood. And that'll bring the riders down on you quicker'n you can turn around. From here, you go on alone."

Kinsett lowered his hands. Then he nodded once and, without a word, turned and went on his way.

After a minute Wellen started back the way they'd come. He knew he should return to where Heldrick had left them, but in this light he didn't know how he could find the spot.

Nothing to do but try, though.

As expected, the quistrils had tightened security. The spyhole opened at Heldrick's approach, and a youngling's voice called:

"Who comes?"

The Vardic words sounded strange on his ear and Heldrick realized that he'd been on the verge of speaking English. Gods!

He pushed back his hood as though he expected the gatekeepers to recognize him and gave the name of the quistril whose clothes he wore. He doubted that these younglings would know the face that formerly went with the name, and in any case he had little choice.

He waited perhaps two seconds, too little for the younglings on duty to begin opening the gate, before shouting:

"Are you deaf? or blind? or both? Can't you see I'm in a hurry, you young dunderheads?" That ought to make them remember him. Now if he could manage to leave again while these younglings still stood guard, they'd think him a known quantity.

The gate began its ponderous swing and Heldrick rushed through as soon as his horse could fit. Perhaps this would proceed smoothly after all. They would have assigned Arrick kitchen duty until his shoulder healed. Heldrick would reach the kitchen shortly before dinner ended. He need only avoid the graycloaks' mess to spirit Arrick away without a fuss.

But when he reached the kitchen, right when he intended, he found it nearly empty. Two younglings mopped the floor.

The dinner hour must have changed. Which meant that Bess had the wrong information.

But what could he do now? They would billet Arrick with the criminals in the barracks. Heldrick could recognize the group of criminals by the presence of guards, but the guards would see Heldrick before he found Arrick and his searching behavior would raise questions he couldn't afford.

Wait. Wouldn't the doctor examine Arrick's shoulder morning and night?

Heldrick's cloak swished as he spun, and he forced himself to slow. His way now would take him to a more dangerous area of the Citadel. He might encounter another mastron, or the Ascendant himself. Any of them would recognize him as an impostor.

Unfortunately, medical was at the opposite end of the Citadel. If he'd gone there first he'd have arrived with time to spare. Now, he'd be lucky to intercept Arrick on the way to the barracks. He had to hurry.

But he didn't dare.

"Do you know where we're going?" Needa asked.

"Not really," Bess answered. "Downstairs somewhere. Here, we're fair game for any quistril who wanders through. Not to speak of the ones Bronli contacted, who want me specifically."

Needa's lips tightened and she nodded.

The corridors were no longer vacant, but they saw no quistrils. Only women, none of whom walked in the same direction as Bess and Needa. They all headed toward the front. Perhaps the quistrils expected them to wait in the bedrooms?

"Did they assign you a job?" Bess asked.

"Yes. Making boots. But I found Corlene last night, in the barracks. She acquainted me to Bronli, and when Corlene started laboring this morning Bronli said I could come to the birthing room. She sent word to my stationmaster that I was took ill, so's I could stay with Corlene. So I ain't done much bootmaking yet."

Needa shook her head. "It's sad about Bronli. Corlene liked her so much—and she seemed so kind."

"Kindness and betrayal aren't incompatible. Look at Heldrick. He betrayed the quistrils, after all."

"Him? Kind?"

"Well . . . yes, when you get to know him."

"Hmph. Not sure I'd want to."

They reached one of the stairwells. All the other foot traffic had passed them by; no one watched. Bess started down.

Needa frowned. "What am I thinking? We can't go down there."

"Why?"

"They doused the lights. We'll see nothing without a lantern."

"I've got one." Bess pulled out her flashlight.

Needa pursed her lips and frowned at the small object, but she followed Bess down the stairs.

Casternack had half a mind to turn around right now and fetch that baby. He'd land in deep trouble if the quistrils learned he'd left a baby in the Nest, instead of taking it straight to the crèche. His explanation would carry little weight if he didn't offer it until after discovery. But if he *did* go back—

No. Too late now. The novice escorting the criminal with the sprained shoulder waited outside his door for the evening check, and had seen him. Probably waited ten minutes for him already.

"Sorry," he said to the escort. "Emergency in the Nest."

He ushered Arrick into his office. "Take your shirt off," he said, and pulled the file while watching to make sure Arrick could get his shirt off without help. Then he felt the man's shoulder for any swelling. He lifted the elbow. "Does this hurt?"

"No. Ah! Yes!"

"Good." Casternack lowered Arrick's arm. "You're improving."

Arrick reached up with his left hand to rub his shoulder. "I think you bend it like that to make it worse, keep me in the kitchen. I don't shirk hard work."

"When you're ready I'll let you go. But if I send you out too soon you'll hurt the shoulder worse than ever."

Casternack went to his desk. "You can put your shirt back on." He marked Arrick's progress in his folder and glanced at the clock. With luck, in forty-five minutes he could finish off that report for the Ascendant on the rising number of females born in the Nest—from one out of a thousand births to one out of three hundred. He was the first to notice the trend; that ought to be worth some points. He would decide after finishing whether to hurry back to the Nest and transfer the baby to the crèche, or wait until he'd presented the report.

Arrick pulled his shirt on, but instead of letting Casternack work, he asked, "Where do they keep the women?"

Casternack set his pen down. "You're kidding. You can't go there. Besides, you haven't spent two days here. You can hardly be desperate already."

Arrick reddened. "No, it's my wife, Needa. Maybe my daughter too, but my wife for sure. They brought the whole family in, see, though they took my girl three years past."

Casternack froze. Dread swept over him. He'd never delivered bad tidings here before. Of all things from his life outside the Citadel, he missed that least.

Arrick noticed his reaction and leaned across the desk on his good arm.

"What? What did they do to her?"

"Nothing! Your wife . . . your wife is well. She's— Your daughter gave birth a short while ago. The baby's fine, your wife has him now. But your daughter . . . died. I'm sorry, I tried—everything I knew. But I couldn't . . . I'm sorry." His voice sounded hollow and insincere in his ears. He couldn't dredge up sympathy any more. After all these years he'd grown immune.

The arm Arrick leaned on trembled. "She was alive tonight?"

"Yes. Please, sit down." Casternack came around the desk and guided Arrick to the chair.

Arrick sagged into it. "I could've been there, if they'd, if I'd—" He banged his knee.

"Take it easy. There's nothing you could have done."

"Nothing except be there!"

"Not even that. You're as far from the women's quarters now as when you were at home on your farm."

Arrick glared. Casternack didn't mind that. Glares he could handle.

After a moment Arrick's expression softened. "You say the baby's with my Needa?"

Casternack hesitated. He shouldn't have said that. But retracting the statement now could give it extra importance in the man's mind, make him more prone to talk about it.

"Yes," he said.

"That'll comfort her."

"I'm sure."

"There's no way I can see my wife then, or the little one?"

He shook his head. "They're in another universe from you."

"Could you take a message?"

"Ah, well—"

"Nothing underhanded. Just tell her I'm fine? Explain about my arm, let her know I'll go to the fields with Wellen soon as it finishes healing. That's all."

Casternack hesitated. The quistrils wouldn't send Arrick to the fields after resisting arrest. He'd go to the mines for sure.

But he said, "No harm in that." He glanced at the clock. "Your escort will wonder what's keeping you."

"Right," Arrick said. "I'm ready." He stood slowly.

The door opened. A mastron stepped in.

CHAPTER 29

CASTERNACK STARED at the mastron in his doorway. Arrick's youngling escort, peering around the mastron, wore a frown of puzzlement. The mastron's eyes swept around the office, as if he were looking for something. He turned to the escort and spoke in Vardic. A dismissal.

The escort saluted and left.

The mastron stepped in and shut the door.

"How's the patient?"

What the hell was this? "I don't—"

"You don't know? Aren't you the doctor?"

These blasted mastrons! So arrogant. But powerful; be polite. "The patient progresses. Three or four days and you can take him for the work force."

"Good. Then he's ready now for what I require." He turned to Arrick. "Let's go."

Arrick blinked at the mastron in astonishment. "But—"

"Move! You'll find out what I have in mind when I decide and not a moment sooner. Do you understand?"

"Aye." Arrick swallowed and, strangely, seemed almost to smile. "Aye. I understand." He stepped to the door and opened it for the mastron, who swished through and then waited for Arrick to follow.

The door closed. Casternack wondered what it meant.

And what message should he deliver to the fellow's wife now?

He made a note in Arrick's file: "Daughter died here in childbirth two days after his arrival." He found it wise to remember these things. One never knew when they might come in handy.

Quistrilian society, Arvinblöd decided, was a shattered mirror. Each Citadel, each fragment, cast its own reflection. Arvinblöd wanted to smooth rivalries and join all quistrildom into a single clear image, but no other Citadel had an Ascendant of like mind.

Most quistrils remained intent on subjugation. What foolishness! They'd concluded the subjugation centuries ago. They ought to work at recovering the science of the Settlers. Much of the lore he desired resided in the Archive, but it lay buried in volumes that no one could now understand. Still, with study, they would yield clues which, combined with experimentation . . .

Norvenmot had the right idea there, but they kept everything they learned to themselves. Arvinblöd's goals called for cooperation; that, in turn, demanded a leader with the necessary vision. In short, himself. Even Lonnkärin lacked the initiative to launch the task, though he might steer it capably enough. What was Lonnkärin up to, anyway? On a wild goose chase, or had he found a lead?

Arvinblöd turned a corner. Would his own death frustrate his plans? His thirty-third birthday had passed months ago. Within a year he might die. Within two, almost certainly. Already his whiskers grew white, his shoulders stooped and his knees bony. His hearing was no better than a cadril's. Could he inaugurate things soon enough?

He had thought to present the two marginals as a hazard which would require alliance, but he couldn't admit their escape to Norvenmot and maintain his credibility. He still didn't know how they'd left the dungeon. What a fiasco! Though at least it gave him more ammunition to use against Pandir. Ollagh deserved punishment more, of course, but Arvinblöd didn't want to dilute the blame. Let it all fall on Pandir. Gods! What a disaster for his plan if that lowbrow became the next Ascendant!

He must find some excuse, some justification to push cooperation on the other Citadels. But he had so little time. Damn! His mind kept running in the same circles. He needed a distraction. Perhaps that cadril doctor had the information he'd asked for.

He turned right, then left at the next passage. Twenty feet down the corridor a mastron emerged from the doctor's office with a cadril behind him.

A mastron escorting a cadril patient from medical?

The mastron turned and walked toward Arvinblöd. He saw Arvinblöd the moment he started to walk and delivered a crisp, automatic salute. Arvinblöd returned it without thinking.

But . . .

Great gods.

Arvinblöd stopped walking and stared. He blinked.

He did not recognize this mastron.

Something was seriously wrong.

DAY SEVEN

The imitation rock door, so realistic it had nearly fooled them, was from its back side an obvious fabrication. Kierkaven walked across the cave to the mirror on the opposite side.

"Close it," he said over his shoulder, but Cranst hesitated.

"You said Pandir wanted us back by sundown. It's already past that and by the time we return—"

"Don't be an idiot. If we ignore this Pandir'll rake us over the coals for lack of initiative."

Cranst closed the wood-backed door. Kierkaven turned to study the reflective barrier.

Even with the cave in near-total darkness he could see nothing through the reflective interface. He put his fingers against the surface, pressed, and watched his dim reflection deform. He tried with the point of his knife, to the same effect. He wished he could see past it.

He put his palm against the base of his knife with the point to the interface and pushed harder; the next moment his hand pressed against the interface. It happened so suddenly that, if he hadn't been watching, he wouldn't have known when the pressure on his hand stopped being from the knife and started being from the interface. He slid his hand down the strange surface, momentarily distorting it.

"I'll try to push through," he said. "If I make it, give me time to step out of the way before you follow."

Cranst nodded. Kierkaven pushed against the surface, leaning hard.

Pop!

Something smashed into the middle of his back with such force that only his quistrilian strength kept his spine from snapping. He pitched forward.

"Cranst! Stay out!" he shouted as he fell, hoping that sound penetrated the interface.

Someone landed on top of him, but his assailant was slow to grab hold, and Kierkaven twisted onto his back. He noted the transparency of the conjunction from this side. Perfect for ambushes. A quistril's hood shrouded his attacker's face, verifying what Pandir had suspected about this world. Kierkaven brought his fingers up straight into the other's midriff, heard "oof," and went for the eyes. But the other had already protected them and managed to clip Kierkaven hard on the jaw. For an instant, he lay stunned—less than a second but long enough for any quistril worth his salt to finish him off. Instead he heard:

"Kierkaven! By the gods!" Hands pinned his arms to the floor and a heavy weight sat on his chest. "What the devil's the matter with you?"

He drew several labored breaths before trusting himself to speak. "Get off me, Cranst."

"Sure. I'm off." Cranst rose. "But don't punch me again."

"What in hell did you expect, jumping on me like that?" He stood.

"I didn't jump on you, I tripped over you. How could I know you'd lie down on the floor? I waited five seconds to let you get out of the way before I came through. You knew I couldn't see you through that mirror."

"Five seconds hell! You rammed me, you fool. You didn't even give me time to catch my balance. What if someone guarded this place? You could have killed us both." —And if Pandir had seen them, two of his own, brawling in the dark over nothing!

Kierkaven could see Cranst's expression now, set and hostile. But at least the man no longer talked back.

He turned and saw his knife, embedded in the underside of a staircase, almost as though it had flown straight there from the strange interface. Puzzled, he grasped it and tugged. It didn't budge. He pulled and jiggled and eventually worked it free.

Kierkaven stepped from underneath the staircase and inspected the small room, ill lit by a dirty window near the ceiling. The conjunction had a doorframe built around it, but the heavy door had been left open. Kierkaven walked across the room, kicked aside the broken slats from some demolished wooden structure, and lifted the window. Bushes blocked most of the view, but he could see a daytime sky, gray with clouds. Yet it was dusk outside the crevice, with a clear sky. They'd found a conjunction all right.

He started back toward the conjunction. At that moment a young boy appeared out of nowhere with a *pop*. The boy held a sheet of paper in one hand. Kierkaven stepped over, grasped the boy by the arm and pulled him away from the door while his mind argued with itself about what he'd seen. The boy hadn't come through the cave. He'd simply materialized.

"Hey!" the boy yelled. He tried to pull free, but Kierkaven held firm. He shook the boy and told him to keep still, then said to Cranst:

"Go out and see if anyone came with the boy."

Cranst nodded. Kierkaven turned back to the boy to question him, but with a *pop,* Cranst returned.

"No one there."

Kierkaven frowned. Cranst couldn't have walked across the cave that fast, let alone checked things out. What was wrong with the man? He'd seemed all right until they reached the conjunction.

"Here, you find out what the boy's up to. I'll check around."

"But I checked—"

"Do what I say!" He handed the boy to Cranst and stepped into the cave, then stopped and turned.

The mysterious mirror had returned. He touched it with his fingers. It pushed back at him as before. But when he'd crossed from that side to this, he'd encountered no resistance at all. How did they do that?

He shook his head, traversed the cave, opened the concealing door and walked to the end of the cleft. Something felt irritatingly out of place, but he couldn't pinpoint what. He could see no one. He stepped out and walked around the rocky outcropping, up the steep hill behind it, and out along the top.

No signs of anyone. But something jangled all his alarms, something so obvious that he couldn't see it.

Sunlight broke through the clouds, startling him.

Daytime! Midafternoon, he'd say. And partly cloudy.

But—

But—

"Great gods." He swung himself over the edge of the outcropping and dropped to the ground below. Two steps into the cleft, he caught himself.

Calm down, he thought. Do your thinking out here. Not until you cross over do you need to hurry. And then fetch Cranst. Simply that. Nothing else matters. Get him out as fast as possible.

All right. He walked back to the mirrored interface, touched it again. Of course. It made sense now. Everything made sense, the knife and Cranst's behavior included.

He took a breath, pushed through, and watched surprise fill Cranst's features. He'd returned before Cranst could look away. "Let's go," he said.

"How did. . . ? It's like you jumped. Except—"

"I'll tell you outside. Come on, hurry."

"But the boy—"

"Forget the boy! He's nothing."

Cranst squinted. He shook his head.

"Something's wrong with you, Kierkaven. Ever since we came in here—"

"That's right. And we have to leave to make things right again. Now." Kierkaven grasped Cranst's arm and pulled. "Move!"

Cranst dropped the boy's arm but resisted Kierkaven's pull.

"I don't—"

Kierkaven drew his knife and placed the point at Cranst's throat.

"I came back in here to bring you out, and by the devil I will. Walk, and walk sharply. I'll hang onto you so that we pass through together."

Cranst stiffened, then turned and walked stiffly to the conjunction. Kierkaven followed, gripping Cranst's arm. Again they met no resistance. Kierkaven glanced over his shoulder and saw the mirrored surface behind him, distorted with the impression of the back of one leg. As if molten, it returned in seconds to its flat, blemish-free appearance.

Kierkaven let Cranst's arm go. Cranst backed away from him. Kierkaven put his knife away.

"We can take our time now. I can explain."

"You can try."

"That conjunction's about to fail."

Cranst frowned. "I don't know what you're talking about."

"Time flow." Cranst blinked and Kierkaven prodded, "We arrived at dusk. What time did it seem when you came out here a minute ago?"

Understanding lit Cranst's eyes. He rushed out the cave to the end of the cleft, raised his eyes to the sky. Kierkaven followed, after closing the camouflage door.

"It's almost dark now," Cranst said.

"We've lost a full day then, at least. Maybe two. Or three. Who knows?"

Cranst rubbed his chin. "So . . . you thought I jumped on you earlier because I pushed through the conjunction a tiny fraction of a second after you."

"Exactly. I'm lucky you didn't break my back, the speed you came through."

"I thought the resistance seemed stiffer than you'd encountered."

"I'm sure. The same effect sent my knife flying into those steps."

"And the mirrored interface . . ."

"Yes. Obvious now." Kierkaven led the way toward the woods.

"The horses will have wandered off to a post house," Cranst said.

"Ye gods, I didn't think of that. We'll have to whistle for a patrol and take theirs."

Cranst said nothing for a moment; then: "I'm still puzzled. How can this conjunction be the one we want? Didn't we expect to find a new one?"

"Yes. That's why I didn't recognize what the reflective interface meant. Maybe we've found a different conjunction altogether. Maybe we followed a false trail that just happened to lead here."

"The odds against that are stupendous."

Kierkaven nodded, and hesitated.

"There's another explanation," he said, finally. "Maybe the marginals in the dungeon aren't marginals at all."

"What do you mean?"

Kierkaven stroked his chin. He said, "I presume you've heard of the Renegade?"

CHAPTER 30

Arvinblöd struggled to control his features. The mastron approached, the cadril a step behind.

He did not recognize the mastron. Yet he knew the face for an important one.

Which mastron was it? He named them all in his mind and could match a face to each. But this face remained nameless.

Gods! Was it happening already? Memory loss! Blood pounded in his ears as he struggled to recall the name of the forgotten mastron.

But no name came. The mastron and his charge passed by, out of sight.

Arvinblöd took a step, then another. He moved his legs automatically, yet with great effort, as if struggling to stand still and failing. With his mind reeling, his feet took him where they would.

In relief, Heldrick removed his hand from the knife under his cloak. They could ill afford the uproar caused by a murdered Ascendant. But why hadn't the Ascendant challenged him? He had stared, unblinking, like a snake. True, he had seen Heldrick's face but once before; he might not have recognized him. But how had he missed noticing that Heldrick did not belong to his select corps of mastrons?

Heldrick drew a deep breath. The Ascendant's eyesight must be failing. Nothing else could explain why he stared so hard at Heldrick without understanding what he saw. Heldrick allowed himself a grim smile.

If he met the Ascendant again he'd know a weakness he could depend on.

Grayvle watched in satisfaction as Horvöl lowered the blunted point of his sword and opened his fencing mask. Anger showed in his eyes.

"Thuvwald told you? That spillbrain!"

"I'm pretty sure I shut him down," Grayvle replied. "Though it's possible he already told someone else."

"All right, so I was stupid to tell him, I get the hint."

"You should have told me instead."

"Right."

"Well, you're going to tell me now." Grayvle opened his own mask. "I want to know how you recognized the girl. You're too young for escort duty and nothing else would have brought you into contact with either prisoner."

"I'm not required to tell you anything."

"Sure you are. If you refuse to give me information which I deem critical to my performance as your mentor I can bring you before the magisterial docent."

"Hah!" Horvöl scoffed. "The hoax revealed! Your true attitude shows itself at last."

"I've always played fair with you, Horvöl. If you'd taken my help in the spirit I gave it, my attitude would still be supportive."

"Kitchen swill. You want that vasik's slot so much you'll do anything, even pretend to a genuine interest in your protégé. But bringing me to the docent will shatter that illusion, don't you think?"

"I don't care." Grayvle had grown intolerably weary of doing his best by Horvöl, only to have his efforts spurned. Horvöl apparently thought him capable of nothing but ambidextrous hypocrisy.

Horvöl shrugged. "I still won't tell you. Report me if you want."

"I'll also report your failure to tell the duty master what you saw this afternoon."

Horvöl's voice lost its sneer. "Bastard. They'd demote me."

"We're all bastards here, Horvöl. Now choose."

For a moment, Grayvle thought Horvöl would attack him. But he only said, "What do you want to know?"

"Everything. When did you first see the girl?"

"In the crypt yesterday."

Grayvle's blood turned to ice and his brain froze on a single thought: Horvöl saw the girl turn down that stressor. He knows I watched and did nothing.

"What's wrong?" Horvöl asked.

Grayvle's mind began to thaw. Horvöl couldn't have seen. Nobody from Horvöl's form, the fourteenth, attended that stressing session.

"Nothing." He cleared his throat. Gods! He couldn't let himself be shaken like that. "Forget it. Go on, I'm listening."

Horvöl frowned. "What makes you so interested in this anyway?"

"That's not your affair. Go on."

Horvöl pinched his nose but nodded. "Of course, I was in the stressor; I didn't notice everything. But I gather that she came to the crypt during the last afternoon session and appropriated some tenth-former's garb. He noticed her first and tried to yell. Of course with the stressor running he barely made a sound, but I occupied the stressor across the aisle. I heard enough to make me open my eyes. And there she stood."

"You reported that, at least?"

"Of course I did! All of us that saw her did. Why do you think I didn't want to tell you?"

Grayvle could believe that. The graycloaks would have instructed Horvöl and the others to keep it under their hoods or else. "So what happened today?"

"I saw the girl in the corridor and chased her. She dodged into the dungeon. I went to obtain a key but when I returned she'd disappeared, I don't know how."

So Thuvwald had reported accurately. The girl remained in the Citadel. And she must have kept her dungeon key.

"You know how she left the dungeon, don't you?" Horvöl asked.

"Of course not. Why do you ask?" And what on earth had made Horvöl suspect?

"You don't act perplexed. Usually you worry a question like that into the ground."

"Ah. Well, I assumed that she used the same method that got her out the first time. And for that matter, if you'd been thinking, you wouldn't have left her alone in the dungeon for that very reason."

Horvöl ignored the recrimination and studied Grayvle for an uncomfortable moment. Grayvle knew he possessed an expressive face for a quistril but could think of nothing to do about it.

"You know," Horvöl said at length, "I don't know what lie you're telling, but I know you're lying."

Grayvle decided his best option was silence.

Horvöl shrugged. "I'll go now. I'd better report seeing the girl."

"What? Have you lost your mind?"

"I don't want you holding anything over my head, Grayvle. I'll tell them I saw her, now, and from a distance. That'll keep them from believing the version I just gave you, should you choose to repeat it later. And they'll start hunting for her. Who knows, if they find her they may give me a commendation."

"Well, wait a minute. I don't think that's a good idea. Uh, if the graycloaks wanted you to keep the other information to yourself, reporting a second sighting instead won't thrill them."

"True. I won't identify her, then; I'll just say I saw a girl in youngling's garb."

"Even so—" Grayvle stopped himself. Horvöl would love an excuse to accuse him of harboring treasonous thoughts. Perhaps he'd already said too much.

Horvöl had his eyes fixed on him, curiosity in his gaze. "What's with you?"

Grayvle closed his fencing mask. "Never mind. Report her if you like. But later, after I finish teaching you how to use that pointed stick in your hand."

"Wait! Why—?"

But Grayvle attacked. The longer he kept Horvöl here, the longer the girl would have for making her escape.

Scraps of cloth littered the room, illuminated by the flashlight beam. "This must be where they make the cloaks," Bess said.

"But they'd've took all the finished ones at the end of the day," Needa answered. "Leastways, that's what they do with the boots."

"Then we'll make do with an unfinished one. Any scissors around here? And needle and thread?"

A quick search turned up both items as well as bolts of cloth. In minutes Needa had cut a panel to match a partially finished cloak. While Bess attached it loosely to the rest of the cloak, Needa cut and basted two smaller pieces for the hood. Unhemmed and unlined, and with the hood merely tucked under the cloak's neck and missing the two brown youngling stripes, it would not stand close scrutiny; but it might, Bess thought, let them travel the less-occupied corridors.

"And now— Needa, what are you doing?"

"Making a sling for Lantry. I can keep my hands free that way, and the cloak'll hide him."

Bess could think of nothing to say. With quistrils wandering the Nest, how could they possibly leave before Casternack returned to deliver the baby to the crèche? She hated to admit it, but she'd be relieved when he took that baby off their hands.

"Bess," Needa said, "I know what you're thinking. Promise me we'll take Lantry when we go."

"Needa, I—"

"Promise!"

"I can't."

"Then I can't go with you."

"Needa, listen. Okay, if I can think of a way, fine, we'll take him. But you should promise me something, too. If the doctor comes and takes the baby while we're still here, then you give up on the baby and come anyway. Fair?"

Needa thought. "All right," she said at last. "So long's you promise to try, and not just wait till the doctor takes Lantry. You promise that?"

Bess was reluctant to make the commitment, though it was a reasonable compromise. Maybe that's what compromise meant, being only moderately unhappy with the outcome. Maybe that's why everybody always talked it up, but nobody really liked doing it.

"I guess," she said. "Okay." But she almost wished she didn't already have some inklings of a plan.

"Which way to the bootery?" she asked.

"You'll find no boots fit to wear."

"That's all right. I've got an idea. Something I saw in an old movie once, on TV."

"In what? Where?"

"Never mind. Just show me the way."

Senoral Durnstaff still hadn't calmed down. Where did these mastrons get their arrogance anyway? Did they acquire it on promotion? The thing that vexed Durnstaff most was the way the rascal had made off with the horses.

But now . . .

He studied the files of Kinsett Wonfall and Wellen Verdanit. This went beyond arrogance. How long had the mastron planned this?

Someone knocked at his door. He lifted his head. "Enter."

The door opened. A novice and a vasik stepped inside and saluted. The vasik said, "Caselvon, Senoral. On duty watch, reporting a new prisoner. Breaking curfew. Thought you might like to know."

"Why? Put him in the barracks with the others."

"Yes, of course, Senoral. But I thought you might like to know about this one."

"Unlikely." The interruption had broken his train of thought, adding to his general annoyance. "I can hardly tell them apart."

"I believe that I've seen this one among the prisoners before, Senoral."

Durnstaff rubbed his nose, stood and opened his file drawer. "All right then, what's his name?"

"Kinsett Wonfall."

Durnstaff slammed the drawer. Really, this was too much. Failure to return a horse suggested carelessness, but letting a prisoner escape indicated rank incompetence. Unless he'd done it on purpose. . . .

By the gods, maybe the mastron really was up to something.

"Who apprehended the man?"

"I," said the novice. "Kessrall, Novice-on-patrol."

"He may have had a companion."

"He was alone when we caught him. But I whistled for help and suggested, on principle, that other patrols stay on the lookout."

"A good night's work. You have the prisoner?"

Kessrall stepped to the door and beckoned. Another novice and two vasiks pushed the prisoner into the office. Three quistrils for one cadril? Durnstaff raised an eyebrow.

"The cadril is quick," Kessrall explained. "He managed to injure my partner during capture."

"Really?" What nonsense. He didn't approve of over-caution. Durnstaff's good opinion of Kessrall began to evaporate. "Was the prisoner hurt during capture?" One of Kinsett's eyes swelled purplishly, but that hardly counted.

"How should they know?" asked Kinsett. "Why don't you ask me?"

The impudence of the prisoner angered Durnstaff; then alarm took its place. Durnstaff's question—the entire conversation, until Kinsett's interruption—had been spoken in Vardic. Had Kinsett learned to understand the language in his three years on the labor force?

No. Impossible. A few key words, perhaps. Anyway, it didn't matter. "You'd better take him to Casternack for a check. Then throw him in the dungeon for the night. You did well to come to me, Caselvon. I want him secure."

Durnstaff saw Kessrall and the other novice exchange glances. "What?"

"It's rumored that the dungeon isn't all that secure."

Durnstaff had heard the rumor also. Utter nonsense, of course. Only novices or younglings would take it seriously.

"Use a high-security cell if you wish." The novices traded looks again but Durnstaff chose to ignore it. "Go on, I'm busy tonight. But if any other cadrils break curfew, put them in the dungeon also. I'll check tomorrow to see if the one I want has been found."

They left, and Durnstaff picked up the prisoner files. He didn't know what game this mastron played, but circumstances demanded action more significant than filing a written complaint. He would complain, in person, to the Ascendant.

Wellen moved cautiously, hands outstretched. Hardly any light from the dusky sky penetrated the forest canopy. He could make out tree trunks before colliding with them, but small branches lurking at eye-level remained invisible.

How long had he been walking? Had he already passed the spot where Heldrick left him?

He heard a soft snuffle. The horses! That would satisfy. Heldrick might worry when he found Kinsett and Wellen gone from the tree, but he would fetch the horses, regardless. Wellen could think of no better place to wait. He'd never find the tree in this light, and it would only get darker.

He saw one of the horses. Far lighter in color than anything else in the woods, it appeared almost bright. Heldrick must have left a dark, rolled up blanket across its back, dangling down the sides.

"Easy, boy," he whispered and took another step.

An evil chuckle stopped him in his tracks.

He realized that the rolled up blanket was a pair of legs, attached at the top to a figure wearing a cloak exactly as black as the shadows. The figure spoke.

"Who are you calling 'boy,' boy?"

CHAPTER 31

ARVINBLÖD STOOD before his office door, hardly able to remember how he had gotten there. He took two deep breaths and opened the door. A failing memory would leave him less time than he'd expected. But as long as his intellect remained he could perfect a plan and perhaps hammer out the details with Lonnkärin. Perhaps.

He cursed silently to himself as he crossed the anteroom and almost missed hearing his assistant say, "Mastron Svent waits in your office."

Arvinblöd stopped with his hand on the door to his inner office and frowned back at the assistant. "Not the conference room?"

"Another visitor waits there. He arrived a few minutes earlier."

"Lonnkärin?" He *ought* to have reported by now.

"No. A senoral. Name of—" The assistant consulted his note pad. "—Durnstaff."

Don't know him, Arvinblöd thought. He must consider the matter important to approach me directly.

And then doubt gnawed at him. —I don't *think* I know him.

"Has Svent been here long?"

"No, sir. A minute or two."

Arvinblöd released the doorknob. Did he know this Durnstaff?

"I'll see Durnstaff first." He ignored his assistant's obvious surprise. "If Lonnkärin should arrive, interrupt me."

He crossed the anteroom and opened the door to the conference room. The senoral stood and saluted. Arvinblöd scrutinized him. Someone he might have seen but never dealt with. He thought.

"Durnstaff, I believe?"

"Yes, Ascendant."

No surprise at the greeting. The senoral didn't expect to be recognized. Arvinblöd sighed in relief. "What's the problem? Sit down."

"I have a complaint about a mastron, Ascendant."

"Really?" Was this Durnstaff some sort of backstabber? Hoping to squeeze into the ranks of mastron himself? "Go on."

"He came to the fields this afternoon and requested two of my prisoners for use in a mysterious project associated with Norvenmot Citadel. He spent some time examining the prisoners and chose these." Durnstaff pushed two folders across the conference table to Arvinblöd.

The fields: Arvinblöd placed Durnstaff now. His assignment to Overseer of the Fields had occurred a few months ago. But what project was he talking about? Arvinblöd frowned. Norvenmot generally kept their projects to themselves. Occasionally they wanted help, but such overtures of cooperation had to go through him, and none had. —Or at least he remembered none.

Play it safe, he thought. "Is that all?"

"He also borrowed two of my guards' horses and promised to return them before evening, but he never did. And he allowed at least one of the two prisoners to escape."

"Escape!"

"Yes. We recovered the prisoner tonight, by chance, in defiance of curfew." Durnstaff reached out and tapped one of the folders. "This one. And I expect that if one escaped both did. Whether the escape resulted from simple incompetence or from deliberate action on the part of the mastron I cannot know."

Arvinblöd gave Durnstaff his best chilling stare. "Deliberate action is a serious charge, Senoral, and one for which you've provided no evidence. I'm surprised you raise such an issue."

Durnstaff drew a deep breath. "Both prisoner files list, as apprehender, the same mastron who took them away. It seems an odd coincidence. More than odd; extraordinary. One is a new prisoner but the other was acquired three years past, which would indicate long-term planning. Perhaps he secretly works for Norvenmot, rather than merely *with* them. I possess no proof, but I thought I should raise the possibility. In any event, the alternative, gross incompetence, seemed sufficient reason to bring this to your attention."

Arvinblöd reached out a hand and opened one of the folders. The first page displayed the information: "Apprehender: Lonnkärin."

"This is nonsense!"

Durnstaff drew back in alarm.

Arvinblöd opened the other folder and glanced inside.

"You say that Lonnkärin did these things? Impossible. He is attached to no such project. He is currently attempting to recover—" —*the escaped prisoners*. "Well, that's of small importance. He would never allow a prisoner to escape, and for that matter he would never break his word."

Durnstaff looked as if he wanted to grab the folders and run but dared not. "I've secured the recovered prisoner in the dungeon. And the mastron stamped his chop for the two prisoners. My chief guard can report how he asked for the horses."

Arvinblöd drummed his fingers. "You have Lonnkärin's name from the chop only? You didn't know him?"

Durnstaff swallowed and shifted in his seat. "Correct. I did not."

"Describe him to me."

"Wide-set, dark eyes. High forehead. Square chin. I didn't see him long."

"That's fine! Fine! Lonnkärin's eyes are light. His chin sports a distinct cleft. You dealt with an impostor."

"But . . . why would anyone do that?"

Arvinblöd shrugged. Who cared why? The description fit the mastron he'd seen earlier. His memory hadn't failed at all. "Clearly a mental breakdown of some sort. We'll find him. Thank you for bringing this to my attention; I'll remember it. —By the way, Durnstaff, if you check your other files you'll find that Lonnkärin is the apprehender of record for over a quarter of your current prisoners."

Durnstaff reddened.

"And now I must take care of this problem you've brought." Arvinblöd stood, turned his back on Durnstaff and left. In the anteroom a sobering thought dampened Arvinblöd's elation: Lonnkärin was probably dead. He would not willingly give up his chop.

Well. Better to lose Lonnkärin than to lose his own memory.

He said to the assistant, "I no longer expect Lonnkärin. If he should arrive anyway send him to my office. But if someone else comes claiming his identity, send him to the conference room. If you tell me on my return that Lonnkärin waits in the conference room, I'll know it's an impostor. All right?"

The assistant knit his eyebrows but nodded. "And what about Mastron Svent?"

"Ah," Arvinblöd said. "Thank you." Pacifying Svent would take perhaps two minutes. Then he would go to Casternack. The impostor came from Casternack's office. Casternack would give him information, willingly or otherwise.

Casternack finished his report and checked the time. Forty minutes remained before his meeting with the Ascendant. To walk to the Nest, then to the crèche, handle the paperwork, come back here to pick up the report and go on to the Ascendant's . . . he could manage. But that would defeat the reason he'd left the baby, without doing much to decrease the risk. Let the woman keep him for another hour.

Maybe the Ascendant would see him early. If so Casternack would have more time to present his report and greater opportunity to ask about the girl.

The door opened without warning. The Ascendant was a trifle grimmer than usual. Casternack, in panic, wondered if he could have misread the time by an hour. Then, remembering himself, he jumped to his feet and said:

"Please. How may I repay this honor?"

The Ascendant shuffled in, sat down. "A mastron visited you earlier. He left with a cadril. Tell me about him."

"Well . . ." Casternack remained standing. Arrick's file still sat on the side of his desk. He opened it and recited the main points.

"Name: Arrick Verdanit. Captured two days ago, shoulder sprained during capture. Doing kitchen work until it heals. Coming along fine. Daughter died—" Casternack caught himself. He hadn't meant to say that. Not before he transferred the baby to the crèche.

But the Ascendant interrupted anyway. "No, no. Not the cadril. Tell me about the mastron. What did he want? Why did he leave with the prisoner?"

Casternack blinked. "I—I didn't think it my place to ask."

The Ascendant fixed his gaze on a spot three inches deep in Casternack's brain. "You will tell me what you know."

Casternack's skin prickled. "Of course." He recounted the incident.

The Ascendant considered the information with a slight frown. "It's not enough. If you think of anything more, no matter how insignificant, bring it to my attention. At once. Do you understand?"

"Absolutely. Uh, the report you wanted. I've finished it. Should I—?"

"Tomorrow." The Ascendant stood. "Tonight I want you to rack your brains for anything, any detail that might help us find this mastron."

"He's missing?"

The Ascendant frowned. "Did I ask you to speculate?"

"No—"

"Then don't. Anything you think of, you let me know."

The Ascendant turned but stopped with his hand on the doorknob. "Did you say that the prisoner's daughter died? During capture? Who was responsible?"

Casternack swallowed once. Don't lie. Don't consider lying.

He forced himself to meet the Ascendant's eyes. "No, during childbirth. Today, this evening."

The Ascendant's hand left the doorknob. "I've received no report from the crèche of any birth today. The baby died also?"

"No. Quite healthy."

The Ascendant kept his gaze fixed on Casternack.

"The director of the crèche is very busy in the evenings," Casternack offered.

"Yes. All right, it's not your concern. For the rest of the evening you do what I've asked." The Ascendant opened the door and left.

Casternack sank into his chair. Did the Ascendant believe him? He hadn't said anything untrue. But he could see his hands shake.

And he'd never asked about Bess. Well, he wouldn't, then. The whole idea had been idiotic from the start; he could see that.

He needed to take that baby to the crèche, now. He gave the Ascendant two minutes to leave the vicinity. Then he reached into his drawer for his keys.

He dared not wait a moment longer.

Grayvle knocked the blade from Horvöl's hand. Horvöl dropped to a sitting position on the floor, head bowed.

"Up!" Grayvle said. "Fight, coward!"

"Grayvle, you're a madman! Enough."

For someone three years younger than Grayvle, Horvöl had done well. But his thrusts had come to resemble those of a drunken man, easily batted aside. Grayvle obtained a smidgen of pleasure by imagining how sore Horvöl's right arm would be tomorrow. He laid his weapon down, pulled his mask off and collapsed on the floor also.

For some minutes neither moved; Grayvle had no wish to hurry Horvöl along. But then, unexpectedly, Horvöl stood over him.

"Why do you protect the girl?" he asked.

Was Horvöl trying to surprise an admission? A fool's trick. Grayvle stood also. "What are you talking about?"

"It's obvious. You've done everything you could to keep me from reporting her. I know you better than anyone does, Grayvle. You can fence like a master and wield your knife as well as anyone. You know twenty-seven ways to kill a man. But you never have, and you never will. You're a weakling, and I'm the one person you haven't fooled. Still, I never thought you'd stoop to helping a spineless cadril! What did she do, beg for mercy when you escorted her back to her cell?"

She didn't beg at all, you contemptible snake. She's got more spine than you have.

But all he said was, "I don't know what you're talking about."

"Oh, but you do. I can see it in your face." Horvöl slapped a hand against his leg. "I wish I knew where she was."

Of course she could only be in one place: the Nest. Obvious, now that Grayvle knew she'd stayed in the Citadel. But he wouldn't do Horvöl's thinking for him. "Whatever you think you see in my face, you're wrong." And after a moment he added, "You're also wrong to think I could never kill anyone."

"I say I'm right. You haven't the grit."

"I could kill *you*, Horvöl. In fact, I think I will."

Horvöl laughed. Grayvle pulled his knife from its sheath.

Horvöl stopped laughing and took a step back. "You're not serious."

"I'm serious."

"You'd kill a fellow quistril before a cadril?"

"I don't consider you a fellow of any sort." Grayvle stepped forward.

"You'll never get away with it."

Grayvle shrugged. "So what? You'll report me for trying to help this girl even though it's not true. If I'm to go down it may as well be for something worthwhile."

"But . . . I'm not planning to report you. I've no proof and you're too popular. Besides, any stain on you will reflect on me. I hope you get that vasik's slot, too. I don't care if you disgrace yourself afterward. When that happens you won't be my mentor anymore. But until then—well, I can put up with the charade for two more weeks. I won't report you."

"A true quistril would never grovel for his life, Horvöl. Prepare to die."

"By all the gods, Grayvle . . ."

Grayvle thrust the knife back under his cloak.

"I've always wondered," he said, "if the biggest bullies were also the biggest cowards. Now I know."

Horvöl swallowed. "You never meant to kill me?"

"Not worth it."

Horvöl's sneer resurrected itself. "So I was right about you after all." He turned and walked off. At the door he had difficulty turning the knob until he used his left hand. Grayvle smiled.

Horvöl opened the door. "But I wasn't groveling, you know. My reasons were authentic. I won't report you." He stepped through the door and paused. "The girl, of course, is a different matter."

He closed the door.

Kierkaven and Cranst thundered up to the gate.

"Ho there! Open up!"

The spyhole opened. A pair of eyes peered out.

"State your names."

Kierkaven and Cranst frowned at each other. "What the. . . ?"

"Regulations," the gatekeeper called out. "New today. Sorry."

They gave their names, a bit grumpily, and the gate opened. They galloped on through to the stables, handed off their horses, and hurried on to the Citadel and Pandir's apartments.

CHAPTER 32

WELLEN FOLLOWED the two quistrils—one with a squint, the other a broken nose—down stairs and through corridors, to a door. Beside the door was a small square plate with a little lever sticking out. The quistrils opened the door on blackness, then flipped the lever. The lights in this place, which used no kerosene and went on and off with a flick of that lever, were awesome. He wondered if he could snitch any before his term ended. Course, he'd have to snitch one of those lever things as well. That might be harder.

This light was dimmer than most. It revealed a spiral staircase and a rock-hewn corridor stretching into darkness.

A voice he'd never expected to hear again hollered, "Who's that?"

"Kinsett?" Wellen called back.

Broken Nose backhanded him across the side of his head.

"Wellen, you damned traitor," Kinsett said. "I should've broke your neck when I had my hands on it."

Wellen decided not to risk another blow by arguing. The quistrils escorted him down the stairs.

"Won't talk to me, eh? I swear I'll kill you. I'll find a way, you see if I don't."

Squint said something to Broken Nose, in their own language. Broken Nose glanced at Squint; then he turned to Wellen and smiled. "Friend of yours?"

Wellen distrusted that smile. "I hardly know him."

"Perhaps you would like to share his cell." They reached the bottom of the steps.

"No! He thinks I betrayed him. He'll kill me. He—"

Wellen stopped. Of course, the quistrils understood that. They'd stop Kinsett from killing him, but they wanted to watch the pummeling. He tried to think how to change their minds, but no ideas came.

They went on to Kinsett's cell, and Squint peered through the grating.

"Stand back. We've brought your friend."

"Bless your black hearts! Let him in here for one minute—"

"Stand back first!"

A shuffling of footsteps.

Squint put his key into the lock, opened the door. He turned his head toward Wellen, and—

Kinsett bounded from the back of the cell, landed a punch in Squint's midriff, under his cloak, and danced back. Watching, Wellen couldn't believe Kinsett's speed, or his stupidity. The quistril gasped in surprise, but despite the solidness of Kinsett's blow he apparently felt no pain.

Broken Nose unsheathed his knife but Squint waved him away. "I'll handle this."

He reached under his cloak and for the barest instant he appeared puzzled. He looked down.

In that fraction of a second Kinsett bounded forward again, this time with Squint's knife in his hand, and with a vicious swipe he nearly decapitated the quistril. Blood sprayed into the cell and over Kinsett, who retreated again. The quistril's knees bent and he toppled forward.

Broken Nose stood motionless for five long seconds, then with his left hand he grabbed Wellen by the back of the shirt. He held Wellen in front of him and pushed in through the small dungeon opening. One after the other they tramped on Squint's body. The quistril, his knife already in his right hand, shoved Wellen to the side of the cell.

"You'll not take me by surprise, cadril."

"You sure? You're by your lone, now. Mayhap you should find yourself another partner and come back."

But Broken Nose had finished with talking. He feinted with the knife. Wellen could see that this quistril moved faster than Kinsett. Kinsett didn't have a chance, unless—

A little bit of distraction's all I need.

Wellen lunged at Broken Nose's nearest hand, but the speed of the quistril's response made him feel like a fly in honey. Before his feet left the ground the quistril's fist struck him in the side of the face. His feet flew from under him, and he knew the quistril's knife would kill him before he hit the ground.

Instead he saw Kinsett crash into the quistril. Then Wellen's head cracked on the stone floor and the contestants exploded in a shower of light.

Wellen tried to regain his feet, but for a few moments he couldn't locate the floor. He found it behind him, pushed himself to his elbows, sat up. The dungeon cell swayed, but somehow Broken Nose and Kinsett kept their feet in the center.

Broken Nose had wrapped his left arm around Kinsett's back, but Kinsett's right hand was somewhere between himself and the quistril, and his left hand kept the quistril's knife hand at arm's length. No way Kinsett had the strength to do that. Except maybe the quistril didn't feel too good. His eyes were closed.

With a shove, Kinsett pushed Broken Nose away, still holding Squint's knife, which had been buried to the hilt in Broken Nose's stomach. Broken Nose fell backward and landed almost on Squint's body. Kinsett sat.

"Good work, lad. I wasn't sure you had it in you."

Wellen reached up and touched his head. He had a lump, sure enough. But at least the cell had stopped swinging.

"How'd you know I wasn't turncoat?"

"Oh, I listened to their talk when they brought me in. They always think none of us can understand it." His voice sounded strained.

"Kinsett, you all right?"

Kinsett waved, his eyes widening. Wellen turned back to Broken Nose, who was still moving.

"Lad. . . ." Kinsett's voice burbled.

Broken Nose rolled over and dropped Squint's dungeon keys into a round hole in the floor. More than a second passed before they struck the bottom.

Wellen heard the hiss of Broken Nose's last exhalation. He crawled forward and reached into the hole, uselessly. He turned back to Kinsett.

The man sat still, watching him, his arms crossed over his middle. Blood had trickled out of his mouth and run down his chin.

"Kinsett? You're hurt bad, ain't you?"

Kinsett didn't answer. Wellen crawled to Kinsett's position, and Kinsett's eyes failed to track.

Wellen touched him on the shoulder, and Kinsett tipped backward, stone dead.

Horvöl paused, and his hand stole into a pocket. He pulled out the set of dungeon keys he'd borrowed that afternoon and stared at them in thought until he noticed the trembling in his hand. Damn Grayvle and his workout! He thrust the keys back into his pocket.

But . . .

Grayvle wanted to protect the girl. The girl had left the dungeon. That ability didn't perplex Grayvle. So he might already have helped her.

Could he have given her keys? Was his depravity unlimited? Perhaps it was, but even Horvöl could scarcely credit this possibility. No one else would consider it; not without evidence.

Still, one other fact tied it all together. The girl had run to the dungeon. She'd known where to go.

Of course! Where else could she hide? He'd asked the question earlier, and Grayvle had kept silent— because he knew. She'd made the dungeon into a base, a haven—a place from which she could come and go with no one the wiser. She might be there now. If not, he could at least find evidence.

He turned away from the duty-quarters, toward the dungeon.

He could be there in five minutes.

Arvinblöd's intuition told him that all the pieces were in his grasp, waiting to be placed. Yet, logically, he knew only three things. One: the impostor's face was familiar and important, but he couldn't place it. Two: the impostor had been abducting (and releasing?) prisoners. Three: Arvinblöd mistrusted that doctor. That was all.

But why should he even consider the doctor important? He reviewed his conversation with Casternack. The doctor hadn't lied, knew nothing of the impostor's plans. And yet—

He had hidden something, something about the baby. But what did the baby have to do with the impostor?

Begin again: the doctor had started by telling him about the prisoner, as if he thought—

Wait. He'd named the prisoner: Arrick Verdanit.

And one of Durnstaff's abducted prisoners had been Wellen Verdanit.

And Lonnkärin had told him about the Verdanits, arrested for aiding the near-quistril.

Ye gods.

In Arvinblöd's mind the impostor dropped his mastron's cloak and lay naked in the stressor: the near-quistril, the devil who escaped from the high-security cell and took the girl with him. Now he was here, in the Citadel, picking up the members of the Verdanit family. And one other family member had been brought in. The wife.

"I'm going to the Nest," he told his assistant on his way out.

"But—your appointment with Pandir in five min-utes—"

"Don't worry about that." Aside from a gift of ruthlessness, the man was incompetent. "Give him my apologies—but don't sound too sincere."

"And with Casternack fifteen minutes later?"

Arvinblöd waved that off. He scuttled a hundred yards down the corridor before it occurred to him that he could do little by himself. But the near-quistril had passed his prime, also—one or two others would suffice. Durnstaff was already involved, but fetching him would take extra time. He needed someone now.

As he thought it, a youngling entered the passage ahead of him. A mere boy, too small to wield a knife effectively. "You," Arvinblöd said, and the youngling turned, startled. "Go find Durnstaff the senoral. Say that I wish him to meet me at the Nest at the earliest possible moment. Have him bring a key. Hurry!"

Doubtless, on the way to the Nest, Arvinblöd would come across someone older to accompany him. But he wished he could walk faster. He'd spend the better part of fifteen minutes getting there.

Needa peered into the infirmary's waiting room, blocking Bess.

"I've told you," Bess said, "Bronli's friends won't be here. They'd have left to search for me the moment they found her. The infirmary's the safest possible place for me right now. Let me in. I hear footsteps."

In a moment, with the door closed, Bess relaxed. She took the cloak off Needa's shoulders and inspected the room for a place to hide it from Casternack when he returned. Needa took it from her and wrapped it round Lantry.

"That'll keep him warm," she said.

The door opened again. Casternack stood there, a large canvas bag in his hand. In shock, Bess looked at the clock. He'd promised them until nine o'clock, but it was not quite a quarter past eight. Another few minutes and he would have caught them out.

"I want the baby now," Casternack said to Needa, his words clipped.

Needa hugged Lantry to her more tightly. "I won't let you."

Bess, recovering from her surprise, found a moment to admire Needa. The woman had retained her composure better than Bess and delivered her lines perfectly.

Casternack's lips thinned.

"Don't make me use force. Understand, my position here is at stake. I've done more than I should already. Hand the boy over."

"No."

"Needa," said Bess, "please. Saying no won't do any good."

"That's right. Listen to your friend. Give me the baby." Casternack reached out his hands.

Needa jerked away. "No!" she said.

The baby woke, started to cry. Bess forced down a smile.

"Now see what you've done," Needa accused.

Casternack nostrils grew pinched, but instead of pressing further he set his canvas bag on the floor and went through a side door to the back area. Bess remembered in alarm the dishes spilled in the middle room. She hoped the doctor wouldn't go in there.

He returned in a minute with a fresh bottle and handed it to Needa. "Feed him. I can wait that long."

Needa took the bottle, glancing at Bess uncertainly. Bess had hoped to follow Lantry from the noise he made. But they couldn't refuse to feed him.

Casternack grew impatient, though a mere twenty or thirty seconds passed before Lantry again fell sound asleep.

So quick. . . .

Bess touched the sleeping, listless infant.

No response.

"What did you—?" She caught herself. She didn't want Needa even more upset.

Casternack said nothing. He turned back to Needa, took the bottle, and put it into the canvas bag.

"I'm taking the baby now," he said, in a tone that tolerated no argument.

Needa stroked Lantry's cheek. "Can I carry him to the door?" she asked.

The doctor hesitated, then shrugged.

"Sure. If you'll come right away. But if you drag your feet, I'll take the boy and go on without you."

At least that part had worked. They had the excuse they required to accompany the doctor to the lounge.

Kierkaven and Cranst didn't find Pandir at his apartments, so they tried his office, with scant hope— Pandir shunned desk work.

But an assistant there told them that Pandir had gone to an appointment with the Ascendant. With misgivings, they convinced each other that their information justified interrupting even such a high-level meeting.

They headed to the Ascendant's office.

CHAPTER 33

PANDIR COULDN'T BELIEVE his ears. "The Nest, you say?"

The Ascendant's assistant shrugged in embarrassment. "That's what he said. He left in a hurry."

"Surely . . ." Surely he's too old, Pandir almost said. But he caught himself. Rumor and innuendo. An Ascendant who skipped a meeting with a mastron and ran off to the Nest supplied plenty of material for chuckles and snide remarks, but not if the mastron himself made a big deal of the matter.

"Has Lonnkärin returned?" he asked.

"No, he . . . no."

"What? Did something happen to Lonnkärin?"

"Not that I know of."

"Well, the Ascendant must have said—ah. Did the Ascendant specify that what he said was confidential?"

"He didn't *say*—"

"Then speak up. You know me."

"Yes." The assistant swallowed. "He said that he no longer expected Lonnkärin, but if someone I didn't recognize claimed to be Lonnkärin, I should direct him to the conference room."

"That's—" and again Pandir held his tongue. Bizarre. Sounds like senility. He smiled and left, wondering: Where should I go to start the rumors?

Horvöl turned the handle—his hand and arm still trembled, but with exhaustion now, or excitement?—and pushed open the dungeon door. If the girl was here, he would kill her himself. If she was out, he would search the cells and use any evidence he found to denounce Grayvle and set up the girl's capture. Either way he would garner the credit.

Down the corridor a cell door stood open.

He sailed down the winding steps, his cloak streaming behind him. Not until he reached the bottom and started toward the cell did he sense the person hidden beneath the final loop of the stairs. He twisted around.

A quistril, a vasik by his cloak, stepped out and walked toward him. Disappointment outweighed astonishment in Horvöl's mind. Too late! Someone else had already secured the credit. But . . .

Did he smell blood on this quistril? Had the girl injured him? Impossible. Yet the man kept both arms folded across his stomach, under his cloak.

"What happened?" he asked, and took a step closer.

Too late he noticed that the vasik's cloak dragged on the floor, and the face was that of an elder youngling.

No! By the gods, a cadril! How many such scum did Grayvle hide?

His awareness shifted. The cadril's knife already plunged toward his abdomen. He skipped back but still received a painful flesh wound. Damn! He would hang Grayvle for this!

The cadril stepped toward him, his knife ready for another strike. He used his left hand; Horvöl had heard that some among the cadrils did that. In a quistril, it might have thrown him off. He almost smiled, despite the pain in his stomach. The cadril moved so sluggishly.

Horvöl reached for his knife. In shock, he realized that his arm moved as slowly as the cadril's. He snatched at his knife with his left hand, but he'd lost precious time. This would not be a killing blow. His knife flashed, slicing his opponent's hand across the knuckles—and then cold fire seared through his left forearm. His fingers lost their grip; both his knife and the cadril's clattered to the ground. What—?

Two knives! The cadril had hidden a weapon in each hand.

The cadril began another slash with his second knife, faster than before, and it dawned on Horvöl that the cadril had used the left hand as a decoy.

Horvöl swung his foot behind the other's ankles and brought the cadril to the floor, but the motion tore at the wound in his stomach and he almost went down himself. He gasped and doubled over, then forced himself upright. He couldn't afford that. And his legs trembled; he'd exercised them almost as much as his arm. Gods! he couldn't have picked a worse time to fight.

He needed to finish this. A swift kick to the cadril's temple before the cadril managed to stand would do the trick.

Except that the cadril broke all the rules and threw his knife. Horvöl barely ducked in time. And two other knives lay on the ground; no wonder the cadril chanced losing one.

Could he kick both out of the way in time? Or should he try to grab one for himself? He couldn't think. That the cadril had inflicted the greater injury baffled him. What should he do?

He remembered Grayvle's frequent admonition: "Indecision is the hallmark of failure."

He straightened and pulled back his leg for as mighty a kick as he could manage. Anywhere. Anywhere would stop the cadril, give him more time.

Too late. The cadril threw another knife. Horvöl, off balance, raised both arms to intercept, but so slow, so slow. The knife went in under his jaw. His kick went wild. He twisted and fell in a heap, spilling his lifeblood on the floor. As he lay there he thought, Grayvle set me up. He knew I'd come here and he wore me out first. He said he'd kill me, and he has.

A cadril could never do this on his own.

His face felt wet. Tears? No—blood from the floor. The cadril tugged at Horvöl's cloak, pulled it off. A better fit, he supposed, than the overlong vasik's cloak.

He must think I'm already dead.

Hands ran over his body, emptying pockets, searching. Horvöl's arms and legs would not move, but he considered growling. Scare the living daylights out of the bastard. He giggled at the thought but without motion, without sound, without breath. And, finally, he understood.

The cadril is right. I *am* already dead.

The cadril had taken his keys. Now he started up the stairs. Horvöl couldn't close his eyes. The cadril spiraled up the staircase, growing impossibly distant, miles, hundreds of miles away. After weeks, or months, the dungeon door opened to let in a furious blaze of light. Then it closed and the light went out.

A thousand years later the sound of the door's closing reached him, a big booming rumble that went on and on in the darkness, forever.

Kierkaven and Cranst found neither Pandir nor the Ascendant at the Ascendant's office.

"Where did they go?" Kierkaven asked.

"They left at different times." The assistant's face was closed, revealing only that he possessed information he wouldn't share with vasiks he didn't know.

"Listen, it's Pandir we want to find. Tell us where he went and we won't ask after the Ascendant."

The assistant considered. "You might try the Nest."

"The Nest?" Kierkaven glanced at Cranst, back at the assistant. "Are you sure?"

"No! I'm not. But it's a possibility." The assistant shrugged. "I don't know any more than that."

The pantry where Heldrick waited with Arrick should be safe until morning, but Heldrick didn't want to wait any longer. He'd only waited this long because, though he knew most quistrils paid their visits to the Nest right after dinner, he had little idea how long they stayed; and he didn't want to meet anyone else, going or coming. But he had to find Bess and Needa before he brought them out.

He touched Arrick on the shoulder. For a moment, in the darkness of the pantry where they hid, he thought the man slept, until he heard, "Anything I can do, let me know."

"Just wait here. I'll be back as soon as I can."

Two minutes later he traveled a passage that dead-ended into another corridor. A left turn there would bring him to the Nest in seconds, but he slowed, hearing footsteps approach in the cross corridor. Latecomers to the Nest?

To his shock the Ascendant passed by, a beefy youngling at his heels. Instinct kept Heldrick walking— the abrupt cessation of his footsteps would attract more attention than the footsteps themselves. But the moment the Ascendant and his companion were out of sight, he lightened his step and slowed. He stopped before entering the intersection.

He peeked around the corner. Halfway to the Nest the passage shifted left, and another corridor branched to the right. The shift almost blocked his view of the end of the corridor, where it turned a sharp left, opposite the Nest entrance on the right.

The door to the Nest opened. Heldrick pulled his head back and listened.

Casternack was, beneath his anxiety, pleasantly surprised. They'd reached the lounge without his once needing to prod them. At the door he set his bag down. "I'll take the baby now."

Bess leaned against the wall near the door while Needa began unwinding the wrap from the child.

"That's not necessary," Casternack told her.

"This wrap belongs to me," Needa snapped. Casternack chewed at his lip and then frowned. Needa had possessed no such wrap when he'd left. At least one of them had wandered around outside the infirmary, when he'd expressly forbidden it. He'd a mind to—

The hell with it. They were there when he arrived.

Casternack took the sedated baby and placed him in his canvas bag, beside the bottle. Then he pulled out his keys and unlocked the door. Needa stepped back and Casternack pulled the door open.

"Doctor." Needa's voice sounded taut. He turned to face her. "The child's name is Lantry. Tell them in the crèche. Will you?"

"It won't do any good—"

"Tell them!" Needa's eyes slid past him and then back. Good God, he thought as he twisted, I'm the prize fool of creation, holding the door open for that girl.

But Bess still leaned against the doorframe. She must have mistaken his expression, for she said, "Please don't be upset. We're not angry with you. I know you'd help if you could."

He took a deep breath, relaxed. Smiled. "That's right. Thank you for understanding."

He stepped out, pulled the door shut behind him and tugged the handle to make sure the door latched.

Then he saw the Ascendant and an elder youngling come to a halt twenty feet down the corridor. He froze.

The Ascendant cocked his head.

"I've never seen you with that bag before, doctor."

"I . . . I needed some supplies for my office," Casternack said, his mouth dry.

The Ascendant shook his head. "Not supplies. A baby."

Casternack swallowed, forced a laugh. "Do you think that I've a baby in here?" He shook the bag. "I'm afraid the one born earlier this evening was the last one today." He knew he protested too much, but he couldn't stop. "Besides, what would I do with a baby?"

The Ascendant shrugged. "You can explain that to me later. In the meantime let's see the bag."

The Ascendant's dark eyes transfixed Casternack. Without meaning to, Casternack took three slow steps toward the Ascendant.

The door of the Nest opened again.

When the leading edge of the door reached the jamb, Bess placed her hands flat against it; when the door stopped moving she leaned on it, hard.

"Not too hard, Bess," Needa begged; but Bess ignored her.

The door jiggled as the doctor tested it, but her weight kept it closed. The moment the jiggling stopped, she stood straight and checked the time. Twenty past eight, but her focus was on the second hand.

"Did it work, then?" Needa asked.

"I think so. I didn't hear the catch click." Bess had already moved to the sofa where she'd stashed her youngling's garb. She couldn't take time to put on more than her cloak, though she also tucked her pants inside the boots.

Needa urged her to hurry. "Lantry ain't crying. If you lose sight of them, how'll you know—?"

"That's the chance we take. If I don't allow Casternack enough lead time, he might see me when I start to follow."

"Well, you've waited plenty. Now go! Go!"

Bess didn't respond. She kept her eyes on the clock. She'd estimated that Casternack would take at least twenty seconds to reach the first turnoff in the longer corridor, the one straight ahead. Sixteen seconds had passed since he tested the door. If she didn't see him, she'd go left.

Bess pulled on the handle and the door opened. Casternack wasn't in sight. She reached high on the casing and pulled off the small square of boot leather that she'd stuck on with cobbler's glue while Needa distracted Casternack. She pulled another off at the height of her knees. The door would latch now. She wondered whether she'd ever remember the movie where she saw that trick.

She stepped out and started turning left before she saw Casternack, still within a few paces. The Ascendant and a youngling stood just beyond him. Her heart dropped like a stone into her stomach. The Ascendant flicked his gaze at her. She turned to go straight again, but too late.

"You!"

The word stopped her in her tracks.

"Come closer."

Bess turned to face him. She couldn't believe she'd been stupid enough to barge out of the Nest without checking the corridor.

"I said to come here."

She didn't see how politeness could help her at this point. "If you want me, you can come get me."

"Ha!" The Ascendant hobbled closer to Bess, ignoring the doctor. The youngling kept by his side.

"I should have suspected you'd be involved in this," the Ascendant said, "but you fooled me. You actually fooled me. I thought the near-quistril was the dangerous one." He shook his head. "Even now I might have believed you never escaped the Citadel, never made it further than this, except I see you've torn your cloak."

He reached into his own cloak and pulled out the strip of cloak Bess had left on the wall.

"Mastron Svent brought this to me within the last hour. We didn't know exactly what to make of it, till now."

To the youngling beside him he explained, "She said that she came to this universe through a conjunction, by accident. She said that she lost her way. And I believed her."

Bess said, "That's what happened."

"Then why did you come back? No, you lied and I believed you. I always know when someone lies to me, but you fooled me. —I don't suppose you wish to tell me how you disappeared from the dungeon?"

Perhaps she could outrun the Ascendant, but the youngling with him would nab her in a flash. Hopeless. Keep talking. "We walked out."

"Ah, of course. Now, why didn't I think of that? Yet, as I recall, those doors were locked."

"We unlocked them." She noticed the youngling's thumb and fingertips rubbing together. Itchy knife hand, probably. She concentrated on the Ascendant.

"You expect me to believe you had keys? And do you also possess a key to the Nest?"

"Well, no—"

"And yet I see you walk out of there also. Clearly you brought some means from your own world of defeating our locks."

Bess frowned. "No, of course that's not so."

The Ascendant's voice changed to a thoughtful murmur.

"Everything you say, every lie, rings true. You are too dangerous for words. You have already escaped from the dungeon once. I would be a fool to think that it would restrict you now."

He stared at Bess for one long moment, then said to the youngling:

"The risk is too great. Kill her. Now. Where she stands."

CHAPTER 34

BUT WHY ON EARTH, Heldrick wondered, would the doctor steal a baby from the crèche?

He heard someone else leave the Nest. The footsteps paused, then headed along the other branch of the passage.

"You!" —The Ascendant's voice, still speaking English. But what cadril besides the doctor could leave the Nest?

He couldn't be sure until she spoke: "If you want me, you can come get me." Gods! No mistaking that.

He stepped out of his boots and pulled his knife from its sheath but kept it under his cloak. Then he moved closer, hidden from view by the zigzag in the corridor. The conversation between Bess and the Ascendant seemed headed in an ominous direction.

He reached the intersection as a senoral arrived from the right-hand passage. Heldrick recognized Durnstaff at the same time that the senoral grabbed him by the arm, hissing: "You!"

From further up the corridor, he heard the Ascendant say, "Kill her."

Heldrick switched the knife to his free left hand, but Durnstaff released Heldrick's arm and grabbed Heldrick's left hand with both of his own. He tried to smash it hard into the wall but merely succeeded in barking Heldrick's knuckles.

And now Heldrick's right arm was free. With extended fingers he punched Durnstaff's midriff.

Durnstaff gasped almost silently. He released Heldrick's left wrist with one hand and reached for his own knife.

Stupid. Heldrick grabbed his knife again with his right hand and plunged it into Durnstaff's biceps.

The senoral staggered back. His arm hung limp; his other hand grabbed at the wound. Heldrick kicked the senoral in the stomach, then chopped him on the back of the neck. Durnstaff crumpled and lay still.

But too late to help Bess. The youngling would already have buried his knife in her belly. Heldrick stepped into the other corridor, knowing what he would see.

And he saw it: Bess's body, anonymous in her youngling garb, motionless on the floor. The two quistrils still faced away from him, the Ascendant bending forward and the youngling crouched to examine the body. The Ascendant, not the youngling, wielded the bloodstained knife. The doctor backed away from them, clutching his bag. No one saw Heldrick.

Rage built within him; his legs carried him forward of their own volition; his hand clenched his knife. This Ascendant would die tonight. His mind admitted no other thought, blocked all consideration of consequences.

Nothing mattered anymore, except that the Ascendant die.

"Kill her. Now. Where she stands."

Bess watched the youngling pull his knife from its sheath. He stopped, then, and looked down the corridor behind him. Bess could see nothing past the bend in the passage.

The Ascendant kept his eyes on Bess but asked the youngling, "Why do you delay?"

"It sounds like—"

"I hear nothing. Kill her."

The youngling turned back to Bess and stared at her. She stared back, really looking at him for the first time. She'd seen him before.

"Faagh!" The Ascendant unsheathed his own knife, quickly for one so old. "I'll do it myself." He took a step toward Bess.

The youngling snatched the Ascendant's wrist and spun him round. He buried his knife to the hilt in the Ascendant's throat, point upward into the brain.

The Ascendant sagged. The youngling withdrew his knife and the blood flowed. The Ascendant collapsed in a heap, face down.

The youngling stared at the knife in his hand, almost as if in surprise. "Wrong again, Horvöl," he muttered.

Bess whispered, "Quick, give me your cloak." She bent down and yanked off the Ascendant's cloak before it absorbed much blood. "And put this on."

"But—"

"Do it."

He handed her his cloak and she crouched to spread the youngling's cloak over the Ascendant's body. They'd need to clean this up, but an impersonation might—just possibly—help them survive if anyone came along before they finished.

The youngling turned at a sound from behind, his bloody knife exposed—hardly the way to succeed at impersonation, Bess thought. Then she saw the quistril who rushed toward them, his knife drawn and a growl rising from his throat, already nearer than Casternack. The quistril's features were so contorted that she barely recognized him.

The youngling crouched, knife at the ready.

"Heldrick!" shouted Bess. She stood and pushed her hood off so that Heldrick could see her, then jumped on the youngling, entangling herself on his arm.

She saw Heldrick try to stop. But his stockinged feet slipped on the floor, and he crashed into them. All three tumbled to the floor.

Something cold and sharp bit into her side.

Pandir had talked to several acquaintances in the corridors but hadn't said a word about the Ascendant's impropriety. He couldn't figure out how, without sounding clumsy and obvious. Sometimes he wished he possessed the slickness of Lonnkärin. He could recognize slickness —it didn't fool him, as it did the Ascendant—but he couldn't imitate it.

He returned to his office, discouraged. His assistant asked, "Did the two vasiks find you at your meeting?"

"Meeting?"

"With the Ascendant."

"Oh. That. The old goat canceled it so he could pay a visit to the Nest." Pandir shook his head angrily, then realized that he'd told someone about the Ascendant's foolishness in precisely the right way.

But it wouldn't do to act overly upset. "Which two vasiks?"

"Kierkaven and Cranst."

Pandir smacked the desktop, and the assistant's eyes widened. "Why in blazes didn't they come yesterday? You say they went to find me at the Ascendant's office?"

The assistant nodded.

"Then they must consider their news important. If they come back here, tell them to wait. I'll return within the hour."

Pandir left his office and started toward the Ascendant's office, then reconsidered. The Ascendant's assistant could not know where Pandir had gone, thus could not have given Kierkaven and Cranst any suggestions. He would receive no help from that quarter.

Where might they have chosen to search for him? His private quarters? Most likely; it's where he usually was at this time. If that didn't work, he'd try *their* quarters. The rumormongering could wait a bit.

Heldrick lifted Bess in his arms. She still breathed, and no blood came from her mouth, but the stain on her shirt was spreading. He opened the door of the Nest and carried her in. Needa, pacing inside, stopped and gaped at him. Tears sprang to her eyes.

"Ah, no. Is she. . . ?"

"She's alive. I don't know more than that. But the doctor will arrive shortly."

Needa put her hand to her heart.

Heldrick set Bess down and pulled her cloak off. Then he pulled a sofa away from the wall by a foot or so.

The door opened and the youngling entered, carrying the protesting doctor over his shoulder, and the bag and a pair of boots in his other hand.

The doctor appeared more offended than anything, until he saw Heldrick. "You!"

"Yes. I have a new patient for you, to make up for the one I took earlier." He motioned to Bess and said, "She was stabbed in the side, but I don't think deeply enough to account for the unconsciousness."

The youngling set the bag on the floor, while the doctor moved to Bess. Needa ran to the bag and pulled out a tiny sleeping baby. Heldrick didn't even try to figure it out.

The youngling held out Heldrick's boots.

"Thought you might want these. Picked them up on the way back. I couldn't carry the senoral."

"Was he moving yet?"

The youngling raised his eyebrows. "He's alive?"

"Yes. I'd better bring him in here before he wanders off." Heldrick pulled on his boots and extended a hand toward Casternack. "Your key to the Nest, please."

Casternack paused. "I'm not supposed to—"

"Don't be foolish."

Casternack pulled out his key ring, started removing a key.

Heldrick twitched the entire ring from Casternack's hands. "This one?"

The doctor nodded and Heldrick headed toward the door. "Come along," he said to the youngling. "You bring in the Ascendant while I get the senoral. Put his body behind that sofa. And take your own cloak back. You look ridiculous in that one." Too bad he hadn't noticed that sooner; he could have avoided the collision.

At least Bess would be all right—if they ever managed to get out of here. And if the conjunction hadn't been discovered by the quistrils. And if it hadn't collapsed.

He left the Nest and loped down the hall to Durnstaff, who now groaned softly. Heldrick lifted Durnstaff's head and cracked it down on the floor. The groaning stopped.

He hefted Durnstaff over his shoulder and rushed him back to the Nest.

"Take his cloak off," he told the youngling. When the cloak was off, he heaved Durnstaff over the sofa on top of the Ascendant's body. Then he pushed the sofa closer to the wall again and placed a chair at each end of the sofa to block the view.

He noticed Bess sitting up. "Bess, how are you?"

Her head turned but she couldn't seem to find him.

The doctor said, "I'd like to disinfect her side and tape it up, but my supplies are in the infirmary. Once I do that, it shouldn't bother her much; it only cut across the ribs. Also, she's swelling right here," and the doctor touched a spot behind Bess's ear. "She must have hit her head on the floor, or perhaps on a knife hilt, in the fall. Enough to daze her. That, coupled with blood loss and mild shock, kept her out till now. She'll regain alertness in a minute or two. You guys should put your knives away before you play tack-ball."

Heldrick drew a deep breath.

The youngling beside him asked, "Aren't you the vasik who was imprisoned with the girl—Bess, you called her?—in the dungeon?"

"That's me."

"You've . . . managed a promotion."

Heldrick shrugged. "I promoted myself. I believe that gives me authority to promote you, as well." He indicated Durnstaff's cloak. "Wear that in the Nest and your own cloak outside. What's your name?"

"Grayvle."

"We're in your debt. But I don't understand why you did this."

Grayvle glanced at Bess. "She deserved it." Then he shrugged. "Given a choice between Bess and the Ascendant, I picked Bess. I was actually on my way here anyway, to tell her that an acquaintance had seen her earlier and was about to report her to his duty master. But I encountered the Ascendant on the way, and he ordered me to accompany him. I couldn't believe it when he came here, too."

Hardly an explanation, Heldrick decided, but more would have to wait.

Bess gazed into Needa's face. "Needa?"

"Aye. You'll be right, soon enough."

"All right," Heldrick said to everyone. "We've little time. Needa, can you fetch a bucket—no, two buckets of water, and some rags?"

"I don't know where—"

"How about the infirmary? Doctor, do you keep buckets there?"

"Of course. But—"

"And a mild cleanser? Also some medicine or disinfectant with a strong odor?"

"Yes. I—"

"Good. Describe the locations to Grayvle. Also where he can find the supplies for Bess's side. Make your descriptions clear, or Grayvle will tear the infirmary apart. Are the cabinets in the infirmary locked? Show the necessary keys to Grayvle. Here, I'll keep the Nest key. Grayvle, you and Needa go together. Run if you can. Needa, you'll go faster if you leave the baby here; Bess can keep it on her lap. The doctor can account for its presence should anyone pass through."

While the doctor instructed Grayvle, Needa handed the baby to Bess. "Can you hold him all right?"

Bess nodded, though with a faint puzzled frown.

Needa reiterated to Heldrick, "Two buckets of water, rags, cleanser, doctor supplies for Bess, something that stinks."

"Right. Go to it."

Kierkaven knelt outside the Nest. The dark floor disguised the stain, but he couldn't mistake the odor of blood. He unsheathed his knife and scraped.

Starting to clot. Just a few minutes since it was spilled.

Cranst knelt also. "What could have happened?"

Kierkaven shook his head. "I don't like this. Go to the duty room and bring back three or four hefty fellows. I'll stay here and watch who comes out."

Bess's side hurt and her head ached. She reached up and touched the spot behind her ear.

Ouch.

"You'd better leave that alone."

She sought for the speaker; saw Casternack. What brought him back?

A tiny baby lay sleeping in her lap. "Did you come to take the baby?" she asked.

"Don't make me laugh."

Where had Needa gone? Bess turned her head slowly from one side to the other. No one except Heldrick, pacing.

She began to remember: the youngling who chased her to the dungeon, Needa and Corlene, the Ascendant dead in the hall, and another youngling—yes, the same one who'd almost seen her turn down the stressor—dumping the body behind the sofa.

"Heldrick. Someone saw me—"

"I know, Grayvle told me."

"Grayvle?"

"Your youngling friend."

"Oh. Is that his name? How did he find out?"

Heldrick shrugged. "Don't worry. We'll leave, or they'll capture us for other reasons, before anything comes of it."

"But why are you here?"

"Later. For now, rest. Soon, we leave. I want you in the best shape possible. The doctor will treat you when the supplies arrive."

Bess turned to Casternack. "Won't you get in trouble for that?"

He glowered.

"Why don't you come with us, then?" she asked.

He blinked. "Come . . . with—?"

"He can't come with us," Heldrick said. "That knock on the head must have affected you more than I thought."

"Of course he can. Couldn't you?"

Casternack swallowed.

"I know! You don't want to leave your daughter. Well, bring her along, too."

"Along where?" he said, his voice a croak.

"To our side of the conjunction." And to Heldrick, "He could help us. He'd know how much of that milk would keep the baby sedated."

"The *baby* is going with us?"

"Unless you can talk Needa out of it."

Heldrick put his fingers to his temples. "This is madness."

"No more so than coming here in the first place."

Heldrick glared. "I can't even tell which side of the argument you expect that statement to support."

Rapid footsteps sounded from the central passage, and Needa entered the lounge with her arms full. She dumped everything on a sofa. "All right, doctor, now fix Bess up."

Casternack and Heldrick both moved to the pile. "Which one's the stuff that smells?" Heldrick asked.

Needa pointed. "Grayvle says this."

Grayvle entered, carrying two buckets full of water.

"Ah," Heldrick said. "Set those down a moment. Let's rinse the blood out of these." He picked up two cloaks and handed one to Grayvle. That's right, Bess thought; Grayvle's cloak had soaked up some blood when she draped it over the Ascendant. But where had he obtained the senoral's cloak he wore now? She shook her head to clear it and instantly wished she hadn't.

Casternack approached her with two small bottles, some cotton, gauze and tape. "Raise your shirt on this side and I'll clean that cut."

"I'm watching you, doctor," Needa said.

Bess smiled. "You needn't worry about Casternack any more. He's coming with us."

"That's good enough," Heldrick said to the youngling. "Now, put this back on before you go out of the Nest. If someone comes by and questions you, send them in to talk to me."

Grayvle pulled off his senoral's cloak and held it out to Heldrick, then pulled it back. "Here. I forgot to tell you what I found in the pocket." He reached into the cloak and pulled out a key.

Heldrick took it and examined it, then pulled out the doctor's Nest key. "They match," he said. "He must have been on his way here, also." He handed the key back. "You keep this one. Needa, time to clean floors."

Needa patted Bess on the knee, then picked up the buckets. Grayvle had already retrieved the rags and brush. Heldrick unlocked the Nest door and they stepped out.

CHAPTER 35

GRAYVLE ALMOST DROPPED his supplies when he saw Kierkaven waiting outside the Nest.

Kierkaven looked almost as surprised. "You again! What's going on here?"

Kierkaven was one of the few quistrils that Grayvle couldn't possibly send in to talk to Heldrick. He quickly invented a vague story, about an argument between two novices, that lost Kierkaven's attention the moment Grayvle revealed that, yes, a mastron was already investigating, and no, it was not Pandir.

And yet Kierkaven remained, with no appearance of imminent departure, even when Needa had almost finished drying the floor. How could Grayvle get rid of him? If he saw Heldrick, he'd recognize him for sure.

"Um."

Kierkaven stopped pacing. "What?"

"Were you waiting for Pandir?"

"You've seen him?"

Grayvle nodded. "He left here with a senoral—"

"When did this happen?"

"Ten minutes ago. Just before they called me in to help with the cleanup. I overheard the senoral mention the Archive."

"The Archive!"

Grayvle immediately wished he'd picked some other location. Everyone knew Pandir never visited the Archive.

But Kierkaven seemed to accept it. "Why didn't you tell me this earlier?"

"You never said you were looking—"

"All right," he said as Needa dropped the last rags in the buckets and stood. "All right." He waved his hand. "Go on about your business."

As soon as Grayvle and Needa left the Nest with their rags and buckets, Heldrick said, "Now to hide the blood scent." Bess watched him open the bottle, sniff, and jerk his head back. "Gods! This should do." He dribbled some over the back of a sofa. A moment later the odor reached Bess, a combination of formaldehyde and rotting cabbage. Heldrick continued around the lounge, spilling lesser amounts of the substance in every corner.

He said, "If someone else walks through here now, we won't have to kill him, too."

As if on cue, another set of footsteps sounded in the hallway. A vasik stepped into the lounge. Heldrick turned to Casternack.

"How long until the odor dissipates, doctor?"

The vasik didn't wait to hear the answer. With wrinkled nose, he fairly flew through the lounge and out the door. Heldrick nodded in satisfaction.

Casternack finished with Bess's side. "Your shirt's still a mess."

"I'll change before we leave," Bess said. "What about you? Do you own any black cloaks?"

"Of course not."

"Heldrick, do you trust that youngling?"

"Grayvle? Why?"

Bess shrugged. "I don't know what to think of him. He, um, he talked to his knife after killing the Ascendant—called it 'Horrible,' I think."

"He seemed quite rational to me."

"Well, good. Because we need more quistril outfits. Do you think he could provide them?"

"We don't have time for that. The sooner we get you and Needa out of here—"

"And the doctor. And his daughter. And the baby."

"Yes, yes. And I suppose Grayvle will want to go also, if he has any sense. And Arrick's waiting for me downstairs. Wellen's the only one already outside the Citadel. Don't you see how impossible this is? We'll never get all those people over the wall."

"That's why we need the outfits. I guess you could pretend to escort Needa and Arrick and the doctor's daughter through the corridors, whatever they're wearing, but nobody'll let them through the gate unless they're dressed as quistrils."

"We can't use the gate either. The gatekeepers would insist that we identify ourselves. It won't be like last time."

"Maybe you could order them to let us through. Wouldn't your mastron's garb convince them?"

"Maybe, but they'd record the irregularity, and when they found the Ascendant's body and started checking gate traffic, they'd come after us. The stuff in this bottle is strong but volatile. It won't last long."

"Long enough for us."

"Hardly. They can track a large party easily. We might reach the conjunction before they even find the Ascendant, but the time differential would still allow them to catch us before we're up the basement steps."

"Oh." She hadn't considered that problem. "What can we do, then?"

The door to the Nest opened. Grayvle and Needa reentered. Heldrick began speaking to Grayvle in Vardic. That irritated Bess a bit, since they could both speak English perfectly well, but her head ached too much for her to bother complaining.

After a couple of minutes, Heldrick opened the door again to let Grayvle out. Then he turned to Needa. "One more job for you. Place these two buckets in the nearest room. But make certain no one occupies the room before you open the door."

To Bess, he said, "Here's the plan. We can't afford to let anyone see us escorting women from the Nest, so Grayvle will procure outfits, as you suggested. Once everyone is appropriately dressed, you, Needa, Arrick, and I go to the dungeon. Casternack and Grayvle go back to work as usual. We'll give the quistrils a day to search the Nest thoroughly, then we'll come back and hide here in the Nest for a week or so while they search the rest of the Citadel."

"A week!"

"By then they'll decide that whoever killed the Ascendant must have escaped the Citadel, and they'll stop searching. Grayvle can let me know when that happens, and he and I will lead the rest of you through the gate in small groups. Then we join together and head for the conjunction."

That plan had holes all through it. Men hiding in the Nest? Of course, quistrils were allowed, so with cloaks they might get away with it, as long as no one noticed that they were here day and night. And they couldn't eat with the women; someone would have to bring them their meals, which might also be noticed.

As for herself and Needa—well, other considerations aside, she did *not* want to spend a week in the Nest. Had Heldrick really not thought of the risk that entailed for women? Maybe he just didn't care. But in any case . . . "I don't think Needa or I could hide here. Bronli's already spotted me and knows Needa is with me."

"Who's Bronli?" Heldrick asked.

"*My* Bronli?" asked Casternack.

Bess nodded to Casternack. To Heldrick she said, "She's the doctor's assistant. She works with the quistrils, and—"

Heldrick frowned and cut her off with a wave. "No woman here would work with the quistrils."

"But she does."

"Bronli hates quistrils," Casternack said.

"Well, she'd already heard about me from that youngling who saw me in the hall—"

"Impossible," Heldrick said. "According to Grayvle he didn't report you until half an hour ago, at most. Forget about it. Right now, I'm more worried about keeping Durnstaff from waking up. Doctor, you must have something injectable in the infirmary that I could use for the purpose?"

Casternack nodded and offered to retrieve it, but Heldrick shook his head. "Grayvle says that Pandir might be somewhere in the Nest. He's the quistril most likely to recognize me. The less time I spend in this lounge, the better, so I'll get it."

Casternack gave directions, and Heldrick left.

In the quiet that followed Heldrick's departure, Bess's headache seemed to grow worse, probably because nothing was distracting her. Or maybe it was that vile smell.

Casternack began to walk back and forth like a caged animal. Bess could hardly blame him for that; her suggestion that he go with them had turned his world upside down.

He stopped abruptly. "I—when should I bring my daughter here?"

"Do you know where she is?"

"If she's not with some quistril, I do."

"Then go now, by all means. The sooner we collect everyone, the better."

Casternack took an obviously relieved breath. "I'll be back soon." He practically ran from the lounge, and Bess took the opportunity to change her ruined shirt for the youngling shirt she'd stashed away.

Soon another quistril came through the lounge. He ignored Bess and Needa but stopped short on seeing Lantry.

"We're holding him for the doctor," Needa explained. "He spilled a batch of medicine—smell it?—and he's gone looking for something to cover it up."

The quistril didn't stay to question the story, and Bess almost wished she could go with him. The fumes had begun to make her ill.

More minutes passed. What kept Heldrick? He should have returned by now.

Heldrick heard a solid thump and turned from the cabinets. The sound had come from the second of a line of three doors. He walked to the door and opened it to reveal an examining room. A trussed and gagged woman, her feet raised to kick again, lay on the floor amid dishes. Her eyes widened and she lowered her feet.

Interesting. "You must be Bronli?"

The woman nodded sullenly.

Heldrick crouched beside her and pried up a corner of the tape on her mouth. "Tighten your lips. Ready?"

He saw the muscles of her face tighten, and yanked the tape off. She gasped, and a reddish square appeared around her lips.

He said, "You were attempting to attract attention?"

"I heard you; I thought you must be the doctor." Bronli continued to watch him with ill-concealed dislike.

"Ah, I see. Unfortunately, Bess—you know Bess?"

"Very funny."

"I didn't know if you knew her name. She failed to tell me she'd immobilized you. I doubt she realizes you're still here."

"I hardly think she'd care."

"She bound you under a misapprehension. She thought you worked with the quistrils."

Bronli glared at Heldrick's cloak and hood. "Surely you jest."

"Rarely." Heldrick pulled out his knife and Bronli stiffened, eyes wide. Heldrick cut through the tape around her arms, then freed her hands and feet.

Bronli stared in astonishment at her cut bonds and then at Heldrick. "Pardon me for pointing this out, but your behavior is highly irregular. Overwork, perhaps?"

Heldrick considered. "There may be an element of that. Do you always speak this impertinently toward quistrils? I'd always heard that women in the Nest were supposed to be afraid of us."

"'Always heard'? You look a little old for this to be your first time here."

"Nevertheless. . . ." He shrugged and extended a hand.

"I don't believe it." She took his hand and he pulled her to her feet.

"That's your prerogative." He wondered whether Bronli was too suspicious of him to help. "I'm looking for a sedative," he said, and told her what Casternack had suggested he use. "Bess said you assisted Casternack. I expect you could find and prepare it faster than I. Are you willing?"

Bronli tilted her head. "I think you're serious." She hesitated. "Tell me why you're doing this."

"I haven't time. If you can accept that I'm on your side, not theirs, fine. Otherwise, go on your way. I'll manage."

Bronli began pulling pieces of tape off her clothes as she walked toward the cabinets. "Actually, I think I can find something better. Though I'm not sure why I should, except I guess I owe you for freeing me."

She went to the rows of medicines and selected one, then filled a hypodermic a measured distance. "Can you insert it in a vein?"

"I expect I could." Heldrick put out his hand. "Though the doctor probably won't demand that task of me."

But Bronli pulled the syringe out of reach.

"Why is Casternack helping you, if you're what you claim?"

"Bess and I have agreed to help him leave this place."

"What makes you think he wants to go?"

"We've invited him to bring his daughter."

Slowly Bronli stretched out her hand and let Heldrick take the hypo.

"That's interesting," she said, "considering he hasn't got any daughter."

Casternack fretted, watching the infirmary door from the end of a long corridor.

What kept Heldrick?

If they left the Nest using his key, he'd be implicated. He'd never explain it away. No one would listen. He needed his key back. And to get it he needed a weapon.

At last Heldrick left the infirmary and headed in the other direction. Casternack hurried toward the infirmary door.

He would find weapons there. Hypodermics and drugs.

Effective use would require proximity, but if they didn't expect anything he might pull it off. And they trusted him now. The lie he'd told Bess about his daughter had served perfectly, though he couldn't claim forethought. Bess's holier-than-thou attitude had provoked him into taking her down a notch, that was all.

He stumbled to a halt when the infirmary door opened again. A woman came out.

Bronli!

He stood frozen. What had she told Heldrick?

Bronli turned in the opposite direction without seeing him. Casternack recovered his composure. Bronli would have told Heldrick nothing. She hated quistrils even more than most of the women here did. She wouldn't have given Heldrick the time of day.

He reached the infirmary, entered his supply room and, as he reached into his pocket, knew defeat. He'd forgotten that Heldrick had taken his entire key ring. Many of the supplies weren't secured, but he kept the drugs and hypodermics—the things the women could use to hurt quistrils or themselves—under lock and key, in heavy steel cabinets.

Then he saw that Heldrick hadn't locked up, and breathed again.

Any number of poisons would kill the quistril, but most would take long enough that the quistril could kill him, in turn, before dying. Casternack decided on a nerve toxin sometimes used as a muscle relaxant. If he injected it near the spinal cord, paralysis of the skeletal muscles would occur instantly. With a large enough dose, lungs and then heart would fail. Killing Heldrick wasn't essential, but he didn't know what dose a quistril could handle and remain mobile. He would use the guaranteed lethal dose for an extra-large human.

It would take a few minutes to dissolve the crystals, and he didn't know how soon his absence might become suspicious. But what choice did he have?

He began the preparations.

Not at my quarters, Pandir thought, nor at their own. Where might they have gone? The Archive? Pandir couldn't abide the place, but Kierkaven went there often enough. Not likely tonight, though, Pandir thought, not if he's searching for me. Besides, it was clear across the Citadel. If he didn't find them there, he'd have wasted a lot of time.

Where might they expect to find him? Perhaps the combat courts. But if they checked there, they'd quickly determine his absence and leave. He couldn't wait around on the chance that they might yet come by.

In the Archive, on the other hand—now that he thought about it—Pandir might find someone who had seen them recently and could point him in the right direction.

Besides . . . it could provide an ideal opportunity to spread his rumors.

At last, to Bess's relief, Heldrick returned. "Where's Casternack?" he asked.

"He went to find his daughter."

Heldrick pulled a hypodermic from under his cloak. He pushed the chair from the end of the sofa and crouched down.

"I found Bronli tied up where you left her," he said.

"Oh! Still? Why didn't her friends—"

"I doubt she has the sort of friends you're imagining. I cut her loose. She told me that Casternack lied about having a daughter."

"That's ridiculous. He told me about her the first time we met. Why would he lie then?"

"I don't know. But Grayvle also told me that the quistrils consider Casternack fully loyal."

"But—why didn't you tell me that before?"

"You'd have given our suspicions away."

"I would not!"

He stood and replaced the chair. "Say what you like. My perception is that, irrespective of your other abilities, you don't know how to hide your anger."

Bess stamped her foot—then clamped her mouth shut. Yeah, maybe Heldrick was right . . . this time.

But her annoyance changed to sick fear as she realized what Heldrick's news meant. Casternack knew their plans. They couldn't go over the wall, they couldn't pass through the gate, and now they couldn't even hide out, unless they found him first. And how would they ever find him?

"You should have told me anyway," she said. "If I'd known, I never would have let him leave to search for his daughter."

"Oh? How would you have stopped him?"

Before she could think of a reply, Bronli entered the lounge. She gave Bess and Needa one glance, then said to Heldrick, "I just saw Casternack hanging around outside the infirmary when I left. I don't think he knows I saw him."

Heldrick stood motionless, whether in thought or surprise Bess couldn't tell. Then he said, "Right. Let's find out what he's up to and put a stop to it."

CHAPTER 36

CASTERNACK KNEW HE would have at most one opportunity, but a needle might bend, or a cylinder crack, or a plunger snap before that opportunity occurred. So he prepared three hypos and taped them to the inside of his cloak, two left and one right.

With misgivings, he left the needles unsheathed for instant availability. The needles wouldn't endanger him if he didn't trip.

He walked through the waiting room to the corridor doorway, closed his eyes and drew three deep breaths. He'd say that his daughter would arrive in a moment. If he relaxed and acted calm, they'd turn away in disinterest.

He must not appear nervous. He must not *be* nervous.

He opened his eyes and reached for the door handle.

But the handle slipped away the moment he touched it. The door opened and in front of him, side by side, stood Bronli and Heldrick.

He grabbed for a hypo but the quistril moved too fast. The long fingers snaked around his wrists and brought his hands smack together.

"See what he has in his cloak, Bronli."

Bronli opened the cloak and pulled off one of the taped syringes. "I wonder what this does," she mused, and put the tip up to Casternack's neck.

"No!" he said, cringing. Then, more softly, "It's a muscle relaxant."

"Like what you suggested I give the senoral to keep him asleep?" Heldrick asked.

"Well, no. Not quite like that." Only Bronli could have told Heldrick that. Casternack decided he'd misread that scenario pretty badly.

Bronli pressed the plunger so that a tiny bubble of fluid formed at the end of the needle. She sniffed. "Ah. This would have kept the senoral asleep, all right." She retrieved the second hypo. "Anything else in there, doc?"

"Nothing."

"Let's see." She reached out her free hand and started patting.

"Wait!" Cold sweat broke out on his forehead. "There's one on the other side."

Bronli removed that one and patted him down.

"That's all I can find," she told Heldrick.

Heldrick released Casternack's wrists and pointed across the room.

"Stand over there, doctor. Face the wall. Touch nothing."

Casternack crossed the room. He could hear Heldrick and Bronli whispering—planning something. Probably deciding the best way to dispose of him. He couldn't understand the words, but it didn't matter. He'd lost the initiative.

Bronli said, "All right, you can turn around." He did, and she beckoned him closer. "One question. Why did you let Needa keep the baby? I thought—when I believed

Bess was some kind of collaborator—that you and Bess arranged that to make me trust Bess—"

"More to make Bess trust me."

"Yes, I see that now. But it hardly justified the risk."

Casternack shrugged. If he'd known for sure that Bess shouldn't have been in the Nest, he would have braved interrupting any quistril and received honors for it . . . but he hadn't known. And if he'd waited until his appointment with the Ascendant to report her, he faced possible condemnation for knowing about her and doing nothing for a few hours. What if she'd escaped by then? Every course held risk.

"I left the baby as an anchor," he said. "Needa wouldn't abandon him, and I hoped Needa would keep Bess here too, long enough for me to check her status. But I never got the chance to check. And I never dreamed they'd consider taking the baby with them. What does it matter, anyway? Why do you care?"

Bronli nodded thoughtfully but said nothing.

"And now, doctor," said Heldrick, "It's time for us to go. I'm sorry, but we can't leave you here to tell what you know, nor can we safely take you with us. I'm afraid you've abandoned all claim to our sympathy. You understand, I'm sure."

He raised the hypodermic. "Bronli, how much of this stuff should we use?"

"Oh, one syringe ought to do. He prepared that hypo for you. But I wouldn't skimp. Give him the whole thing."

Seventy units. Casternack watched in despair.

"And where's the best place to inject?" Heldrick asked.

"Here," Bronli said. "Let me. It'll be a pleasure." She took the syringe and stepped up to Casternack. With her back to Heldrick, she tipped the needle, pressed the plunger to eliminate air bubbles . . . and continued, squirting the toxin onto Casternack's cloak.

Casternack watched in disbelief. Bronli emptied all but five units of the dose. Five units! It might fail to fully paralyze him, and in any case the paralysis could last for as little as ten or fifteen minutes. Though hours would pass before he could dance again.

Bronli! He couldn't believe it.

She gave him a broad wink in an otherwise deadpan expression. "Better turn around, doctor."

He did, making certain to keep Bronli between Heldrick's gaze and the damp spot on his cloak.

Bronli pulled down the back of his cloak and shirt collar and the needle bit into his upper back, right above the shoulder blades, near the spine. So whatever happened would happen—

—*Fast.*

In spite of himself, Casternack was unprepared. His face smashed into the floor so suddenly that he might have believed he'd been decapitated, except that his head didn't roll.

—But I'm still alive, you bastard. I'll get you yet.

Pandir stepped into the Archive already regretting the time spent en route. He made a quick survey of the central room: no one there that he knew well enough to talk to socially, nor anyone who would likely know the whereabouts of Kierkaven and Cranst. He could wander the stacks . . .

Oh, to hell with it. He didn't possess the knack of spreading rumors, and Kierkaven probably waited for him right now in his office. He turned to go but heard his name called out. To his astonishment, Kierkaven and Cranst themselves came out of the doorway to the stacks.

"I heard you'd come here," Kierkaven said, "but we'd about given up finding you."

"Heard? From whom?"

"A youngling you passed in the hall near the Nest. Name of Grayvle."

He'd heard the name. Supposed to be the most promising of the graduating form. But— "I haven't been near the Nest," he said, realizing as he spoke that he was near the Nest now. But surely Kierkaven meant closer than this.

No matter. A youngling had misrecognized another mastron as himself; so what?

"Where have you two rascals been?"

Kierkaven said, "I think we'd better speak in private."

Pandir nodded and led the way to a study room. He waited till Cranst closed the door. "Well?"

"We found a margin conjunction," Kierkaven said. "A large one."

Pandir swallowed his smile before it showed. "I'd hoped for no less. A message sent last night, as I requested, would have been appreciated."

"The conjunction is not what you expected. It's old. We spent about a minute on the other side, while a full day passed here."

Pandir narrowed his eyes. "That makes no sense."

"I believe it does." Kierkaven told their story, including his speculations about the Renegade.

"But we've seen no Renegade activity for years!"

"Exactly. I'd guess that years pass here for each day spent across the boundary."

Could it be? "What about the girl? She's definitely a marginal. The things she brought . . ." And hadn't she told the Ascendant that she came here by mistake? That would fit. "You left the conjunction unguarded?"

Kierkaven said, "It didn't seem a danger, in its present state. And with the marginals in the dungeon . . ." He shrugged. "It seemed more important to get back here with the information."

Of course. Kierkaven and Cranst were *there* but hadn't known to keep a lookout. Pandir made a fist in frustration. "The marginals escaped from the dungeon yesterday, while you were in limbo."

Cranst frowned. "Escaped from the dungeon? How?"

But Kierkaven straightened, seeing the implications. "We must return at once."

"If it's not already too late," replied Pandir, glumly. "They escaped more than a day ago."

"They couldn't have passed through while we were there."

Pandir drew a sharp breath. "By the gods, that's so! Is the passage large enough to roll boulders through?"

"A small explosion might do the trick more easily."

"Of course!" Pandir picked up a book from the room's small desk and tore out the flyleaf. Kierkaven winced, but in silence at least. Pandir wrote a note, stamped it with his chop and handed it to Kierkaven.

"Take this to the armory. Requisition a couple of men to go with you to the conjunction. Cranst, stay at the armory until they've readied the explosives, then lead them to the conjunction. While you wait, draw a map in case I need to follow before you return. Kierkaven, determine first of all if the marginals returned to the conjunction after you left. If so . . . hmm."

"They can't have crossed the boundary more than a few seconds ago, their time. We can catch them just the other side, if the conjunction still exists."

"Excellent! Bring them back alive, if possible. —I'm sure you can decide how to place the explosives, Menodral."

Kierkaven's eyes barely widened at the promotion, but he smiled. "Indeed I can. In two hours we'll have them, if not in our hands then at least trapped on this side."

Bess winced to see Heldrick uncap the bottle of atrocious-smelling stuff, even as he stepped into the lounge.

"Heldrick, must you? My head's swimming."

He raised a sardonic eyebrow. "Would you rather—"

"Oh, I know, I know. Go ahead. Did you find Casternack?"

He told her what they'd found in Casternack's cloak. "Obviously he intended to do some of us in. But he's been taken care of."

She bit her lip, knowing what "taken care of" had to mean, but she didn't see what other course Heldrick could have followed.

"Oh," he said, recapping the bottle, "Bronli's decided to come with us."

"Bronli! *You* asked her?"

"Well . . . I thought, why not? She can help keep the baby sedated. Now, I'm a bit behind schedule. If Grayvle should arrive before I return with Arrick, tell him that the doctor's been neutralized and that I'll return soon." He retrieved the senoral's cloak. "And if he wants this, let him know I've borrowed it for Arrick."

He used his key to let himself out of the Nest.

Needa said, "I'm glad Bronli's turned out all right. I hope she ain't mad at me."

Bess snorted. "She'll be too mad at me to bother thinking about you, if you want my opinion."

Not long after, a quistril walked into the lounge, this time from outside the Nest. He stopped, wrinkled his nose. "Smells like medicine in here."

"Yes." Bess repeated their story.

The quistril frowned at Needa, who sat holding the baby, then stepped over to Bess and lifted her chin with a finger.

"Young, aren't you?" A spark of cold understanding shot through Bess and left her too stunned, for a moment, to resist or protest. The lounge was for women who wanted to cooperate. Volunteers. Why hadn't Heldrick warned her?

Because he didn't know. Neither did Grayvle. Younglings were never allowed in the Nest. Casternack could have warned them, though.

Bronli entered the lounge carrying a cloth bag in one hand. She nodded curtly at Needa, then saw the quistril and Bess. Her eyebrows drew together.

The quistril looked up at Bronli and stared for a moment. "Tempting," he said. "But this one got here first."

"Where's Heldrick?" Bronli asked Bess.

"He should be back in a minute," Bess said. "I think—"

"He's not here now," said the quistril, "so he's lost his chance." He yanked Bess's hand and pulled her to her feet. Needa sat with her mouth open, beginning to understand.

Bronli set her bag down, put her hands on her hips. "She's practically a boy!"

The quistril glowered. "Don't insinuate anything."

"Oh, pooh! I meant—"

"I don't care what you meant. Just shut up."

"Why should I?"

The quistril paused and turned to look full at Bronli. "I've heard about you. You're the one who thinks you can say whatever you please, just because we're not supposed to injure the women."

Bronli lifted her chin. "What if I am?"

"I know ways to hurt you that will never show."

Bronli's mouth opened; this time nothing came out.

But the door opened, and Heldrick stepped in, followed by Arrick in the senoral's outfit. The quistril, glaring at Bronli, paid no attention until Heldrick, after a quick moment to take in the situation, said, "The girl is mine."

The quistril turned slowly until he saw the color of Heldrick's cloak, then he practically tossed Bess's hand back at her. He spoke in his own language to Heldrick and then hissed at Bess, "Why didn't you tell me you expected a mastron?"

Bess didn't answer. The quistril shrugged and left the Nest, anger and embarrassment striving for dominance on his features.

The moment the door shut Bess ran to give Heldrick a hug, while Needa hurried to Arrick and showed him the baby. Bess turned to Bronli.

"Thank you for trying to help me there. I'm sorry I tied you up, I—"

"Forget it." Bronli shrugged. "I'll forgive you anything if we make it out of here."

The door opened once more. Grayvle stepped in, wearing a rather incongruous backpack.

"I don't know who just left," he said, "but he sure didn't look happy."

CHAPTER 37

KIERKAVEN AND CRANST left, but Pandir remained sitting in the study room, tapping his fingertips together. Almost as soon as the other two had left, his elation had damped and he began to worry he'd done the wrong thing. Not that he knew anything else to do, but—

It didn't make sense. Things didn't hold together. The escaped marginals should have gone straight back to the conjunction. Why hadn't they arrived while Kierkaven and Cranst were there? What could they be up to? Could the boy who had crossed the conjunction have anything to do with it? Not likely; probably a local exploring the cave. He wished Kierkaven had brought him back—but Kierkaven had acted rightly. The two seconds the task might have required could have delayed their arrival at the Citadel by an hour.

He shook his head. No matter what the marginals were up to, Kierkaven was correct. In two hours they'd either be captured, or trapped on this side.

He finally rose and left the study room. His old form-mate Rüdnor entered the Archive at that moment and stalked toward a table where someone else had left a book. Rüdnor sat and roughly flipped pages.

Pandir walked over beside him. "Now, now. Don't tear the paper."

Rüdnor looked up. His eyes widened, clearing the furrows from his brow. "What are you doing here?"

"I could ask the same," Pandir said. "I don't remember you as the type to read just any book lying about."

"Nor I, you, as the type to read a book, period."

Pandir acknowledged the rejoinder. "But allow me to pull rank; tell me first. What brings you here?"

Rüdnor's face darkened. "I've suffered enough rank-pulling for one night. From one of your fellow mastrons, no less. You think I'm angry now, you should've seen me then."

"Really? Which mastron?"

"How should I know? You're the only mastron I'd recognize. Took the girl I'd picked out."

"Ah!" Pandir could scarcely believe his good fortune. "You came from the Nest?"

"Mm-hm. But I lost my taste for it after the mastron bullied me. 'The girl is mine,' he said, except in English. You'd think he'd pick on someone his own rank. Like you."

Pandir nodded impatiently. "You didn't see the Ascendant there?"

"Oh, sure. The fellow can't even *stand* straight."

"I'm serious. Skipped out on a meeting with me to go there."

Rüdnor lowered his eyebrows. "You mean this?"

"Certainly. I thought you might've run across him."

"Amazing." Rüdnor shook his head slowly. "Really amazing. That's almost funny. Wait'll I tell Würner." He squinted at Pandir. "Sure you're not tugging my cloak?"

Pandir forced his features back into their usual wooden scowl. "Absolutely."

"All right, all right. Too bad I didn't stay a bit longer." But at that Rüdnor frowned and changed the subject. "Say, whatever became of that prisoner? The one you invited me to watch you interrogate in the stressor? I've heard . . ." Rüdnor stopped, swallowed and stared at Pandir in disquiet.

Pandir realized he was letting his feelings show and again recomposed his features. "Why do you ask?" he asked, his voice tight.

"Nothing. Nothing. That mastron resembled him, brought him to mind. That's all. Really."

Pandir took a breath. "All right. I'm on edge, forget it." But now something bothered him, he didn't know quite why. "You say the mastron spoke in English?"

"That's right."

"Why?"

"Got me. You're the sharp one."

Rüdnor had always thought that about Pandir, which only proved to Pandir that Rüdnor must, in fact, be rather stupid. "Perhaps for the girl's benefit," he suggested, and drummed his fingers on the tabletop, vaguely dissatisfied. "Well. I must go. Business to attend to." He raised a hand and started off, but his feet slowed and he halted, not fifteen paces from Rüdnor. It struck him that no mastron bore a close resemblance to the near-quistril.

And the near-quistril had sometimes spoken English during the interrogation.

Could it be? Still in the Citadel?

He spun, shouted, "The girl, what did she look like?"
Heads turned from all over.

Rüdnor looked up in surprise. "Well . . . real young. Too young to be in there, almost. I thought—"

But Pandir stalked back to Rüdnor and pulled him to his feet, all thoughts of rumormongering flown from his head.

"Follow me," he said. "—And hurry!"

Grayvle pulled off his backpack, then his cloak, to reveal two pair of boots strapped to his back.

"I brought the boots for Needa and Arrick," he said.

"Boots!" Heldrick said. "Good thinking, I'd forgotten to mention them. Here, Needa, try these on."

Grayvle glanced at Bronli. "I didn't know about her."

"Don't worry, she's provided for. What's in the backpack?"

"I've six youngling outfits in the backpack, of varying sizes. No one need look too ill-tailored."

Heldrick pulled the garb from the pack. He selected the largest shirt and pants. "Arrick, put these on and change cloaks with Grayvle."

Bess selected an outfit for Needa and a new, untorn cloak for herself. They couldn't change in the lounge, though. There'd be no explaining it if a quistril came through. "Needa, show us to the room where you left the buckets. We can all change there."

Bronli brought her cloth bag, which turned out to contain a complete quistril outfit, including boots.

"How did you come by that?" Bess asked.

"Made it from scraps."

Taken from under the noses of the quistrils. And Bronli had no flashlight to enable after-hours thievery. "How long did it take you?"

"Years. I started the week after they brought me here."

"Boots are big," Needa said, looking down at her feet.

"Tell Heldrick," Bess said. "Let's get back."

Needa's boots clomped with each step on the way back. She didn't even need to say anything to Heldrick—he poked his frowning head into the corridor before they reached the lounge. When they got there he'd just finished tearing an unused shirt to shreds.

"Here, Needa. Wrap your feet. Bronli, your clothes fit well, but that cloak looks like patchwork. Better use this." He tossed her one and turned away to help Needa with the boots.

Bronli glared at Heldrick's back. Then she noticed Bess watching her and took a deep breath.

"The cloak took me longer than anything but the boots. But it's getting out that's important, not how it's done." She replaced her cloak.

Bess stuffed the rest of the outfits behind another sofa. "Whoever cleans this place in the morning is going to get quite a shock," she muttered.

"All ready?" Heldrick asked. "I'll spread this stuff one more time."

"I'll do it." Bess retrieved Needa's earlier makeshift garb and selected the sling. "Put this on, Heldrick, to hold the baby."

"*I?*"

"You're the biggest, you'll hide it best. And you're wearing the mastron's cloak. People will stare at you least. Put it on."

Heldrick glowered at Bess and Needa both, but unfastened his cloak. "Pure idiocy," he said.

Needa smiled.

Bess held her nose and spread the rest of the odoriferous substance. Enough remained for a double dose, and she used it all. Her stomach churned, but in moments they'd be out.

Needa arranged Lantry in Heldrick's sling, and Bronli placed the bottle of drugged milk alongside him.

"If he wakens, give him some of that."

"But not much," Needa said.

"No. A few swallows will put him out."

"All right, all right." Heldrick glanced around. "Are we ready?"

No one demurred.

Heldrick said, "The less time we spend in the corridors the better, and together we're too large a party to hurry without attracting attention. Grayvle, take Arrick and Needa. Follow the left corridor and stay on this floor as long as you can. I'll go down a floor with the others. Hoods up, everyone." He opened the door and they filed out.

Bess, alongside Bronli, followed Heldrick at a near trot down the corridor.

Grayvle led Arrick and Needa along the passage. They turned left at the first branch, and Grayvle nearly ran into a mastron and vasik who hurried by so fast they didn't notice Arrick and Needa's failure to salute, so fast they disappeared around the corner themselves before Grayvle recognized the mastron as Pandir.

Hurrying. To the Nest?

No one else walked the corridor. Grayvle picked up the pace and hissed: "Faster!"

The lounge was empty: an odor almost strong enough to make Pandir gag assaulted his nostrils.

"Gods!" he said to Rüdnor. "Hold that door." He blocked it open with an end table. "Wander around. See what you can find. I'll guard the exit and impress into service any of our people who pass by."

Pandir sat down to wait but stood again and walked to the door. The stench was horrid.

Three minutes passed. Either the odor faded somewhat or his nostrils became desensitized. From the middle passage he heard someone running heavily, not with the light tread of a quistril. He moved to the passage and saw Rüdnor approaching. The body of a man in Rüdnor's arms accounted for the heaviness of his step. The man wore a tan cloak.

Casternack!

A moment later Rüdnor arrived. He dropped the doctor's body on a sofa and struggled to regain his wind. Shamefully out of shape. He panted, "Found him crawling in the hallway on his belly like a worm."

"He's alive?"

"Yeah. Paralyzed. Tried to tell me something but I couldn't understand a word."

Pandir heard the doctor mumble, "Mmmahmmnnn-nammmmuh." He crouched by the sofa.

"Do you remember the girl you examined the other day? The marginal?"

"Aahhhh."

"Have you seen her tonight?"

"Aahhh! Aahhh!"

"Where?"

"Ehhh."

Pandir grimaced. "I'm not sure we profit by this."

"Thuffa! Thuffa!" Casternack's eyes protruded with effort.

"Thuffa?"

"*Thuffa!*"

Pandir looked around the lounge. He closed his eyes and tried to imagine the sounds that a semi-paralyzed mouth might convert to *thuffa*. "Thuffa, thofa, thiffa, thufa, suffa, sofa, siffa . . . sofa! Sofa?"

"Aahhh!"

Pandir frowned. "You're lying on a sofa."

"Nnhhh!"

"You saw the girl on a sofa?"

"Nnhhh. Aahhh. Nnhhh."

Pandir thought. "You did see the girl on a sofa, but that's not what you want to say."

"Aahhh."

"Did a quistril accompany her?"

"Aahhh. Thofa!"

Why did he keep harping about the sofa? They all *looked* normal. Maybe . . . Pandir rose from his crouch, stepped to the end of Casternack's sofa, and pulled it away from the wall. Behind it was a shapeless mass that looked, in the darkness, like a heap of rags. He reached his hand in.

"Great gods!" he muttered as he pulled out a suit of youngling garb. "Any of the women could . . . Rüdnor, look at this!" He reached again and pulled out more. Finally he heard Casternack grunting:

"Nnuhhh! Nnuhhh! Nnuhhh!"

"This isn't what you wanted us to see?"

"Nnuhhh."

"I don't think there's anything else—"

"Nnohhh! Uthah thofa." Casternack moved his arms spastically.

"A different sofa?"

"Ahthhh."

Pandir walked to another sofa and pulled it from the wall. Nothing. Behind the next he found a youngling's cloak, damp and with a strip torn off the bottom. He held it up and cocked an eyebrow.

"Nnoh. Uthah." Casternack waved weakly, meaninglessly.

Pandir moved on. The next sofa again hid nothing, but the last one—

The stench emanated most strongly from here.

He moved the chair that blocked the sofa's end, shifted that end of the sofa, and recognized the profile of a senoral, one whose name he should recall. Dunstaff? Dunsturf? He wore no cloak and a sleeve of his shirt was torn up past the elbow. Pandir could smell the blood now, even over the other scent.

Pandir grabbed the senoral under the arms and pulled. He met resistance, indicating that the senoral shared his tight quarters. He tugged harder.

The senoral came out, unconscious but, to Pandir's surprise, still alive. Pandir pulled him out of the way and turned back to the sofa. He grabbed a pair of boots, and the feet in them, and pulled.

Ye gods!

"Rüdnor, look at this."

Rüdnor did; his face went bloodless.

Pandir turned to Casternack. "Do you know when this happened?"

"Vivdy minth."

"Fifty minutes ago?"

"Yaahth." Casternack tried to sit up.

Pandir rubbed a hand across his forehead. "That means they must have left maybe half an hour before Kierkaven."

"Nohnohnoh."

"What? How would you know when Kierkaven left?"

"Den minth, vivdeen, did thiz. Me."

"They paralyzed you less than fifteen minutes ago?"
Casternack managed to sit up.

"Yahzz. Doog my gie."

"You imbecile! Why didn't you tell me that first?"

Pandir turned to go, but Casternack said, "Goan duh dunzhin. Waydle zursh uv nezdun, then gumbag ear. Avder a view daze, dried a leave ziddudel." Pandir stared, at a loss, until Rüdnor broke in:

"He says they're going to the dungeon. They'll wait till the search of the Nest is done, then come back here. After a few days, they'll try to leave the Citadel."

Pandir blinked at Rüdnor in surprise, then turned back to Casternack. "That's what you meant?"

"Yahss."

"They don't plan on leaving the Citadel tonight?"
Casternack shook his head.

"But how will they know when they can return to the Nest? How can they leave the dungeon? What will they eat? And where did they obtain these outfits?"

Casternack mumbled and Rüdnor translated. "One's a genuine youngling, name of Grayvle—"

"Grayvle! A traitor!"

"Yes." Rüdnor listened to Casternack. "He's who killed the Ascendant. Then there's a marginal named Heldrick, who wears mastron's garb—"

"That's who took your girl. The girl herself is the other marginal." Pandir recalled the senoral and two younglings he and Rüdnor had passed on the way in. So that's where the senoral's cloak went. They'd passed within an arm's length of him.

But a thrill of exaltation went through him. His quarry would never reach the conjunction before Kierkaven, even if they left this moment. And they didn't plan that. Instead, they'd put themselves in his power. He need only collect a few men to take them from the dungeon without incident.

Casternack spoke again and stood up, a bit unsteadily.

"Rüdnor, what's he say?"

"He wants to go with you."

"He can walk? You can walk?"

Casternack nodded.

"And you require someone to let you out of here. Come along, then." He glanced at Durnstaff, on the floor. Might as well leave him for now.

Casternack staggered at first but managed to keep up. At the Archive, they paused—though not for Casternack's sake. Pandir went in and ordered several men to come along with them. By the time they started on toward the dungeon, Casternack was walking almost normally.

At the dungeon door, Pandir took his knife in hand. One of the vasiks flipped the light switch as Pandir pushed open the door. The bulb cast its feeble illumination down the dungeon corridor. The door to one cell stood ajar.

Pandir started down the stairs. He kept his attention fixed on the open cell as he spiraled around, until Rüdnor touched his shoulder and pointed to the floor at the base of the stairs.

A youngling lay in a pool of blood, a knife in his throat. He wore no cloak.

"They must be here," Rüdnor whispered.

But Pandir shook his head. He didn't like this at all. "They had no need of more cloaks."

He hurried down, touched the blood. Already well-coagulated. The youngling's skin looked waxy, his lips and nails pale.

"This happened more than five or ten minutes ago. Two of you, stay and guard the stairs. The rest follow me." He headed along the corridor to the open cell.

CHAPTER 38

HELDRICK OPENED a doorway to the night.

Whoa, Bess thought. "Heldrick—how will going outside help us reach the dungeon faster?"

"We're not going to the dungeon," Heldrick answered.

"But—you said—"

"That story was for Casternack's benefit." He pushed Bess and Bronli ahead of him. Grayvle, Arrick and Needa already waited outside.

"I don't understand. How will we—?"

"Can't you wait for once?" Heldrick closed the door to the Citadel. "Just accept that we have a chance if we can exit the gate before they begin pursuit."

Grayvle said, "Pandir went by us at a run, soon after we separated, heading for the Nest."

"Damnation! He may find the Ascendant sooner than I'd anticipated. Or Casternack, even before he's recovered."

"Recovered?" Bess asked. "Casternack?"

Bronli said, "Heldrick suggested I give him just enough toxin to paralyze him for ten minutes or so."

"You mean you left him alive? Why?"

Heldrick frowned at her. "How could feeding him a false story help otherwise? His information should delay a search for us outside the Citadel, but it won't help if we're still here. Let's go."

Heldrick led them across the compound toward the stables. Bess kept beside him. She pulled her cloak tight against the chill breeze that blew through the dark compound. When they drew near the stables, Heldrick halted, turned to Grayvle, and spoke in Vardic.

Grayvle nodded and headed into the stable. Heldrick turned to the rest and spoke, still in Vardic. Bess watched, understanding nothing, silent. She supposed he instructed them in the details of some imaginary task.

But what did he actually plan? How did he expect to prevent the quistrils from tracking them?

Grayvle led two horses from the stables. Bess doubted that he could have saddled them both himself in that time; the stable hands must have done the work. That would speed things up. Heldrick took the horses and passed the reins to Arrick.

"But," Needa whispered, "I don't know how to ride a—"

Heldrick spun and clapped a hand over Needa's mouth. He twisted to look over his shoulder. No one came running from the stables to investigate the sound of spoken English. Heldrick removed his hand and nodded to Grayvle, who went back for the next two horses.

But then a dark shape detached itself from the shadows alongside the stable and began to walk toward them. In the dim light, Bess couldn't distinguish the quistril's rank. She saw Heldrick reach under his cloak for his knife. The quistril stopped a few paces away.

For a moment no one moved. Then the quistril spoke. "Ma?"

The cadril and two quistrils that Pandir found in the cell had died at about the same time as the youngling, he decided: between thirty minutes and two hours ago.

The marginals, and Grayvle the traitor, must have found these bodies and decided not to hide in the dungeon after all. But where did they go?

And who had murdered the quistrils?

"There must have been more than the three of them," he muttered.

"Six," said Casternack thickly.

Pandir turned on him, lifted him by his shirtfront with one hand and slung him against the rock wall. *"Why didn't you tell me?"*

Casternack's mouth opened and closed, slowly, like a blind eye winking in the darkness. At last he managed, "You never asked. Thought you knew."

Pandir smashed the doctor another time against the wall, then released him. Casternack slid to the ground.

Pitiful. "Stand up."

Casternack struggled to his feet.

"Tell me about the other three."

Casternack swallowed. "Two cadrils, a fellow and his wife." Pandir listened with half an ear while Casternack gave him the details on the couple. "And Bronli, too."

"Who?"

"My assistant. They don't know that she works for us—"

"Don't be an ass. None of the women work for us."

"But she's the one who emptied most of the nerve toxin before injecting me. Heldrick planned to give me a fatal dose."

"Perhaps she's formed a romantic attachment to you."

"Impossible."

Pandir appraised the doctor. "You may be right. Though I've heard of stranger things. Rüdnor, let's go. —No," he said to Casternack. "You stay here."

"But—"

"Did you think you'd go without punishment for giving up your Nest key?"

"But they paralyzed me!"

"So? A night spent in the dungeon with these—" he waved toward the bodies "—will remind you that extenuating circumstances don't negate responsibility."

"But—"

Pandir stepped out after Rüdnor and closed the door on the doctor. Through the grate Casternack shouted, "They took the senoral's key too! It wasn't just me."

"Really? Interesting." He would have to check on that senoral, but not now. Marginals, murderers and traitors . . . who knew where they might have gone? Yet if the worst happened and the marginals managed to depart the Citadel, they'd still find their conjunction exploded by Kierkaven.

But that juncture should never be reached. Soon every quistril in the Citadel would be on the lookout for the marginals. The Ascendant, with his subtle plans and desire for secrecy, had chosen the fool's course. He, Pandir, wouldn't make that mistake.

"Rüdnor, go to the gate. Run all the way. Tell them to watch for Grayvle, if they know him, and in any case not to allow any younglings through the gate without positive identification. They should especially scrutinize parties of six. And they should stop any senoral they don't recognize. Tell them that the order comes from me, and that in a short time I'll arrive myself. Clear?"

"Yes."

"Then go. I'll initiate a search of the Citadel. They'll not escape us."

Enfarad watched Corck pace within the confines of the gatekeep and wondered whether he, himself, would remain as solicitous of his own protégé as Corck had of him, these last three years.

"It took an entire day to move through channels and start some action when I brought them the key and artifact," Corck said. "Who knows how long they'll spend this time? Especially since the scrap of material had no unusual feature other than its location atop the wall."

"You're suggesting that, after escaping, the marginals came *back?*" Enfarad asked. "And that, instead of returning through the gate they came in over the wall? Even though they had cloaks and coming in through the gate should have been easy?"

"I know, it sounds crazy. It makes *them* sound crazy. But if they knew that gate security would be tightened— as it has—then coming over the wall starts to make sense. Coming back at all is still crazy, but how else would a piece of cloak have found its way to the top of the wall?" Corck shook his head. "I doubt they can scale the wall from the inside, though. If they decide to leave again, and they don't have any confederates outside to throw them a rope, they'll almost have to use the gate and trust that none of you have seen them before—"

"Which we haven't. Still, the new regulations—"

"But they won't know about those, not for sure. I remembered you had gate duty and thought I'd warn you."

Enfarad heard footsteps on the stairs just before Corck said, "Who's that?" He opened the door to a vasik who stood a moment, panting, before managing to say, "Message from Pandir."

Needa gasped and pushed past Heldrick to hug Wellen.

Heldrick swore, sheathed his knife, and stepped forward to separate the two. "You'll kill us all," he muttered to them.

Grayvle brought two more horses. Heldrick spoke a few Vardic words and gestured at Wellen. Grayvle turned to Wellen, then rubbed his nose, shook his head, and returned to the stables.

Heldrick indicated that they should mount. Needa turned frightened eyes toward Bess. Bess could think of nothing to do, except to help Needa get her foot in the stirrup. Perhaps Needa's joy at Wellen's unforeseen arrival would dampen her fear of riding the horse. It sure had Bess in a tizzy.

Arrick and Wellen managed to mount on their own, and Bronli did so without clumsiness. Grayvle returned with the last three horses. He, Heldrick, and Bess mounted. Heldrick took the reins to Needa's horse. Grayvle took the reins to Arrick's, and so Bess took Wellen's. Bronli seemed able to manage on her own. Perhaps the quistrils permitted the town people to ride horses.

They progressed at a walk for a hundred yards, then Heldrick stopped and, for the benefit of Arrick's family, whispered quick instructions for directing the horses.

"We'll ride fast for only a short distance. Grayvle, Bess, and I will stay on the outside. If you simply hold the reins loosely, your horses will follow our lead. All right? Let's go."

In moments the entire group raced at a gallop, heading for the gate.

"Your slide, Enfarad," one of the others said, as Enfarad closed the door behind Rüdnor. But he was no longer in the mood for three-handed slipshuffle and left his tiles on the table.

"What's Grayvle tangled himself up with?" Corck asked.

Enfarad shook his head. "It must be some mistake." He walked back and forth several times and peered twice out the spyhole. Then he turned, listening. The others pricked up their ears and one said:

"Someone's in a hurry."

Enfarad stepped to the small platform over the inner courtyard. Seven horses and their riders came into sight. Enfarad counted five younglings, a senoral and a mastron. He hoped the mastron was Pandir. He didn't enjoy this type of responsibility. At least he didn't face a group of six, with Grayvle in the lead.

The horses drew up. "Quick!" the mastron shouted. "Six prisoners over the stockade wall!"

Six.

And from inside the gatekeep, Corck muttered, "Over the wall again!"

One of the others began to turn the windlass that pulled the massive gate open.

"Wait," Enfarad said; then, "Forgive us, but the new rules demand that we identify everyone passing out the gate. If you'd—"

"Don't act the fool, Enfarad," Corck said behind him. "Seconds count!"

And below, the mastron flipped back his hood. He glared. "The prisoners run the strip this moment, and you want our names?"

With a jolt, Enfarad recognized the ill-tempered mastron who'd come through the gate earlier in the evening.

"Lonnkärin," he said.

"Open the gate!"

Enfarad waved his hand and the other two proceeded. What did they expect? First they made the rules, and then they asked you to break them. At least he recognized the mastron. He turned and started back into the gate station, but Corck stopped him and squeezed onto the platform with him.

"Where's Lonnkärin?" he whispered. "I've heard he's to become the next Ascendant."

The gate creaked open. Before Enfarad had a chance to point out the mastron, the senoral glanced up at him, then hurriedly looked away. Enfarad tightened his fingers on Corck's arm.

"Grayvle!" he hissed.

"What! Where? Are you sure?"

"No—but . . ."

The horsemen shook their reins and galloped out the gate. Corck pushed into the gatekeep ahead of

Enfarad and looked through the spyhole. He spun and headed for the door.

"On your lives," he said to the other two, "keep the gate open until we've a party after them!" He clattered down the steps.

Enfarad rushed to the spyhole. The group of horsemen ignored the strip, where anyone who'd just gone over the wall would be, and galloped full speed down the road.

"Call the alarm!" he said to the other two; and to himself, "Damn!"

The other mastrons Pandir had called to his office now listened intently, despite their initial doubt.

"Do you see? The Ascendant joined forces with the near-quistril from the start. Once I understood that, all the pieces fell into place. The original 'escape' never occurred. You notice that Ollagh never received so much as a reprimand."

Ollagh, right arm in a sling, shot to his feet. He trembled with anger. "Do you accuse me of treason, then? I'll have you know—"

"Not treason, no. Incompetence. The Ascendant knew that you'd be too slow and careless to stop the marginals at the gate—if it was them. But either they never left, or they returned later. In any case, they hid for a time within the Citadel: the girl in the Nest and the near-quistril in the dungeon. The Ascendant went to the Nest tonight, to meet with his confederates. They suffered a falling out, with the Ascendant landing the hardest. When Durnstaff stumbled upon the incident, the Ascendant's former allies drugged him and left him with the Ascendant's body as a possible scapegoat."

Several mastrons remained dubious. "I wish Lonnkärin would return," said one. Pandir smiled; he'd waited until that very remark to serve his last bombshell.

"Lonnkärin may have been involved also. You'll recall that the Ascendant placed him in charge of recovering the prisoners. And, earlier this evening, I learned that the Ascendant gave his assistant instructions to send someone pretending to be Lonnkärin—the near-quistril, obviously—to the conference room. Is it any wonder a promising student like Grayvle succumbed to corruption, influenced by two such powerful men?"

By now everyone but Ollagh was nodding. Pandir felt pleased with his reasoning, especially since he knew reasoning was not his greatest strength.

Rüdnor, wheezing and gasping, burst into Pandir's office.

"Gone!" he said; then gasped, round-eyed, at the assemblage of power in the room. "I'm sorry, I didn't know—"

"Forget that. What are you talking about?"

Rüdnor explained. He had already delivered Pandir's message and left the gatekeep when seven riders galloped past. Suspicious, he went back, arriving moments after the group rode off.

"We know it was them. Enfarad, the gatekeeper, recognized Grayvle as they rode out. Corck was there as well; he organized a pursuit party instantly."

All the mastrons had bounded to their feet, but Pandir snapped, "Sit down!" The marginals should never have slipped past the gate. Either Rüdnor or the gatekeeper had failed him, and when he found out who, that person would pay. But for now he must maintain the appearance of utter control.

"It doesn't matter," he said to the group. "We know where they're headed." He turned to Rüdnor.

"Didn't you tell them to detain Grayvle and anyone with him?"

"Enfarad says he didn't identify Grayvle soon enough. The mastron with them claimed Lonnkärin's identity and had already ordered him to open the gate." The other mastrons murmured at this unlooked for support of Pandir's theory, but Pandir hid his smile with a scowl.

"Claimed! He broke protocol on a claim? I'll turn his hide into a pair of boots."

"Actually," Rüdnor said, "Enfarad says he *recognized* Lonnkärin."

"Recog—" Pandir stopped. "You say the party numbered seven?"

"Yes."

"By thunder!" Pandir's fist smashed down on his desktop. "It was him. Lonnkärin himself. I'll bet you anything that *he* killed the quistrils in the dungeon and the others didn't find out until they arrived." The others broke into a confused gabble, clearly on his side now. Yet as soon as he'd spoken, Pandir knew it couldn't have happened as he'd said.

He and Rüdnor had left the Nest five or six minutes after the marginals. But in order for the marginals to reach the dungeon, meet Lonnkärin and learn of the killings, then travel back across the entire Citadel, on to the stables, ask for seven horses and ride to the gate— they'd have lost double that time at least. Rüdnor had beaten them to the gate, but barely.

Without doubt, they'd headed straight to the stables.

So Casternack had lied about their plans. And what about the paralysis? Did Casternack feign the condition to keep Pandir asking questions while the marginals escaped? And to explain, too, how the marginals had obtained Casternack's key?

Yes. An economical lie, serving two functions. Treason, again.

Pandir lacked proof. But who required proof? He would recruit another doctor altogether and move Casternack to the work crew.

In the meantime, Enfarad the gatekeeper could testify that Lonnkärin had participated in the Ascendant's treasonous machinations. With the Ascendant dead and Lonnkärin a proven traitor, Pandir's rise to the position of Ascendant was assured. The Citadel would receive some much-needed tightening up.

But right now the marginals and traitors rode loose. Corck's group would never catch them before they reached the conjunction.

"Rüdnor, go to the armory. If you find Cranst still there, tell him that it is essential—no, vital, I'm sure he'll understand how the distinction applies to him—that the explosives arrive at the conjunction before the marginals. Tell him that the marginals head there this moment, accompanied by Lonnkärin the mastron, Grayvle the youngling, and three cadrils."

Rüdnor hurried off, and Pandir smiled at the other mastrons. "While the marginals and their friends meander about in the dark, hiding their trail from Corck and his crew, the explosives will arrow straight for the conjunction. If by some freak of luck the marginals reach the conjunction first, they'll still find it already guarded by Kierkaven, one of my menodrals.

"We have them boxed in."

CHAPTER 39

BESS AND GRAYVLE followed Heldrick's lead and directed their horses off the road, into the woods. The other horses stayed with them.

Heldrick reined in and listened for a moment before nodding. "Less trouble losing them than last time."

"But we're such a large group," Bess protested. "I know we didn't go as fast as yesterday."

"They took longer to start after us. The head start gave us a big advantage, and the darkness helped more. The moment I knew our distance put us out of earshot, my worries ended. Though of course we didn't stop right away, even so." He unclasped his cloak. "Is everyone all right?" He pulled the sling over his head. "Needa, you can carry this now."

"What's that?" Wellen asked.

"Lantry," Needa said. "Your nephew. Born today."

Wellen sat silent, dumbfounded; then said, "Corlene? Is Corlene—" He searched wildly in the dark.

Needa placed her hand on Wellen's. "No. Died giving birth." She sighed. "Free, now."

Wellen said nothing for a moment. "But not free like us, eh?"

Bess doubted that they were free themselves. The trail they'd left would become obvious with daylight, or earlier. How brightly would the moon shine tonight?

"Can't they still track us, Heldrick?"

"Certainly. But the moon will rise late and give little light. Tracking us before daylight will prove difficult. We can obscure our trail before then, despite our numbers." He shrugged. "You'll remember Casternack was present when I told you the other story. I think we could reach the conjunction in an hour."

He rubbed his nose, thinking. "We needn't obliterate the trail entirely, you understand. If they take a day to find the conjunction, that'll give us a full minute to exit the house. They may choose to follow us out, but if we're no longer in sight they won't go far. It's not easy to track someone on paved roads and sidewalks. If nothing stops them sooner, I expect they'll give up at the sight of their first car."

He reclasped his cloak. "Let's go."

Cranst stared at the gatekeeper in disbelief. "You *what?*"

"I'm sorry." The gatekeeper wiped his brow, uncomfortable but immovable. "Neither I, nor my companions, recognize you, or yours. If you wish to leave the Citadel, you must find someone known to at least one of us who will vouch for your identities. Until then, I will not open the gate."

"You . . . you—" Cranst couldn't believe this. If the marginals reached the conjunction before he did, Pandir would have his head, and all his other parts for that matter.

He swallowed. "Let me explain one more time. I am on an urgent mission. Time is of the essence. Pandir himself has placed the highest priority on this. If you fail to let us through, he will see that you regret it."

The gatekeeper sagged. Cranst had a moment of hope. Maybe the dimwit understood.

But the youngling shook his head. "I regret it already," he said. "But my instructions come from Pandir also. The gate stays closed. No one else will pass through the gate without positive identification."

Cranst had half a mind to barge into the gatekeep and slaughter the three younglings on duty. Pandir would support him, if it came to any sort of inquest. Unless, of course, the younglings had indeed received their orders from Pandir. Hell and damnation!

Wait a minute. What had the gatekeeper said? "No one else will pass through. . . ."

Else.

"You fool! You let the marginals out. And now you're keeping us in? They're the ones we're after!"

The gatekeeper sighed. "I've heard that one before. I wish I hadn't. The gate stays closed."

Kierkaven, satisfied that no one had come to the conjunction since he and Cranst left it, paused. He moved his torch toward the reflective interface; touched it; pushed into it. The interface deformed and his torch began to smoke, but when he pulled the torch away the mirrored surface remained bright. He placed his hand on the spot and felt no heat. Amazing. He'd learned about this but had never seen another failing conjunction anywhere near this size.

He pressed his hand into the interface, against the resistance of the sluggish, time-slowed atmosphere on the other side. He kept his hand in position, and the pressure faded as the air moved out of the way. The interface oozed to fill the space between his fingers. He snatched his hand back, and for the briefest instant could see his fingerprints etched in the surface; after a few seconds, even the outline of his hand faded, leaving his reflection clear and bright.

How long would he need to stand in one place before the boy on the other side could see him? The interface reflected so perfectly, he'd learned long ago, because the photons piled up on themselves and interfered with their own wave functions. Of course, nobody understood what that even meant, but they still taught it to the younglings, and maybe one day someone would find the answer in the archives. In any case, the effect was that the time differential kept all but a tiny fraction of light from crossing the conjunction in that direction—and a good thing for the boy, or the light from Kierkaven's torch, turned into a tiny sun by the time compression, would incinerate him.

Who was the boy? What lay across the conjunction, besides that one room? No one would ever find out by gazing at the interface. Light traveled this way without hindrance, but the time differential dimmed it to invisibility. Kierkaven squelched an almost irresistible urge to push through and snatch the boy out; but in the few seconds that would take, hours would pass here. Cranst could arrive, and the armorers could place and explode the charges, before he returned.

So he would have to be satisfied by having been through the conjunction already. He would wait here. But he wished Cranst would hurry. He had an uneasy feeling; he didn't know why.

He wouldn't relax until he'd destroyed this conjunction.

"After I found my way out of the Citadel," Wellen said, "I hid out behind the stables. I figured you'd want horses before you left, and I hoped I'd see you on your way out. But I couldn't see much in the dark. Ma's voice gave you away."

Good thing nobody else heard her, though, Bess thought.

Heldrick had led them into a stream some time back. Now he said, "Everybody off your horses. Bess, you know the routine."

"But Heldrick, how will we reach the conjunction as soon as you said if we walk all the way?"

"I didn't say we would reach it that soon; I said we *could*. That estimate gave us no leeway. If we only have a minute to get out of the house and someone trips and hurts themselves, they could be caught. The worst thing we can do is to hurry to the conjunction. I would like our trackers to spend at least a couple of days getting to the conjunction, and for that we need to hide our trail more thoroughly. Anyway, you'll notice that recently we've only been traveling at walking speed. At this point, the horses are just making us easier to track."

Bess dismounted. Heldrick was right. But impatience danced between her shoulder blades like an itch she couldn't reach. This close, she wanted to gallop straight to the conjunction and back home. No detours, no delays.

Besides, she had an uneasy feeling; she didn't know why.

Enfarad hadn't thought he could feel any worse.

He hadn't dared to step out on the inner platform and face the derision of the men remaining, once the vasik had gone off to find someone to vouch for them. But at the sound of more horses approaching, he had to.

And at the sight of the lead horseman, he almost lost his supper.

Pandir, himself. The other, of course, was the vasik who wanted to leave.

Enfarad gripped the rail. Suicide was an option. At least, if he didn't wait until they stripped him of his weapons.

Pandir pulled his horse to a stop and looked up at him. "Do you recognize me?"

"Yes, sir!"

"Who am I?"

"Uh . . . you're Pandir. The—the mastron."

"Are you sure?"

Enfarad was afraid he might faint and pitch over the railing. He squeezed the rail tighter. "I'm sure."

"What? Speak up!"

"I'm sure!"

"And you recognize none of these other men?"

"Yes. I mean, that's right."

"You're sure?"

Enfarad couldn't believe this. "I'm. . . ." He cleared his throat. "I'm sure."

"Good. Will you accept my word that these men are who they say?"

"Of course, I—"

"Open the gate, then."

Enfarad didn't dare let go of the rail. He turned his head to give the order, but the others had already started. He turned back.

Pandir watched him. The others rode out the gate. The gate closed.

Pandir watched him.

Enfarad couldn't have moved if his life depended on it.

At last Pandir said, "You're Enfarad?"

He nodded, his knees trembling. Pandir already knew his name!

"I understand that you saw Lonnkärin leave earlier? You recognized him?"

"Um. That's right."

"You're sure?" Pandir leaned forward. His expression hardened, and his posture turned threatening. Even his voice changed. "Absolutely sure?"

Enfarad swallowed. "I'm sure. He came in shortly after the dinner hour and left about forty-five minutes ago. I'm positive."

Slowly, Pandir smiled. Enfarad had never seen *that* before.

"That's good," Pandir said. "I'll require your presence tomorrow. Be ready." He turned his horse and called over his shoulder, "The marginals are gone. Consider the new gate protocols canceled henceforth."

Behind Enfarad, one of his mates said, "What was that all about?"

For a long moment Enfarad didn't answer. At last he said, "I'm . . . *not* sure." He began the painful task of uncurling his fingers from the rail and hoped the delay he'd caused would allow Grayvle to escape.

"I think I hear them," Kierkaven's companion said.

Kierkaven stopped pacing and cocked his head, listening intently.

The other grunted. "A bit on edge, aren't you?"

"Shut up." Kierkaven's anger at Cranst's tardiness had turned to worry and then distress. What if the marginals had companions in the woods? What if they'd waylaid Cranst's party and taken the explosives? They could be approaching now, with only himself and one other quistril to stop them. What if. . . ?

He heard the horses approaching and drew his knife. "Arm yourself."

"Aw, c'mon, Kierkaven—"

"Do it! They should have arrived half an hour ago. We don't know who this is."

Grumbling, the other drew his own knife.

The riders pulled into view and rode up to the crevice, Cranst in the lead. Kierkaven thrust his knife back. "What the blazes took you so long?"

"You won't believe me," Cranst said. "They wouldn't let us out the gate. They made me fetch Pandir first." He shook his head. "Strangest thing is, Pandir didn't even sound angry."

"Okay, okay, you can tell me the rest later. Right now, I want these explosives placed and set off. I don't know why, but I'm worried."

"I don't blame you. The marginals came back to the Citadel."

"What?"

"And left again. That's why they gave us such a hard time at the gate."

Kierkaven let his jaw hang for only a moment before snapping it shut. "Who's in charge from the armory?"

"Naidro." Cranst pointed.

Kierkaven walked over to the man. "Naidro—I want the conjunction destroyed but not buried. Can you do that? I want to be able to clear enough rubble away afterward to verify the conjunction's closing." If the entire outcropping collapsed, it wouldn't be the end of the world. But Pandir would doubtlessly send a team of men to clear the rubble and make sure a conjunction wasn't still hiding in there somewhere—and he wouldn't be happy about having to do that.

Naidro dismounted. "You'd better show me the formation."

Kierkaven picked up a fist-sized rock and raked it horizontally above the top edge of the conjunction, leaving a long pale scar on the cave wall. Then he stepped on a small outcropping, so that he could reach higher, and drew another line, shorter, a hand's length above. He reached still higher and drew one more, shorter yet.

"That should do," he said, taking the torch. "Set the timer."

Naidro said, "Drop the torch over there. If you try to bring it out, you'll blow us all to smithereens."

"All right." Naidro knew his business. "Set it and let's back off."

Naidro turned the dial on the clock. Kierkaven dropped the torch where Naidro had suggested and walked out of the crevice. He said to Cranst, who waited outside, "Three minutes," and kept walking. Cranst hurried after him.

They didn't go far. Naidro hadn't had to use much explosive. "Lots of cracks," he'd said, which meant both that he could set the explosives without drilling and that less explosive would propel more material through the conjunction.

"All right," Kierkaven said to Cranst when they stopped. "Tell me about the marginals now."

"They murdered the Ascendant."

"Great gods!" That opened up all sorts of possibilities. No one could stand in Pandir's way now but Lonnkärin. "How did they manage that?"

"They possessed garb, and help from some traitors. A youngling named Grayvle—"

"Grayvle!"

"You know him? Wait! Isn't that who you said told you that Pandir was at the Archive?"

Kierkaven cursed himself. The blood outside the Nest must have come from the Ascendant himself. If he'd stepped into the Nest he might have caught them all: not a fact he'd want Pandir to discover.

"Never mind that," he said. "Any others?"

"Yes. Lonnkärin. He left the Citadel with them. That's how they got out the gate."

"Lonnkärin! You're mad."

Cranst shrugged.

Kierkaven didn't know what to think. Cranst usually had his facts straight.

He'd sort it out later. For now, destroying the conjunction would satisfy him.

He said, "It should blow any second."

CHAPTER 40

WALKING IN THE darkness, everything appeared the same to Bess. It took her by surprise when Heldrick stepped close to her and whispered in her ear, "We're almost to Glasshugh's." He led them into the woods and stopped.

"Everyone wait here. Try not to make any noise. I'll return in five minutes." He turned away without another word and disappeared into the shadows.

"Is he fetching Kale?" Needa asked. Arrick shushed her before Bess could answer.

The minutes passed, and finally Heldrick returned alone. "Let's go on. We're almost to the conjunction."

"But where's Kale?" Needa whispered.

"He's already across the conjunction."

He began walking and they followed him. Once out of the woods, he increased his pace, then stopped abruptly as a distant rumble filled the air. "What's that?"

Bess checked the sky, but stars gleamed hard and bright. "Could it be an earthquake?" she asked. "I thought the ground trembled, a little. . . ." She broke off at the expression on Heldrick's face. "What is it?"

"I don't know. Damn!" He walked faster.

Kale stared into the mousehole. The two quistrils had stepped through and disappeared. He didn't see Bess and Heldrick either, or after a moment, anything. The conjunction had become a dead black oval.

He stepped to the doorway. After a few seconds he could see hints of the cave again, lit faintly by momentary streaks and spots of light.

What was going on? Nervously he glanced over his shoulder.

He heard a sharp crack accompanied by a flash of light so brief that he barely perceived it; before he could think of looking back at the conjunction, a torrent of rock, gravel and dirt smacked into him, knocking him flat, covering him, filling his mouth and blocking his nostrils. His legs tangled, and the weight of the avalanche snapped both bones in the lower part of his right leg. He wanted to scream but couldn't; his throat clogged with grit, and hundreds of pounds of rocky detritus squeezed the air from his lungs.

In seconds, the shock and pain rendered him senseless.

Kierkaven entered the crevice as soon as the dust settled, Cranst and Naidro at his heels.

Naidro had warned that the whole formation might collapse, though he doubted it. But he'd done his work well. Some large hunks of rock obstructed the end of the crevice, but Kierkaven and the others climbed over them. The cave had changed shape; rock and rubble lay piled high against the conjunction, hiding it, leaving an enlarged bean-shaped area covered with debris. Kierkaven held his torch high and did a quick eyeball check. "Looks like none went through."

"That means the conjunction closed right away," said Naidro. "No surprise, from what you said. The first half-ton probably did it. Satisfied?"

"Not quite." Kierkaven handed the torch to Naidro and crawled up the rubble pile. He could still see the top two lines he'd scraped. He slid down a couple of feet, pulled out a rock, and avoided the gravel and dirt that cascaded down.

"What are you doing?" asked Naidro. "After that explosion, this cave isn't exactly safe."

"I won't know till I see."

"Waste of time."

Kierkaven shrugged. Naidro didn't work for Pandir. "I just want to dig out the top here. It's shallow. Cranst, help me."

Cranst dutifully climbed up and began pawing at the heap of rock.

Minutes passed. Naidro grew restless.

"Come on, Kierkaven. Time to pack up."

"A bit longer. Hand me the torch." The torchlight showed those parts of the lowest scratched line that the explosion hadn't obliterated. Below it . . .

He held the torch close. A glittery type of rock filled the top of the space that the conjunction had occupied.

Kierkaven rubbed his finger against the rock: rough, hard and scratchy. He picked up a stone and smashed it against the new portion of the cave wall with all of his quistril strength. The stone in his hand cracked in half.

Solid rock. The conjunction was closed.

"I'm satisfied. Let's get out of here."

"That's what I've been saying for five minutes," Naidro grumbled.

Back outside the cave, Naidro got all his materials repacked. Kierkaven told Cranst to return with Naidro. "Tell Pandir, as soon as you get back, that the conjunction is closed. I may return late, depending on when the relief shows up, and I don't want the responsibility either for waking him or for letting the essential news wait. And tell him I'll have a full report in the morning."

Cranst set off and Kierkaven settled down for a long wait, but as it turned out, his relief showed up within minutes, walking out of the woods.

"Where're their horses?" his companion asked.

"Don't be an idiot. In the woods, where we should be." Kierkaven felt like an idiot himself. With the conjunction closed, the prime task naturally reverted to catching the marginals. And the marginals would never approach with a couple of quistrils in plain sight.

"Gods! It's a mastron and a senoral."

"Shut up." Though Kierkaven hadn't expected that either. Pandir took this seriously.

When they got close enough, Kierkaven saluted. The senoral approached, while the mastron angled off to examine the crevice.

"You're Kierkaven?" the senoral asked. Kierkaven could barely see the hooded face in the dark.

"Yes."

The senoral glanced around.

"Whom do you expect to catch, out in the open like this?"

"The armorers just left. I was about to relocate to the woods," he lied.

"You can relocate to the Citadel instead. A half-dozen vasiks wait in the woods. Anything they should know?"

"Yes. The conjunction's closed. I checked. The marginals won't escape that way."

The senoral stood motionless. "Well done," he said at last. "All right, on your way."

"Closed," Heldrick said.

Dear Lord. Bess's legs trembled. She would never reach home. And Kale—

"Kale?" Needa's voice rose with a wail.

"Silence!" Heldrick's hiss cut through her cry. More gently he whispered, "I'm sorry, Needa, but we must still worry about ourselves." He pushed back his senoral's hood; he and Grayvle had swapped cloaks before confronting the quistrils.

Bess blinked back tears. To have come this far—and Kale, stuck on the other side, in a strange world without his family.

"They used explosives," Heldrick said. "That's what caused the rumble earlier. The faster any material travels through the conjunction, the less it takes to close it." He rubbed his temples. "And Kierkaven'll come back when he finds that no relief's been sent. Of course, they may be a bit disorganized at the Citadel. We could have till morning, or only an hour. We should spend the time leaving this vicinity and hiding our trail completely."

Needa sat down.

Heldrick said, "Needa—" but Bess put a hand on his arm.

"Give her at least a minute or two, Heldrick." She could use the time herself. She'd rejoiced so when

Heldrick had trapped Kale, but now Kale was stuck in her world and she in his. She remembered the last she'd seen of him, the back of one leg silvered by the conjunction, motionless. . . .

Frozen.

The tightness in her throat began to ease.

"Heldrick," she whispered. "How could an explosion drive anything through the conjunction quickly?"

He frowned. "Explosions happen quickly. It's their nature."

"Yes, but wouldn't the first bits and pieces to pass through slow down so much—compared to this side, that is—that nothing else could go through behind them?"

Heldrick stared at her.

"Well?"

"Kierkaven said he checked. Grayvle! What did you see down the crevice?"

"Too dark. I couldn't see a thing."

Bess reached in her pocket. "I have a light."

Bess squeezed past Heldrick and clambered up the pile, ignoring the pains she still felt in her wrist. She caught her breath. Near the top a curved bit of mirror stuck four inches out of the grit and rubble. She pushed it with a finger.

It yielded but pushed back.

"The top's right here," she said. "They can't have checked closely." She began digging, but in seconds her heart sank. Below the small mirrored area that she'd first seen, the conjunction transformed into a hard, glittery rock.

"Can a conjunction collapse part way?" They could never fit through the small bit of mirror remaining.

Heldrick climbed beside her and ran his finger over the nubbly surface. "Fascinating. No, it's what you said before. The material already through has stopped, from our viewpoint, and blocks the rest. This top bit fell through since they checked. The stuff lower down shows you what they must have seen when they looked at the top, earlier. The rock and dust on the other side distort the conjunction on such a fine scale that it's lost most of its reflective properties. But, slowly, that material will fall out of the way. There's a landslide going on in my basement right now and we're sitting on top of it and don't notice a thing." He thought a moment. "To stop the avalanche on the other side will mean clearing this entire pile. For that we'll want tools. Everyone start on the easy stuff; I'll return shortly."

By the time Heldrick returned, everyone's fingers were sore, and the pile was barely diminished. But Heldrick brought tools from Glasshugh's: pickaxes, shovels, and gloves. The pace of work trebled. They filled the opening to the crevice as they worked, except for a ventilation window at the top.

"Whoever comes back will check in the crevice to the end and see it empty," Heldrick said. "Even Kierkaven, and the others who saw it after the explosion, will think that the cave collapsed, blocking the crevice completely. At least, I hope they will."

He and Grayvle each did the work of three men. Half an hour later, they'd dug enough of a pit in the pile to expose half of the conjunction—but the bulk of the pile still lay untouched.

A small rock suddenly dropped out of the conjunction into the pit.

"Ha!" Heldrick said. "We're finished, then."

"How's that?" Bess asked.

"It's spilling back. We've dug below the height that the pile's reached on the other side. All we have to do is wait a few minutes for the surface to smooth out. Then we'll know exactly how high to step when we go through."

He turned the flash off. No one said anything. When he turned the light back on it was clear where the top of the pile across the conjunction was.

He paused. "I think we can go through in pairs. Bess and I will go first, since I can lead you to the best hiding place. Needa and Arrick, wait ten minutes before coming through; that will give us about a second to vacate our position on the other side. Wellen and Bronli follow, then Grayvle. Grayvle will let each of you know when the ten minutes has passed." He clicked off the flashlight again.

"Bess," he said.

She pulled off her sweaty gloves and took his large, calloused hand. Together, they climbed into the pit. "Keep your head down, Heldrick," she said.

"And step *up,*" he answered.

The mirror waited before them, smooth to the touch but invisible in the dark. They leaned against the interface.

"Now!" Heldrick said.

They pushed hard, and *pop pop pop pop!* someone bumped into Bess from behind and they all slipped and fell down the pile. Somehow she kept from hurting her wrist further. She hopped to her feet and ran toward the stairs, Heldrick a step in front of her. They'd already reached the steps when Needa called:

"Where's Kale?"

Bess felt ashamed. She'd forgotten all about him.

Everyone turned toward the pile of rock that they'd trampled over without thinking. The tips of four dirty fingers extended past the edge of the pile.

Needa reached Kale first, though in her hurry she nearly dropped Lantry. She scrabbled at the pile like a madwoman. Within seconds everyone else joined in, working twice as hard as before. Bess's fingers began bleeding within twenty seconds, her wrist was on fire, and she realized they worked at a hopeless task. Before, with picks and shovels, they'd worked over half an hour to open the way. If they'd at least brought the gloves with them! This pile, though smaller, nevertheless rose two and a half feet against the conjunction. If Kale still lived, he would suffocate within minutes.

Heldrick stopped. "Fool!" he muttered. He strode over the rubble and through the conjunction.

The light in the basement illuminated nothing across the conjunction, and if Heldrick used the dim flashlight he did so in such brief bursts that no one could see. But the rock pile covering Kale began to spill out through the conjunction, eerily like sand through a funnel.

Grayvle roused himself and leaped through the conjunction also. The level of the pile dropped faster, poured through the doorway into blackness. In seconds the edge of the pile close to the conjunction nearly reached the floor. Grayvle and Heldrick popped through the conjunction again, as exhausted as Bess had ever seen them. Arrick jumped over the remainder of the pile and pawed through the shallow part.

"I got his legs," Arrick cried.

Everyone else attacked the still hopeless task of uncovering Kale's head and chest, but Heldrick pushed

Arrick aside, grabbed Kale high on the legs and pulled. The rocks that sat on Kale ripped his clothes, tore his body and cut his face, but he was out.

Kale coughed once. He breathed in.

Then he screamed. The scream degenerated into more coughing.

Bronli pointed. "We should splint that leg."

Heldrick said to her, "Follow me, I'll show you what I have, take whatever you can use." Bronli followed him upstairs.

Kale didn't scream again. He hadn't, in fact, fully regained consciousness, and his breathing remained rough, but he lived, twisting his head back and forth and moaning. Wellen took one of his hands; Needa, with Lantry once more in her lap, grasped the other.

Grayvle found an empty spot on the floor, lay down and fell fast asleep.

Bronli returned, clattering down the steps. She went to Kale and cut away his pant leg. Heldrick flipped on a light switch at the top of the steps before descending. He looked washed out.

"They didn't follow us through," he said.

Bess swallowed and turned toward the conjunction. She'd forgotten that possibility, forgotten how soon it would have happened.

"We'd better leave the house right away," she said.

Heldrick shrugged. "A week's passed for them. If they haven't come already, they won't."

He paused for the space of a few breaths, as if talking tired him out.

"The conjunction must posses a remarkably stable configuration. I expect the time differential's doubled or tripled, with all the activity it's suffered. Yet it endures. Well, it can't last much longer."

Bess's eyes widened as a thought struck her. "It could have closed while you and Grayvle worked on the other side. You could have been trapped there." On impulse she stepped to Heldrick and hugged him. It seemed silly in a way, after all the bad things that might have happened; but right now, not seeing Heldrick again was the worst possible thing she could imagine. Heldrick seemed embarrassed and she let him go.

"You'd better go home," he told her. "Ten minutes may have passed since you disappeared behind my shrubs. Your brother must be panic-stricken, with all the stories told about me."

"Oh gosh." She laughed. "Only ten minutes. For once I made friends faster than my little brother. But don't you think we should try to close the conjunction first? We could throw these rocks back through—"

"Don't bother. Nobody's coming. Besides, throwing them through one at a time wouldn't do much, and would take us hours." He shrugged. "In a while, if it's still open, I'll fire my shotgun. The speed of the blast will more than make up for the smaller amount of mass."

Bess wasn't sure that was the best idea. "Won't that be noisy? It's bad enough you already fired it once before coming after me. You don't want someone calling the police."

Heldrick waved that down. "If I stick the muzzle past the doorframe, stretching the conjunction out on the other side, the blast will carry the sound through. Very little, if any, will make it back here, even if the conjunction doesn't close. Now, you should go home and reassure your brother you're fine."

"All right. But I'll come back in the morning. You're going to need help adjusting to life in this world. Well, *you* know what it's like, but none of the others can even talk here yet."

Heldrick closed his eyes. "That sounds like a good idea." He really did look tired.

She ran halfway up the steps. "Good night, everyone," she called. "I'll see you tomorrow."

CHAPTER 41

Bess reached the front door as someone began pounding on it. For the briefest of moments she thought, *quistrils!* Then she opened the door. Her father stood before her, fists still raised, an expression of anger and desperation on his face that Bess had never seen.

"Oh, Dad!" She wrapped her arms around him, and the pent-up energy in her father's fists flowed into the tightest hug Bess could remember. She couldn't breathe.

This one time, she didn't care.

Her father loosened his hug but didn't let go.

"Are you all right?"

"Sure, you didn't squeeze me that hard."

"Jeff said you'd been shot."

"Oh!" So Jeff *had* heard Heldrick's shotgun. "No, I'm fine. Everything's wonderful." She let go and smiled up at him.

He scowled and glanced into the house suspiciously. "How did you hurt your face?" He touched her cheek, frowning in puzzlement. "Odd . . . this doesn't look like it just happened."

She'd forgotten about that. "I must look a fright." She raised a hand to her cheek, and her father, eyes widening, said, "Don't touch it with those fingers." He grabbed her arm to pull her hand away, causing needles to shoot through her wrist. She gasped, and he let go, alarm all over his face.

"Don't worry," she said to reassure him. "It's nothing. I just turned my wrist. It'll be okay." She glanced at her hands, and the sight of her cracked nails and bleeding, dirt-crusted fingers shocked her. It looked a lot worse than she'd expected.

But it was all worth it.

Her father took her hands, gently. He said, "You'd better clean these up. You can tell me about it afterwards," and she remembered how much she loved him for never boxing her in with questions. "If you're *sure* you're all right, that is. . . ." He frowned darkly into the house again.

"I am. I promise." She pulled the door closed behind her.

He rubbed the cloth of her youngling cloak between his thumb and fingers and peered into her face, past the dirt. "You look . . . older."

"Yeah," she said, and couldn't help but giggle a little. "I suppose I do." She hugged him again. "Let's go home."

Her mother, who generally pestered her with unceasing questions—"Did you do your homework? Have you brushed your teeth? Did you have a good day at school?"—hadn't returned from the grocery store. Jeff tried to substitute, but her father ordered him from the house till suppertime.

Her father helped her clean her hands and found some antibiotic for her fingers in one of the still unpacked moving boxes. She considered telling him the story right then, but she couldn't think how to start, and she was so tired. Instead, she drank a big glass of milk, kicked off her boots and lay down on her bed. She fell asleep at once, and slept past supper, and all the night through.

SATURDAY

She awoke from a dream of quistrils. The thunder of hoofbeats collapsed into a pounding at her door.

"Bess, wake up!"

She opened one sticky eyelid, pushed herself into a sitting position. Jeff, always impatient, gave up knocking and burst into her room.

"Hey, you're awake."

"Mmm."

"Say, what happened in Heldrick's house yesterday?"

Bess blinked. The real events had merged with her dream. Or . . . was it *all* a dream? She clenched her fists in panic.

They hurt.

Bess looked at her swollen, scabbed fingers. She still wore the youngling outfit. The boots stood by the side of her bed.

No dream, then. Her heart sang.

She sat up. "I've got to go."

"Go where?"

"Heldrick's house." She pulled on her boots, and her mother preempted Jeff's position at her bedroom door.

"Oh, good. You're awake," she said. "I wanted to call the doctor but your father insisted you'd be all right."

"I was just tired, Mom."

"That's what he said, but he couldn't tell me why. What could wear you out like that? And what happened to your hands? Your face is filthy. How long has it been since you washed it?"

"I'll tell you later, Mom. I've got to check on something." Bess pulled her hood up without thinking.

"And where did you find that monk's cloak?"

"It's not a monk's cloak, Mom."

"But where did you get it?"

Bess sighed. This could go on forever unless she came up with an answer that wouldn't make her mother think of another question. "I stole it."

While her mother gaped, Bess slipped past. Ignoring her mother's strident orders to come back, she hurried down the stairs and out the front door.

Bess rang the bell, then pounded the knocker without waiting. What if the quistrils had come back after all? She had been so worn out that she'd listened to Heldrick's assurances. But why had they run the risk? Everyone should have come to her house.

Back up the street, she saw her mother stride round the corner, then her father. He caught up with her mom, stopping her. They spoke, then her mother began walking again. Her father, shaking his head, followed.

She pounded on the door again. "Hey, it's me! Bess!" Not until that moment did it occur to her that, if the quistrils had returned, they could be on the other side of the door this minute.

The door opened a crack and Bronli peered out.

Bess sighed in relief. "Thank God you're still here."

But Bronli grabbed her, pulled her inside, and closed the door.

"I thought you'd never come," she said. "Heldrick said you'd help. He told me how to reach your house and pointed it out from his upstairs room. But I only have these youngling clothes. If they caught me . . ." She shook her head. "I won't go back to that life. Not ever. I'll die first."

"Help?" Bess asked. "How? What kind of help does he need?" And why couldn't he come to her himself? He must be hurt. "Take me to him. What can I do?"

Bronli stared. "Help me, I meant. He said you would."

"—Oh. Sure, I'll help you. I'll help all of you. But—Heldrick's all right?"

Bronli didn't answer fast enough.

Bess stepped close to Bronli and grabbed a handful of cloak in each hand. Heldrick was gone. She felt certain. "The quistrils took him back through the conjunction, didn't they?" Tears blurred her vision and she bit her lip so hard it hurt.

But Bronli shook her head, frowning. "No. The quistrils—"

The doorbell rang. Bronli turned to the door, her eyes wide, and lifted a hand. For the first time Bess noticed that it held a kitchen knife. Bess let go of Bronli's cloak and wiped her eyes. "For God's sake, put that away. It's just my parents."

"How do you know?"

"I saw them coming. Relax, there're no quistrils out there."

"That's what he said. . . ."

Bess opened the door and saw that Jeff had managed to catch up with her mom and dad. "Listen," she told them, her tongue almost tripping over the switch from Otherworld to Homeworld. "I'll explain everything, but give me a few more minutes first, okay?"

Her mother opened her mouth but closed it again when her father put a hand on her arm.

Bronli frowned. "I thought you spoke English here?"

"Yes. It's different sounding, but you'll adjust. Now, put that knife down and tell me where Heldrick is."

"He and Grayvle crossed over to clear the crevice."

"Clear the crevice! Did they *want* the quistrils here?" She couldn't believe they'd risked the conjunction closing on them for that. She would twist Heldrick's ears. "They might never have made it back."

"Oh, they returned. They cleared the crevice for the Verdanits."

"For the—?"

The house was so quiet.

"The Verdanits went back? But why?"

"Bess, listen. Heldrick went with them, and Grayvle too."

Bess waited for more, but nothing came.

"And they're still not back?"

"No. Bess—"

"But the conjunction could close any second." Bess pushed past Bronli and raced to the basement door, tore it open, and ran down the steps two at a time without stopping to turn on the light. She scrabbled over the remains of the rock pile to the conjunction's framed position and put her hands up to it.

Felt it. Saw it.

Rough concrete. Solid wall.

"Oh, no. Oh, no." Bess pushed against the wall, then struck it with her fists. *"No!"* She pounded more, and her fingers began bleeding again, but the concrete didn't yield. She slid to her knees, disbelief keeping grief at bay. "No, no, no," each word punctuated by a slap at the rough wall until her father reached her, took her arms in his strong but gentle grasp and pulled them from the wall without a word.

Everyone had followed her down the stairs, but no one spoke. Not her mother; not even Jeff. Bess's eyes brimmed, but she blinked the tears away and swallowed with an aching throat.

"Why?" she asked Bronli, her voice a croak. "They knew this could happen. Why did they take the chance?"

"Bess. I'm sorry. They wanted to go back. Heldrick showed me how to use his shotgun and told me to fire after him through the mousehole until it closed. I had to reload twice." She rubbed her shoulder.

Bess stared, speechless.

"Here," Bronli said. "He left a letter."

"Oh, great." Bess stood, snatched at the envelope and crushed it in her bleeding fingers. "That makes everything hunky-dory." Tears no longer threatened, but her eyes still burned. Bitterness bottled her grief and shoved it deep inside where it couldn't hurt her. After all she'd done to bring them here, they'd turned around and left without saying goodbye. Arrick and his family she could almost understand, afraid of a new place, a new way of life—and a chance to go home months after the quistrils stopped searching for them. But Heldrick considered this world his, as much as the other. He'd always planned to stay here. What changed his mind?

She had, of course. She remembered the hug she'd given him and the way he'd pulled back. Her promise to return and his unenthusiastic response. Her cheeks burned. He didn't want her around. He'd left to avoid her.

And she'd thought he considered her a friend.

He chose; that's what rankled. Not hurt. Not dead. Just up and left. She shoved the envelope into a pocket.

"Bess," her mother said and then floundered, apparently faced with more questions than she could handle. She snatched at the nearest. "What language was that?"

"It's a kind of English, Mom." Bess's fingers began throbbing; or she began to notice them doing so, at any rate. She wiggled them and sighed, but the sigh stuck in her throat, turned into a whimper that she stopped only by letting the tears course down her face. She couldn't even wipe them away without leaving bloody streaks on her cheeks.

Bronli reached her first, put her arms around her and held her tight.

"I'm sorry, Bess. I didn't know how much they meant to you."

"No." Bess swallowed. "Neither did they, Bronli." She had never felt so alone in her life. Then, abruptly, she was ashamed of herself. *She* had made it back home; she still had her family. Bronli had nothing, nobody, alone in a strange world, too frightened to go outdoors. It didn't make Bess any happier, but if Bronli could offer her comfort under those circumstances, surely Bess could return the favor. She wiped her nose and straightened.

"Mom, Dad, Jeff. This is Bronli. I've said I'd help her. But I can't do much by myself. She doesn't even speak regular English right now. Will you help me help her? She'll need to live with us for at least a while."

And to her surprise it was her mother who answered, without asking any questions at all, "Of course we'll help. Whatever we can do. She's welcome." She took Bronli's hands and said, "You're more than welcome."

Bess translated, and Bronli gave Bess another hug, but it didn't help. She still felt dirty and crumpled; discarded, like an empty cigarette pack.

"I can hardly believe it," Mom said, many times, and Bess didn't blame her. Without the existence of Bronli, even her father might have doubted her. In her own house and her own clothes, she found it a bit hard to believe, herself.

But back in her room, on the desk, the crumpled, bloodied envelope waited for her.

When she excused herself early to go to bed, no one else even expressed surprise. She went through the kitchen and slipped a book of matches into her pocket on the way to her room. Then, when she was all ready for bed except for turning out the light, she got the matches from her pants, went to her desk, and picked up the envelope. She could open the window and hold it outside as it burned.

A minute passed . . . two. She stood there, the letter in her left hand, the matches in her right. She couldn't make herself move, couldn't quite bring herself to do it; not tonight.

Not any night.

She sighed and admitted to herself that she'd break down and read the letter eventually. She might as well do it and be done.

As if awaiting permission, her right hand dropped the matches and leaped enthusiastically to the letter. She winced as her swollen fingers split the envelope. The pain in her hands seemed a part of her now, something that would last long after the swelling vanished.

Heldrick's tall, angular handwriting covered several sheets. She closed her eyes, heart pounding. She didn't want to know what this letter said. She hurt enough already. Maybe ignorance was bliss, after all?

But she couldn't help herself. Her eyes opened and she read.

Dear Bess,

I feel, as I write this, that my entire life has been a prelude for the moment when I step through the conjunction for the last time. A week ago, I would have found such an idea preposterous. But recent events have changed me—no, turned me, made me see what I never, before, found worthy of a glance.

Why have I gone back? Why have any of us? I can't intelligibly answer in a word or two, so bear with me while I explain.

Understand, first, that where my loyalty to the Citadel was broken many years ago by fear and hatred, Grayvle's was not broken at all but redirected—by the kindness, and courage, and honor, and duty of the bravest girl I have ever known.

Many quistrils, it's true, see kindness and honor as weaknesses, places to attack. But you've shown me that not all quistrils are alike. Quistril society, rather than any quistrils acting on their own, is the culprit; and it perpetuates itself because those most successfully shaped by that society are the ones put in charge. But others like Grayvle exist. They can be found.

I'm sure you see now what Grayvle and I must do (and the Verdanits hope Lantry, when old enough, will join us). The Citadel cannot be brought down by hatred; on the contrary, hatred upholds it. Instead, we will enter the Citadel again and again, searching out likely younglings and doing our best to divert them from the Citadel's warped path.

Failure will mean capture and death; but success will create an inner society within the Citadel that will grow over time until it becomes significant enough to change the Citadel's policy. How much time? Perhaps a hundred years, perhaps twice that. Neither I, nor Grayvle, nor even Lantry will see the fruits of our labors. But, for me at least, the labors will be enough.

I discussed this with Grayvle while digging out Kale. We could have presented the idea to the Verdanits and you on our return. But I feared that, if we did, you would want to stay until we were gone; feared that you might even say you wished I wouldn't leave, and then nothing could have induced me to go. Even now I keep putting off the moment, a part of me hoping that the conjunction will close on its own before I depart.

But I am sure it will not. I am not one to acknowledge fate, but you have shown me what I *must* do; I believe nothing besides you can keep me from it. Therefore I choose this cowardly and impersonal method of saying goodbye, and still it twists my heart.

In the short time since we met, you have become the best and truest friend I have ever known. I can only hope you will forgive me for leaving this way. I know you, as I have known few others; and I am sure, deep in my heart, that you will indeed forgive me. I will die believing it. Even so, I will always miss having heard it from your own lips.

With great love and affection,
Heldrick

  Bess smoothed the crinkles and folds from the letter, wiped her eyes, read it again, and thought: Of course I forgive you, Heldrick. She thought it again, trying her best to project it across the worlds directly to Heldrick's mind and heart; and though she expected no response, a weight lifted from her soul. The urge to cry ebbed.

  Oh, the permanent separation still broke her heart, and probably would for a long time. Still—she remembered last year when Gram, her mom's mom, died. Someone trying to console her mom had said, "But you still have your memories." She'd thought it to be, at the time, a weak and foolish comfort, an emotional consolation prize. In fact, she realized now, it was far worse: the memories were a *cause* of the pain, not a balm for it. Without her memories of Heldrick, after all, the separation would have been inconsequential.

  Yet, at the same time, those memories brought her far more joy than the separation could ever take away. She wouldn't willingly give them up, no matter how much pain they caused. She *would* remember Heldrick, always, as long as she lived; and he would remember her. Those were the things that mattered. What would have been truly, unutterably sad would have been if she had burned this letter unopened, as she'd intended.

And now there was hope for Heldrick's world, hope that hadn't been there before she went. Would Heldrick's plan work? She felt the corners of her mouth tugging upward, for the first time since learning that Heldrick was gone. Of course it would! If anyone could pull it off, it would be Heldrick. And he was doing it because of her—she had brought hope not only to that world, but to Heldrick himself. The thought made her wish that she'd crossed the conjunction with him that last time, to help—

But no. This was her world. Her family was here. This was where she belonged. Besides . . .

Her smile broadened.

Besides . . . there were plenty of problems to solve in this universe, too.

The End

Do the World a Favor

IF YOU ENJOYED *Cloaks* (and I gather you enjoyed it at least enough to finish it), consider leaving a review at the place where you purchased it.

Many authors have a note here where they tell you how important reviews are to them, and it's entirely true. But reviews are also important to *you,* and to other readers like you. They help you find the books that you might be interested in. The more people who write reviews, the easier it becomes for you to find what you want.

Also, leaving reviews lets authors know which books they should write sequels to, and which are better left alone. That can have a direct effect on what books you'll find available next time you go book browsing.

So, sure, do me a favor and write a review. But do yourself and the world a favor at the same time.

Also, if you're interested in signing up for my newsletter—no spam, just information on when new books come out—you can do so at *fafisher.com/newsletter.php.* Or scan the code below with your phone:

And look at the next page if you want to read a sneak-preview of *Pandir Decloaked.*

EXCERPT FROM

PANDIR DECLOAKED

CHAPTER 1

LORANN KNITTED by the fire, thinking about the cow and two goats they'd lost already to this winter's fierce cold.

"Mama?"

The anxiety in Jeniele's voice seeped through Lorann's concerns, and she looked up. Jeniele was sixteen now, and the sweetest girl ever, though not much to look at—except when she smiled, which was near all the time, so it hardly mattered.

She wasn't smiling now. "I hear something. Still far-off."

A layer of ice formed around Lorann's heart. Quistrils? She stepped to the door, opened it, and listened, ignoring the snow flurries and biting cold air that swirled in.

Hoofbeats. And getting louder. She shut the door and said, "Get your pa from the barn, send him in, and *don't come back.*"

Jeniele nodded, eyes wide. She grabbed her coat from the rack and ran out the back door pulling the coat on.

In the short time before her husband reached the house, the flurries thickened to heavy snow. Lorann couldn't hardly see the end of the lane from the window. Good thing she'd sent Jeniele out before it really started; her tracks would be covered.

Ibon came in, brushing flakes from his coat. "Jeniele said riders are—"

"Yes." Lorann didn't turn from the window. "Get your coat and overshoes off. We don't want it to look like you been up to anything outside."

"But why?" he asked, anguish in his voice. "Why do they take—"

"Oh, Ibon, why do you *think* they take girls?" For the first time, she regretted marrying Ibon. If she'd found a town man, like her ma wanted, this probably wouldn't be happening. Everyone knew the quistrils took farm girls to "work" in the Citadel five times as often as they took town girls.

But the regret vanished faster than it took to think of the reason for it. If she hadn't married Ibon, she never would have had Jeniele, or Zane or Shalla either.

"I'm sorry, Ibon. I'm distraught."

He nodded and took her hand. "I just don't fathom why they can't leave us be. Why they have to treat us this way."

Lorann shook her head. To her, the answer was plain. The quistrils treated them this way because they could.

She remembered her mother, long ago, trying to convince her that it could be worse. "At least they follow their own rules. When they take a girl, they hand out a plaque. A family that can show a plaque won't have another girl taken." Lorann never had reason to doubt her mother, though it was certain that if the quistrils chose to break their own rules, there wasn't nothing anyone could do to stop them.

Besides, Mama, there *is* only one Jeniele. How am I supposed to make that seem better?

Two shadows in the whiteness of the snow suddenly resolved into dark-cloaked figures on horses. She stepped back from the window before they saw her watching. "They're here."

"Right. I told Jeniele to—"

Lorann clapped a hand over Ibon's mouth and tapped her ear. She didn't know if the quistrils really heard as well as some said, but she didn't want to find out at Jeniele's expense. "Just open the door, Ibon."

Ibon nodded, and did so. Lorann stood behind him. The quistrils had dismounted but hadn't yet started up the walk. Still, Ibon held the door open, despite the snow that blew in. Always safer that way, Lorann thought. Mustn't shut the door on them once they'd seen it open. Mustn't ever make them knock. Do everything possible to make them happy. Everything except give up Jeniele.

A wild thought struck her. Maybe, maybe they could be bribed, bought off. . . . No. In the first place, her mother would have told her if that were so. In the second . . . bought off with what? Farmers dealt almost exclusively in trade. The townspeople had money, but the only money in a typical farmhouse was the pair of coins, hammered together where they overlapped and fixed to a small board saying "Bless this couple," that hung just over the front door. She could see it now from where she stood.

The two quistrils strode in, glanced at her and Ibon, and walked past them to the fireplace. At least they hadn't smiled. Those slightly sharp quistril teeth—the merest shade too sharp to seem really human—gave her a chill.

They pushed back their hoods, pulled off their gloves, and held their hands out to warm them. She noticed that one wore a senoral's cloak, though the other was the usual vasik. Had Ibon noticed the difference? Probably not. To most farmers, the quistrils were all "riders." But her ma had grown up in town and had taught Lorann the ranks and subtle cloak markings. It did no good now; she couldn't think why someone ranked as high as a senoral would ride on an errand like this, nor how the knowledge could help.

The senoral spoke over his shoulder. "Please assemble your family."

"Yes, sir." Ibon glanced at Lorann, and she hurried to the top of the stairs and down the hall. Shalla'd had fever, but the worst was over, thank God. Still, she had Zane watch during naptime, in case her breathing clogged.

The room was at the back of the house, and the door was shut. Zane likely hadn't heard a thing. She opened it and stepped in. "Go downstairs, Zane," she said, and as he turned she grabbed him and leaned down to whisper in his ear, soft as she could, "Riders. Don't mention Jeniele."

Zane's eyes widened, and he froze. Then he nodded once and headed out.

Lorann picked up Shalla gently, trying not to waken her. She was so *light*—over three years old but as easy to lift as when she'd been two. Still, she'd survived. That was the important thing.

"Mama?"

"Shh, it's all right. Go back to sleep." Shalla rested her head on Lorann's shoulder. Lorann considered telling her not to mention Jeniele but, like as not, that would make her question the reason, which would be just as bad. Better she went back to sleep. Quietly, she carried the girl downstairs.

The quistrils moved to the table and sat. Lorann, Ibon, and Zane remained standing, of course, with eyes lowered.

F. A. Fisher

"This is your entire family?"

"Yes, sir," Ibon said.

"Have you a plaque?"

Lorann's head snapped up in shock. Why did he ask, when they had no girl to be taken? He couldn't know about Jeniele; he hadn't searched the house.

—Surely they don't plan on taking *me.*

She'd always understood they only took girls around Jeniele's age—never wives, unless they'd committed a crime.

Shalla? Dear God, they wouldn't. She was too young for them, it wouldn't be worth it. . . .

"Have you a plaque?" The same words but this time with steel in the voice.

She realized she was staring and dropped her gaze. Ibon stuttered, "No, sir—"

"All right. You have now." The senoral spoke to the vasik in the quistril language. The vasik pulled a thin, inscribed piece of wood from a pocket in his cloak, and a sharp-tipped implement along with it. The senoral took them.

"But . . ." Lorann knew she shouldn't say anything but couldn't stop herself. "But Senoral—"

Both quistrils looked at her sharply. The vasik spoke for the first time. "You're town-born?"

Should she lie? Would it help? She couldn't see how. "No. No, sir. But my mother was." She didn't see how that could help, either.

And then she wondered, Help with what? Who are they taking?

"Well." The senoral pursed his lips. "That's of no import at the moment." He carefully scratched a few more marks onto the plaque.

She'd never heard tell of anyone who knew what the marks meant, but every plaque was marked differently, she knew that.

"You understand that possession of this plaque will only protect the remaining females of your family if you keep it. Should you lose it, or destroy it, or try to loan it to someone else—and I guarantee that would be detected—the protection is gone."

"Yes, sir," said Ibon. "But *who*—?"

"I take it your daughter is in the barn." The senoral looked up from the plaque at Ibon and then at Lorann. "Yes. I suspected as much."

Lorann turned to Ibon. The shock on his face was plain as day. She supposed her own expression must match.

"It was foolish of you to try to hide her," the senoral said, "especially without her overshoes."

Lorann glanced at the overshoes by the wall, next to her own, and above them the empty peg that usually held Jeniele's coat.

"And that was only the most obvious sign. I knew the moment I came in the door how many were in your family. Had I been forced to search for her, I might have been very angry. Furthermore, by trying to hide her, you've committed a criminal act. I could now take the entire family to the Citadel."

Lorann hadn't thought her blood could get any colder.

The senoral shrugged and pushed the plaque across the table, then stood and pulled on his gloves. "Some people keep the plaque on the mantle, where it can be easily seen. I do not recommend this in your case."

He spoke a quistril word to the vasik. They walked to the door.

There, the senoral stopped and said to them, "Since you have not, in fact, lost a daughter, neighbors seeing the plaque would instantly know that something strange was going on, and the word would spread. Therefore, you would be well advised to hide it in a safe place and not pull it out unless threatened by other quistrils. And don't forget to fetch your daughter back from the barn. It must be cold out there."

The quistrils pulled up their hoods, opened the door, and stepped out into the snow. The senoral looked back with his hand on the knob. "Have a nice day."

The door closed.

Lorann's and Ibon's mouths stayed open.

CHAPTER 2

GRAYVLE BRUSHED SNOW off his saddle, mounted in a single movement, and started off without waiting for Heldrick. Heldrick knew where they were headed as well as he did and, even in snow this thick, they wouldn't get lost. That was almost impossible for quistrils—one result of the genetic alterations that distinguished them from cadrils. Besides, he wanted to get back to Needa and Arrick's place—but with the limits on vision, the horses couldn't travel as fast. And they'd need to be changed out more often, as well.

Also besides . . . he was just a little annoyed with Heldrick.

Heldrick caught up with him at the end of the lane.

They rode in silence for a while before Grayvle asked, "Why do you do that?"

"Do what?"

"Scare the cadrils like that. Why don't you tell them honestly you want to give them a free plaque and be done with it?"

"Oh, that. I don't want them asking a lot of questions that I'm unwilling to answer. So I let them think we're for real until we're ready to leave."

"Hmm." Grayvle didn't buy it.

"What—do you think I enjoy frightening them?"

"I get that feeling. Yes."

Heldrick turned his best glare on Grayvle, but Grayvle kept his eyes ahead and pretended not to notice.

Heldrick grunted. "I suppose there's a bit of truth to it. What I enjoy is the shock on their faces when we leave without the girl. If we did it your way, they'd be no more than puzzled. Not nearly the same. But mostly, I don't want to answer their questions, and I don't want to refuse to answer them, either. My way is best."

He saw Heldrick's point but still found the practice irritating and the man's enjoyment of it, though it wasn't his reason for doing it, disappointing. "All right." Somewhat pettily, he added, "You're the senoral."

"I'm not a senoral and you know it. In fact—" Heldrick laughed. "Technically, you outrank me. When I left the Citadel I was a couple of years younger than you, when you left."

That was true, wasn't it? "Then, as your superior officer, let me ask you another question. Where did you pick up that 'Have a nice day' nonsense?"

"Oh. From Bess's universe, across the conjunction."

"Really?" Grayvle glanced at him. "I never heard Bess use the expression." Which was a silly thing to say, and he realized it the moment he spoke. Bess had hurtled into his life, lifting and tumbling him like a flash flood; and when she was gone, the course of his life was in a different channel, tied to Heldrick instead of the Citadel. That didn't change the fact he'd hardly exchanged a dozen words with her.

"Not from Bess, herself," Heldrick said. "From her world. Remember, I spent years there."

Yes, before they'd met. Before Bess. "It would be nice to find another conjunction."

Heldrick didn't answer that. He didn't need to. Conjunctions made for a convenient access to another universe, but most were an inch or less in diameter. It was only once every few centuries that one formed somewhere on the planet large enough for a person to step through, and the odds of another forming nearby, this soon, in a place that was sufficiently well-hidden that they could keep it secret, were minuscule. The odds of *them* being the ones to find it in such a place were tinier still.

Grayvle went on: "I still wonder if we did the right thing in closing that conjunction when we did. Bess's universe made a great hiding place."

"It would have closed soon on its own anyway."

Heldrick's voice held a bit of snap, and Grayvle bit his lip, chagrined. He *knew* Heldrick had done a lot of soul-searching regarding the conjunction . . . not about whether to close it, but about which side he wanted to be on when he did. So when Heldrick changed the topic, he didn't protest.

"I don't know why you should be perplexed by the origin of that phrase. I'm sure the cadrils here have similar pleasantries."

"You're kidding." Frankly, it was a bit hard to believe. "I can't imagine Needa or Arrick saying anything like that."

"They don't talk that way to *quistrils*. Not likely to tonight, especially. With this snow, we're bound to be late. Needa will be in high dudgeon."

True. Needa had a sharp tongue when you didn't live up to her expectations, unlike her husband Arrick who would likely say nothing. Just glare. But they, and their sons Wellen and Kale, were fine people. A year and a half ago he'd known nothing about them except that Heldrick and Bess had risked their lives to save them. Now they were family.

"If we didn't have to go so far—" But Grayvle didn't finish the complaint. Heldrick had made the point often enough: unlikely as it might be that anyone would become aware of their distribution of unauthorized plaques, it was crucial that, should it happen, the areas of activity be far removed from their base of operations.

The snow continued until past nightfall. When it finally stopped, the sky cleared as well; but the wind, if anything, picked up, occasionally sounding to Grayvle's ears almost like . . .

Was that—?

Heldrick pulled his horse to a halt and raised a gloved hand for silence, though Grayvle hadn't been talking.

Grayvle halted as well. From his horse's nostrils billowed clouds of moonlit steam, backlit by the snow and tattered by the wind. He pulled back his hood, exposing his cheeks to the pinpricks of airborne ice crystals, and listened for a repeat of the scream he'd heard, or imagined.

Heldrick was also listening. After a moment he shook his head.

So Grayvle said, "I heard it too."

He wondered what Heldrick would do. Needa would already be fretting, and checking this out would take extra time. More importantly, they were close to home now, and Heldrick felt uncomfortable taking actions this close to Arrick and Needa's that might eventually be discovered. But— "If this is a simple curfew violation, there should be no risk." They could act, even in the presence of other quistrils, exactly as quistrils ought to act, and still do something useful.

Heldrick nodded. "Let's go."

They set off at a gallop, their hoofbeats muffled by snow.

The woods forced them to slow their pace. Although the moonlight shone brightly through the high leafless branches, the trees grew thickly enough to limit visibility to thirty paces. The cry couldn't have come from much farther than this.

Grayvle spotted the fresh hoof prints at the same moment that Heldrick pointed. Striving for silence, they followed the trail to a clearing. One man sat mounted on the opposite side, wearing a vasik's cloak, his back to them. He held the reins of his partner's horse, while his partner, also a vasik, tied a tall dark-haired woman's wrists together. A gag had already been pulled across her mouth. Grayvle glanced at the tracks in the snow. The woman had run. She must have decided to dash across the clearing—a poor choice. The horses had less advantage in the woods. Heldrick edged his horse forward, and Grayvle followed. Not until halfway across the clearing did anyone hear them. The woman looked up an instant before the two men turned their heads. She had sharp hearing, for a cadril; and, of course, all women were cadrils. Quistril women didn't exist, another result of those genetic alterations—in this case, the one that resulted in quistrils taking women in the first place.

The vasiks saluted on seeing Heldrick's senoral's cloak.

They rode closer. "On patrol?" Heldrick asked, in Vardic.

"Yes, Senoral," the one afoot said. "Found this woman violating curfew."

"You must have been pleased with your prize."

"Sir?"

"Both of you staring at her, letting us slip up behind you like that."

The two glanced uneasily at each other. Grayvle repressed the urge to grin. Heldrick had the senoral's attitude down perfectly.

"When does your shift end?" Heldrick asked.

"Not for a few hours," the mounted vasik said. "We planned to drop her off at the nearest post house—

"And to pause, perhaps, for a bit of food, and then warm up by the fire?"

"No, Senoral!" the other vasik said, earnestly if unconvincingly. "Just to drop her off."

"Commendable. We'll save you the trouble. Bring her here."

The vasik's shoulders drooped a bit. "Yes, sir." To the woman, in English, he said, "Come along." He took a step. When the woman didn't follow, he turned back, raised a hand and slapped her.

"Stop that!" Heldrick snapped in Vardic.

Both men looked at him in surprise.

"You know better than to hurt a woman."

"It was just a slap—"

Heldrick rode close, leaned over in his saddle and struck the vasik open-handed across the face. "Tell me that didn't hurt."

That, Grayvle decided, was well-deserved. They *weren't* supposed to hurt the women. Women were too valuable.

Heldrick straightened and said, "That cavalier attitude contributes to the early death of so many women in the Nest. You are always to use the *minimum* amount of force on a woman. Is that clear?"

"But ... she didn't move when I asked." The vasik's eyes were resentful.

"So ask again, more clearly." Heldrick leaned forward in his saddle and stared at the gagged woman, until she met his eyes. In English, he said, "One way or another, you will come with me. If you think it through, you will realize that. You can make it difficult for me, but not as difficult as I can make it for you. I would suggest you choose your battles wisely."

The woman stared back for the space of a few heartbeats, then she began to walk forward.

"Ride with my companion," he said; then, to the mounted vasik, in Vardic: "Help her up."

Grayvle rode closer as the woman and the mounted Vasik approached. He reached out and took hold of the woman's bound hands. The vasik also leaned forward to assist, then straightened and shouted to his partner, "It's Grayvle, the traitor!"

Damn! He looked at the other and recognized Thuvwald, his old form-mate, already raising his knife high over his head.

He dropped the woman's hands, pressing both knees against his horse. The horse stepped back; the knife flashed by within an inch of his nose.

The tip caught his thigh, slicing a line of fire along it.

By that time he had his own knife out. Thank the gods it was Thuvwald who'd recognized him. The man was such a idiot. Anyone else, and Grayvle would be dead by now. All this time and the man hadn't learned not to use that overhead stroke! If Thuvwald hadn't taken him by surprise—indeed, if Grayvle hadn't been off-balance and holding that woman's hands—this fight would have ended already, and Thuvwald would never have had another opportunity to make a fool of himself.

He and Thuvwald jockeyed their horses for position, and he got a momentary glimpse of Heldrick and the other man, rolling in the snow.

Then his horse didn't move quite as he'd intended, nearly putting him in range of another of Thuvwald's thrusts. If the man weren't so clumsy, Grayvle might have been in serious trouble.

It happened again. What was his horse doing? He glanced down, thinking that first thrust of Thuvwald's might have injured his horse as well. Instead he saw that the wound in his leg was worse than he'd realized. Far worse, well beyond his quistril body's automatic ability to stem blood loss, gaping wide and bleeding profusely, the blood soaking his pant leg and filling his boot.

The horse wasn't misbehaving; his leg was.

He grabbed the reins with his free hand. He'd planned to use that hand to pull Thuvwald off balance at a crucial moment, but that was no longer an option.

And he worried about Heldrick. His own fight with Thuvwald seemed to have been going on for long enough that he had to wonder whether Heldrick and his opponent had each incapacitated the other.

At that point, though, Thuvwald glanced aside, turned his horse, and galloped off.

Grayvle felt unexpectedly dizzy.

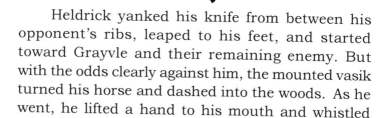

Heldrick yanked his knife from between his opponent's ribs, leaped to his feet, and started toward Grayvle and their remaining enemy. But with the odds clearly against him, the mounted vasik turned his horse and dashed into the woods. As he went, he lifted a hand to his mouth and whistled once for help.

"After him, Grayvle!" Fat lot of good the whistle would do the man; by the time help arrived, they'd be elsewhere. Heldrick turned to retrieve his own horse but stopped when he realized that Grayvle wasn't giving chase.

He turned back to see Grayvle leaning on his horse's neck. As he stepped closer, he saw the snow spotted with blood around the area where the fight had occurred and the steady drip ... drip ... drip from the toe of Grayvle's right boot.

Want To Keep Reading?

Get *Pandir Decloaked* right now. Here's the link:
https://www.amazon.com/gp/product/B01N9GKDPV/

Or scan this code with your phone:

Want Notice of Future
Book Releases?

Sign up for my newsletter. You can either go to *fafisher.com/newsletter.php*, or scan the code below with your phone. No junk emails, promise! Just info on when future books are going to be available for purchase (and occasional prizes).

About the Author

T HE COURSE OF F. A. FISHER'S LIFE was decided in utero, as he was introduced to science fiction and fantasy while his mother was reading *The Chronicles of Narnia* to his older sister. Though he grew up among the first generation where television was commonplace, he was of a contrary nature and spent most of his time reading. That contrariness continued in college, where he ignored his adviser and chose an area major, which allowed him to take whatever he wanted, with the result that his degree didn't prepare him for any job whatsoever—except perhaps writing.

He was raised in an era without computers or even hand calculators, so naturally he got his first master's degree in Computer Science. And though he loved learning he always hated school, so of course he got his second master's in Education. He'd wanted to become a writer from an early age, so it followed that he went through several other jobs, including two self-start companies, before putting out his first book.

Somewhere along the way he developed a deep and abiding hatred for typos. Fortunately, by this time his contrariness has abated, so if you find any typos in any of his books, let him know, and he'll fix them.

    Cloaks is his first novel. His second, *Pandir Decloaked,* is also available..

ALSO BY F. A. FISHER

The second book in the *Cloaks* series:

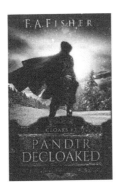

PANDIR DECLOAKED

Get it now at:
https://www.amazon.com/gp/product/B01N9GKDPV

Or scan the code below:

An EQP Book

E-QUALITY PRESS
http://EQPBooks.com/

Made in the USA
Middletown, DE
24 September 2023

39226592R00252